ALONG
A
BRETON
SHORE

also by

ARLEM HAWKS

Georgana's Secret

Beyond the Lavender Fields

ALONG
A
BRETON
SHORE

ARLEM HAWKS

SHADOW
MOUNTAIN
PUBLISHING

Visit us at shadowmountain.com

This is a work of fiction. Characters and events in this book are products of the author's imagination or are represented fictitiously.

Library of Congress Cataloging-in-Publication Data

Names: Hawks, Arlem, author.
Title: Along a Breton shore / Arlem Hawks.
Description: [Salt Lake City]: Shadow Mountain Publishing, [2023] | Summary: "A soldier must choose between his heart's desire or his duty to country in this gripping novel of friendship and survival."—Provided by publisher.
Identifiers: LCCN 2022060042 | ISBN 9781639931071 (hardback)
Subjects: LCSH: Soldiers—France—Fiction. | Man-woman relationships—Fiction. | France—History—Revolution, 1789–1799—Fiction. | BISAC: FICTION / Historical / General | LCGFT: Historical fiction. | Novels.
Classification: LCC PS3608. A89348 A79 2023 | DDC 813/.6—dc23/eng/20230125
LC record available at https: //lccn.loc.gov/2022060042

Printed in the United States of America
Publishers Printing

10   9   8   7   6   5   4   3   2   1

For Caledon and Matheson—

Je vous aime, mes fils. *Don't you ever forget that.*

CHARACTERS

BERNARD (bair-NAHRD) FAMILY
Armelle (ahr-MEL)
Cécile (say-SEEL)
Gabriel (gah-bree-EL)
Gustave (gew-STAHV)
Henri (on-REE)
Jacqueline (jahk-LEEN)
Julien (joo-LYEN)
Ranée (rah-NAY)
Yanick (YAH-nik)

COLBERT (kohl-BAIR) FAMILY
Alana (ah-LAH-nah)
Jean-Baptiste (jon bah-TEEST)
Louise (loo-EEZ)
Noël (noh-EL)

DAUBIN (doh-BAHN) FAMILY
Angelique (on-jel-EEK)
Émile (ay-MEEL)
Marie-Caroline (mah-REE cah-roh-LEEN)

ÉTIENNE (AY-tyen) FAMILY
Aude (ode)
Claire (clair)
Gilles (jeel)
Jeanne (jahn)
Lina (LEE-nuh)
Maxence (max-AHNCE)
Oscar (oh-SCAHR)
Rosalie (roh-zah-LEE)
Victor (vik-TORE)

OTHER CHARACTERS
†Barbaroux (bar-bah-ROO)
†Carrier (car-YAY)
Evennou (ev-en-NOO)
Florence (flohr-AHNCE)
Froment (froh-MOHN)
Hirel (ee-REL)
†Marat (mah-rah)
Martel (mar-TEL)
Nadon (nah-DOHN)
Nicole Richaud (nee-KOHL ree-SHOHD)
Père Quéré (pair kay-RAY)
Pierre (pee-YAIR)
Prado (prah-DOH)
†Robespierre (robes-pee-YAIR)
Roulin (roo-LAHN)
Savatier (sah-vah-tee-YAY)
Tanet (tah-NAY)
Trouard (troo-AHRD)
Voulland (voo-LAHND)

†*Historical figures*

PLACES

Blain (blahn)
*Chapeau Rouge (sha-POH rooj)
Dinard (dee-NAHRD)
*Ilizmaen (eel-eez-MAEN)
Loire (lwahr)
Lorient (loh-ree-OHN)
Marseille (mar-SAY-ye)
Montpellier (mohn-pel-YAY)
Nantes (nont)
Nozay (noh-ZAY)
Provence (proh-VAHNCE)
Rennes (ren)
*Le Rossignol (luh ross-in-YOLE)
Saint-Domingue (sahn doh-MAHNG)
Saint-Malo (sahn mah-LOH)
Savenay (sah-ven-AY)
Tuileries (twee-luh-REE)
Vendée (vahn-DAY)

*Fictional places

FRENCH TERMS

Adieu: Literally "at God," meaning an expectation of meeting after this life.

A demain (ah de-MAHN): Until tomorrow.

Aristo (ah-ree-STOH): An aristocrat.

Aurevoir (oh-rev-WAHR): Literally "until the next meeting." Used to say goodbye.

Bien sûr (byun sur): Of course.

Biniou (bin-YOO): Breton bagpipes.

Bonne nuit (bon NWEE): Good night.

Bonsoir (bon-SWAHR): Good evening.

Bonté divine (bon-TAY dee-VEEN): Literally "divine goodness." Goodness gracious.

C'est bon (say bohn): It's good.

C'est naturel (say nat-ur-EL): Literally "It's natural." Of course.

Charmeur (shar-MUHR): Charmer.

Chef-de-brigade (shef duh bree-GAHD): Brigade chief. In the republic's army, this rank was equivalent to a colonel.

Cher/chère (shair): Dear.

Chéri/chérie (shair-EE): Dear one.

Chouan (shoo-AHN): A Breton counterrevolutionary, named after the sound the French use for an owl's call, which was said to be their signal.

Chouannerie (shoo-ahn-air-EE): The Breton counterrevolutionary movement.

Chut (shoot): Shush.

Cidre (SEE-druh): Cider. A Breton drink with low alcohol content made
 from apples. Because of potential contamination, during this time period it was safer for people to drink water that had acidity added (such
 as lemonade), was brewed (such as for tea, coffee, or chocolate), or
 had some level of alcohol (like *cidre*). These treatments killed micro-
 organisms that would make people sick, though people at the time
 did not know the science behind why it was healthier not to drink
 straight water.

Ciel (syel): Heavens.

Cirier (seer-YAY): Candlemaker.

Citoyen (sit-wah-YUN): Citizen (masculine).

Citoyenne (sit-wah-YEN): Citizen (feminine).

Citrouille (sit-roo-EE): Pumpkin.

Demi-brigade (demi bree-GAHD): Literally "half brigade." The new
 military units created in 1793 to replace Old Regime regiments. At
 this time they included two companies of *fédérés* and one company of
 national guards.

Diantre (dee-ON-truh): Literally "the devil." Good heavens.

Dieu merci (dyuh mair-SEE): Thank the Lord.

Émigrés (ay-mee-GRAY): Immigrants. The name given to French royalists who fled France to escape the revolutionaries.

Fédéré (fay-day-ray): Literally "federalist." The name used for militiamen.

Fichtre (FEESH-truh): Gosh.

Fusiliers (foo-sil-YAY): Another word for soldier.

Galette (gal-ET): Breton crêpes made of buckwheat flour.

Grandmère (grahn-MAIR): Grandmother.

Grandpère (grahn-PAIR): Grandfather.

Gouvernante (goo-vair-NAHNT): Governess.

Habit national (ah-BEE nah-shyun-AL): Literally "national dress." Used
 to describe the national guard uniform of a blue coat with white lapels, red piping, and red collar. It was adopted by other branches of
 military starting in 1793.

Jacobin (jack-oh-BUN): A member of the Jacobin club, one of the most
 influential political factions of the French Revolution. Against
 the monarchy and the old ways, members of the Jacobin club like

Robespierre are largely blamed for the Reign of Terror and execution of Louis XVI and Marie-Antoinette.

Je t'aime (juh-TEM): I love you.

La patrie (la paht-REE): The fatherland.

Le rufian (luh roo-FYAHN): The ruffian.

Levée en masse (lev-AY on mass): Mass draft. In 1793, the republic drafted all able-bodied, unmarried men between the ages of eighteen and twenty-five who were not fathers into the army to fight enemies in France and abroad.

Livre (LEE-vruh): Pound. The unit of money used before the franc became the official monetary unit in 1795.

Louis Capet (loo-EE cap-AY): The civilian name given to Louis XVI by revolutionaries.

Maman (ma-MAW): Mama.

Ma femme (ma fem): My wife.

Ma fille (ma fee): My daughter.

Marseillais (mar-say-YAY): Literally "person from Marseille." The name given to the group of volunteers who marched from Marseille to protect Paris from royalists. The Marseillais made up a majority of the force that stormed the Tuileries Palace and took Louis XVI and his family into custody.

Menhir (men-EER): A standing stone.

Merci (mair-SEE): Thank you.

Mère (mair): Mother.

Messieurs (may-SYUH): Plural form of *monsieur*.

Misérables (mee-zay-RAH-bluh): Unfortunate souls.

Mon ami/mon amie (mohn ah-MEE): My friend.

Mon amour (mohn ah-MOOR): My love.

Monarchiste (mohn-ahr-SHEEST): A monarchist.

Mon chou (mohn shoo): My cabbage. A term of endearment, like "honey" in English.

Mon fils (mohn fees): My son.

Mon frère (mohn frair): My brother.

Neveu (nev-EUH): Nephew.

Oncle (OHN-kluh): Uncle.

Pain d'égalité (pan day-gal-ee-TAY): Literally "bread of equality." The bread everyone in France was supposed to eat, which had a fixed price throughout the country.

FRENCH TERMS

Parfait (pahr-FAY): Perfect.

Parfumeries (par-fewm-air-EE): Perfume shops.

Pas possible (pah poh-SEE-bluh): Not possible.

Passepied (pass-pee-YAY): A Breton dance performed in a circle.

Patriote (pah-tree-OHT): Patriot. Used to refer to revolutionaries.

Père (pair): Father.

Petite sotte (puh-TEET soht): Fool, silly, idiot.

Pitié (peet-YAY): Literally "pity." Have mercy.

Potage (poh-TAHJ): Thick soup. Usually savory, but there are a few instances of sweet potage in eighteenth-century French cookbooks.

Que diable (kuh dee-AB-luh): What the devil!

Que diantre (kuh dee-ON-truh): Literally "what the devil!" Good heavens.

Quel démon (kel day-MOHN): What a demon!

Quel niguad (kel nee-GOHD): What a simpleton!

Regarde (re-GAHRD): Look.

Remercie le ciel (re-mair-SEE luh syel): Literally "thank the sky." Thank heavens.

Répresentat-en-mission (ray-pray-sahnt-AH on mi-SHYON): Literally, "representative on mission." These government officials were sent from Paris to oversee various regions and make sure the Republic's rules were being upheld. Many were responsible for allowing large numbers of executions.

République (ray-pew-BLEEK): Republic.

Révolutionnaire (rev-oh-loo-shun-AIR): A revolutionary.

Royaliste (roh-yahl-EEST): A royalist.

Rue (rew): Road.

Sacrebleu (sah-kruh-BLUH): Literally "sacred blue." Oh my gosh.

Sans-culotte (son kew-LOHT): Literally "without breeches." Breeches were a symbol of the upper class, and the sans-culottes rejected the style as a sign that they did not support the aristocracy. This group of revolutionaries was one of the most feared, as they were often the group to start violence in the streets. Their symbol was the red liberty cap.

Savon de Marseille (sav-on duh mar-SAY-ye): Soap of Marseille. A type of olive oil-based soap made exclusively in Marseille. Its process and name has been protected since the seventeenth century, and it is still famous throughout the world.

Savonnerie (sav-on-eh-REE): Soap factory.

S'il te plaît (seel tuh play): The informal form of please.

S'il vous plaît (seel voo play): Literally "if it pleases you." The formal or plural form of please.

Si vous voulez (see voo voo-LAY): If you want.

Soldat (sohl-DAHT): Soldier.

Sous-lieutenant (soo lyuh-ten-AHNT): Under lieutenant or second lieutenant.

Talabard (tah-lah-BAHRD): A Breton instrument similar to a trumpet.

Tante (tahnt): Aunt.

Tricolore (tree-koh-LOR): Literally "tricolor." A name for the French flag.

Une noble (oon NOH-bluh): A noble.

Vendéean (von-day-AHN): A person from the Vendée region. Also used to describe a counterrevolutionary from that region.

Vivre le roi (veev luh rwah): Long live the king.

BRETON TERMS

Breizhadez on (breyes-ahd-ES own): I am Breton.

Demat (day-mat): Hello.

Kannerezed noz (kahn-er-es-ED noze): Ghosts from Breton mythology similar to banshees of Irish mythology. They are said to wash the shrouds of those about to die.

Kenavo (ken-ah-vo): Goodbye.

Noz vat (noze VAHT): Good night.

Trugarez (troo-GAR-es): Thank you.

PROLOGUE

25 June 1792
Marseille, Provence, France

Paris. It called to Maxence Étienne as he tore apart his bedroom, attempting to decide what to bring. Robespierre, Barbaroux, Marat—all the people who had a hand in bringing liberty to France were in Paris making their mark on history, and now it was his turn.

Maxence threw a new jacket on the bed. That wouldn't be going, much as it pained him to leave it behind. This wasn't a grand tour for young *aristos* with money to burn. His red leather mules echoed across the floor as he moved to his trunk. Those would be staying as well. There wouldn't be any use for them in a dirty camp.

He shoved aside a stack of books he'd hardly read, searching for another shirt in the depths of the trunk. His younger brother, Gilles, was the scholar in the family, despite not having started his studies at the university. If Gilles weren't coming with him, Maxence would happily have given him these tomes.

Ah, there was the shirt. He pulled the wadded fabric out from under the books. The linen was terribly wrinkled. Perhaps Maman could be persuaded to press it before he left. No doubt she'd already mended, washed, and pressed Gilles's clothes. He was, after all, her baby.

A familiar clenching in his stomach warranted another glass of wine. He went to the bedside table where an empty glass and half-full bottle sat. Maxence poured a generous serving and took a sip. There was no need for childish envy against his brother. In a matter of days, they'd be off to Paris to protect the city from the threat of invasion from foreign powers who thought they knew what was best for France.

He twisted the stem of the glass in his fingers. Their friend Émile Daubin would also be with them. Barely a week ago all three of them had sat in a nearby courtyard, listening to the stirring songs of liberty. Barbaroux had called for six hundred Marseillais who knew how to die to stand up in defense of *la patrie*. The three of them had immediately volunteered to join the *fédérés* and march to Paris, leaving southern France and all its troubles behind.

Someone tapped on the door, and Maxence returned the glass to the table. As he made his way to answer it, he tripped over a book on the floor. Detestable thing. He kicked it under the bed.

With a deep breath, he grasped the door handle, hoping it wasn't his mother to give him a disappointed stare over the state of the room. Their long, comfortable talks—when he'd shared his heart and she her wisdom—had ended when he left for university and Gilles returned from the sea. Maxence regularly tried to convince himself he didn't miss those conversations. He swung the door open to reveal his younger brother. Thank the stars.

Gilles was much shorter than Maxence, but the hint of laughter in his eyes more than made up for it where girls were concerned. Though they looked similar—same dark curls, same brown eyes, same swarthy complexion—Gilles had a softness to his demeanor that women found irritatingly irresistible.

Maxence grinned. "*Mon frère*, I thought you'd gone to bed. Come in." He motioned behind him. Not that there was a place to sit in the disarray. At least Gilles wouldn't judge Maxence for the mess. Even as tidy as Gilles was, he'd understand the struggle to pack for a rough journey of unknown length.

But Gilles's usual playfulness had fled tonight. He sighed, and his solemn countenance brought back the clenching in Maxence's stomach. Perhaps his brother was simply subdued by the weight of their responsibility to the new nation.

"You are lucky, you know," Maxence said, hoping to put him at ease. "You did not have to cart home all your belongings before setting off for Paris." All those heavy books, none of which had helped him excel in his medical studies. Gilles was already a better physician without the formal study.

"I wish to speak to you on that subject," Gilles said. Something in his voice piqued Maxence's unease.

"Our departure?"

"The whole venture." Gilles dropped his gaze to the floor.

Maxence hesitated. "What venture?" Surely he wasn't reconsidering.

Gilles licked his lips. "I have decided to remain in Marseille and help build up the Club here." His voice was low, hesitant.

Maxence straightened, his head spinning and not just from the drink. "You aren't joining the *fédérés*?"

Gilles picked at the sleeve of his shirt. "We can't all go off to follow our convictions and leave Maman on her own."

Maman. No, of course not. Gilles couldn't go off and leave the woman who coddled and praised him. How would he keep up his confidence without her holding his hand each step of the way? Heat rose in Maxence's chest, and he looked away. "Hang Maman." His brother would have to learn to make his own decisions. Never mind that several years ago Maxence would have done anything to get the same regard from his parents that Gilles enjoyed. Père hadn't given it during Maxence's years at sea on *le Rossignol*. And once he'd gone off to Montpellier for university and Gilles had returned home from their father's ship, Maman stopped giving it as well. She disapproved of Maxence's dallying.

"France needs you more than Maman." Maxence wiped a hand across his mouth. He didn't know how to inspire the same zeal they'd all felt listening to the songs of revolution. Émile was the one who could recite stirring speeches. "You had no qualms running off on *le Rossignol*. And now you're worried about her being alone? She has Rosalie. The girls." Their oldest brother's wife and daughters visited constantly. He slapped his palm against the doorframe, ignoring the sting it sent across his skin. "France needs you, Gilles."

"One man is not going to make a difference." Maxence could hear the seething in his brother's voice. He'd gone too far with the comment on their mother, but he didn't care. Losing one man wasn't the issue, because it wouldn't be just one.

"How many others are making that same craven justification?" He smacked the doorframe again. "The *fédérés* are counting on you. The Club is counting on you." And the sinking in his stomach belied the fact that *he* was counting on Gilles too. Gilles was the only one who seemed to think him worthy of notice in this family. Worthy of esteem. "If we do not stand between Paris and her enemies, what will this country come to?"

"Paris's enemies, or the Jacobins'?" Gilles muttered.

"What did you say?"

Gilles lifted his head, shaking it. "I was never the best on the gun crews. I think the *fédérés* will hardly miss me." He shrugged, a glimmer of his usual humor lighting his eye.

A bald-faced lie, and Père would agree. There was a reason their father continued to hound Gilles about rejoining his ship's crew. Maxence snorted. "Never the best? You practically were the gun crew. Père made you a crew captain before you were even an able seaman."

"I'm pathetic with a musket."

More excuses. "You think the *fédérés* won't have cannon? You're exactly what they need." Maxence growled and pulled at his hair. "Don't do this, *mon frère*." They were supposed to go together. As brothers.

"What about Maman? Rosalie? The girls? What if there's an attack by sea, or what if the *révolutionnaires* are overrun by the *monarchistes* while we are away?"

Their mother again. Maxence gave a mirthless chuckle and turned away. He needed to pack. There wasn't time for this.

He moved to the stack of books on the bed, limbs suddenly leaden. Gilles had made up his mind—or perhaps more accurately, Maman had made it up for him—and Maxence wouldn't be able to change it. Perhaps Émile could. He tossed the books to the floor one by one, each thud ramming home the realization that he wouldn't have his brother by his side as they marched.

None of his jokes or optimism. When they'd both worked at sea, Gilles had been a calming, reassuring presence when it was time to face the enemy's guns. Maxence wouldn't have that in Paris.

"You refused to go recruit for the cause with Martel," Maxence said after he'd removed every book from his bed. "You refuse to go to Paris to help us maintain peace and liberty. And you call yourself a Jacobin." He spit at the floor. If Gilles wouldn't come, then Maxence didn't need him. France didn't need him. They'd do better without tepid loyalty.

"I am no *royaliste*. I wish for freedom and a new France. I simply . . . What will we do in Paris? If the army holds the Prussians and Austrians, I mean."

"What we do here. Advance the cause with every waking breath." Maxence threw a cravat over one shoulder, then another. He'd only need one neckcloth. Or perhaps two. Those wouldn't take up much room.

"But what does that mean? Stir up riots? Beat into submission those who disagree?"

It meant to defend liberty for themselves and their countrymen. Did Gilles not see that? "Whatever is needed."

"I left *le Rossignol* to help people, not to hurt them."

Ah, yes. Let's be noble about our weakness. Maxence gathered his clothing into a small pile on the bed. He'd just suffer the wrinkled shirt. He wasn't above sacrificing personal comforts for greater causes. "Sometimes a little pain is what is best for them."

"But you cannot force it. Do they not still have the right to choose?"

No, his brother wouldn't last a day in the *fédérés*. Not with this womanly concern that had been instilled in his heart by their mother. "You are a coward, Gilles Étienne," Maxence said over his shoulder.

"It is not cowardice to be wise."

Maxence stiffened. Those were not Gilles's own words. Those came from the man they'd both learned to detest. Maxence turned, lips pulling into a sneer. "You sound like Père. Fitting for someone who cares only about his own safety and gain."

"I'm not the one leaving home to prey on those who cannot defend themselves," Gilles said through gritted teeth.

Something snapped. Maxence couldn't say what. His brain was a fog of disbelief and anger that propelled him toward the door. He'd heard enough.

Gilles crouched, fists raised. But Maxence caught himself against the doorframe, snarling. "Then stay and hide behind the women's skirts," he bellowed. "And may your impure blood water the fields with that of every other enemy of France."

He seized the door and slammed it shut, banishing his brother's hollow stare. The door crashed against its frame, and the force reverberated through him. He didn't need Gilles or the chance to rediscover the companionship they'd once shared. He had Émile, a true friend and Jacobin, and he had France.

Maxence gasped for air as though it had been sucked from the room. The *fédérés* would become his brothers, more dear to him than Gilles or their eldest brother, Victor. His comrades would be the support he couldn't find anywhere else. This journey would be the start of a new life.

Yet as Maxence stood amid the debris of his last twenty-four years, the gaping void inside threatened to swallow him whole.

CHAPTER 1

One and a half years later
25 February 1794 (7 Ventôse Year II)
Nantes, Brittany, France

Funny how the sun always sensed elation and seemed to clear the skies in response.

Armelle Bernard turned her face toward its warmth, closing her eyes to block out the somber city streets around her. The bubble of joy inside her chest continued to swell, threatening to burst.

Dockworkers and sailors and businessmen passed by, their eyes on the ground. Thank the heavens. Few had reason to be joyful these days, especially in Nantes, and she'd surely draw stares if they weren't so preoccupied. No one deserved this much happiness, not when so many lives had been destroyed in these times of terror. She couldn't fathom how her family had received such luck.

Oh, come, Nicole. Her friend, usually so prompt, had not been punctual for their Tuesday morning meetings of late. Today Armelle had hoped Nicole would be on time. The wait was making her want to shout her news to every passerby, and what a disaster that could prove.

She rocked forward and back, the wooden heels of her shoes clacking against the cobbles. Between the buildings, the Loire River crept drab and grey through the city. It didn't reflect the brilliant sky. How could it, after all the drownings?

Armelle snapped her gaze away and dug her hand into her pocket. A folded corner of paper pricked her finger and brought a smile to her lips. The poke might have hurt if the letter hadn't been softened from being unfolded and refolded a hundred times since last night. That graveyard of a river would not keep her in melancholy a moment longer. She drew out the letter once more and opened it. There was no mistaking the familiar writing that told of life at sea on the Provençal brig *le Rossignol*, as though nothing had happened and his entire family didn't think him at the bottom of the river. He'd even made a carefree little drawing of a ship and nightingale to match the name of the vessel.

Nicole's bonnet appeared through the crowd, and Armelle couldn't stand still. She released the letter in her pocket and dashed toward her friend. The bucket she carried sloshed water across her red cloak and the trousers of men she passed. Grunts of annoyance erupted in her wake, but she paid them no mind. That was the peril of walking in the streets—one never knew what they'd be splattered with. At least her bucket was only full of water.

"What kept you?" Armelle fell into step with Nicole, going back the way she'd come.

Her friend sighed, a heavy, slow sound like the groan of a rusty prison gate. "Nothing unusual." The sparkle that had once graced Nicole's eyes had vanished in the last year, replaced by dark circles and worry lines and drooping shoulders.

Armelle's good news caught in her throat. Nicole looked old. Not twenty-four hours ago Armelle must have looked the same. She had certainly felt ancient until last night. How strange that one day could change a person from feeling eighty to her true age of twenty.

"Your work is taking a toll on you," Armelle said, decreasing her pace to match her friend's. The previous summer the République had laid siege to Nantes, forcing out counterrevolutionaries—Vendéeans from the south and Brittany's own Chouans—before arresting, imprisoning, and then executing anyone connected with the rebellion. With the uprising still alive in some parts of the region, the arrests hadn't slowed.

Nicole's lips pressed tightly together, and she looked away. "I'm not suffering more than those people I feed. We need the money, and Papa needs help." Her voice dropped so Armelle could barely hear. "There are so many."

They continued for a moment in silence toward the coffee warehouse where Nicole and her father worked. Once such an innocent establishment, the place had been turned into a jail for thousands of Bretons and Vendéeans the government had determined were traitors to the republic. Feeding all those people waiting to be taken to their deaths had buried Nicole's smile, much like being the final resting place of the same people had erased the Loire's beauty.

Armelle's bucket tapped against her leg, as if to remind her of the news begging to be shared. "Perhaps there is some hope." Hope that this infernal war would end, that neighbors would stop turning in neighbors, and that her family would be whole again.

Nicole's eyes narrowed. "You, of all people, should know there isn't any. No one escapes the jail."

At least no one had yet. They hadn't had the opportunity to attempt their plan, or that record might have been broken. Not that they would have succeeded. "No." Armelle leaned closer. "But someone escaped the ships."

Nicole stopped, forcing the workers behind her to swerve around them. "You've heard of someone? Who?"

Armelle mouthed the word "Père" and couldn't bite back the grin that pulled at her lips. A blank expression settled on Nicole's face. A moment passed. With a cry, she seized Armelle's arm and dragged her to the side of the road. They squeezed behind a stopped cart. Nicole's fingers trembled as they dug into Armelle's shoulders.

"Your father is alive? He survived the drownings?"

Armelle's eyes burned. "We received a letter. Mère opened it last night. He was vague about his escape, but we think he was able to pull free from his bindings when they sank his ship. He must have swum to another because he talks about life at sea as though he's always been there." A month ago, just after Père had been taken, the government decided to send its prisoners out on the river in old Dutch ships and sink them. Armelle and Nicole had plotted to break him out of the prison, but the execution had been ordered before they were ready. Armelle shuddered, remembering the smothering despair when she had learned they were too late.

"This is impossible." Nicole released her and held her hand to her head. "I thought we'd failed him."

"We didn't." Armelle squeezed her arm. "And if he escaped, perhaps one of those prisoners you feed each day has a chance as well." She set down her bucket and wrapped Nicole in a hug, the chill February air nipping at her damp cheeks. "We can't give up hope. This will pass." A day ago, when she still believed her father was dead, she would have scorned these words. Giddiness had made her bold. Perhaps a little too bold.

Nicole stepped back, wiping at her eyes with her mitt-covered hands. "I should hurry. Papa will have started bringing the morning meal. Oh, Armelle. I'm so happy for you."

Armelle retrieved her bucket and linked her free arm through Nicole's. She didn't care if anyone saw the evidence of her crying. "It hardly seems real, after so much grief."

"I think I would go mad with happiness," Nicole said, voice still shaky from tears. "But where are you off to? You don't have your market bag today."

Armelle gave a wicked smile. "I am not going to market today. Today is a day of celebration. I am going to church."

"I don't understand."

They reached the coffee warehouse's iron gate. Its black bars swallowed the morning's light, and the yard behind it remained a patch-work of shadows. *Here*, it seemed to say, *hope comes to die.* That was certainly what had happened to Nicole's hope as she trudged through this gate day after day. But Armelle would not let this place's austerity damper her resolve.

"I happen to know of a priest who insists on muddying our church with his presence."

Nicole's eyes narrowed for a moment. She glanced at the bucket in Armelle's hand and the brush hanging from the waistband of her petticoat. Then understanding dawned in their brown depths, and she moaned. "You wouldn't do that."

"And . . . ," Armelle went on through her friend's dismay. "I intend to rid our church of his filth, if only for a day." Breton women hadn't harassed constitutional clergymen since the beginning of France's attack on religion. Today she intended to resurrect the practice. The priest may have torn their family apart for a moment, but that charlatan would not win in the end.

Someday her family would be back together. She'd make sure of it.

If Maxence closed his eyes, he could almost imagine he occupied a seat at Maison Valentin instead of this dirty, overcrowded café in Nantes. In this vision he had good coffee, intelligent companions, pretty serving girls, and a brilliant Marseillais sunset through the windows.

Instead he sat on a rickety chair drinking tepid, brown water not worthy of a better name and listening to Martel and Froment compete for control of the conversation. Seven soldiers in blue coats lounged about the café, which at this time of morning sat mostly empty. Maxence sloshed his drink about his cup as Martel launched into over-zealous denunciations of counterrevolutionary forces.

"Did they think they could win a fight against a professional army?

Or that the army wouldn't hunt down and eliminate every last Vendéean or Chouan rebel?"

It was getting confusing who the army meant for them to fight. Their *demi-brigade* had been sent from Paris to Normandy to fight the Breton rebels who called themselves Chouans. But shortly after they arrived, they were sent to Nantes, where they were meant to oppose the combined forces of rebels from the Vendée region and Brittany. Now there were competing rumors that they were to cross the river and march south, deeper into the Vendée, or they were to march north, crossing sparsely populated countryside, to the Emerald Coast of Brittany.

"These rebels hide in plain sight and shoot at us from the trees," Froment said, taking a drink from his cup. "It is not the soldiers themselves but the people supporting them who we must crush under our heels if we are to finish this war." He spoke deliberately, as though trying to show both his charisma and his rationality.

Maxence pretended to drink but smirked into his cup. Though barely twenty-three, Froment clearly had his eye set on promotion. Whispers through the company of officer advancement meant several positions could be vacated very soon. This peacock, who did not even wear his *habit national* well, wanted to recommend himself to his fellow *fusiliers*.

"The Bretons say they want liberty," Martel said, thumping the table, "and yet a majority sympathize with these counterrevolutionary dogs. Who are led by the very *aristos* keeping these peasants from wealth and comfort." Martel also jostled for promotion consideration, though the egret-like man had few things to recommend him besides intense ardor.

What neither man knew was their captain had approached Maxence about being made *sous-lieutenant* after their company's current lieutenants received promotions.

"Is something funny about this counterrevolution, Ross?" Froment asked.

Maxence set down his cup and pushed it away. "If you wish for advancement, perhaps you should learn to call your men by their real names."

Froment inclined his head, a patronizing look on his pretty boy face. "I should have thought you would be delighted to be called after your father's ship." The man saw it rankled Maxence, but he didn't understand that Père's conceit and lack of interest had made being nicknamed after *le Rossignol* tedious at best.

"Come, Ross," Martel said. "At this rate you'll be worse than Gilles."

Maxence leaned back in his chair. "I will never be worse than Gilles. He stayed home." His brother had hardly looked guilty when the *fédérés* departed from Marseille. Martel still insisted their mother had been the one to convince Gilles to stay, but Émile Daubin once suggested a pair of long eyelashes had dampened his brother's enthusiasm. Maxence couldn't help thinking Émile had been right. Never mind the girl would never accept his interest, even if Gilles had a thousand years to try.

A shadow crossed Martel's eye, one that Maxence couldn't decipher. Martel and Gilles had been friends once, both members of the same Jacobin chapter. But something had happened before Martel came to Paris with the second wave of *fédérés*; he'd never said what. "This is true, but you are far less lively now than you were before Daubin got himself shot at the Tuileries."

Smoke. Shouting. His breath cut off as Émile's bloodied face flashed before his eyes. Maxence blinked, fighting to expand his chest for air. Explosions echoed through the courtyard. Red and white and blue swirled in utter chaos around them as he dropped to the ground beside Émile's lifeless form.

"Ross?"

Maxence blinked again. He wasn't at the Tuileries Palace with Marseillais volunteers swarming toward the king's red-coated Swiss guards. And he wasn't surrounded by gunfire with his greatest friend dead at his feet. He was in a grimy café in Nantes. He shook his head, partly to clear his mind and partly in irritation at the continued use of the name.

"What is wrong with you?" Froment asked. He couldn't have looked any less concerned.

"Nothing." Maxence rose swiftly and pushed in his chair. He threw the price of his coffee on the table and strode from the café into the hum of Nantes.

Bretons in embroidered clothing, some in wooden shoes, trudged past in the street, throwing him glances and then hurrying along. He'd like to have thought they admired his appearance. It had cost a hefty sum to outfit himself in the deep sapphire coat of a national guardsman, with its pristine white lapels and red collar. But even though the army had repelled the rebels last summer and saved the city in the Battle of Nantes, few Nantais citizens saw the army as their saviors.

It was just as well. He'd failed as a mariner, then failed as a student. Failed as a *fédéré*, as a son, as a friend. Though his current path had taken a promising turn toward promotion, he couldn't help questioning whether his passion for the betterment of France would also fail in the end.

CHAPTER 2

Armelle slipped through the door of the old church, memories rising like a morning mist of masses and weddings and baptisms and holy days with her family. The musty smell of disuse filled her nose. So few people worshipped here anymore, the new priest had started to complain.

She lowered her pail to the floor and pulled off the mitts Mère had embroidered as her eyes adjusted to the dimness. Nicole was right. This was stupid. And when she'd stopped by her father's carpentry shop on the way to the church, her uncle—Oncle Yanick—had told her the same thing. But Père was alive, and even though she could not breathe a word of it to the priest responsible for turning him in, she would remind that pompous intruder that Nantes did not want him. What was the worst he could do? A false priest couldn't condemn her soul.

A little man in black scuttled back and forth behind the altar, mumbling. A sermon, perhaps? Armelle allowed herself a wicked grin as she stuffed her mitts in her pocket, untied the brush from her waist, and retrieved the bucket of water. She strode toward the front, chin raised. Her footsteps echoed in the still chamber, pounding down whatever fear had followed her from the carpenter's shop.

The clergyman turned, an elated smile on his face. The imbecile.

Few people in Brittany trusted these government-installed priests. Without parishioners, he must have been crazy for something to do. "Ah! How may I be of service, *citoyenne*?" he asked, spreading his arms as though to embrace her.

Citizen. That was how the Parisians wanted everyone to address each other these days. She continued her march to the dais and plopped the bucket down so that water sloshed over the floor. She dipped her brush into it, knelt, and scrubbed the marble tiles with vigor.

"Oh, you must be mistaken," the clergyman said. "The floors were cleaned yesterday." Armelle continued scouring, moving in his direction. This was for Père, and for every Breton broken by the government this man represented.

Her brush neared his shoes, and he stepped back. Adjusting her course, she plowed forward, the wetness soon seeping through all layers of her petticoat and shift, making her knees cold.

"Pardon . . . I . . . What are you doing?" he cried, shuffling to get out of her way each time she changed directions to follow after him. His brows pulled together until they were one long, thick line above his beady eyes.

She couldn't really scrub away the filth he'd brought into this church, but pretending to scrub his footprints from the floor allowed her to imagine for a moment that she could erase what he'd done. Erase his discovery of the Chouan rebel and his family hidden in Père's workshop. Erase the soldiers dragging Père off to the coffee warehouse prison. Erase the newspaper recounting one of many nights that hundreds of prisoners—her father included—had been loaded into boats, sailed to the middle of the river, and sunk into its depths. Armelle gripped the brush so tight her knuckles turned white.

The clergyman huffed. "*Bonté divine.* Not this again."

Oh, yes. It is definitely this again. It had been a few years since Breton women had badgered constitutional clergy this way, and he probably thought he'd seen the last of it.

He walked briskly to one side of the church. Armelle scrambled off the dais and quickened her pace. She whistled a cheery tune, not looking up.

"This will gain you nothing, girl." There was a whine in his voice like her younger sister Jacqueline's whenever she discovered a spider on the floor.

Armelle bit her lips to keep back a retort. She was only here to make a show of washing the floors. If she let her tongue loose, heaven only knew what trouble she might get herself in.

"I . . . I must insist you leave, *citoyenne*. Leave right now. Through that door."

She peeked up to make sure she was still moving in his direction, increasing the length of her strokes to cut down the distance. Mère would be horrified at her cleaning technique, but a thorough washing was not the aim of this exercise.

The priest pressed himself against the wall. "You will bring down the wrath of heaven on your head for mistreating one of His servants."

Armelle paused. One of His servants? He who sent members of his parish to their deaths and hardly mentioned religion except when it helped his image? Heat roiled in her chest, as searing as the day they'd taken her father. The fences that held it safely back crumbled.

She wound up and spat. It didn't come close to hitting him, but the clergyman recoiled as though the spittle were venom. She met his gaze evenly, then gave the stone beneath her an emphatic swipe of her brush.

The man's lip curled. "You're the carpenter's daughter."

Armelle sat back on her heels, warning bells pealing in her mind.

"I did you a favor," he said. "I could have suggested they take you all for your father's treachery."

Armelle's mouth went dry. They'd all prayed each morning, each night, practically every waking moment that the République's soldiers wouldn't come to take the rest of them away. The men in power in Nantes had proven they didn't take into account a person's age or sex when determining who deserved punishment.

His oily tone continued. "You, your mother, your sisters, your brothers. Especially that little ruffian who will no doubt grow to be as much a scourge to the republic as your father."

She pressed her fingers into the unrelenting stone floor to steady herself against the torrent mounting within. Thank the saints she hadn't let Julien follow her from the carpentry. Barely seven years old, he would have pounced on this devil, for what good it would have done. It was all she could do not to throw herself at the blackguard. She needed to calm herself.

"His corpse should be floating in the Loire right now beside your father's."

Something snapped within her. A shout tore from Armelle's lips as she snatched the bucket and slopped its contents across the floor. With a yelp, the clergyman dashed for dry ground in vain. He sputtered, hopping from one foot to the other and trying to shake the wetness from his shoes.

"So much filth today," she said, oozing as much pleasantry as she could, and gave another brush. *Que diantre*, why couldn't she keep control under obvious provocation?

The man's hands formed into knobby fists. His mouth worked for several moments before anything came out. "Backward, ignorant, obstinate peasant." His shoes squelched as he pivoted and stomped toward the front door, Armelle trailing behind him.

That is all you have, intruder? The satisfaction of justice tempered her turbulent heart. She was stronger than his empty threats. One day her family would enter this chapel, whole and restored, with both her parents and all five of her siblings together, as they were meant to be. A real priest would stand at the altar, and all traces of this man and his government would be washed away. She simply had to keep holding onto hope that things would be right again.

The clergyman pulled the door open and motioned to the blinding light through the entrance. "Out. Leave me."

Armelle wagged her brush at him. "But, *monsieur*, I have not finished."

"You have done enough," he said through his teeth.

"I will leave when you graciously rid us of your presence." She beamed and could practically see the steam rising off his face. She'd add this memory to the lovely ones already painted in her mind forever. Unlike the sweetness of those times with her family, this would carry the sweetness of victory over the man who had almost destroyed them.

He stuck his head out the door and began to shout for help like a coward. But if a passing citizen were to take pity and save him from the terrible young woman scrubbing his floors, she'd eat her brush.

It was turning out to be a satisfying morning.

Maxence leaned back against the wall of the café. Carrier, the *répresentat-en-mission* sent from Paris to oversee Nantes, had not come out of his meeting, nor had their *chef-de-brigade,* Voulland. Carrier had insisted on an armed escort that morning. As his power over Nantes had grown, so did the *citoyens'* dissatisfaction. In a world where one minute a man could be at the peak of public approbation and the next lie under the blade of the guillotine, a man of Carrier's standing could not take too many precautions.

Maxence took in a deep breath of dank air. At least outside the air held a hint of freshness from the river. Inside he'd nearly suffocated, first under Froment and Martel's battle to prove who held more revolutionary fervor and then under the weight of that blasted memory.

Maxence rested his hand just over the breast pocket of his coat. A little ribbon, twisted into a rosette, lay under the blue wool—the only thing he had left from his friend.

Gilles should have been there at his side when Émile died. Maxence rubbed his hands over his face. He could never forgive his brother for abandoning both him and Émile. If Gilles had been there, perhaps he would have made that shot. Perhaps Émile would still be with them.

They would have left the *fédérés* and joined the national guard together. But no. Gilles put other things above defending *la patrie*.

"Who do you think Carrier and Voulland are visiting?" Martel's nasally voice whined in his ear the way a curious fly buzzed about one's head in the midst of summer. But he couldn't so easily swat away this annoyance. Martel took position beside him, and Maxence wished he'd stayed inside. The man could never tell when Maxence wanted solitude.

"I don't question what our superiors do," Maxence said. "I do what I'm told for the good of *la patrie*." With one rather major exception no one had caught yet. He fought back the nightmarish images of the Tuileries again. Why were they suddenly springing up after he'd reined them in months ago?

Martel made a face. "Froment struts about and makes speeches as though he were already *sous-lieutenant*." Martel wasn't likely to take Maxence's promotion well. He had led *sans-culottes* and Jacobins in raids on counterrevolutionaries in Marseille, but only because he knew how to whip a crowd into a frenzy.

Maxence pulled his bayonet from its sheath on the strap across his chest. "Let him play the idiot." He turned the blade over. Though it was new to him since they had merged national guard and *fédéré* units into *demi-brigades* a month ago, the blade had a knick on one side, suggesting it had been well used. He ran his nail along the edge. Still plenty sharp.

A little blur of green and blue barreled around the corner of the café and smacked into them. Martel shook the boy off, sending him rolling to the street. "You scamp," he hissed, brushing off his white breeches as though the boy had stained them.

Maxence hauled the boy up and set him on his feet. "Are you hurt?" His green shirt, a little too big for him, skewed to one side, and his cap had nearly come off. The boy stared at him with wide, pale-blue eyes, shrinking back from Maxence's touch. "No harm done." He adjusted the boy's cap over his brown hair. "Where are you off to in such a hurry?"

The boy looked to be about seven or eight, the same age as Maxence's niece Aude. He backed away, glancing between Maxence and a grumbling Martel. It was clear he saw only soldiers, not men who would care about a Breton boy. Maxence wasn't surprised when the boy pivoted and fled, vanishing behind the church across the street.

The look of fear on the boy's face burned into his mind. He hadn't joined the *fédérés* for this, to terrorize his fellow Frenchmen. Gilles had been right on that point. Saving France and pulling her from the villainous grasp of despots and traitors had pushed him to sign on. Maxence had hoped the national guard would prove different.

A tall man in a finely tailored coat exited a building a few doors down, accompanied by a shorter man in blue. Martel slapped Maxence's arm, and they both straightened as the men walked in their direction. The taller man—Répresentat Carrier—pulled out a handkerchief and coughed into it, mumbling a pardon.

"*Soldats*," Carrier greeted them in a gravelly voice after he'd recovered. He had gained a brutal reputation in Nantes, and the blunt lines of his face only enhanced that perception. Carrier wore his hair wild and without powder, as Maxence preferred as well, though he was not allowed to do so in the national guard. The man's olive skin and dark features belied a southern heritage. Another commonality to recommend him.

Martel saluted. "I'll get the others." Of course he'd jump to anticipate commands. As head of their *demi-brigade*, Voulland was the man to impress. But as Martel turned to enter the café, a shout from across the street brought them all around. On the church steps, a short man in black waved frantically.

Carrier raised an eyebrow and motioned for Maxence and his comrade to investigate. They led the *représentant* to the church, winding through passing Nantais who hardly spared the agitated priest a glance. Maxence shared a smirk with Martel, who had no love for clergymen after chasing a nonconforming priest relative all around Marseille before he'd left. But even the constitutional clergy were insufferable.

The clergyman did not bother with greetings. "I did not come all

21

the way from Paris to suffer such disrespect and humiliation as I have been forced to endure in this forsaken city."

"At least we both agree that this city has been forsaken," came a bright voice from the door of the church.

Maxence tilted to see around the priest. A young woman knelt in the doorway. Her copper-brown hair peeked out from under a white cap, and a cardinal cloak covered her shoulders. Though she appeared to be scrubbing the floor, the brush she held and the stone around her was dry. Her face blanched when she raised her head and spied the detail approaching.

"I am a devoted clergyman, loyal to the republic and the cause of liberty," the priest continued. "I hardly deserve the treatment I have faced every moment since my arrival."

Maxence found Martel's whining irritating, but this man was insufferable.

"You do not like your floors clean?" Carrier asked, his tone scornful.

The clergyman's hands balled into fists. "Not when the women are wiping my footsteps from the floor of the church, suggesting my presence is defiling it."

Voulland chuckled. "Étienne, help this good *citoyen*."

Without a word, Maxence brushed past the squat priest. The young woman scrambled to her feet and retrieved an empty bucket. "Your services are no longer needed," he said, reaching for her.

Her hazel eyes bored into him as though daring him to touch her. "I can see myself out, *merci*."

Maxence paused, fingers hovering above her linen sleeve. Something about the set of her lips gave her an impish look. Not the suggestive kind he'd seen on so many girls with whom he'd interacted, the ones he and Émile had made wagers about kissing. She appeared rather unimpressed with the soldier standing before her. It was certainly a ruse. He'd seen the fear on her face when they'd walked up. "After you, *citoyenne*." He gestured gallantly toward the street.

The young woman didn't move. "I do not need an escort."

"Filthy Chouan," the clergyman hissed, squirming, clearly eager to have her extracted from his domain.

"Devil's minion," she shot back with a defiant throw of her head.

Now Martel marched forward. "Enough of this. Get out, girl." He snatched her by the arm, a slimy sneer on his narrow face as he looked her up and down. Maxence took her other arm, with half a mind to pull her from Martel's grasp.

A yell sounded from the street, and a moment later a rock bounced off the wall of the church, worryingly close to Martel.

"Let her go!" The boy in the green shirt who had stumbled into them a moment ago ran forward. He paused to launch another rock that barely missed Maxence.

Martel released the girl and rounded on the boy, jaw working.

"Julien, stop!" she cried. "Please, let him alone. We'll leave." The pallor Maxence had observed earlier returned.

"Children of the republic need to be disciplined," Carrier said. "Teach him a little respect, *soldat*."

"Gladly." Martel stormed toward the boy, who froze for a moment before taking off down the street and darting around a lumbering cart.

Out of the corner of his eye, Maxence caught a blur of movement in his direction. He ducked, but not fast enough.

CHAPTER 3

The edge of the young woman's pail glanced off the crown of Maxence's head, knocking off his hat. He cried out as the impact rang through his skull. A clank and grunt alerted him that he was not the only victim of the woman's assault. To his left, Carrier clutched his face and stumbled back, tripping over a dead shrub. His string of curses turned into a fit of coughing. Voulland made to move toward his companion, but Carrier waved him off.

Reddening, Voulland pointed at the young woman, who stood motionless, seeming just as shocked as the rest of them at her actions. "Traitor."

Maxence rubbed at his sore head. The blasted bucket had loosened his queue from its tie, causing an unsightly bulge in his hair.

The young woman backed away from the officer, eyes round and face pale.

"Étienne, take her away. Dispose of her." Voulland's greying brows sat low.

She dashed for the crowd, but Maxence caught her around the waist, his arms working mechanically. "Dispose of her?" His body had acted, but his mind scrambled to catch up.

"River. Musket. Bayonet. However you wish." Voulland turned back to Carrier and motioned to their carriage driver across the street, who brought the coach toward the writhing *représentat.*

"No!" The young woman wrenched against his arms. "Let go of me!"

Dispose of her. If he'd learned anything in his nearly two years of service to the fledgling République, it was to follow orders. Numbness overtook his limbs in a way that hadn't happened since that August day at the Tuileries. She kicked and clawed at him, but he overpowered her attack and secured her hands with a cord. Voulland regarded him with approval as he helped Carrier into the coach.

Dispose of her. Like dumping refuse in the river. The words rang through his head, louder than the reverberations of the bucket, making it difficult to think. The young woman shouted at him, hate in her vivid eyes, but it wasn't the sight of her face that registered in his mind.

The memory of the last time he'd aimed a gun pressed against his consciousness. The slip. The missed shot. The returning fire that found its mark. Émile's pale face filled his waking vision, and the cold steel of a useless musket weighed in his palms.

Armelle jerked against the soldier's iron grasp. Her shoes caught in the cobblestones beneath her, but instead of helping her hold ground, it tipped her weight forward until she lost her balance. She stumbled, the cord biting into her wrists.

Julien. Where was Julien?

The man pulled her into the street and passersby gave them a wide berth. They glanced at her with heads lowered and quickly looked away if she met their eyes. Objecting or attempting to intervene meant sharing in the offender's fate.

She scanned the crowd for Julien, but he and the other soldier had disappeared. She whispered a prayer under her breath that he'd made it home.

Home. Her breath caught in her chest. She'd never see home again. What would her family—what would Mère—do without her? They'd never be all together again. A fiery surge overwhelmed her, burning its way through her core. No. They had to reunite. She dug in her heels and tried to wrench away from the man who held her arms. This would not be the end. She had to go home.

The soldier tightened his grip around her arms. Armelle kicked at his pretty, spotless gaiters, but he sidestepped. She threw her shoulder into him, as she used to do when her brother Henri would try to wrestle, then threw herself in the opposite direction. His fingers cinched around her arms, unyielding as the stones beneath them. The force made her snap back toward him.

What had she thought would come of this? Her throat clenched. Harsh words, that's what she'd expected. Perhaps getting thrown from the church. But they were surrounded by a war in which the clothes you donned or the greeting you gave could send you to prison. Tears smudged her vision. What a dunce she was.

The memory of Mère stricken with grief from Henri's absence and Papa's arrest filled Armelle's mind. She'd be one more family member taken from home. This time never to return.

No. They needed her, stupidity and all. Armelle cried out as she swung her bound fists toward the soldier's head. He easily ducked but lost his grip on one of her arms. She wrenched away, heart cantering.

Break his hold. Make for the river. She'd lose him in the alleyways and backstreets of Nantes. She kicked back, her shoe connecting with his knee.

His arm hooked around her waist as curses blared in her ears. Her vision blurred. She pushed and yanked and slapped and kicked. But she might as well have been battling a mountain. The cobblestones gave way to a dirt road that slipped out from under her shoes. Her strength slipped out with it. Her body ached from his parries, and her heart ached more. As strong as she wanted to be, she couldn't overpower this servant of the République. Nantes soon disappeared behind barns and trees.

The sun had hid its face behind a sheet of clouds by the time their feet crunched on old snow. She slumped in his arms as ice filled her shoes, and she willed its numbing cold to fill her soul.

Dispose of her. The words throbbed in Maxence's head in time with the throbbing of his arm where his captive had driven in her elbow. Voulland had given his command to a soldier he thought perfectly capable of executing an order. Someone recommended for promotion, who should be counted on to destroy enemies of the République.

This woman wasn't an enemy.

They advanced into a clearing ringed by colorless trees. His chest rose and fell in rapid breaths. The musket over his shoulder pulled down like an anchor sinking into the deep. If he didn't do this, he'd fail as a guardsman. Just as he'd failed at everything else.

Maxence tied her hands above her head to the branch of the nearest scraggly, empty tree. His limbs shook as much as hers did. He hadn't signed on for this. She'd thrown a bucket; she hadn't gathered an army to fight against the republic like the Chouans or murdered one of their leaders in cold blood like Charlotte Corday. She hadn't attempted to free despots and renegades.

Dispose of her. He retreated several paces, legs stiff. She didn't deserve this. Neither did he.

Maxence unslung his musket. *Bite off the cartridge end. Pour powder in the pan. Stuff the cartridge through the muzzle. Ram it home. Slide the ramrod back into place.* He'd done this countless times for drills and street skirmishes with *royalistes.* And he'd gone through the same process just before his missed shot allowed a Swiss guardsman to gun down Émile. He had to hurry in case Voulland sent the rest of his comrades after him to be sure the job was finished.

He cocked the musket and set the butt of it against his shoulder, then eyed the young woman. What his *chef-de-brigade* didn't know was that though Maxence had fired a musket many times, he hadn't aimed a loaded musket at a person, *royaliste* or otherwise, since the attack on the Tuileries, where he'd failed his friend.

She stood, eyes closed and perfectly still but for her murmuring lips. The red of her cloak in the pale winter morning practically glowed against the muted scenery about them. He brought up the musket barrel several degrees to her left.

This was not the day he'd change his ways.

"You aren't going to have a bit of fun first?" Martel's jarring voice made him flinch.

Maxence whirled around, nearly dropping the gun. His sharp-faced companion sauntered toward them. What was he doing here? Curse Martel. Curse him! Had he seen Maxence's obvious aiming for the trees? Martel always arrived at the worst of times.

"Really, Ross, I'm shocked. That is not at all like you."

The young woman's lips stilled. Her eyes opened as Martel's footsteps advanced through the snow in her direction, and she shrank back as much as the binding would allow.

"Get away from her," Maxence growled, gut twisting. His limbs quavered as he stepped forward to cut Martel off.

His comrade stopped. "Says the man who's kissed every girl within the boundaries of Marseille. When did you lose your taste for it?"

When the friend who had goaded him into the pastime had fallen dead at his feet. "It wasn't every girl." He needed an excuse. Anything to get Martel to leave.

"Ah, yes. The little Daubin vixen gave you and Gilles trouble, didn't she?"

He meant Marie-Caroline, Émile's *royaliste* sister. Maxence gripped the musket. "Where is the boy?" Bile rose in his throat. He couldn't carry out his ruse with a spectator. Martel wouldn't let him.

"I lost him." Martel abandoned his course for the helpless young woman and put distance between himself and Maxence. "Carry on, then, and we can at least raid her pockets."

Even at the height of his Jacobin fervor, surely Maxence hadn't been this vile. Sweat gathered between his hand and the musket barrel. His head ached from grasping for ideas. If he didn't shoot her, Martel would. He'd probably shoot them both. "You should get back to Voulland. He'll want a report."

"I will return when we've finished our orders." He watched Maxence intensely.

Maxence's pulse thundered so loudly he could hardly hear. "*I* was given these orders," he snapped. "Go back and lick Voulland's boots, and perhaps he'll make you lieutenant."

Martel folded his arms. "And let you get the whole prize, when I lost that brat despite my efforts?"

"Yes, you lost him, so you don't deserve a prize." He'd have to really aim. Not doing so would forfeit all he'd struggled to achieve the last two years.

"Get on with it." Martel kicked snow at him, sharp crystals glinting in the air. "What has happened to you? You really have turned into a killjoy."

The tightness in Maxence's shoulders made it difficult to lift the musket back into place. It was his life or the girl's life. They both couldn't walk out of this clearing alive. He sighted down the barrel. Drew a breath. Stilled his quavering hands. "War changes us all." He pulled the trigger, and flint snapped against steel. There was a flash and echoing crack. Birds flew from their perches. The young woman yelped. A branch crashed to the ground from the group of trees on the opposite side of the clearing.

"Idiot," Martel cried, throwing up his hands. "How did you miss at that range?"

"My hand slipped." He didn't look at the woman as he lowered the musket. If he got them out of this disaster alive, it would be . . . well, a miracle, as his mother would say.

Martel shook his head, as though *he* could hit anything farther than a dozen yards away. "You are pathetic, Ross. Do it again."

Maxence planted the butt of his gun in the snow. "That was my last cartridge." At least the last one he'd pulled from the box at his hip. Even if it weren't a lie, Martel would have more. He needed a distraction.

With a huff, Martel unslung his musket and fumbled with his cartridge box. "Then I will finish the job."

"Voulland told *me* to do this." *Think, Maxence.*

"And you, veritable dunce that you are, failed your order." Martel shoved the cartridge into the muzzle.

Maxence's heart leaped into his throat. He snatched the man's gun and yanked it from his hands, earning him a squawk of surprise. "She's had enough terror for one day. We should just take her to the coffee warehouse." Then he wouldn't have to see her demise. And she'd have some small chance of someone taking pity and letting her out.

"Enough?" Martel sputtered like he'd taken a face full of ocean water. "A traitor to the République?"

The young woman pulled at the cords, wiggling her hands back and forth as though trying to loosen the knot. Unfortunately for both of them, knot tying was one of the few things Maxence had excelled at during his time at sea. She threw him a wary glance. He had to keep Martel occupied. If she got herself free, she might have a chance to escape on foot.

"She threw a bucket. That's hardly worthy of execution. By tomorrow Voulland won't remember his orders. Everyone who has served with him before attests he's temperamental. We don't need to fear his wrath if we let her go." Maxence backed up slowly with both muskets in hand.

"Let her go?" Martel's eyes narrowed. "You never intended to follow the order from the start, did you?"

"She isn't a Chouan or a Vendéean. We shouldn't be wasting our time on—"

Martel launched forward, slamming into Maxence and sending them both into the snow.

Maxence dropped the muskets to push him off.

"Traitor," Martel howled. He swung for Maxence's head, but

30

Maxence easily dodged. "You Étiennes can't resist a pretty face. If she isn't a Chouan, she'll spawn them."

"You're mad." Maxence rolled, but Martel's wiry frame somehow forced him back. He tried again to take the upper hand by rolling. Martel scrambled out from under him.

"Coward."

Maxence pulled his feet under him, ready to defend. Snow slipped under his sleeve cuffs, biting his skin. Strands of hair fell over his eyes. He brushed them back just as Martel attacked again. Maxence threw his weight toward the man, but a lucky fist to the jaw sent him reeling backward. The ringing in his head from getting hit with the bucket now pealed out like a city's worth of church bells sounding an alarm. He sat back hard.

Martel was on him in seconds, and it was all Maxence could do to prevent another hit. "You . . . will . . . pay," Martel said as they grappled for position. Maxence tried to lock his arms around the other man's neck. Martel wrenched his head away. He pulled at the strap on Maxence's chest and brandished the bayonet with its wicked notch in one side.

"Stop," Maxence said, reaching for his knife in his boot. "Can't we discuss—"

Martel's knee drove into Maxence's stomach. The air flew from his lungs. Maxence gasped as another kick kept him from drawing breath.

Martel jumped to his feet and took a step back to regard his opponent. "I don't discuss orders with weaklings like the Étiennes."

Maxence pushed himself up, coughing.

"I'll finish the command, and then I'll drag your sorry skin back to Voulland so he might see how fine a soldier Ross Étienne truly is." Martel sneered as Maxence tried to rise. "You're no better than your brother." He stormed toward the girl with Maxence's bayonet in hand, the long, sharp blade pointing skyward.

Maxence threw his leg out, planting his foot to trip the rat. Martel's boot struck Maxence's knee and forced it backward. Pain flashed from his knee and flew the length of his leg as it bent the wrong way. He choked down a shout as his vision bleared. Martel's body tumbled over him and hit the ground hard, but Maxence barely registered it.

He grabbed at his knee, writhing in the snow. The pain seared through his consciousness, and for several moments it was all he knew. The rocking did nothing to bring relief. He couldn't even get out the string of curses that sat waiting to be released on his tongue.

Maxence finally collapsed on his side, panting. His knee screamed. He curled into a ball, cradling the injury as best he could on the cold, hard ground.

Martel had won. She was dead.

With great effort, Maxence pried his eyes open. Sweat dripped into them, and he blinked to make sense of the bleary scene. Martel lay on the ground before him. He wasn't moving.

Maxence raised his head, his muscles responding stiffly. Martel hadn't made it to her. The young woman's eyes bulged as she stared at Martel's still form. Had he hit his head?

"Martel."

No response.

Maxence called his name again, but the man remained immobile. With a groan, Maxence pulled himself onto his hands and good knee. Dragging his useless leg, he crept toward his comrade. Each movement sent a fresh wave of pain radiating from his knee.

"Martel." He braced himself before using one hand to turn the man over.

Blood as bright as the young woman's cloak stained the melting snow beneath Martel. Maxence's arms went weak, almost dumping him to the ground. "Martel!" Maxence's voice cracked. The base of his bayonet protruded from Martel's white waistcoat. The man's face had gone ashen, his eyes glassy and unfocused. A faint, raspy breath rattled from his chest.

Maxence's stomach leaped to his throat. A frenzy of diagnoses flooded his brain, ghostly voices of professors he'd tried to forget. One word swirled above the others—fatal. This was fatal. It didn't take a clear mind to diagnose the damage of a seventeen-inch blade angled upward from the abdomen.

He pulled the edges of Martel's coat farther to the sides with hands so jittery they could hardly grasp the wool, the echoes of his medical training insisting something must be done for the patient. But no. There was nothing to be done. Maxence's arms gave out, and he sat back hard, dropping his forehead into his palm.

"Is he . . . ?" the young woman said.

"Not yet." But it wouldn't be long. Maxence's lungs wouldn't expand. He couldn't very well carry Martel back to the barracks. Not that he would survive the journey, even if Maxence could walk. He tried to swallow, but his throat felt like it had been coated with sand.

"Can you take it out?" she asked.

"And speed up his bleeding? Wonderful idea." Maxence swiped his hand down his face.

The least he could do was staunch the blood. Taking out the bayonet would kill him quicker. Martel's breathing declined steadily as Maxence searched for a makeshift bandage.

A laugh rang through the quiet, coming from down the road. Maxence went rigid. Jovial conversation followed the laughter. All men's voices. And the loudest of them . . .

Froment.

Maxence snapped his head up and met her eyes. A chill worse than the snow seeping through his clothing settled into his heart. He had to get her out of here.

Maxence scrambled around Martel. Mud streaked his once pristine uniform as he crawled through uneven patches of snow and dirt. He stopped at her feet, using all the strength he had left to push himself up to stand on his uninjured leg.

"What are you doing?" She shied away from him, just as she'd done with Martel. Wisps of hair that had come loose during their grapple now framed her face.

He tried to put weight on both legs, but his injured knee instantly buckled. With a grunt, he grabbed for the tree branch, almost knocking into her before righting himself. "At least one of us shouldn't have to die today," he said, gasping. He tugged at the cords, unwinding them in the correct order until the bindings slid from the branch and dropped between them.

She rubbed her hands, which had taken on a pallid hue, and hugged them to her chest. "Why are you doing this?"

Maxence glanced over his shoulder. "Go!" He didn't have an answer, but his efforts would be for naught if she stayed another moment. Sounds grew ever louder around the corner of the barn.

A soft touch on his arm halted time. He brought his gaze around slowly. "Come with me," she said. When was the last time someone had touched him like this? As though they cared about his sorry existence?

He shook his head sharply. "I'll slow you down. Go."

She hesitated, brows knit as she studied his face.

"Run!" He pushed her toward the barn. Only then did she turn and flee.

She darted behind the barn just as five soldiers, Froment in the lead, came around the other side of it. Maxence sank to the ground. Shouts replaced the laughter and merriment. Would he even make it back to the barracks alive when they realized what had happened? Did it matter if he died here or in town? It was his bayonet in the man's stomach, and no one else was around. He closed his eyes and let his body fall to the earth, the only small comfort coming in the thought that this would be his last failure.

Armelle huddled between freshly made barrels behind a cooper's shop, willing the familiar scent of wood shavings to calm her galloping heart and settle her stomach. Nicole had told her her plan was idiocy.

Oncle Yanick had told her. Heavens, she'd told herself. Someday she would listen to reason.

Her stomach hadn't let her travel far from the clearing that the soldier—Ross?—had taken her to before ejecting its contents, leaving her whole body quavering too much to run. The reality of her escape did not soothe her terror. Instead her mind fixated on Ross and his look of defeat. The cooper's shop was close enough that she could hear shouts and grunts and cries of pain she could only assume came from him. She tensed for the sound of gunfire. A bullet that had been meant for her.

Not two hours ago she'd stood with Nicole, exulting in the news that Papa had survived. They'd won a victory against the tyranny that had taken over Nantes. Now she quailed in a corner under the shadows of her own stupidity.

She pressed her brow against her knees. The priest knew who she was. Even if the soldiers didn't discover her now, they could easily track her like a rabbit in fresh snow.

A commotion on the road made her shrink back into the shadows. She pressed against the wall of the cooper's and held her breath. Through the space between barrels, she spied one light-haired soldier marching tall and proud. Behind him came two soldiers carrying a third. Martel, Ross had called him. His waistcoat was one large scarlet stain. A chill raced down her spine.

She leaned forward to see farther up the road. Two more soldiers hauled a lethargic Ross between them. His head lolled forward and back as they moved. Blood from a cut on his brow covered one side of his face. His unfocused eyes blinked as he stumbled between the soldiers, who seemed to carry much of his weight. His left leg dragged behind him.

Armelle pressed her hands to her mouth. He wasn't dead—for that she should have been grateful. But the sight of him beaten for trying to protect her wrenched her heart. Before that morning he'd never even seen her. As a soldier of the new République, he had no reason to want to protect her.

"It'll be the coffee warehouse for you," she could hear the first soldier say. "If Voulland spares you long enough for court-martial." She scooted forward to keep Ross in view, but the party quickly disappeared into the city.

The coffee warehouse. That only delayed the inevitable. Instead of getting shot in a field, he'd get shot in a prison courtyard or sent into the Loire on a sinking boat like her father. Armelle hugged herself tightly. All this because she wanted a moment of triumph over a pompous clergyman.

She didn't know how long she sat there before pulling herself out from behind the barrels and rushing for home. Earlier she would have been elated at the prospect of returning to her family. Now guilt compounded in her chest, blocking out the barest flickers of relief. She owed her life to Ross, the soldier now headed for his own death.

CHAPTER 4

Armelle burst through the door of her home. Mère looked up from the pile of mending on the table, face pinched. In the corner, her younger sisters shrieked. Voices erupted in a worried cacophony as Armelle shut the door. She hardly had time to open her arms as Julien shot into them, his cheeks red and tear streaked.

Mère pulled them both into a fierce embrace. "Julien said the soldiers carried you off. Where have you been? It's been hours. Did they hurt you? Why did you not come home?" Her mother's frantic questions tumbled out like clothing from the overstuffed bags of laundry they collected each week.

Armelle held on to Julien, burying her face in his hair. How close she'd come to never hugging him again. A piercing realization made her breath hitch. When would she next be able to hold him after today?

Mère's interrogation bordered on hysteria. "Julien said you were washing the floors of the church. What could have possessed you to do that? After what that man did to your father. What did they do to you?"

"I'm sorry," Armelle managed to say. She could barely make her mouth work as it should.

"We need to know what happened." Mère took her by the shoulders and turned her, forcing her to release Julien.

One by one they were being pulled from home. First her older brother, Henri, had been compelled to join the army by the government's *lêvée en masse*, and then Père had sheltered Chouan rebels running for their lives, leading to his arrest. Memories of happy evenings full of dance and song shimmered before her eyes. Now *she* would have to go.

"The soldier who took me didn't intend to hurt me," she said.

Mère scoffed. *"Pas possible.* What were his orders?"

"To dispose of me." Her voice came out leaden. She'd ruined everything. They'd never be a family again, working through the hard times and laughing through the good.

Her mother's hands tightened around Armelle's shoulders. One of her sisters whimpered. "How did you escape?" Mère asked.

"It looked like he was going to shoot me, then his friend came. He pretended to aim and missed, but when his friend told him to try again he said he wouldn't. There was a fight." Armelle swallowed, the image of Martel's ashen face against the snow sending a shudder through her. "The friend was wounded. The first soldier made me run before his comrades came."

Mère's arms fell to her sides. The tiredness in her features, which had vanished on receiving the letter from Père, returned in an instant. "I am grateful for his sacrifice, but he sentenced himself to death. I don't understand why he would do such a thing. People die for much pettier offenses."

"Perhaps there are good men among the army's ranks." The look in Ross's dark eyes as he urged her to go without him was evidence enough of that. He knew what would happen to him.

"Henri is the only one." Mère turned away, rubbing her forehead.

Armelle murmured an agreement, even if it wasn't entirely true. Mère didn't know Henri's secret, but now was not the time to share that detail with her family.

Mère sighed, her usually proud posture slumped. "You cannot stay."

"Why not?" Jacqueline and Cécile cried from the corner.

Armelle bit her lip and nodded. They'd come looking for her. The longer she waited, the greater danger they'd all be in. A long, lonely road lay ahead, leading to somewhere far from the ones she loved. Julien's stiff arms encircled her waist again. She squeezed him, fighting to keep back the sobs.

Maxence sat in the darkness, his back against cold, wet stone. The pounding in his head made thought difficult. It was just as well. Once in a while the coughing or shifting of other prisoners pulled his focus from the pain in his head and his swollen knee. Not twelve hours in prison, and he already found himself hungry for the company of other humans. That hadn't happened often since Émile's death.

He tilted his head back, then side to side, trying to relieve the tension. Would the army inform his family of his fate, or would he simply slip from their memory and be lost to the shadows of time? He hadn't responded to Mère's last letter. None of them knew he'd transferred to the national guard, then got sent into the army and assigned to Nantes. Gilles would continue happily clerking at the Daubins' *savonnerie*, Victor would continue happily commanding a company ship, and Père would continue happily plundering under a dubious letter of marque, oblivious to the fact that Maxence was rotting in some unmarked grave.

Footsteps echoed down the hall, and faint lantern light painted the stone wall through the bars of his cell. Maxence didn't know the time, but a pretty girl had already brought the evening meal—a scant helping of tasteless porridge—and retrieved the bowl. Perhaps it was a night guard making his rounds.

A figure came into the narrow view he had from his cell and stopped. In the light his white lapels glowed orange. Froment.

"Martel is dead."

As expected. And Maxence would swiftly follow.

How could this have happened? One minute he was on his way toward promotion, and the next he was lying on a straw-covered floor. His inability to shoot someone, his unresolved weakness that set in at Émile's death, had finally turned into a liability. If he'd have just shot the girl, Martel wouldn't have died. Much as he disliked the man's company, he hadn't wished him such an end. But Maxence hadn't had the guts. Not after the way she had looked at him. "Why are you here? No one is allowed to speak to prisoners."

"I received permission from the warden." The ice in his voice only confirmed what Maxence had feared. No one in the army sympathized with him. "You murdered your own friend and have no remorse."

Martel was actually Gilles's friend, but correcting Froment would do nothing to help his cause. Maxence shifted, and his knee protested the action. Would he even live to see it healed? A knee strained from being bent the wrong direction needed rest more than anything. Weeks of it. Something told him Voulland would want him dead sooner than that. "I told you it was an accident."

"You'll understand if no one believes that, when it was your bayonet." Froment sneered. "And to think, you were the favored of the company. Everyone spoke of your loyalty. Your bravery. Maxence Étienne, who stormed the Tuileries and brought Louis Capet and the rest of the royal vipers to justice." He made a flourish with his hand. "You were destined to rise through the ranks. And now you're sitting in a cell waiting to die."

"What do you want from me?" This was not the sort of companionship he'd been craving.

Froment leaned casually against the cell door. "Chef Voulland says if you confess and tell us where you hid the girl, he'll give you a swift end before a firing squad instead of letting you languish here until they decide to send the boats out again."

Clearly Voulland didn't care to bother with a court-martial. "I did not hide the girl anywhere. Martel could have told you that."

"But he didn't," Froment said with a shrug. "And now you have no witnesses."

"She escaped the cords, just as I said, and ran off."

Froment threw him a withering look. "A mariner who can't tie knots. Really, Ross."

Something skittered across the cell. The lantern light threw its scraggy shadow across the dirty floor. A rat. It shot through the food hatch at the bottom of the door, and Froment backed away with a curse. Maxence envied the creature's freedom to move about and repel unwanted attention.

His former comrade returned to the window too soon. "What will it be, *soldat*?"

"Martel's death was an accident, and I don't know where the girl is." Whatever happened, he wouldn't go to his grave groveling.

"Very well." Froment pushed off the door and gave a sloppy salute. *"Adieu*, Ross." His footsteps sounded back down the corridor and faded into the silence of the prison. A heavy door pounded shut, and Maxence felt the force in his bones.

Then stay and hide behind the women's skirts. And may your impure blood water the fields with that of every other enemy of France.

He slumped to one side until his head met the floor, shackles around his ankles clinking. Straw scratched the side of his face, and the stone chilled his bruised skin, still covered in dried blood from his cut. He scrunched his eyes tight as images of home swirled through his mind.

Sitting in the kitchen sipping chocolate with his mother. Lounging in a café with his brothers. Chasing his nieces through the salon. Even standing on the deck of *le Rossignol* with a warm Mediterranean sunset before him and his father's husky laugh in his ears.

It wasn't Gilles's blood that would water the fields.

It was his.

"Gabriel, get the market bag. The big one." Mère's commands rumbled through the house like an approaching storm, and the footsteps of Armelle's siblings pattering up and down the stairs were the rain. "Jacqueline, your cloak. She can't wear her red one."

Armelle looked up from stuffing supplies into her pockets at the kitchen table. A little lamp sat in the middle of it, their only defense against the early-morning darkness. "Why not?" She'd only just finished making it. Plenty of women wore red cloaks.

Mère's hands flew to her hips. "You'll be on the run. You'd draw attention like a peacock in the henhouse."

She was right, but Armelle hated letting the new cloak go to her little sister. Fabric for new clothing didn't come into the house very often, especially not in stylish hues.

Her mother brought bread and cheese to the table and wrapped it up in paper. "You should make it to Savenay by tonight if nothing delays you." She paused and looked up. "Don't let anything delay you."

Armelle ducked her head as though examining the contents of her housewife, the little sewing kit she'd made with her mother as a child, even though she'd already checked for needles and thread. How did Mère always sense Armelle's plans before they were even fully formed in her own head?

"The Colbert family lives on *rue des Tulipes.*" Mère tied string around the paper-wrapped food.

Armelle folded the housewife and tucked it into her pocket. "Yes, of course." Père's former apprentice had left Nantes a few years ago, but they had occasionally visited him and his young family on their way to Lorient.

Her brother spread the pillowcase-like market bag on the table and helped Mère place the food into one side of it. Oncle Yanick, Mère's brother, pulled the curtains tight across the front windows. Jacqueline hurried down the stairs with her dark green cloak, biting her lips in a poor attempt at hiding her excitement over getting the new, fashionable cloak. The younger siblings, Cécile and Julien, followed her with heavy eyelids and tousled hair. Julien was still in his nightshirt.

All this commotion for her. A lump formed in Armelle's throat. The earliness of the hour and little sleep during the night had put her in a bit of a fog. Now the weight of the situation crashed down on her shoulders. She was leaving. Just like Henri in the autumn and Père last month. How many more would be forced to leave this crowded, busy, wonderful place?

"The Colberts will help you get to Grandmère and Grandpère in Lorient. Jean-Baptiste travels there frequently for his supplies. Stay until you hear from us." Mère's tone had the same strict calmness she employed when they tended to laundry. "You're wearing enough petticoats?" Mère packed stockings, a shift, and one of her own bedgowns into the market bag, opposite the food. The loosely shaped jacket would be far too big on Armelle, but it was warmer than the one she owned.

"Yes. I think I have plenty." A little hand slipped into hers. Armelle had to swallow hard before meeting the upturned gaze of its owner. "Did you sleep well?"

Julien held up a little wooden cube he'd carved with Père and fashioned into a die. He always carried it in his pocket and liked to roll it through his fingers when he was forced to wait. He and Armelle played their special game with it each night before she tucked him into bed.

"For me?" Tears gathered in her eyes. *Fichtre.* How could she leave this boy?

Julien nodded. He found the slit for her pocket and plopped it in. "Will you come back?"

She squeezed his hand. "I hope so." What else could she say?

"I remember the time before the bad," Julien said, leaning into her. "I miss that time."

The time before the death and brokenness seemed like another lifetime. "It won't always be this way. I promise." Someday she would restore her family to what it was before the revolution had ripped them apart, if only so she could see a smile return to Julien's face. He'd seen too much in his seven years.

"Food, water, clothing, coins," Mère muttered as she ticked things off on her fingers. "Can you think of anything else?"

The skeleton key. Armelle sucked in a sharp breath. She'd nearly forgotten. "One more thing." She kissed Julien's hand and released it before dashing up the stairs. With a quick glance to make sure she hadn't been followed, she tiptoed into the room her brothers shared.

Last month Gabriel had borrowed a skeleton key from the locksmith who had employed him to do extra chores to help with the family income. He still hadn't returned it, and Armelle thanked the heavens for the forgetfulness of youth. Her plan wouldn't work without it. She pulled it out from under his mattress and transferred it to her pocket. Mère's voice sounded in her head, scolding her for another dangerous plot.

Never mind that. She had to try.

Armelle hurried down the stairs. At the window, Oncle Yanick straightened. "There's a lantern coming up the road. They have uniforms."

The room fell silent. A patrol on the hunt? They didn't have time to find out. "Hurry. Out the back, and we'll cause a distraction." Mère twisted the market bag to secure it as Armelle tied on Jacqueline's cloak and grabbed her bonnet. She only had time to kiss Julien's head as their mother shooed her into the parents' bedroom. Mère threw open the window, which faced an alleyway. Then she turned to Armelle.

A hot tear escaped Armelle's lashes as she threw her arms around Mère. "I'm so sorry, Maman." She hadn't used that name in ages, but as she looked at this woman for the last time in who knew how long, she felt very much like a child.

"My dear, wild girl." Mère's voice was scratchy. Her embrace tightened until Armelle could barely breathe. "How we will miss you."

"I'll write as soon as I arrive."

Mère nodded solemnly, then released her. "You must leave now."

Armelle settled the market bag over her right shoulder and her roll of blankets over her left, then hoisted herself onto the windowsill. She swung her legs to the other side so they dangled above the dirt. "Thank you," she murmured with one last look back.

Mère stood with arms folded, eyes glinting with wetness in the azure light. "Godspeed." Then she turned, making for the kitchen. Mère didn't like taking time for emotions. "Cécile, start crying. The rest of you, to your beds. Pray your hardest those soldiers don't intend to stop here."

In a moment, a convincing wail blared from the main room, the perfect start to a chaotic distraction. Despite it all, Armelle laughed at her youngest sister's acting before pushing herself from the windowsill out into the street.

CHAPTER 5

Morning slithered through the quiet city as Armelle ran toward the Savenay road, but once she'd cleared a few streets, she turned and made for Nicole's house. It was the opposite direction from where she should have been going.

She kept her head down as she passed others. The brighter the skies became, the more people filtered out from houses, ready to suffer through one more day of wondering if they'd be taken by the Jacobins or the *sans-culottes*, the Jacobins' even more radical allies. The citizens of Nantes wouldn't be looking for her. She didn't even know if the soldiers were looking for her, but it was wise to take care.

Nicole's house came into view as Armelle rounded the next corner. Père had made the pretty shutters that hung from the upper windows. She found the door to the stairs leading to the living quarters above the ground-floor offices and tiptoed up to the tiny apartment Nicole's father rented from the office owners. A jailer's salary did not get them much, even with Nicole and her younger siblings helping with the work.

No one answered her soft knock. She tried again, gnawing her lip. What if Nicole had left early for work today? Armelle closed her eyes. She couldn't stay another day, but how could she leave him in there?

Finally the door opened to Nicole's curious face. "Armelle? What is it?"

Armelle pushed her way in and quickly shut the door. The main room was still dark but for a lone candle. The hearty scent of porridge filled the air.

"What's happening?" Nicole wrung her hands. Across the room, her younger brother and sister looked up from the washbasin with dishes in their hands.

She could simply bid her friend goodbye and run for Savenay. Anyone would say that was the smart thing to do. And she certainly shouldn't be dragging her friend into her scheme. But the plan wouldn't work without Nicole, and she wanted her conscience clear. "You remember our plan to break my father out of prison?" Armelle kept her voice low so only her friend could hear.

Nicole paled. "Yes, but—"

"I need your help."

"This is madness," Nicole whispered as they hurried toward the coffee warehouse. Its austere gate loomed up ahead.

Armelle pulled up the collar of Nicole's father's old coat with jittery hands. A sloppy felt hat borrowed from Nicole's brother shadowed her face, and a cloak covered the fact that none of the clothes she wore—from trousers to waistcoat—fit her. She just needed the ensemble to convince the gatekeeper for a few minutes.

"You don't even know him," her friend said.

Armelle took Nicole's arm to stop her. "You don't have to follow through with this." She meant it. Nicole was jeopardizing herself and her family.

Nicole took a shuddering breath. "He knew what he was risking when he let you go. He accepted the sacrifice. And if you're both captured, then it was all for nothing."

"I suppose . . ." Armelle looked back along the street at all the down-turned, dreary faces. No one looked up. Few greeted each other. One never knew what random act would draw the ire of those in power. "I suppose I saw a kindness in him that I have not seen in a stranger for a very long time, and I want to return it." She locked gazes with Nicole. "I wouldn't wish anyone to go through the anguish we experienced when we thought Père was dead. I don't want his family to suffer that grief. And I couldn't leave knowing I had the chance to try to save the man who saved me but did nothing."

Her friend nodded slowly. "What if he's already dead?"

Armelle swallowed and offered a silent prayer that was not the case. She'd already considered it. "Then we did our best."

"Come." Nicole continued toward the prison. "We don't have much time. The guard should be changing now." An essential part of their plan was entering and exiting during the distraction of the shift change. Nicole tugged at the sleeves of the jacket she wore. It was Armelle's and a bit too short in the arms. The petticoat was also too short, especially since it was thrown over the top of the petticoats Nicole was already wearing. The men wouldn't look too closely, but it was vital the new guard saw both her and Nicole's clothing in passing.

The gate creaked open as they approached, and the sound made Armelle flinch. It was all she could do to keep moving when her limbs wanted to freeze in place. Two men stood talking just inside the gate.

"Hurry," Nicole hissed. Armelle practically ran to keep up with her stride. They slipped through the gate, and Nicole called out in greeting.

"Citoyen and Citoyenne Richaud." The men glanced at her, glanced at Armelle, then returned to their conversation with a wave of their hands.

They'd taken her for Nicole's brother without question. Armelle's breath rushed out. She turned her head to grin at Nicole, but her friend's eyes focused straight ahead. She continued walking calmly into the prison yard, her lips pressed firmly together. No time to celebrate yet.

Dead leaves rustled about the packed dirt under their feet. The yard was empty except for a cart. Armelle spared a glance to see what sort of goods would . . . The long, still forms were unmistakable. She tore her eyes away. Those were not supplies covered loosely by canvas. Not all deaths in the prison came from execution.

"This way." Nicole passed the cart without looking. Was it here every morning to take the dead to mass graves? She steered them toward the back corner of the yard and down a little alley. They paused before a narrow door, and Nicole scanned the pathway before pulling it open and practically throwing Armelle inside.

Armelle caught herself against the wall as Nicole shut the door and leaned against it. Broken crates, bits of rope, and a few chains littered the ground. They were in a storage room of some sort. They listened in the faint light from a barred window for any sounds in the alley that would indicate someone had followed them.

"Well, here we are," Nicole whispered. "There's no way to turn back now." She pulled a pin from Armelle's jacket.

The first—and unquestionably easiest—step was done. Armelle pulled off the cloak, trousers, coat, and enormous shirt they'd found in Nicole's rag pile. All were torn and patched, except Jacqueline's cloak. She threw them in a mound with the waistcoat and neckcloth on top of a crate. Standing in her chemise and stays, Armelle shivered as Nicole removed her jacket and petticoat and handed them over. On the way back out, they hoped the guard would see the clothes and not scrutinize the wearers.

"The pins are stuck in the right side," Nicole said. She straightened her jacket and petticoats, which had rumpled from being worn under Armelle's.

Furiously tying and pinning, Armelle tried to right herself as fast as she could. Nicole pulled a cap from her pocket and fussed over Armelle's hair while she worked.

"I'll make the first round of meals and see if I can find him," Nicole said. "There were empty cells in the east end yesterday. He's probably in one of those." Once they knew where he was and Nicole gave him the key, Armelle would sneak in and transfer him back to this room.

Armelle felt for her pockets before remembering she'd left them at Nicole's. "You have the skeleton key?"

Nicole fished it out and showed her. "What does he look like?"

"He's tall, and I think his hair is dark, but it was powdered." Armelle racked her brain for any details that would set him apart. She couldn't very well tell Nicole about his deep brown eyes or the secrets so obviously hidden behind them. She wouldn't be able to see the color in the dimness anyway. "He had blood on his uniform. And his leg was injured."

Nicole's shoulders rose and fell. "I hope I find him."

Armelle grabbed her hands, willing some of her strength into her friend. Nicole gave half a smile and said, "Stay silent. This room isn't used, but others nearby are." Then she crept out and shut the door.

Alone, Armelle pressed her hands together and brought them to her lips. *Please let him be here.* She moved her lips soundlessly in prayer. If he wasn't here, she'd endangered herself and her friend needlessly. And if he was, she'd need all the help she could get to smuggle a man of his stature through that iron gate.

CHAPTER 6

The scrape of wood on stone signaled the impending arrival of food, but Maxence didn't rise. Moving toward the door would make his knee flare up again. Besides, his stomach was too twisted to fathom eating anything.

The rock beneath him pushed against his head, his joints, his aching knee. Stale air clouded his cell, but every so often the faintest gust of a breeze touched his nose from the tiny opening—barely the length of his hand and half as wide—in the wall near the ceiling.

Wood tapped against the floor and slid toward him. He didn't turn, even to get a glimpse of the pretty face of the girl who brought the food. The Maxence in Marseille would have sidled up to the door for a few flirtatious words with her. But that Maxence had died with Émile.

A scratching sound pulled his attention to the door. He lifted his head. The girl stared at him with face on the floor to see through the slot and shoved his bowl back and forth. Was she trying to get his attention? In the twenty-four hours he'd been here, they'd made it clear prison workers and inmates were not to speak to one another.

She pointed with an exaggerated gesture to something sticking up out of his bowl. It had a metallic sheen to it. A spoon? He raised a brow.

How generous. They'd given him something to eat with. Last night he'd gulped his gruel straight from the bowl.

The girl withdrew her hand but continued to watch him. Perhaps she'd supplied the spoon. With a groan, he rolled onto his stomach. This could be the last kindness he received, small as it was. He used his arms to drag his body toward the waiting food, since he couldn't bend his injured knee and the shackles wouldn't allow him to crawl on one leg. Still she didn't move, as though she intended to watch him eat.

He stopped over the bowl and sat back with some difficulty. That was a strange looking spoon. He plucked up the bowl and lifted the metal from the grey slop. Though slender like a spoon, instead of a scoop it had teeth at the end—like a key.

He clutched it tightly, a flicker of life racing through his veins. It couldn't be.

Through the food hatch, the girl wrapped her fingers around one wrist then the other, almost like . . . shackles? She made a motion like turning a key. Then she held out a flat hand as though telling him to halt.

Maxence turned the key over in his hand, unsure what she could have meant. She repeated the gestures. Fingers around one wrist, then the other. Shackles? He didn't have shackles on his wrists. But he did have them on his ankles. She turned an invisible key.

Unlock his shackles. That must be it.

The young woman held up a hand. Then she repeated the sequence again. Unlock the shackles and wait? He couldn't think of anything else it could mean. Maxence nodded, and the girl nodded back. She disappeared a moment later, and he heard a bowl scrape against the floor at the door of the next cell.

His pounding heart threatened to choke him. That girl wanted to help him escape. Why, he couldn't comprehend. Whatever insanity had possessed him to sacrifice for a stranger the day before must have infested her. They'd surely both meet the guillotine, but even that thought could not dampen the thrill coursing through him. His hands shook as he fit the key into the lock of one shackle. A click sounded when the key engaged, and pressure dissolved from his ankle. He attacked the other shackle with a giddiness that his normal self would have sneered at. Never mind he still sat in a dirty cell. He had to rein in the surging emotions to keep himself from unlocking the cell right then and ruining the young woman's whole plan.

A lifetime seemed to pass before he heard the bowl collection, this time coming from the opposite direction. He hadn't stood since Froment and the others had thrown him in this cell, but the lightness in his chest buoyed him up to standing on his good foot. He leaned against the wall near the door for support. The grinding of wheels and sound of sliding bowls got increasingly louder until it finally reached his cell.

But the face that appeared through the bars was not the same young woman. Maxence's blood ran cold. Here he stood inexplicably without shackles and with nowhere to hide. She'd tell the guards, and they would end him without a second thought.

As he stared at the newcomer, squinting through the prison's dimness, a pair of hazel eyes held his gaze. Her lips curled softly. Brown hair with the barest hint of red poked out from under her cap in the faint light from the window.

The girl from the church. He pressed his hands against the door. A familiar face, one he never thought he'd see again. He could practically feel her tender touch on his arm from the day before. Of course she would be crazy enough to attempt this.

Praise the stars.

Armelle watched the alley as she pulled the storage room door closed. Behind her Ross gasped, no doubt from straining to walk normally from the cell. Frankly, she was shocked they'd made it here without detection with only her cloak covering him and how badly he limped. Getting through the gate would not be so easy.

He sat down heavily on a crate before she could warn him. With a crack, the wood collapsed beneath his weight. Armelle winced and scrambled toward him. Her pulse roared in her ears. If someone had heard that, they'd come running.

Ross moaned, and though his mouth moved in what seemed like curses, Armelle couldn't make out words. She grasped his arm and helped him sit up. He held onto his knee for a moment, eyes scrunched shut.

"How bad is it?" she whispered. If they couldn't get out the gate, this would turn into a disaster.

Ross opened his eyes and released his leg with obvious effort. "What is your plan?"

"We have clothes here for you." She motioned to the pile.

He sighed and shrugged out of his blue coat, which was much dirtier than when she'd first met him yesterday morning. Dried blood caked the side of his face and stained the collar of his shirt, trailing down the front of his waistcoat. Nothing a little scrubbing and sunlight couldn't get out, Mère would say. But they didn't have time for that.

"They won't suspect a strange man walking out of the prison?" He unbuttoned his waistcoat and pulled his arms through. Bruises and cuts marred his face. He was lucky they hadn't shot him on the spot.

"I came in wearing these," she said. "We'll leave when the gatekeeper changes, and no one should suspect."

Ross reached for a crate, then seemed to think better of it, and awkwardly pushed himself to his feet with the help of the ground. "You are significantly shorter than I am."

Armelle dug through the pile of clothes and pulled out the overlarge shirt. Nicole's father was a big man. When she wore the shirt, they'd had to stuff it into the coat and trousers to keep it from billowing out.

Ross untucked his stained shirt and pulled it over his head. Armelle halted in the middle of handing him the other. Her breath caught. Shadows crossed his chest and stomach, outlining lean muscles. His arms were equally well formed, no doubt from drilling with his unit. He balled up his shirt and tossed it to the floor. An image of a ship under sail marked the skin of his right upper arm just below the shoulder. The ink-formed vessel crested a wave that traced the ridge of his muscle, its sharp angle giving the impression of a storm-tossed sea. He didn't have quite so bulky a physique as the men in her family had gained from hard labor. Still, the view of his bare torso, even in this light, was enough to make any unmarried woman stare.

"Enjoying yourself?" He snatched the shirt from her hand.

Armelle blinked, heat flooding her face. She scooped up the pile of old clothes and shoved them at him. "Here." So he was one of those young men who thought very highly of his looks. She turned her back quickly. With three brothers, a father, and an uncle who all worked at the carpentry, it wasn't as though she hadn't seen a muscled man shirtless before. Fatigue had muddled her senses. Nicole was the one who giggled and blushed over men. At least she used to. Armelle was the one who teased her about ogling.

"I can't say I mind," he said.

"The gruffness in your voice would suggest otherwise." She locked her eyes on the door.

Of all the stupid things to be caught doing, watching a man dress. Nicole wouldn't be back for some time since she was helping her father in the kitchen, but in all their years of friendship Armelle had never desired her company more than she did just now.

"It was a common occurrence at home," he said. There was a faint lilt to his words, more like the melodic speech of southern France than the nasally accent of most soldiers who came from Paris. But his voice didn't have the warmth she usually associated with the merchants and mariners of Provence.

"You often went out shirtless?" Her attempt at nonchalance was almost convincing.

"Not at home, no. But I drew my fair share of looks regardless."

This streak of vanity had not been apparent the morning before. "You're certain they were admiring your looks?" Armelle shifted her weight from one foot to the other. His injured leg would make dressing difficult. She'd have to remain standing, gaze trained on the door, until she was certain he'd managed it.

"The kisses that followed suggested they were."

Ciel. He was worse than she'd imagined. Which made her staring all the more humiliating. The only thing worse than getting caught doing something so embarrassing was boosting his ego in the same act.

"It is fortunate none of those girls are here now, as they would certainly change their minds," he grumbled.

Armelle tried to swallow a satisfied grin. A dandy such as he would not appreciate the collection of clothing she and Nicole had scrounged up. "Our aim is not to impress today, *monsieur*. Only to survive."

"*Citoyen.*"

She ignored the correction. "Are you dressed?"

"One could say that."

She turned. He tugged at the oddly fitting clothes with clear displeasure. The hems of the trousers were pulled awkwardly over his boots. Powder still streaked his dark hair. Armelle stepped up to him and batted at the whiteness.

He ducked. "What are you doing?"

"You look like an *aristo*." The powder sticking stubbornly to his curls would undoubtedly draw suspicion. Surprisingly he let her brush at his head.

"And you are acting like my mother."

She dispelled most of the powder before allowing him to straighten. "There. Perhaps those girls would at least spare you a glance."

He answered with a grimace as she settled herself onto the ground.

"And now?" he asked.

"We wait for Nicole. Do you need help sitting?"

Ross waved her off. With some effort he lowered himself to the floor and stretched out his injured leg. He planted his elbow on his other knee and kneaded his brow. "Why did you do this?"

"You shouldn't die for helping me." The same reason her *père* didn't deserve to die for helping a Chouan family. He didn't support the *chouannerie*; he was simply doing his best to love his neighbor.

Ross grunted, jaw working. He seemed to have something else to say, but he didn't continue the conversation.

Armelle traced the embroidery on her mitts, attempting to dispel the tension in her shoulders. Fop or not, he didn't deserve death, but she would not complain when they parted ways. *The kisses that followed suggested they were.* It was enough vanity to make a person gag.

In her head, Mère's voice launched into a stream of scolding on the naivety of risking her life again so soon after being handed a second chance. Not to mention the folly of doing so for a man she didn't know. If her mother had realized what Père was doing before his arrest, she might have said the same things to him. Trepidation seeped into Armelle's middle, and she hugged her arms against her stomach to try to make it go away. Mère might be right, but they'd already made it this far. She couldn't batter her confidence with doubt in the middle of the mission.

An hour or more passed in silence before footsteps drew near. They both stiffened when the sound stopped in front of the door. There was a pause. Then Nicole darted inside.

"You made it," she breathed.

Armelle rose and hugged her friend. "Is it time?"

"The gatekeeper is pacing. His replacement should come soon." Nicole removed the bonnet she wore, which also belonged to Armelle, and placed it on Armelle's head. She handed her the pin to secure it.

"They haven't suspected?" Armelle pulled the dark-blue bonnet low over her face before sliding in the pin.

"No alarms yet." Nicole regarded Ross and leaned in. "You failed to mention your soldier was handsome," she said so only Armelle could hear.

Her soldier. She snickered. He would appreciate that title as much as he appreciated being called *monsieur*. "You know I care little about that."

Nicole pulled back, but her brows were raised. As though Armelle was in peril of losing her heart to a coxcomb with too high an opinion of himself. Especially one who was such a libertine as he boasted to be.

The young man pulled on his uniform coat. Armelle scowled. "You cannot wear that." Only an imbecile would think the gatekeeper would overlook a military uniform.

"The other coat will hide it."

"*Quel niguad*!" Being a fop was one thing. Being daft was another. "If they catch one glimpse of that, we will all be dead."

"I'll turn it inside out." He took it off and flipped it so the beige linen lining hid most of the blue wool, then put it back on and tucked in the collar.

Nicole stared with wide eyes, looking close to tears. Armelle pressed her fists to her head. "What sort of idiot risks his life for—"

"The same sort of idiot who throws a bucket at the government official who sends his enemies to the bottom of a river."

Armelle snapped her mouth shut. That man had been Répresentat Carrier? Cold rushed over her skin. *Répresentats-en-mission* held in their hands the fate of every citizen in their districts, and Carrier had allowed so much bloodshed on his watch. No wonder she'd angered his army officer companion. "It will get you arrested," she said, voice quivering. "If not now, then later."

Ross pulled Nicole's father's coat over the top of his uniform. The dirty brown thing did cover it, but if he swayed too much, the blue wool and white turn-backs of the coattails might show through.

"You cannot go traipsing about France in the *habit national* if you're on the run." If she couldn't bring her cardinal cloak for fear it would draw attention, he certainly had to abandon his coat.

"I'm not leaving it."

"Please, just let it go." She stepped closer, catching his brown eyes. "It can't be so important to you that you'd risk everything."

Armelle didn't expect the flash of pain that crossed his eyes, like lightning against a tempestuous night sky. This coat meant more than his pride. She couldn't fathom why. What she did comprehend was the panic on his face, that same petrifying fear of the unknown road ahead that had gripped her since yesterday.

"You must hurry," Nicole whispered. "The guards will change soon."

Armelle sighed as Ross fidgeted with the coat. Another rebuke lodged in her throat. "Keep it tight around you," she finally said and turned to her friend. She should refuse to help unless he gave in, but that look on his face rattled her. Only Julien had ever affected her like this, bending her will to his over something so ridiculous to her yet important to him. "Will you stay here?" Armelle asked. Nicole needed to give the others who worked at the prison time to believe she'd left.

"I'll keep to this corner. At least as long as it would take for me to go home and back." Nicole helped Armelle tie the cloak around her shoulders, then drew her friend into another embrace. "You'll write?" Nicole's voice was thick. Her arms tightened around Armelle.

"Of course." She'd find a way like Père had. "Thank you, *mon amie.*" Memories of carefree days made it hard to hold back tears. What more would this new *république* take from her before people came to their senses? The sands of the life she loved sifted through her fingers, and the fiercer she held to them, the faster they fell. She had to let go and take the new path ahead of her. Perhaps distance would give her the clarity of mind to determine how to recover what she'd lost.

But first she had to get this troublesome soldier through the gate.

CHAPTER 7

Maxence clamped his jaw shut as he strained not to limp. He kept his eyes on the ground, following the hem of the young woman's green petticoat, which was all he could see with the floppy hat pulled so low. Why was she walking so fast? Had she already forgotten how difficult it had been to get from his cell to the storage room? And then they'd had the help of a food cart. The throbbing that had plagued him since the previous morning heightened with each step toward freedom.

"Can you slouch any more?" the girl whispered over her shoulder.

"I'll look like a hunchback."

"Better that than . . ." She paused her rapid pace. "Is it getting worse? Your leg."

Maxence stopped, hands on his hips. His labored breathing alone would give them away. "Of course it is. We're practically running."

She set her lips and glanced toward the gate, where two men stood talking in the open passage. "We need to get through as quickly as possible. Lean on me. I'll help you."

"That won't look as suspicious as limping?" His blasted knee would get them all killed. He should have told them just to leave him. His sacrifice would be for nothing if she died trying to save him.

Her arm slipped around his waist. He stiffened, her reassuring touch sending a strange sensation through him, one he might have found comforting in different circumstances. He laid his arm across her shoulders, though it hardly fit. Leaning too heavily on her would knock them both to the ground.

"Keep your head down," the young woman said, plowing forward. Maxence had no choice but to hold onto her to keep pace.

"Another round of illness running rampant through the prisoners," an older man's voice said, growing louder as they drew near.

"At least we get to stay outside instead of working among them," another voice said. The guards changing watch.

Maxence drew in a shaky breath and risked a glance from under the brim of his hat. Two men stood just inside the narrowly open gate. If his rescuer hadn't been leading the charge, Maxence would have balked. They had little space to make it past, and if either guard got a good look at him, face still scratched and bloodied, they'd be done for.

"*A demain*," the young woman mumbled, lifting an arm in greeting. Until tomorrow. Maxence hoped that wouldn't be the case. They meandered around the pair of gatekeepers, keeping Maxence on the far side of them. His pulse thundered in his ears.

"If we aren't careful we'll all . . . Citoyenne Richaud!"

Her arm stiffened around him as they halted. He clung to her shoulder. She had to get them out of this. One word from him, and they'd forfeit their disguise.

"Where are you going?" one of the men said. "The day is only half done."

Her fingers gripped the side of Maxence's coat. "My . . . my brother is sick. I think it's what the prisoners have. I must see him home, and then I'll return for the evening meal."

Maxence chewed his lip. Had the gatekeepers caught the disparity between her greeting and her explanation? His whole body tensed, waiting for them to pounce and uncover the deception.

Shoes shuffled against the dirt, and the men's voices sounded farther away as they muttered something indistinguishable. "Ah, yes. Take him home quickly. We cannot afford more illness."

"Of course," the young woman said. "*Merci.*" Almost as swiftly as he'd dragged her out of the city the day before, she dragged him into the street. The gate gave a thrilling screech as the leaving gatekeeper pulled it closed behind them. They'd made it. Maxence slowed, his arm slipping from her shoulders.

"Hold the gate!" He flinched at the shout behind them. Someone had caught them. Now they'd both get arrested. Maxence stumbled forward, trying to quicken his pace. Where could they hide?

The young woman pulled his arm back in place over her shoulder. "Steady."

His lungs wouldn't expand. "We can't run." The thought of returning to the dark, wet cell stifled him. The gate opened again behind them, its noise taunting his already frazzled nerves.

"If you act suspicious, they'll get suspicious." But he could hear a waver in her tone as well.

Fate was cruel, giving him a taste of freedom only to squash hope like an early sprout under the weight of a late snow. "No doubt they've found the empty cell."

"Close your mouth and watch the road," she said cheerily.

What good would that do? Rattling filled the street, followed by calls to clear a path. She looked over her shoulder. "It's a cart."

A cart to haul them back to prison? They shuffled to the edge of the road against the prison's wall. A lone horse passed pulling a roughly made cart. It didn't take much imagination to guess what the tarpaulin covered. The driver was headed for the cemetery.

Maxence's stomach turned. He might have been in that heap, if not today then some day soon.

"You see?" The young woman grinned. "No reason to fear." She sighed contentedly, as though she were curled up by the fire in thick blankets with a warm mug of coffee instead of limping along a chill and mucky street with a disgraced soldier.

"There are still plenty of reasons," Maxence grumbled. He had to get out of the city and decide where to go from there with no supplies, no direction, no plan. But his limbs relaxed the smallest amount as they walked. He wouldn't be at ease until he made it beyond the borders of the city.

"Have a little faith."

He grunted. "Faith has never been one of my strengths." His mother had been the only one in the family who put any effort into religion, and that had faded after the start of the revolution.

She tilted her head so that the day's soft, grey light caught her eyes. "Everyone has faith in something, Ross."

Ross? Where had she heard that?

Before he could correct her, someone rushed by them, nearly bowling them over. Maxence's knee protested the sudden impact, and he crashed into his rescuer. She threw her other arm around him and somehow managed to keep them both upright. The youth who'd hit them rushed through an apology before taking off again.

"What is it?" she called after him.

The lad turned as he ran. "A prisoner's escaped. They think he's in the corpse cart." He spun and dashed after the cart, which was rounding a corner ahead.

She went still, meeting Maxence's gaze. They'd discovered his empty cell. In the distance the prison gate slammed shut, and though no one followed after them, it was only a matter of time before someone remembered they'd just let "Citoyenne Richaud" and her brother out. The girl's tight expression hinted she was thinking the same thing. Or perhaps she worried her friend would be connected to the disappearance.

"Your faith seems to have done well for you," he said, scanning for alleys and crossroads. Was there anything close enough to help? "Now should we start trying to run?"

She pressed closer against his ribs, as though worried he'd try to bolt. "No. We walk calmly."

"That sounds like a terrible idea if they are looking for us." The jailers would run them down in moments.

She patted his side as though she were comforting a child. "We cannot outrun anyone just now. Keep your head down, and we'll make it to Nicole's shortly." She turned them down another street, opposite the way the cart had taken.

"How shortly?" More shouts sounded behind them, and it took all Maxence's effort to keep his head pointed forward.

"On second thought, I am quite interested in that side of pork in the butcher's window. Shall we take a look?" She tugged him into the *boucherie* and greeted the butcher in the Breton language.

Maxence didn't try to listen to the conversation. Outside men ran past, and every second he expected them to dash through the door as easily as the flies. He wanted to vomit, whether from the metallic scent of blood in the air or the prolonged fear, he couldn't tell. The butcher turned away and exited the front room of the shop. Was she really trying to buy meat?

"Don't worry," she whispered, guiding him back toward the door. "We'll get out of this, even if we have to hide in each shop the entire length of the street."

"How can you be so optimistic?"

"Faith." She shrugged, tossing her head to one side with a playful look, as though they weren't running for their lives.

"If we live through this, I'll be sure to investigate its qualities." But as he looked at the queue of doors marking their path, the probability that they would survive this seemed dismal. They made toward the next door on the street. Many shops lined the road. It would take a year to get to the next crossroads.

Unless the young woman could work some sort of fairy magic, he did not like their odds.

They wouldn't make it far today. Armelle adjusted the market bag on her shoulder and took in the darkening sky above them. Retrieving her things from Nicole's apartment had taken longer than expected, what with having to explain the situation to Nicole's brother and sister and trying to convince Ross once again to give up that deuced national guard coat. He had not budged in his opinion despite the fatigue etched across his features.

He hobbled beside her on the uneven dirt road. Though they'd cleaned his cuts and bruises briefly at the Richauds' home, he made a pitiful image. At least she'd managed to convince him to travel with her. "For a time," he'd said. He wouldn't make it far on his own in this state. They moved so slowly Armelle could hardly count it as walking. But now that the danger had somewhat lifted, he refused to let her help him move. She couldn't decide if it was because of a manly urge to prove he didn't need a woman's help or if it was just in his nature to be ridiculously obstinate. Based on the glower he wore and their repeated arguments about the coat, the latter seemed more likely. Or perhaps he was just angry she'd dragged him to half the shops in Nantes before determining no one had followed them and taking him to the Richauds' dwelling.

No matter. They'd part ways soon, and he could take his sullenness with him. She didn't know why a former mariner with a melodic Provençal accent would want to travel to Lorient with her, so she didn't mention it, but she hoped he would stay with her long enough to settle her fears that he wouldn't get caught again. He could rest in Savenay and come up with his own plan on where to go from there.

His flushed features belied the effort to walk this flat stretch of road. Poor man, even if he was a dandy and a cad. "You're from the south," she said. Perhaps a little conversation would help take his mind off the pain.

His head snapped up as though she'd fired a pistol. He took her in, eyes searching her face. Was he worried? As if hauling him out of a prison wasn't enough to prove she could be trusted.

"What does it matter?" he finally asked, dropping his head again.

His dark curls fell across his brow, a subtle sheen of white powder still clinging to them. Or perhaps the strain of the last two days had caused his hair to turn an early grey.

Armelle bit back a laugh. He couldn't be more than twenty-five or twenty-six, and she didn't see him appreciating such a joke. "Home would be the most logical place for someone in your situation to go. It's where I would go, if there wasn't a risk of them searching for me there." Her throat tightened. Home. With Mère and her younger brothers and sisters and Oncle Yanick. Someday Père and Henri would return as well. She bit her lip. The memory of their smiling faces made her heart ache. She'd seen her family just that morning, but it felt like weeks had passed.

"If I was from the south, I wouldn't return. There's nothing for me there."

"If?" Armelle raised her brows. "Your accent gives you away. Not many Frenchmen make use of all the vowels in their words. You are from Provence, *monsieur*. Don't deny it."

Ross paused his limping and balanced himself on his uninjured leg. His army coat, turned inside out and bundled into an oddly shaped knapsack, dangled from his fingers. He wouldn't be this tired if he'd just let her help him. "If you know vowels and spelling, that must mean you can read."

This man did not wish to talk about himself, did he? Armelle folded her arms. "Did you think Brittany was a land of unintelligent and illiterate peasants?"

"Your support of the *royalistes*, specifically the Chouans, would suggest that to be the case." He started walking again, perhaps trying to make a grand exit to end the conversation. But he could only look so haughty when he could barely walk, and what's more, she had not finished with their chat.

"Of course, all intelligent people believe the same way." She gave her voice an air of innocence and leaned toward him. "It's so they don't have to think, isn't it? How very clever of them. They let someone else think for them, and then they are free to spend their time in other pursuits."

She tapped her chin. "Perhaps if we Bretons engaged someone else to do our thinking, just as the *aristos* engage someone else to do their hard labor, we would have more opportunity to establish the financial stability the *révolutionnaires* keep talking about."

The muscles of his particularly square jaw tightened.

Armelle switched her market bag to her other shoulder and her bedroll to the now vacant one. Mère always insisted on regularly rotating one's load for an even distribution of effort. "Come, Ross. I am simply trying to understand what we lack." She almost said it with a serious face.

"My name isn't Ross."

Armelle narrowed her eyes. The other soldier had called him that yesterday morning. "Then what is it?"

"Étienne."

"Ay-tyen . . . or Ay-tyen-uh?" she asked, mimicking his accent.

He fixed her with what should have been a withering gaze. Given a few more hours together, Nicole certainly would have fallen in love with this man, with his swarthy visage and brooding disposition. Not Armelle. She didn't know what sort of man would turn her head or flutter her heart, but this one certainly wouldn't do the job. Even if she could admit he was handsome. She threw him a wide grin.

He set his sights back on the road, and Armelle could practically hear his internal groan. She should stop. Let him alone. But where was the fun in that? "How does one get Ross out of Étienne?"

"Ross has nothing to do with Étienne. It comes from Rossignol."

Étienne Rossignol. She supposed it wasn't a bad name. How very forward for him to suggest she use his first name, especially when he had not asked her name at all. Mère would find that rather rude, but perhaps he wanted it that way, in case the army caught him and questioned him. Or maybe he was just grumpier than an old tomcat.

He wiped his brow with his shirtsleeve. Despite the February chill, sweat had formed at his temples. It was time to halt before they depleted all his strength.

"There's a barn up ahead." She nodded toward a structure a little way off the path. The hedges so commonly used as fences between fields were now little more than stumps of bushes they could easily step over. One more casualty of war. "I don't think we'll make it to Savenay tonight." At this pace, they'd be lucky to make it to Savenay tomorrow.

"A barn. How agreeable." Despite his gruff words, he sounded relieved.

"Surely it's better than where you slept last night, with its rats and damp floor."

"Who's to say this barn doesn't have those as well?"

"You can't tell me you aren't used to rats and the damp, Monsieur Mariner." Unbidden, the memory of the ship on his arm rippled across her mind. It wasn't a common practice to mark one's skin with tattoos—not in Nantes—but the only men she'd ever seen with them were sailors.

"I am not a mariner."

"But your—"

His eyes hardened as he turned to her. "I am *not* a mariner," he repeated slowly. Something smoldered behind his glare—a strange anger. But Armelle sensed something deeper, like she had back at the prison. A hurt, an injustice, a spurn. He'd suffered something at sea.

She let him have his peace as they found their way to the barn. It was unoccupied except for tools and grain, though it looked as if it might have housed animals once, judging from the empty stalls and troughs. There was little debris on the floor at the front of the barn, as though someone had recently swept it clean. No house sat nearby, but the land's owner must have used the building frequently enough. She just hoped he wouldn't need it between now and their morning departure. Best to keep their presence unknown, even if the farmer wouldn't mind lending a roof to weary travelers.

Armelle led them to a back corner and cleared away dead leaves, twigs, and straw from the dirt floor. The stone walls held in the cold, but with their blankets and clothing they'd survive the night. The day had warmed despite the cover of clouds. They'd no doubt face a storm soon, but that was tomorrow's worry.

Étienne lowered himself to the ground near the wall with some difficulty. He dropped his bundled coat beside him, loosened the stained neckcloth he'd borrowed, and lay down on his side with the coat serving as a pillow.

"Do you want to eat?" Armelle asked, sitting and crossing her legs under her petticoats.

He mumbled inaudibly and shook his head, eyes closed. She slipped bread and cheese from one side of her market bag. There wasn't enough for two people for two days, since Mère had planned on Armelle's arriving in Savenay tonight. She'd have to ration it.

"One question before sleep," she said. How odd that sounded— sleeping in the same room with a man she'd just met. She tried to banish the thought before the embarrassment turned her cheeks pink. They couldn't avoid the situation, and yet the thought of anyone in her family discovering it made her insides squirm. They would never know. Any of them.

He cracked one eye open.

"It's a tradition. My father always asked me one question before bed when I was small, and now I do the same with my youngest brother." Her stomach twisted as she tugged at the knot Mère had made in the string around the food. Pulling one of Mère's knots the correct way, the string would fall away easily. The wrong way, and it became an unyielding vice. "He would ask all sorts of —"

"What is the question?" His voice was muffled by the bundle of wool.

Fichtre. Armelle gave up on the knot and unceremoniously yanked the string off the packet of food. Mère wasn't around to be appalled, and Armelle's mouth watered so much, she feared at any moment she would start to dribble like a slobbering street dog. She peeled back the paper and broke off a piece of cheese.

"My question is this." The sharp aroma tickling her nose made it difficult to remember what she'd been about to ask. Did it always smell this good, or did the cheese and bread seem like a great luxury because of the events of the day and lack of nourishment? She pulled her attention away from the meal and back to her companion. "Why didn't you shoot me?"

He looked away quickly, then closed his eye and nestled his face further into his coat. "I didn't shoot. Nothing else needs to be said about it."

Armelle bit into the cheese. Its salty, smoky flavor skipped over her tongue as she chewed. "There has to be a reason."

"It isn't one I wish to discuss with you."

He said it with such finality. She swallowed her bite quickly. "If you do not tell me something, I shall have to invent a reason. You wouldn't want that."

"I couldn't care." His voice got weaker, dreamier.

"You should." The cheese disappeared at an alarming rate. She'd have to force herself not to tap into tomorrow's ration. "I have a grand imagination."

"I do not doubt that." Before long, Étienne's breathing slowed and deepened. Very well. She'd let him sleep.

He looked terribly uncomfortable in his boots and thin borrowed shirt. The bulky waistcoat from Nicole's father draped awkwardly around him. Only his white breeches, which he'd worn under the trousers when they escaped, fit him well. Quite well, Nicole would have noted. He'd returned the rest of the clothing to Nicole's family, which meant he had to walk around without a coat since his national guard coat was the only other article of clothing he possessed. Foolish man. What possessed him to cling to a garment that could so quickly lead to condemnation? She might never discover the reason since they would likely soon part paths.

She tore off a morsel of bread and set what remained of her cheese atop it. Étienne hadn't turned out to be what she'd imagined yesterday morning as he'd fumbled with the cords tying her to the tree. She'd assigned him all the courage and chivalry of a Perseus or a Galahad. What other sort of man would endanger himself to save a woman he'd never met? This surly man she'd spent the better part of the day with seemed almost a different person. She paused her nibbling. Even heroes had their irritable moments, she supposed. Injury, fatigue, hopelessness, and fear were not conducive to a cheery humor. And then there was the way he sidestepped questions of his home and life.

Armelle cocked her head as she regarded his sleeping form. He'd catch cold in his shirtsleeves. She popped the rest of her portion of bread and cheese in her mouth and untied the roll of blankets she'd brought from home. They weren't terribly thick, but the wool would keep them warm enough. She pulled the larger blanket free and tiptoed over, then gently draped it around him.

She sat back down and burrowed into the other blanket. Tomorrow night they'd be in Jean-Baptiste and Alana Colberts' warm house. She pulled off her bonnet and covered her head with her cloak's hood. Then she drew out Père's letter, which had remained in her pocket all this time. In the near dark she traced the little ship and nightingale, which Père had drawn in one corner of the page for her younger siblings. Night eased in through the little barn windows until the images and Étienne's tranquil features faded into blackness.

Whatever thought had stayed his hand that morning, she was grateful. Beneath the ill temper and rough appearance hid a good heart.

CHAPTER 8

Maxence awoke to the young woman's vigorous yawn. He cracked one eye open. She stood not far from him, reaching toward the rafters in a long stretch. The grey light of dawn peeked in through windows and slits in the roof, and not far away the bright whistle of a lark announced the beginning of the day.

He reached up to rub at his eyes, arm slowed by the weight of . . . a blanket? He sat up, body groaning at the effort, and pulled it off. The cool, stale air quickly enveloped him. He didn't remember her offering him a blanket last night. The fatigue of the day must have caught up to him.

"*Demat, monsieur.*" She held out her hand to him.

Why did she insist on using that antiquated form of address? He waved her away.

Sleeping on a barn floor was only slightly more comfortable than sleeping on a prison floor. "Standing is easier with help. Especially in your state."

His knee throbbed in support of her statement. Maxence sighed and took her hand. He wasn't sure how much a young woman could help someone of his size, but he would— She yanked on his arm with both hands and hauled him to his feet so quickly he nearly fell on his face.

"Steady." She grasped his arms. "We don't want you to injure yourself again."

Maxence muttered his gratitude as she released him and began digging in her market bag. He couldn't understand such blitheness this early in the day. Gilles acted the same way in the morning. Mère was similar. Just one of many things they shared that recommended them to each other.

"We have only a little bread and cheese," she said, placing the food into his hands. "It will have to do until we get to Savenay. The Colberts will feed us well tonight."

"Who are the Colberts?" He bit into the meager breakfast. It was good bread, if a little stale. It certainly wasn't the dense *pain d'égalité* the République had commanded all bakers and citizens alike to make in order to fix the price of bread. No one, *révolutionnaire* or *royaliste* enjoyed eating that. Her family must have hoarded white flour.

"A family we are friends with who will take me on to my grandparents' in Lorient." The young woman knelt and placed her blanket on his. Had she eaten before he awoke? She rolled the blankets together.

Maxence stopped chewing. She hadn't eaten. "I can do that." Here he stood like an ungrateful wretch eating her breakfast and watching her work.

"Nonsense. You're injured." She tied up the bedroll and slung it over her shoulder, then draped her market bag over the other.

"You don't have to do all of this for me," he said. She'd broken him out of prison, risking her life and her friend's in the process. Whatever debt she thought she owed had already been fulfilled.

"You seem uncomfortable being served." She came toe to toe with him and cocked her head. "You needn't be. Friends help each other, Étienne."

Service wasn't something he'd experienced often in the last two years. Not without paying for it. "Friends? We've known each other for barely forty-eight hours." He didn't even know her name. His muddled brain hadn't thought to ask yesterday, and asking now seemed so awkward. His stomach grumbled, and he lifted the bread and cheese to his mouth again. He hated to admit that he wouldn't get far without eating her food.

She laughed. "Well, I certainly wouldn't call us enemies. Shall we go?"

Maxence collected his coat and followed her out of the barn. His knee wasn't much better, but she didn't seem in a hurry.

They'd almost made it back to the road when the light pounding of hoofbeats on dirt hit their ears. His companion swiveled her head to stare back down the road toward Nantes. A man in worn clothes ambled toward the barn, not paying them any attention. The farmer, perhaps? Had he seen them? Before Maxence could suggest they hurry in order to not catch his notice, two horses appeared in the distance. Though they didn't gallop, their pace implied they weren't out for a leisurely morning ride.

"I think we should stay off the road," she said.

Maxence nodded. "It wouldn't hurt to exercise caution."

She led them to what had once been a stand of trees. Roughly hacked stumps covered the ground. Most of the trunks had been removed. She pointed toward a trunk at the back that had fallen among brush. As they moved in that direction, she looked back at the road.

Her sharp intake of breath brought his gaze around. "Soldiers," she hissed. Their red collars were just visible over the heads of their mounts.

Maxence's heart leaped into his throat. He shuffled as quickly as he could around the tree and dropped to his good knee behind the brush. She crawled up beside him, face taut.

"Do you think they're looking for us?" she whispered.

Maxence tried to swallow with a dry mouth. "I hope we don't find out." He sat, facing the direction of the riders. He couldn't see them, but distant voices carried across the barren fields. "It would be easier to hide if these trees were still here to block us."

"You have your comrades to thank for that," she said. She pulled her knees up to her chin and tucked her skirts around her. "After the battle with the Chouans at Savenay in December, the army cut down the trees and hedges along the road to prevent fleeing rebels from hiding."

Maxence had heard soldiers talk about the battle. Nearly eighteen thousand of the République's troops against six thousand Chouans. The battle had gone as one might have foreseen and ended with the Army of the West hunting down as many Breton insurgents as they could. "That is to be expected," he said, stretching out his knee. Dried leaves from last autumn crackled at the movement. He paused, listening for a moment before he continued. "If something is hindering you, then it is aiding your enemy."

"I suppose. But I cannot agree that all things the army deems to be threats are truly that." She said it with a grim set to her lips.

"Such as?"

"Wives and children of Chouan soldiers," she snapped. "Neutral citizens who simply wish to help anyone in need, regardless of their views."

Maxence held up a hand to quiet her and glanced toward the barn, though he couldn't see anything through the brush where they huddled. Her voice might carry across the field. She hadn't shown such anger since their first meeting. "One cannot remain neutral," he said. "Not in this age."

"There are some who think there should be another choice besides *royaliste* and *révolutionnaire*." She sighed. "My father believed we could stay out of the fight."

She'd spoken in past tense. Maxence studied her as she wrapped her arms around herself. Her fingers dug into the sleeves of her coat. "What happened to your father?" It wasn't his business—he hardly knew her— but her defeated tone drew the question out before he could stop it.

"He was taken for sheltering a Chouan family who had nowhere to go. A man, his wife, and their baby." She stared at the ground with an icy gaze. "He was reported by that imposter priest."

"The shrill little clergyman you were harassing?"

She nodded. "He was—" She blinked and pulled back her head, rubbing a water droplet from the top of her nose, then looked toward the sky. "Ah, here comes the rain."

Cool drips tapped at Maxence's face, gentle and sporadic for a moment. Then the cadence increased. He groaned, ducking his head and holding up his bundled coat to protect his face. The pattering would make it harder to hear the soldiers if they came this way.

"Take this."

Something fell around his shoulders and covered his hair. Her deep green cloak. "I can't take your cloak."

"You'll be soaked to the skin in minutes," she said. "I have a jacket and bonnet. You only have your shirtsleeves because you were too stubborn to keep the coat from Nicole."

"I am not in need of charity." But he held still as she tied the ribbons at his neck.

Her brow rose. "Except when you needed to be rescued from prison. You cannot tell me you had plans to escape on your own." Her fingers stilled, but she didn't remove her hands from where they brushed his collarbone. The gesture was merely incidental, but he struggled to pull his mind from the soft tickle of her touch. It wasn't as though he'd never had a young woman adjust his cravat or tug at his lapels before.

"I might have been able to explain the situation to my superiors given time." Froment hadn't seemed to think so, but what trust could he put in that lout? If she'd left him in the cell, perhaps his captain could have been persuaded to change his mind and in turn convince Voulland to set him free. Then he wouldn't be sitting in a February rain in the middle of a forsaken country with a girl he hardly knew.

"Or you might have been tossed in the river." Her eyes locked on his, her gaze so intense that he wished he could turn away.

"Like your father?" he asked slowly.

She let go of the cloak and sat back on her heels, drawing away some of the warmth with her. The dark rain spots on the dirt around them multiplied until the whole ground was damp. The tapping swelled to a rattle loud enough to drown out all sounds around them.

"I take it you are in support of the Chouans," he said. It was just his luck that he had gone from impressing the region's representative and his *chef-de-brigade* to cowering in a downpour with a *royaliste*.

Her brows lowered. "I had no love for Louis Capet."

He blinked. She wasn't in support of the king? Not that it mattered, since the king and queen were both dead and their heir imprisoned.

"But neither do I condone the actions of the current government." She sighed and rested her chin on her hand. "Or its armies." A bead of rain dripped from a strand of her hair and ran down the kerchief about her neck. She shivered.

"If you aren't a Chouan, what were you doing harassing a constitutional priest?"

That confident beam he'd already come to know lit her eyes. "Getting my revenge."

"And now you've returned to your usual chipper self," he muttered. Never mind that they were sitting in the mud during a rainstorm. He had to look away. She might see a bright future for herself with her grandparents, but what future did he have? He couldn't return to the army. He'd rather jump in the Loire than return to his parents. Especially as the whipped dog he had become.

"I don't let the République keep me down."

"That isn't what the République does," he grumbled. He should have kept his gaiters, even though they would have given him away as a runaway soldier. Though he tried to sit still, somehow the sides of his boots were already coated with mud. How had his life so quickly come to this?

They tensed as hoofbeats cut through the rain, getting louder and louder until the riders seemed to be moments from cantering right through their hiding place. Her shoulder touched his. Whatever happened, she wouldn't abandon him. She could have left him to die, but she hadn't. The thought warmed him despite the chill wetness around them. Not since he and Émile had rushed the gates of the Tuileries Palace had he counted on someone like this.

They sat still as statues until the pounding faded into the patter of raindrops. Her shoulder slackened against his. One more escape. One more stroke of luck.

"You will have difficulty convincing me the République is not trying to hold its people down." She turned away, breaking their connection and any companionable feelings with it. "All evidence I have seen suggests that this government does exactly that."

Rain muffled Maxence's groan, and he stamped down all thoughts comparing this girl to Émile. He hadn't slept long or well enough to handle incessant teasing and contradicting. This day, like this rain, couldn't end a moment too soon.

So close. Armelle glanced at the steely skies. She didn't know this road well, but she hoped it wouldn't be much longer until they reached the Colberts' home, or they'd have to try to find it in the dark.

Étienne sat beside her massaging his knee, his eyes clenched shut and his breath strained. Poor man. He needed rest, and more than the quick breaks she'd given him that day. Once they were safely in Savenay, she'd allow him all the time he wished to recover. Then they'd part ways, never to meet again. How strange, after all they'd been through in three days.

Armelle pushed herself to her feet and brushed little bits of bark from her hands. She watched the bend in the road not far behind them. Étienne had insisted they stop here, even though they could easily be surprised by another pair of soldiers riding up around the corner without much warning. The possibility didn't allow her to relax much during their rest. "We need to keep moving. It's not much farther."

His hands stilled, but he kept his eyes closed. "That is what you said the last time we stopped."

"If I keep saying it, one of these times I'll be correct." She extended both hands to him. He grasped hers more willingly than he had that morning. His skin was warm from rubbing his knee. She pulled him up slowly and held on until he caught his balance. Then she handed him his bundled coat.

"How are you always this optimistic?" He shoved the coat under one arm. "It's exhausting."

"It should be exhausting to me, or it's exhausting to you?" Either way, his disgruntled muttering bolstered her step as she returned to the road. She shouldn't tease. He'd had a trying few days and clearly did not battle heaviness with frivolity as she did. But the way his brows lowered incredulously every time she opened her mouth . . . It was a temptation she didn't try hard to parry.

He took a few shuffling steps behind her without responding. Probably trying to think of something scathing or witty to take the upper hand. He hadn't had the last word yet, and she didn't intend to give it to him. Whichever card he played, she had one card that would always trump: laughter.

A lightness she hadn't felt for several days quickened her pace. Though she hadn't been to Jean-Baptiste and Alana's home in some time, the thought of being somewhere familiar—and with dear friends— made her want to run the rest of the way. It wasn't home, but it would have to do while she planned a way to get her family all back, safe and happy, to that sweet little house in Nantes.

"Don't try too hard to think of something to say, Monsieur Mariner," she said over her shoulder. "You'll . . ." A rumble behind them hit her ears. She pivoted, stomach plummeting. Étienne stopped to listen. They hadn't seen any more soldiers since the two who had passed the barn that morning.

"A wagon," he said. "Or a coach."

There was little foliage to speak of along the side of the road. Just a few trees and stumps. Nowhere to hide. Étienne unslung the waterskin from his shoulder. It had long been empty, but whenever they came upon another traveler, they'd used it, pretending to pause and drink so no one noticed his terrible limp. He pulled her cloak, which he still wore, to conceal the bundle under his arm.

A horse rounded the bend followed by a wagon. A grey-haired man in a brown cap held the reins. Armelle pulled her eyes back to her companion, willing her pulse to slow. It wasn't a soldier. That gave them a better chance of not being noticed.

Étienne unstopped the waterskin and leisurely brought it to his lips. The wagon moved steadily toward them. They'd have to feign drinking slowly, as it would take some time before the driver was far enough away to not notice Étienne's ailment. They didn't want to give any passerby something to remember them. Who knew how far the soldiers would search?

He handed her the waterskin and wiped his mouth on his sleeve. If she hadn't known the truth, he would have convinced her he had just taken a long, cool drink. She didn't think her efforts would be as convincing, but the wagon would pass before it became apparent.

The driver pulled back on the reins as his wagon passed and called for the horse to halt.

Armelle choked on the water she wasn't drinking.

"*Bonsoir, mon—*" The man cleared his throat. "*Citoyens.*"

A *royaliste*-sympathizing Breton? She hoped so. She nodded a greeting and then turned away. Perhaps he'd leave quickly.

"Have you come from Nantes?" he asked.

Étienne started to respond, but Armelle spoke over him. "No, we skirted the city." She lowered her voice. "Trying to avoid trouble."

The man's bushy eyebrows lifted in understanding. "A wise choice." He glanced behind them, then up the road. "Did you hear about the . . ." He nodded, as though she should know.

Her eyes met Étienne's. "Hear about what?" She held the waterskin toward him. This wasn't an inconspicuous encounter.

The older man leaned toward them. "There was another drowning last night."

Étienne's hand closed around hers and froze before he could take the waterskin. "A drowning?" he repeated.

The traveler bobbed his head gravely. "Mostly women and children. A few men. Terrible business."

Étienne paled despite his olive skin. His throat tightened beneath his neckcloth as if he were trying to swallow.

"What horrible news," she said. The downward spiraling sensation in her chest threatened to push her to her knees. So many innocents gone. Drifting in the Loire. Just like she thought Père had. Just like Étienne should have, if she hadn't freed him. His wide, brown eyes showed he had a similar thought. It lay between them, thick as a winter storm.

She almost didn't hear the man ask if they wanted to ride in the back of the wagon to Savenay. Images that had haunted her mind since Papa had been sent to die at the bottom of the river swirled. Splashing. Screaming. Shadows flailing in starless waters. Lantern light receding as the executioners rowed back to shore, taking all hope with them.

"Yes, thank you." The words didn't sound like they came from her mouth. They were too distant.

Étienne didn't move, and she had to take his arm to guide him toward the wagon. "I don't know why this is . . . ," he whispered. "After everything, this shouldn't . . ." Affect him. She'd question his sanity if it didn't. The likelihood that he could have been thrown in the mix of *misérables* was high.

She hushed him as she set her market bag and blankets in the wagon bed. "It's been a tiring day." She grasped the side of the wagon and pulled herself up before reaching back to help him in. The wagon rolled forward, and the old man's voice picked up again.

They'd come so close to death once again. The increasing pressure against her lungs made it difficult to focus on the man's chatter. Étienne closed his eyes and dropped his head, and it was all Armelle could do not to grab his hand like she would do for a frightened Julien.

With the world as it was, would they ever be rid of it, this feeling of always being just one step ahead of their demise?

CHAPTER 9

Maxence limped on sore feet down the darkening lane. That was the problem with sitting after so much walking—one's feet protested even louder when they were forced into action again. The old man had left them at the edge of town with a merry farewell from Maxence's companion. His hope that they didn't have far to go was for naught.

"Come along, *monsieur*. We're nearly there." How did she still have energy to move?

"Why must you use that address?" Maxence's words came out as little more than a grunt as he tried not to stumble on the uneven road. "Do you not care about the law? *Monsieur. Madame.* Those are all words of a different time." Each house they passed he hoped would be the one, but she kept ignoring them, which soured his spirits even more.

She twisted her face into an ogreish snarl that he could just make out in the waning light. "*Citoyen!*" she spat, then huffed. "It sounds so loving, so friendly."

"And *monsieur* sounds any better?" When had his coat become so heavy? His fingers could barely grip it anymore. Wherever they were going, he'd have to find a place to lay it out to dry. All their clothing was still damp from the morning's rain. "It conjures the image of bowing and scraping before a lord."

She shrugged, then leaned forward as though inspecting a house a little farther down. Their destination? *Please let it be so.* "It shows deference when you greet another person," she said. "How can that be wrong?" A man came from what appeared to be a nearby shop and walked toward the house. Warm light peeked through the windows in front.

"You don't care about the threat of getting in trouble, do you?" he asked.

She lolled her head back, speaking to the murky skies. "Would we be together in the streets of this town after dark on a cold night if I did?" Exasperation edged her voice. Was she kicking herself for her little display at the church? A small part of him hoped so.

"I suppose that was a stupid question to ask," he said.

"It hasn't been your first."

Before he could protest, she cried out and ran toward the house just as the man was entering through the door. "Jean-Baptiste! Jean-Baptiste!" The bags over her shoulders bounced and jangled.

The figure stopped and took a step back toward the lane. "Who are you?" His voice was deep, his build short and stocky.

Like Gilles.

A sudden, strange longing pierced his core. Maxence swallowed against a lump trying to form in his throat. This was ridiculous. He hadn't wanted to see his younger brother in nearly two years. He hadn't looked back when he marched from Marseille with Émile and the other *fédérés*. Now he was about to walk into the home of a man he'd never met in a town he'd be glad to never see again, and he wanted to be with the brother who had abandoned him?

"It's me! It's Armelle!" She embraced him, nearly knocking him through the doorway as he gave a laugh of disbelief.

Maxence shook off the odd emotions and shuffled to catch up. The door opened wider behind their host, letting more light into the lane.

"*Sacrebleu*," the man said. "Armelle Bernard, what are you doing here?" He had dark skin and short hair under his three-cornered hat. His sleeves were rolled up to his elbows despite the chill.

A light-skinned woman stepped through the doorway. "Armelle?"

Armelle. Maxence halted. So that was her name. He hadn't heard it much in Provence. Armelle Bernard. It suited her.

"It is too long a story for the doorstep," she told her friends. "May we come inside?"

Colbert gestured to the house. "Please come in."

His wife hugged Citoyenne Bernard. "I hope it isn't serious. Is your family well?"

"We are all well enough, but much has happened since we saw you last." Maxence's companion of the last three days glanced back at him. "I must introduce my friend."

Her friend. Something about the softness of her gaze, or perhaps it was the promise of a fire waiting for them in the hearth, sent warmth through his chest. Émile had often introduced him in a similar way, but it had been so long since someone had said "friend" when describing Maxence and truly meant it.

"Ah . . . Your friend." Colbert glanced at his wife with raised brows. *Ciel.* Their hosts thought they were engaged, or at least romantically inclined.

Armelle waved him over. "This is Étienne Rossignol."

Maxence's face twisted of its own accord. What had put that name into her head? He opened his mouth, grasping for words, but Colbert thumped him on the back. "Welcome, *citoyen*."

"Oh, please be careful," Armelle said as Citoyenne Colbert pulled her through the door. "Monsieur Rossignol is rather delicate just now."

Maxence flushed. Of all the people he could have wound up entangled with, it had to be a saucy Chouan sympathizer with a propensity to poke fun at everything. He closed his eyes as Colbert ushered him inside, a curious look on the man's face.

Delicate. Of all the insults . . .

Armelle closed the door to Jean-Baptiste's workshop and secured the lock. She'd volunteered to return a tool while he helped Alana get their two children to bed. Of course, Jean-Baptiste had been trying to find a way out of helping. Armelle grinned as she backed away from the carpentry door. She hardly blamed him. The Colberts' children were almost as good as Julien at finding excuses to stay awake.

The stars didn't gleam that night. Clouds had stayed through the day, keeping everything damp and cool. But Armelle had visited the Colberts with her father often enough that she could find her way from the house to the neatly kept carpentry and back without difficulty.

She paused in the small yard that separated the two buildings and tilted her head back, searching for the tiniest glimmer that might indicate a thinning in the clouds. One little star's light, just to remind her what was beyond the gloom. Something in the skies that perhaps Mère or Julien, who was no doubt going through his nightly barrage of excuses just then, could also see from Nantes.

A swelling in her throat, sharp and paralyzing, threatened to choke her. She started humming an old tune, but when that didn't help, she switched to singing.

> *Dans les prisons de Nantes*
> *Y avait un prisonnier.*
> *Personne ne vint le vouère*
> *Que la fille du geôlier.*

"What are you singing?"

Armelle flinched at the unexpected voice. Étienne. When had he come out? The tall figure moved slowly toward her. She cleared her throat and laughed. "A song."

He grumbled something she couldn't understand. A common occurrence with him, she'd discovered. "A song about a jailer?" he asked.

"A jailer's daughter, rather."

He paused at the edge of the house and leaned against the wall. Alana had fussed over his injured leg during dinner until he looked thoroughly humiliated, much to Armelle's satisfaction. But with Alana distracted by the children, he must have slipped out. "That sounds like a lovely song," he said, clear incredulity in his voice.

"It is." Armelle wandered over to him and mimicked his pose against the house. "She befriends a prisoner in Nantes and helps him escape."

For a moment, he didn't respond. "Fitting."

"It has taken up residence in my head for much of the last two days, if you can believe it." She couldn't see his face, but she easily imagined his scowl. "Have you never heard it? Often the sailors would sing it when my father helped with repairs on ships."

"Why would I have heard a song popular with sailors?"

Still denying his maritime past. Armelle crossed her arms in front of her. He was a puzzle, this man.

He shifted. "What happens after she frees him?"

"He vows to marry her if he ever returns to Nantes." Her breath shook as she uttered the last words. Return to Nantes. She'd always loved returning home after traveling to Lorient to visit her grandparents. Reuniting with Nicole and her family members who had stayed behind, filling their ears with stories of adventures and mishaps, crawling into her familiar bed after so many nights away—it was almost as exciting as the actual travels. But home had never felt like such a faraway dream as it did now.

Étienne snorted. "If I ever return to Nantes, don't expect a proposal."

"I would laugh at you if you asked me and immediately refuse." Heaven forbid she marry a man even half as grumpy as he. "But you would have to be daft not to make an offer for Nicole. She's the true jailer's daughter anyhow." And as sweet and as loyal and as pretty a girl as Nantes had ever produced. "Of course, you would shatter the dreams of all your girls back home."

"Dozens of broken hearts." He said it so wryly Armelle snorted.

"Why are we always talking about the girls from Marseille?" If he hadn't boasted his prowess, she wouldn't have found the need to tease him mercilessly. "How many boys did you leave in Nantes?"

He was from Marseille. She'd heard about the southern port city, with its perfect weather and impossibly pretty girls, but how much of it was exaggerated tales from bored mariners, she couldn't say. "I didn't leave any boys in Nantes." He couldn't turn the tables so easily.

"A lie."

She'd accuse him of flattery if he'd spoken with a little more conviction instead of his usual flatness. "You will find it hard to believe that I do not go around sampling the sweets before deciding which to buy."

"Oh no," he groaned. "You aren't one of those girls who's saving her first kiss for the man she marries."

Armelle pushed briskly off the wall. "And if I am?" Just because he went about kissing half of Marseille didn't give him the right to criticize her choice not to do the same in Nantes.

She turned on her heel. The Colberts would be wondering where they'd gone. She needn't linger with someone intent on making her feel foolish.

More frustrating than his criticism was the fact that after three days, he'd finally found a way to rankle her. She supposed he had to win sometime, but she didn't like it.

"Do you think they traced my disappearance to her?" he asked.

Armelle's stomach lurched. Their flight from Nantes had made it easy to banish that fear to the corners of her mind. But here in the safety of darkness, visions of what the *révolutionnaires* could do to her friend flashed before her eyes. "She knew the peril. She agreed to it. But I desperately hope . . ." If anything had happened to Nicole, how could she live with herself? She clutched her hands together. They'd grown cold in the evening breeze. "The only thing we can do is pray, Monsieur Rossignol."

He cleared his throat. "My name is *not* Étienne Rossignol." He sighed, as though gathering patience. "It is Maxence Étienne."

Armelle turned back around. How had she botched that? She raised her hands. "You can hardly blame me. *Étienne* on its own is far more common a given name than a surname. And then there was the Ross and Rossignol business with your friends."

"*Rossignol* is the name of my father's ship."

She froze, hands still in the air. *Le Rossignol.* She let her arms sink to her sides, and without thought her fingers found Papa's letter in her pocket, with its picture of a ship and a nightingale. There must be several ships called *le Rossignol.* The possibility that this man could be the key to tracking her father's whereabouts made her chest expand with a weightlessness she'd lost while running for their lives.

"Why . . . why did your friends call you that?"

"I don't know that I can call them my friends," he said. "But soldiers like to give each other nicknames related to where they're from."

"And you're from the sea." Would he know where his father's ship was now? Surely he'd know if his father had been in the same city as he. He might have news about where they had headed after Nantes. Her thoughts jumbled together like laundry in a cauldron. The last three days had seemed to take her family several steps in the opposite direction of being reunited, what with Henri in the north, Papa somewhere at sea, and Armelle on the run. But perhaps this mishap had taken her closer to bringing them all safely home.

"I am most definitely not from the sea."

She stuck out her hand, not certain he could see it in the dark. "It is good to meet you, Maxence Étienne from Marseille." She reached out until her fingers bumped his arm.

"What is this? We've already met."

"Not properly. My name is Armelle Bernard. You never asked for my name, either." Seconds ticked by, but she was in no hurry to end the awkwardness of standing with her arm outstretched between them. Let him make the next move. She wished she could see him squirm.

His hand wrapped around hers, strong and firm. He shook once. "Citoyenne Bernard."

She tightened her fingers, not letting him pull away. "I also haven't properly thanked you for saving my life that morning. It would have been easier for you to follow your orders."

"It was nothing."

"It was *something*," she insisted. "It meant the world to me. To my family. You didn't have to protect me, but you did. And I am grateful."

She could feel the tension in his hand. He wanted to retreat. Brush it off. She wasn't going to let him. "This is the part when most people say, 'You're welcome.'"

Another pause. Was it so difficult to say? To accept someone's gratitude? "You're welcome." She waited for him to shake free from her grasp. "And thank you."

Her brows shot up. Gratitude? He'd hardly shown any thanks on their journey.

"I didn't think anyone on this earth cared I was sitting in that cell." His hand slid out of hers, and he hobbled past her toward the door.

Armelle's heart sank as she watched him go. His words were heavy with meaning, filled with that same hurt she'd sensed the day before. She wanted to make him spill it out and let her examine it, like Julien showing her all the new rocks and twigs he'd collected for his little box of treasures. No one should have to carry such burdens alone.

Chère *Nicole,*

I am anxious for word of your safety. I have little to tell beyond that we are more or less well and have made it to our first destination. You'll forgive the false name on the front of this letter. We cannot be too careful.

Please send your response to my relatives at our final destination. I will be sick with worry until I hear from you. I pray for your protection and won't cease to do so until I see you again.

A. B.

One last thing—I fear our friend better aligns with your ideals for what a man ought to be: contemplative, serious, and enigmatic. It is a pity our roles are not reversed. But I do not find him quite so insufferable as when we first set off. Perhaps if I can manage not to drive him mad with my vexing, I shall have the opportunity to properly introduce you one day.

CHAPTER 10

Citoyenne Colbert retrieved another pillow to squeeze under Maxence's injured knee. "I can make a poultice easy enough," she said. The second time she'd offered, and he again shook his head. "To think, you walked all the way from Nantes like this."

Maxence reclined on the lone sofa, which sectioned off the small sitting area from the finely crafted dining table. Heat from the fire before him made his eyelids heavy, but he wouldn't have a chance to sleep until the woman of the house stopped her ministrations. Satisfied his knee was properly elevated, she brought a blanket and draped it over him.

Footsteps on the ladder announced the return of Colbert, but he halted halfway down at a chorus of giggles from above. He trudged back up, his pace as haggard as Maxence's had been when he'd arrived in Savenay.

His rescuer—Citoyenne Bernard, she did have a name—sat at the table with quill and ink. She turned her gaze upward as though she could see through to the floor above and laughed softly as the pattering of little feet rushed from one end of the house to the other.

"They are very naughty this evening." Citoyenne Colbert reddened. "Having guests always gives them more energy than we can match."

Maxence believed it. The little girl and boy hadn't sat still through dinner, and Citoyenne Bernard had egged them on.

"I cannot speak for Monsieur Étienne, but they do not bother me. Julien is close to Louise's age, so I have plenty of experience." She set down the pen and blew on what she'd just written.

She called him "Monsieur" just to exasperate him, didn't she?

"Would you like some *cidre*?" Citoyenne Colbert asked, wringing her hands. She seemed to have run out of ideas for how to make him more comfortable. "I have it warming in the kitchen."

"Yes, *merci*."

When she'd disappeared into the kitchen, Maxence let out a sigh.

"You could act a little more grateful," Citoyenne Bernard whispered across the room.

"I am grateful," he whispered back. Just not used to such attention. He shifted. Perhaps he would have better been able to feel gratitude if other feelings did not press so harshly against his chest. The warmth and friendliness lulled his senses into a comfortable stupor, but guilt had niggled at the back of his mind all evening. If the Colberts knew who he was, they'd have every right and reason to throw him out.

"You had me fooled." She folded one side of her letter, then the other.

The man of the house finally returned and sat heavily in a chair by the hearth. "I didn't know I was agreeing to this when I married." He motioned upstairs.

"I'll remember that if ever faced with the choice," Maxence said. Did his voice sound tense? The man had given him a strange stare through dinner, as though he saw through Citoyenne Bernard's explanation of Maxence being a friend of her family.

Colbert leaned back and propped his elbow on the chair, resting his head in his hand. "Some days I find it more exhausting than carpentry."

"You're a carpenter?" He should have guessed it by the well-made furniture, which seemed too expensive for a house this size. Colbert had the thick shoulders and strong arms for carpentry, and the look of suspicion he now wore made his appearance all the more intimidating. Maxence hoped amiable conversation would calm the man's suspicions.

"He's a talented woodworker as well. Jean-Baptiste was my father's apprentice several years ago," Citoyenne Bernard said. "Before he married Alana."

"When you and your brothers were running around like those little urchins." Colbert lifted his voice. "Who should be tucked into their beds if they fear the wrath of their father." He watched the ceiling for a moment and then shrugged. "Perhaps they've finally settled."

Citoyenne Colbert returned, bearing a tray with small bowls. She set one in Maxence's hands first before giving one to her husband and then to Citoyenne Bernard, who had brought a chair from the dining table into the sitting room.

"How is your father, Armelle?" Colbert asked.

Maxence dropped his eyes to his steaming drink. The clear, amber liquid—nearly the color of Armelle Bernard's hair—allowed him to see into the depths of the bowl. Her father was in the Loire, along with hundreds of others. Where Maxence should have been but for the daughter's kindness.

"We think he is well," she said.

Maxence's head snapped up. Well? Her gaze flicked to his.

"We have not seen him for more than a month." Was she lying to her friend? Though she talked to Colbert, she studied Maxence. "He was on board one of the drowning ships."

Colbert straightened. "He escaped?"

Citoyenne Bernard nodded slowly, drawing her attention away from Maxence. Her father had survived. Maxence pushed himself to a more upright position. She hadn't mentioned that vital information. He couldn't explain the thrill that pulsed through him at the news. The man had been a traitor in the eyes of the République, but seeing the relief in her eyes, he couldn't help sharing it. Where was her father now? Hiding, no doubt. As Maxence should be.

"What under the heavens did he do to get thrown in the Loire?" Colbert's eyes were wide.

She shrugged. "It doesn't take very much to lose favor with the République. You can wash the floors in a way they dislike and find yourself at the wrong end of a musket barrel."

That sort of carelessness had earned lasting consequences for more than just her. Maxence's stomach soured. "You were asking for trouble," he growled. Why hadn't she told him about her father? She didn't seem the type to beg pity, but she had been decrying the government when she mentioned her father before. His escape hadn't fit the portrayal she'd attempted to paint.

"My father sheltered a Chouan family in his workshop," she said, as though she hadn't heard him. "They fled the Battle of Savenay."

She didn't trust him. That had to be it. Maxence swallowed, a pit forming in his gut. He shouldn't have cared whether she trusted him or not, since they wouldn't be long acquaintances, but the more he mused, the harder the sinking sensation became to ignore. He had no one to whom he could divulge that information. She could have told him.

Colbert nodded slowly, face impassive. "Many left after the fighting."

"Where were you?" she asked the Colberts. She sat tall in her chair, hands folded around her bowl. Calm as though she were asking after the weather. Was she avoiding looking Maxence's way, or was he simply imagining it? Though they'd been forced to trust each other in certain ways the last few days, that didn't mean they were confidants. Still, the thought that she'd kept this from him smarted.

"We evacuated with most of the town. Only Chouans and their families remained." Colbert took a long drink from his bowl. "We were lucky to escape most of the damage. They broke in our door and up-ended furniture to search for rebels and put a few bullets through the walls, but our home looks much better than those near the church." He shook his head. "The Chouans set up artillery at the church. The aftermath isn't pretty."

Maxence brought the drink to his lips. The sweet taste of apples hit his tongue, tempered by an acidic tang. The liquid washed down his throat, taking the awakening thoughts of battle with them. It didn't matter that he hadn't seen Savenay's battle. He could imagine it too well.

"Mère was relieved to receive your letter, Alana," Citoyenne Bernard said to the hostess, who had returned from the kitchen with her own cider. "We were so worried you'd been taken."

"We don't side with the Chouans," Colbert said firmly.

"Surely you don't side with the République." Citoyenne Bernard's voice had an edge to it Maxence had rarely heard in their time together. Her hands tightened around her drink, which she hadn't yet tasted. "Do you know what the troops did after the battle?"

Colbert's face hardened. "We all know, Armelle. I don't condone the arrests, especially not of the Chouans' families, but the Chouans have participated in equally terrible things."

"Not on so great a scale." She bit her lips. "Who knows but the little family Père sheltered were your neighbors? Former friends? Now they're no more." As quickly as the fire had erupted in her eyes, it died down. She stood and wandered back to the table where her letter sat and set down her drink.

"I don't excuse them," Colbert said, stroking his jaw. "But I do find it difficult to oppose the people who have finally recognized the equality of all men, whether we live in France or Saint-Domingue."

Maxence nodded. In the last month, the National Assembly voted to abolish slavery in any land under French rule, including Caribbean islands like Saint-Domingue. Previously it had been outlawed only in mainland France. "Good is coming from all of the Jacobins' work." At least he had an ally in their host, even if Citoyenne Bernard thought differently.

"Does one good thing excuse all the horrifying things they've done?" Her hands slid up her arms as though she were cold.

"One?" Maxence threw up a hand. "How can you say it has been only one good thing? The king is gone and with him the tethers of the past." An old passion, one grief and duty had suppressed for too long, blinked to life inside him. Nights of conversation in bustling cafés humming with revolutionary fervor. A sunlit evening in a crowded courtyard thrumming with the melody of a musical call to arms. A long walk out of Marseille toward glory and freedom in Paris with Émile at his side. These were moments never to be forgotten.

She didn't respond but picked up her drink again, her back toward them. Citoyenne Colbert moved to her side and put an arm around her shoulders. "We're grateful your father survived. Where is he now?"

"On the ship that rescued him from the Loire."

No wonder she'd been so obsessed with his sailing past. She wanted to know about her father's new life. Nautical carpentry included many intricacies that would be unfamiliar to a landsman in the same line of work, but a ship's captain wouldn't turn away a man with talent who had nowhere to go.

Colbert downed the last of his *cidre* and sighed contentedly. "That is the safest place for him right now. Most are not so lucky." He traced the rim of his empty bowl with his thumb. "Gustave was never one to leave people out in the cold."

Gustave must be Citoyenne Bernard's father. His daughter had a similar philosophy.

Citoyenne Bernard turned quickly, her countenance once again exuberant. "How is your knee after a little rest, *monsieur*?"

"It is fine." No better or worse than it had been the last time she asked.

"Is there anything more I can get you?" the hostess asked, crossing the room to hover over him once more.

It took all of Maxence's strength to not glare at his companion for reminding Citoyenne Colbert of his injury. "No, I am well."

The younger woman cleared her throat expectantly.

"*Merci*," Maxence added. Citoyenne Bernard gave him a proud smile, and it was all he could do not to glower back.

"You should have returned to Nantes when you got injured," Colbert said. He rose and made for the kitchen. "Your recovery will take longer." He paused beside Citoyenne Bernard and patted her shoulder, as though to apologize for the earlier disagreement. Though no words passed between them, the warm gestures and expressions spoke forgiveness.

Just like that, they'd restored friendship. Maxence's brows lowered. It had been too easy. She had accused those Colbert supported of terrible things. He had defended the same people who had nearly killed her father. How could friendship exist, when they were on such vastly different sides of the argument?

"Where are you going after this?" Colbert asked as he returned from the kitchen.

"I am off to Lorient, whenever you go next for supplies," she said. "That is, if you do not mind a companion with plenty to say and little restraint." Her eyes found Maxence. "I know some would refuse."

It wasn't the talking but the teasing that had nearly driven him mad. He wasn't about to say it, however. He settled back into the couch, the warmth of the drink in his belly making it difficult to keep his eyes open. They'd sparred enough today.

Colbert chuckled. "I just returned from Lorient last week. It will be a couple of weeks until I travel there again."

"I don't mind waiting. My grandparents will be happy to see me, no matter when I come. It will give Monsieur Étienne time to heal."

"He's going with you to meet your grandparents?"

Maxence wanted to protest Colbert's suggestive tone, but he couldn't open his eyes or his mouth. His head sank into the back of the couch, so much softer than stone and dirt floors, and his limbs seemed anchored in place. He'd set their host straight tomorrow. Tonight his body had decided that after three painful days of little rest and little food with a fiery companion, it couldn't take another moment. He let himself drift into sleep, her happy natter twirling through his mind.

"Your friend isn't going to Lorient, then?" Jean-Baptiste asked.

Armelle glanced at the couch, where Étienne seemed to have dozed off. His head was nestled against the back of it, his grip loosening on his bowl of cider. "I don't know where he is going." She walked quietly over to him and took the bowl. He didn't stir. His chest rose and fell slowly under the too-large waistcoat. He deserved this rest after all they'd been through.

She paused beside him. Three days without the means to shave had left his angular face covered in stubble. Firelight ebbed and flowed across his olive skin, tracing the line of his jaw.

Was there someone in Marseille worried about this man? A mother? A sister? A sweetheart?

Armelle blinked. No, not a sweetheart. He'd made it clear he preferred the benefits of not being attached to one woman. She frowned and pulled her gaze away.

Jean-Baptiste stepped in front of her as she headed toward the kitchen with Étienne's and her bowls. "I find this journey rather suspicious." He folded his arms and raised an eyebrow. "You arrive on our doorstep at night unannounced with a man battered, bruised, and limping, then you tell us you're simply paying a visit to your grandparents." He didn't say it, but his look told her what he was thinking. He couldn't be too cautious in who he allowed into his house these days.

She turned her gaze to Alana—honest, believing, doting Alana—who was also giving her a questioning look. Armelle sighed. "I don't want to wake him."

They followed her into the kitchen, where she crouched by the washbasin to rinse out the bowls. Étienne hadn't finished his *cidre*, so she quickly drank the rest before plunging the bowls into the now-cold water. The coldness seemed to seep into her fingers and up her arms. She was asking her friends to do the same thing that had put her father in prison.

"I think it might be better if we only stay the night," Armelle said. Perhaps they'd find another kind driver who would allow them to ride toward Lorient.

Alana knelt beside her, the light from the fire in the other room outlining her profile. "Are you in trouble?"

After the conversation with Étienne about Nicole, a knot had formed in the pit of Armelle's stomach. She'd endangered one friend while seeking help. How could she put the Colberts at risk as well? She nodded as she rose and sought out something to dry the bowls. Before springing Étienne from prison, it would not have been so dangerous to stop here, but a runaway soldier heightened the risk.

"Are you covering for him?" Jean-Baptiste asked.

Alana handed her a rag. Armelle couldn't see either of their faces in the shadows of the kitchen, and she hoped that meant they couldn't see her blush. "It is much more the other way around. But I fear if I tell you more, it could make things more dangerous for you. At dinner you said there are still soldiers stationed in Savenay."

"There will be until the Chouans are no longer a threat."

Alana took the bowls from her and returned them to her chest of dishes. "*Chéri*, that doesn't matter," she said quietly.

"It does matter if there's a threat." Jean-Baptiste's voice held no anger, only concern.

Armelle couldn't blame him.

She swallowed. Everywhere she went, she brought danger to her friends and family. She rose to her feet. "We can leave now." Where they'd go, she couldn't say. After dark was hardly an easy time to find lodging in a small town, especially one still occupied by the army.

But Alana was shaking her head. She gestured to the front room where Étienne slept. "He's in no condition to walk far enough to find shelter."

Her husband shrugged. "He walked from Nantes." He drew in a sharp breath. "There were soldiers here this morning looking for a deserter from the city. Tell me it's not your friend they were seeking."

Armelle flinched. This had been a terrible idea. Why didn't she think these things through? "We'll leave at first light. No one needs to know we were here."

"A *deserter*, Armelle?" Jean-Baptiste hissed. He covered his face with his hand. "Of all the sorts to take a liking to."

"I haven't taken a liking to him." Why did people always assume some sort of attachment when they saw two young people together? She huffed. Jean-Baptiste was going to pull the truth from her, whether he wanted it or not. She might as well get it out now. "He was supposed to shoot me, he refused, there was a fight, someone was killed, they blamed it on him, and they sent him to jail. I got him out, and here we are."

A deafening silence filled the kitchen. Alana and Jean-Baptiste stood unmoving while Armelle struggled not to fidget. She waited for his fury; she deserved it after forcing all of this on his family.

Armelle started when Jean-Baptiste let out a low, mirthless laugh. "I shouldn't be surprised. Will you ever grow out of getting yourself into disasters?"

"It would appear not." Armelle shoved her hands into her pockets. One hand found the letter from Papa, the other the little wood die from Julien. If the Colberts couldn't let them stay, they would find another place. Her father's situation had been hopeless, and he still found a way out. They were not in as dire a position. Yet.

Alana crossed to her husband's side and took his hand. "We can't turn them out into the cold. Not after all Gustave and Ranée did when you worked for him. Surely there's a way."

Dear Alana. Armelle wanted to embrace her.

Jean-Baptiste nodded slowly. "If the soldiers return, we will say I've hired him to work temporarily at the carpentry. I haven't been able to replace my last employee who left for the army. It's a logical story. As long as we keep you close to the house until I leave for Lorient, you should be safe."

Tears gathered in Armelle's eyes, and it was all she could do not to blink and send them running down her face. Papa always said that there were still good people in the world, despite the division that had upended their homeland. After three days of distrusting almost every person she saw, the weight of fear finally began to lift.

CHAPTER 11

A little finger poked Maxence's arm. Softly at first, but after a few moments the tapping intensified. Ignoring Citoyenne Colbert's morning clamor the last three days since their arrival hadn't been so difficult. This, on the other hand . . .

He cracked one eye open to a head of curly black hair and brown eyes. "What is it?" His words scratched and caught on their way out.

"Citoyen Étienne? Are you awake?" The four-year-old boy tilted his face in the same direction as Maxence's.

"What do you think?" He resisted the urge to roll over and try to go back to sleep. The Colberts had supplied him with an old mattress pushed into the corner of the main room, for which he was grateful. The bed was softer than any he'd slept on in some time, the room held the lingering warmth from the hearth late into the night, and if it could provide slightly more privacy from early-morning visitors, Maxence would not ask for more.

"Armelle said that you like to wake up early."

Maxence grunted. She would say that. "Is she still in bed?" She was sharing one of the two upper-floor bedrooms with the Colberts' daughter and son.

101

"She and Louise didn't want to be awake yet." The little boy lifted his shoulders.

So she'd sent him downstairs to rouse someone else. Maxence, specifically. He sighed and opened both eyes. Dim light from the windows suggested it was still early. Citoyenne Colbert stirred something in the kitchen—wooden spoon scraping metal—but the house was otherwise silent. With a groan, he flipped to his back and stretched. Three mornings here had taught him that the youngest Colbert would not leave his side until he rose, though usually the boy waited to awaken Maxence until breakfast was nearly ready.

"Noël!" Citoyenne Colbert cried through the doorway. "Let him alone. I'm very sorry."

Maxence waved a hand. His nieces, Aude and Claire, had done similar things before he left. At least when Gilles wasn't around. If he was home, they stayed glued to his side. Gilles was everyone's favorite— favorite uncle, favorite shipmate, favorite son.

He sat up quickly, rubbing his eyes. The blankets fell from his shoulders, letting in the cool air. Citoyenne Colbert hadn't lit a fire in the main room this morning, and the loose linen shirt he'd borrowed did not keep him from shivering.

"Papa is making us a real bed for our mattress," Noël said. "It's in his shop. Do you want to see it?"

Maxence prodded his injured knee through the blankets. Still sore, but not as much as when he'd first arrived. Their hostess had hardly let him walk their first day in Savenay. A walking stick loaned from her husband and Citoyenne Bernard's reassurance had finally convinced her he was capable of moving around without further injuring himself.

He buttoned the collar of the shirt, wondering how long it would be before the loose button popped off. The cravat had likewise seen better days. He tried not to look too closely at the unstylishly discolored sections as he tied the strip of cloth at his throat. Then he pulled on the oversized waistcoat. He didn't have a mirror to inspect his appearance, but he quickly determined he did not, in fact, want to see the sight.

He shuffled toward the door with the help of the walking stick, Noël hopping at his side. To have that sort of energy before breakfast . . . It was a pity people lost it by age twelve. Well, *most* people. Footsteps on the ladder announced the arrival of one of the few people he could think of who hadn't lost that vivacity despite growing older.

"Good morning, Monsieur Étienne!"

"Noël made it sound as though you wished to sleep longer," Maxence said. If she was going to come down only a few minutes later, why had she sent the boy?

Citoyenne Bernard crossed the room, heading for the kitchen. "I thought it would make you feel more at home. Surely you had to rise early in the army."

Maxence paused before the door, swallowing a sigh. She seemed to think her teasing was funnier the louder he sighed, and he would not grant her another victory. "I think Citoyenne Bernard would like to see your new bed, Noël."

The boy snatched Maxence's free hand. "Armelle saw it yesterday." The boy's wide, pleading eyes wouldn't let him say no. Maxence nodded toward the door, and Noël hurried to open it.

"You're going out there without even a cloak?" Citoyenne Bernard asked from the kitchen doorway. "It's barely March." His national guard coat was safely bundled by his mattress, and he did not want to wear her cloak again. It hit awkwardly short on him.

He paused before stepping out the door. "You misspeak, *citoyenne*." Not that he would gain anything by correcting her, but he couldn't help it. "I believe the name you are searching for is Ventôse, not March." The calendar of the République, with its newly named months, did not directly correlate with the antiquated Gregorian calendar, since the République began its years on what had been September 22. Even he sometimes struggled to remember the new dates, but it was for the good of the nation to put everything related to the old regime in the past, where it belonged.

She threw him a gleeful grin. "You had to think about it." Then she disappeared into the kitchen.

She always had to have the last word, even when she was wrong. Maxence followed Noël into the yard, lips pursed.

"Armelle doesn't like *la patrie*," the boy said as they turned toward the carpentry. He swung his arms forward and back, contentedly matching Maxence's slow pace.

Maxence almost agreed but caught himself. That wasn't entirely true. She'd said she didn't like Louis Capet on the throne. "What makes you think that?"

"She's always quiet when you and Papa talk about *la patrie*." Noël stopped and gave Maxence a very serious look. "Armelle is never quiet."

Maxence bit his cheek to keep a straight face. The perfect description of that woman. "It is true. She does not agree with what the government is doing."

"Maman says someday the war will be over." Noël led the way around the carpentry toward the back door. "We were in a war. See?"

Maxence followed the boy's finger to a speckling of holes along the wall of the shop. Rags filled the bullet holes to keep some of the cold out of the building. "You weren't here, were you?" Colbert had mentioned their flight on a few occasions.

"Papa ran in and said we had to go fast. We got in Pierre's wagon and left." The boy shrugged. "Pierre's old horse isn't very fast. Do you like horses?" He chattered on about animals, leaving the harrowing topic of the Battle of Savenay in the dust as he directed Maxence into the carpentry.

Someday the war would be over, but it seemed a faraway dream. Someday friends wouldn't die at the hand of foreigners. Someday there wouldn't be fighting between neighbors. Or brothers.

"You're awake early," Colbert said from his workbench. "How is the knee?"

"Mending."

Noël scampered to a corner of the workshop where a collection of posts leaned against the wall. One had been smoothed and shaped, but the rest awaited their turn. "You see? This will be our bed."

Maxence ran a hand over the even wood. The design was simple, but it seemed well executed. Not that he was versed in carpentry. The only woodworking he'd observed was repairs to *le Rossignol*.

"What will you do when you've healed?" Colbert asked. "Return home?"

"Home is in the south." Though he didn't have much to return to. His last months at Montpellier's prestigious medical school had been more drink and conversation than studying. Gilles probably knew more than he did on the subject of medicine and healing, and Gilles hadn't even started his university studies when Maxence had left with the *fédérés*. Surely Gilles had saved enough to begin by now, though the *levée en masse* would have foiled his brother's plans for school. Unless he'd figured out how to get himself married and escape the army. Maxence forced down the wondering thoughts. It didn't matter what Gilles had done with his life the last two years.

"Will you go with her to Lorient?" Colbert pushed a sharpening stone across the blade of an axe in little circles. The soft whirring of his work filled the shop.

"I don't think that would be wise. Her grandparents might get the wrong impression."

"As we did?" Colbert laughed. "A young man traveling with Armelle from Nantes. I don't know how we could have made the wrong assumption." He brushed grit from the blade, then dipped the sharpening stone into a pail of water. What a life it would be to have control of one's time and efforts. Maxence couldn't pull his eyes from Colbert's simple task. The man could decide when to cut wood and when to sharpen his tools. He didn't answer to anyone.

Even kicked out of the army, Maxence was still answering to someone. That hazel-eyed shrew, who had taken it upon herself to direct his life now that she felt indebted to him. "Rest assured that there is absolutely nothing between us." He couldn't imagine being married to someone with so much spunk.

"Then what are your plans?" Colbert held up the axe, sighting down the blade.

If only Maxence knew. He felt as though he was standing at the edge of a coastal cliff, fog obscuring the water below. He didn't know what lay before him. "A week ago my only plan was to do what I could to rise in the military. I haven't had time to create a new one."

Colbert lowered the axe, fixing his eyes on Maxence. "The world we're in now doesn't allow us the luxury of having time to make careful decisions."

Maxence nodded. Two years ago he'd chosen to join the *fédérés* and left Marseille within two weeks. Failing to make up his mind would have meant getting left behind like Gilles. Or worse. The political uproar that had overtaken the country meant one wrong decision could land someone under a guillotine blade. Maxence pulled his gaze away from Colbert and glanced back toward the house. Even right decisions, like his choice to protect her, could get a man killed. But what was he to do now? The Colberts were very generous to allow them to stay until he was healed, but he couldn't stay forever. And Citoyenne Bernard would leave for her grandparents' in a week.

"Do you know anyone in Brittany?" The whirring of the sharpening stone started up again.

Not many, though he had been to Brittany on several occasions. "I have an uncle in Saint-Malo." He liked Oncle Oscar. He wasn't as oppressive as Père.

Oncle Oscar. Maxence rubbed the back of his neck. His uncle was the nearest family member. He didn't know where Oscar stood when it came to the revolution, but surely he would help a nephew. He could assist Maxence in finding employment in his office or even on a ship, where the army would have a difficult time finding him. And then . . .

Maxence froze. Employment on a ship? Or for a shipping company? What was he thinking? He hated the sea and its harsh life. He let his hand fall to his side. It would only be temporary. When he figured out a better situation, he'd leave. Perhaps he'd find a new life somewhere far from France's shores. The thought sent a pang through him. Everything he'd hoped for as a Jacobin, everything he and Émile had sacrificed for—he'd be turning his back on it.

He leaned into the walking stick and gave a short nod. "I'll go to Saint-Malo. My connections there will help me determine my next course of action." Even if he stayed in the city, a den of privateers and smugglers, he'd be safer than in southern Brittany. No one would recognize him, no one would care that he was within the draft age and not conscripted into the army, and no one would ask questions.

"Saint-Malo?" asked a voice behind him. "I've heard that's a lovely city." The bright face Maxence had rarely been separated from in the last week poked around the doorframe.

"Is breakfast ready, Armelle?" Colbert asked. He set down the axe and stone on his bench.

"Alana is just slicing the bread." She entered the shop, pausing to take a deep breath. A small smile lit her face. "What is in Saint-Malo, Étienne?"

"A port."

Noël ran for the door, nearly knocking the walking stick out from under him. The corners of his lips twitched. That boy was so full of life. Colbert also watched Noël go, and though he didn't smile, a softening around his eyes spoke of deeper feelings than a smile could portray—love and sacrifice and protection. Things Maxence longed for from his own family.

The boy darted into the yard, arms flailing as though he hadn't a care in the world. Maxence's little nieces had been like that, always moving and unconcerned of dangers that awaited. How did one protect such innocence? He hadn't envied men like his brother Victor and Colbert the task before. It seemed too great a responsibility. But now, watching their host with his son, this boy who had already seen so much ugliness in the world and could still find joy in it, Maxence wondered if that depth of love made the responsibility worth it.

"Of course I know that," she said as Colbert followed his son, throwing them a suspicious look before departing. She moved to Maxence's side, head tilted expectantly. "Why would you want to go there?"

"I have family there." They stepped out into the sunlight. A little bird hopped across the eaves of the house. It regarded them for a moment before flitting away. "My uncle owns a small shipping company in Saint-Malo. My father likes to make land there, so I know the city well."

Her brow raised. "Oh . . . On *le Rossignol*?"

"Of course." His father had captained that ship for years. In fact, Père's uncle had willed it to him, though Maxence had his doubts that the old man would ever die.

"How often does he dock in Saint-Malo? Do you know when he will be there again?" She stared at the front door ahead, but her gaze seemed far away.

"Do you plan on booking passage?" What was this fascination with sea life? She wouldn't stop mentioning it. "Living on a ship is not as romantic as poets and artists make it seem."

She blinked. "Oh, I do not expect it to be. I only wondered if you would be reunited with your father before long." She tucked a strand of hair under her cap.

"He comes a few times a year." But Maxence would not seek him out unless he had nowhere else to turn.

Citoyenne Bernard opened the door and held it for him. "Then I hope you will see him soon."

Maxence shuffled through the door. He very much hoped the opposite.

The next morning, Armelle bounded out of bed before even Noël. She'd hardly slept the night before and shouldn't have been able to wake this morning, but her head had swirled with thoughts of Saint-Malo and finding Papa since yesterday.

Henri was in Saint-Malo. And in the next few months it was very likely Papa would be too. She grinned as she tied on her petticoat and slipped into her jacket. They could be together. She paused in pinning up the front of her jacket. Papa would find out Henri's secret. Would he tell Mère? She finished placing the last of the pins. It hardly mattered. They hadn't seen Papa since before the drowning. Having someone from the family meet him, see him, talk to him would make the surprise of Henri's activities inconsequential.

She shoved her stockinged feet into her shoes and hurried down the ladder. The more she thought on it, the more determined she was that she should be there in Saint-Malo to greet her *père*. Étienne was her passage there.

"You're exceedingly happy this morning," came a grunt from the corner. Étienne lay on his mattress, peeking out from under one arm that lay across his face.

"It's a beautiful day, isn't it?" Had Alana not started breakfast? The kitchen looked dark, as though the curtains hadn't been opened yet. She couldn't hear anything moving.

Étienne pushed himself up to sitting and rubbed the sleep from his eyes.

"I thought you didn't like waking early," she said. She might as well start breakfast since she was ready for the day.

"Do you think I could sleep with you around?" That was teasing she could not find a flippant response to. He hadn't shaved in the week since the altercation with the priest, and his face was well on its way to being shadowed with a short beard, giving him a rugged and fierce aura. His shirt hung open almost to his waist with how large it was, and one didn't have to focus too closely to see beneath it. Armelle pried her eyes away. Heat skipped across her cheeks at the memory of the last time she'd stared at him in such a state of undress.

"I think I'll start the fire," she said, hurrying toward the kitchen.

"What is this?" he asked. "No saucy response?"

She halted. "I apologize. Did you wish for one?" She slowly glanced back. He'd buttoned his collar, which mostly closed his shirt. Thank the heavens.

"I expected one. I can't say I wished for it." He held up Nicole's father's waistcoat, a look of disgust on his face. She bit back a smile, unable to blame him but thoroughly enjoying his revulsion.

"I think I could adjust it for you," she blurted without thinking.

Étienne pulled it on. "I wouldn't want you to put so much work into something I will cast off at the earliest opportunity."

"Seeing as you have little to your name, that might not happen for some time."

He paused, the waistcoat only half buttoned. The murky light from the window by the door touched his hardened face.

Armelle's heart sank at his grim look. She went to the kitchen window to pull back the curtain and let in the hope of morning. The yard and road beyond it were still. Waiting for something to happen.

Did he regret not following his orders? It was a horrible thing to consider, both for what the result would have been for her and what such a thought would imply about him. She retrieved the tinderbox and knelt by the cold, empty hearth. Even driven from her home by her own stupid decision, Armelle had so much to be grateful for. Friends, family, places she would be welcomed, food, even a little money. Étienne escaped with only the clothes on his back, and most of them weren't even his clothes. That coat still bundled and hidden in the corner was practically all he had left.

Armelle swallowed, staring unseeing at the flame she'd coaxed to life in the kindling. She'd stolen him out of the coffee warehouse. Most would consider her debt repaid. Why did it feel as though he'd sacrificed more? In the end, she'd be comfortably situated with her grandparents until it was safe to return. He had nowhere to go and nothing to his name.

"That would be very kind of you."

She startled, rocking back on her heels and nearly falling over. She hadn't heard him come to the kitchen door. He leaned against the door-frame, features still somber, but with an appearance of ease she hadn't seen in all the time she'd known him. His eyes—dark and severe—held her gaze as they had that fateful morning a week ago on the church steps.

Something strange twisted in her stomach as she took him in. Something bright and buoyant and dangerous and terrifying. Armelle swallowed. The billowing clothes didn't hide his well-built frame as much as she would have liked. He seemed so tall from where she crouched. In the soot.

Her cheeks instantly flamed. She pushed herself to her feet, brushing at her petticoat. "What would be kind of me?" The baby fire at her feet fizzled out. *Fichtre.* He'd completely unsettled her.

"Taking in the waistcoat."

"Ah. Yes." She rubbed at her brow with the back of her wrist and wandered to the corner by the window. Was her forehead warm? She couldn't remember what Alana had planned for them to eat that morning. "We can measure it just after breakfast. I should have it done in a day or so." This was ridiculous. He'd seen her in more humiliating situations than crouching before a fire gawking at him. At least he had his shirt on this time. Armelle straightened and forced her hands to her sides. Lack of sleep had made her head fuzzy. She turned to finish her task of building the fire.

"*Merci,*" Étienne said, running a hand over the short hair that covered his jaw. The word came out hesitantly, as though he wasn't used to saying it often.

"It's nothing." She bent toward the hearth, gathering more kindling into a little bundle.

Fitting his waistcoat would put her in very close proximity to those eyes. *Petite sotte.* She was being a fool.

Of course she would make Maxence stand in the middle of the floor like a prisoner waiting for his sentencing. Citoyenne Colbert sat on the couch with some mending, her gaze flitting often to Citoyenne Bernard as she danced about the room readying pins from a little striped house-wife and chattering about the waistcoat. She almost reminded him of his parent's hired help, Florence. Although Citoyenne Bernard always had a look of intent about her. Florence's words seemed to surprise even herself half of the time.

"Very well." She stepped up to him and grabbed the front of his waistcoat, which she'd made him put on inside out. "Let us button this first." She made quick work of the first few buttons despite the awkwardness of needing a hand both inside and outside to pull through the buttonholes.

Maxence fell back a step, brushing her hand out from under his waistcoat. "I can do that."

She waited silently, eyes fixed on his hands in a way that caused him to fumble over the task. The shouts of Noël and Louise playing outside filtered through the window, which Citoyenne Colbert had opened a crack after breakfast. When he'd completed the task, he dropped his arms to his sides.

"Finished?" Without waiting for an answer, she moved forward again, taking up the bottom seam of the garment. "I'll pull out these stitches along here. Just enough to get in to work on the inside." She let it fall and grasped the side seam. After adjusting so she wasn't holding onto his shirt, she pinched the seam close against him and pinned it there.

"I don't know how you will get this to look presentable." He lifted his arm so she had better access to the seam. She backed away to look at it, then adjusted the pins before moving to his other side.

"My mother has done washing, mending, and sewing for upper-class patrons most of my life, even after Papa's shop became more established.

We had to help." She stuck a pair of pins between her lips before pulling the waistcoat tight on his other side. Her hands halted in their work. "Do you hear that?" she mumbled through the pins.

Shrieking and protests exploded from the yard. Maxence couldn't tell which child was crying and which was yelling, but the noise crescendoed as they listened. Citoyenne Colbert sighed and dropped her mending to the couch. "Children are a blessing," she muttered as she wearily pulled open the door.

"I can easily believe it," Maxence said, his oddly sudden desire to have his own children from the day before dimming.

"Children *are* a blessing." Citoyenne Bernard stared after her friend and pulled the pins from between her lips.

A blessing he hadn't minded putting off whenever he watched his sister-in-law, Rosalie, attempt to wrangle his nieces. "I don't see you jumping for a chance at raising some of your own."

Her mouth pressed into a line. "I will quite happily raise children of my own when I find the right man to . . ." Her face flushed, and she seized his waistcoat once more.

He'd gotten to her. Maxence clamped his teeth together to keep from laughing at her discomfort. For all the times she'd riled him with her teasing, she deserved a little embarrassment. "Tell me more about this right man who will share your first kiss," he goaded.

Her mouth twisted as though she were contemplating sticking the pin straight into his side. None too gently she took his arm and lifted it out of her way. He'd rolled his sleeves up prior to breakfast and forgotten to take them down afterward, leaving the skin of his forearm exposed to her rough treatment.

Maxence wasn't about to back down, even though he stood with his arm at an awkward angle in the air where she'd positioned it. "Is he a carpenter in your dreams? Or perhaps a merchant?"

She straightened and locked eyes with him. "Neither. He's a mariner."

Maxence's insides wriggled under her stare. The intensity of her expression, which warned him against continuing down this path of conversation, made him swallow his next quip. "Is he?"

"If you knew me better, you would know that I haven't thought on that subject at all. I could not care less about his profession. Now, please, hold still."

As though she hadn't already turned him to stone with her withering glare. "It has been only a week since we met," he said after a moment of her pinning and repinning. She ran a hand along the front of the waistcoat, smoothing wrinkles. Her touch was so light he could hardly feel it through his shirt.

"Then perhaps when we are done with this journey, you will have better ammunition with which to tease me. Until then, keep practicing. I daresay the skill of intelligent jesting will come to you eventually."

Maxence clenched his jaw. How did she always win? No matter the subject, he somehow found himself bested.

She lowered his arm but didn't release it. "What's this?" She rotated it until the inside of his forearm faced up, the familiar raised line on his skin from wrist to elbow catching the light.

He looked away, fighting to keep his breathing steady. "A scar."

"I can see it's a scar. Where did you get it?"

Maxence flinched as her fingers traced the length of it. The wound didn't hurt anymore. The passing of a year and a half had seen to that. If only the wounds inside him—the ones she couldn't see—would heal as quickly. He shrugged. "I can't remember." He *wouldn't* remember. He tried not to every day. And until that morning in the Nantais café, he had been able to suppress the memories.

"That's a rather large scar to not have a story."

Gunpowder. Smoke. Red coat Swiss guards and shouting *fédérés*. "I can't remember," he repeated through grinding teeth. He tried to block the impending memory from his mind, but it advanced through his defenses. Émile's pale face, haloed in crimson blood.

"Étienne?"

Hard, dusty stone under his knees. A scream of agony that might have been his. The wild face of the man he'd intended to shoot, who had turned around and killed the only person Maxence could truly call a friend. He hadn't felt the slash of the guard's bayonet across his arm; he'd been too concerned with deflecting the intended fatal blow.

"What is wrong?"

Maxence gasped for breath. The Swiss guard suddenly dropped before him, gunned down by a *fédéré* who ran past with hardly a glance. His gun. Where was his gun? He had to get Émile to safety. Perhaps something could be done. Never mind the years of medical training that shrieked it was too late.

He'd missed his shot. He'd failed him. His greatest friend. The only one who cared whether he lived or died.

"Maxence?" Soft hands encircled his arms, jerking him from the torrents of his mind like a ship's anchor catching too quickly on a reef. Hazel eyes wide with concern filled his vision, pushing away the vivid imaginings of the past. His chest heaved.

"What is it?" She squeezed his arms. "You can tell me."

"I . . ." His voice scratched against his throat, which was raw as though he'd just inhaled the fumes of battle at the Tuileries. "I failed him."

CHAPTER 12

Why did the heaviness ease as he told her? It all came spilling out—the fervor to get to the palace, the tense and then bloodthirsty chaos, the anger at missing the shot and then fear at the soldier's response. Shock and disbelief that turned into numbing emptiness at Émile's death.

He couldn't take it back.

Her hands stayed on his arms, her thumb smoothing up and down his scar. Maxence paused his recounting. He'd known her for barely more than a week, and here he was baring his soul. The urge to recoil tightened his throat and almost convinced him to pull away. But her touch, with its promise of safety, kept him rooted to the floor.

"Even if you hadn't missed the guard, you might not have saved him," she said softly.

He dropped his head, breaking away from her gaze. He'd practically been staring. What had she seen in him? Panic and weakness, no doubt. Something about looking into her eyes, the gentleness and eagerness he saw in their depths, had intoxicated him to the point he couldn't help telling everything. She didn't blench at the hideous wounds he uncovered. The steadiness of her touch seemed to insist she wanted to know.

She wanted to bear this burden with him, never mind their short acquaintance.

He hadn't felt this sort of closeness to another person, this desire to divulge all, since the nights he'd spent in cafés with Émile and sometimes Gilles, talking and laughing over several rounds of drinks until there was hardly a thing they didn't know about each other. Those nights he hadn't minded throwing in embellishments here and there. This morning Citoyenne Bernard received the whole story, raw and unadorned with heroics or bravado.

"I know that," Maxence finally said. "We were in battle. Either of us could have fallen."

"It was not your fault, though I know it feels that way."

Maxence moved his arms from her grasp, and she didn't resist. "Perhaps not." She couldn't know. She'd never been in battle.

"Did you write to your friend's family?"

It had taken several days to heal enough to even grasp a quill. "I wrote to my family. My younger brother is employed by my friend's father. I assume he delivered the news and Émile's last letter." Maxence brought his head up. He fought to keep his breathing steady. The drowning sensation threatened to overwhelm his control. "Is that all you need to do to fit this?"

"I think I will need to take in the back seam as well." He didn't meet her eyes as she searched his face one last time before stepping behind him. "Stand straight, please."

Maxence squared his shoulders. Her footsteps retreated then returned. Going for more pins, he presumed. Her fingers tickled the nape of his neck as she pinched the back seam. He straightened even more.

"I suppose you didn't miss again," she said, almost whispering. Her hands trailed down his back as she pinned and repinned. A shiver ran over his spine, tingling his skin and halting his breath as it went.

"Miss what?"

"Another shot."

He'd been fitted for waistcoats and jackets dozens of times

throughout his life, but he'd never been this exceedingly aware of his tailor's work. So aware that he struggled to say the words that sat on his tongue, though perhaps that came more from the fact he'd never admitted to anyone what he intended to say next.

She thought him to be just another obedient soldier filled with unquenchable revolutionary avidity, but then . . . Wasn't she the only person left on this earth who had witnessed the falseness of that persona he'd tried so desperately to uphold?

"On the contrary," he said. "I've never shot at anyone since."

Her hands stilled midway down his back. "Why not?"

He shrugged. How could he explain? "Lest you think it an act of nobility or pity, my forbearance comes from . . ." Maxence licked his lips. It didn't matter if she knew. Nothing really mattered anymore. He had no life to return to. For years he had tried to pry doors open, hoping to find some place or entity where he fit. Once again his efforts had fallen short. "From a trepidation I cannot seem to shake."

The tickle of her fingers' movements started up again, both soothing and enlivening all at once. "What do you fear?"

He snorted. "What do I not fear?" He feared his weapon, falling short of finding his own way in this world, disappointing his family.

Her hands reached the small of his back. "You didn't fear the consequences of letting me go. Not enough to follow through on your orders."

"I couldn't have shot you if I wanted to," he growled. Had she finished? He needed fresh air. The room had grown warm despite the fire in the hearth dozing off to embers. Perhaps it was just her warmth from standing so close behind him.

"Did you want to?" Her voice—small, hesitant, and too close—flooded his mind with images of trudging through the streets of Nantes, dragging her with him. Those wide eyes filled with hate, and then with fear. He saw her lips moving in silent prayer while standing tied to the tree. His throat tightened at the memory of the unexpected concern on her upturned face as he insisted she leave him behind.

"No," he said. He couldn't say what it was about the copper-haired sprite scrubbing the clergyman's filth from the church's floor, but from the moment his eyes had fallen on her, he wished her no harm. He hadn't expected her to return the sentiment, let alone risk her life to protect his.

The door opened to a weary Citoyenne Colbert. Citoyenne Bernard dropped the back of his waistcoat and hurried around him.

"Children are a blessing. *Pitié*." Their hostess sank onto the sofa and took up her mending. "Have you finished?"

"I think I will need to take in the shoulder seams as well. But nearly there." Citoyenne Bernard reached up to adjust the waistcoat, a carefree grin once more on her face as though he hadn't just borne his soul to her.

Their hostess nodded. "*C'est bon*. He shouldn't be standing much longer if he wants to be healed by the time you leave."

His friend glanced at Citoyenne Colbert, a strange look in her eye. He opened his mouth to ask but thought better of it. He detected an air of secrecy in the glance. She was planning something. Though he hadn't known her for long, it seemed she was always plotting, from punishing constitutional clergymen to breaking traitor soldiers out of prison.

"Why are you smiling?" she asked.

Maxence lowered his brows. "I wasn't smiling." Though a peculiar lightness had nestled into his chest. It must be relief after harboring those overwhelming memories for so long. To finally be able to share them with a friend . . . A friend? After so willingly sharing his burden, ugliness and all, it only seemed right to consider her that.

"It was the start of a smile at the very least." She cocked her head. "You know you could ask Jean-Baptiste to borrow his shaving kit." The fervent distress on her features from their earlier conversation had dissolved into her usual impish mien.

Maxence ran a hand over his face, covered in a short, dark beard. He must look positively wild. Even on the road from Marseille to Paris with the *fédérés*, he'd managed to keep his face fashionably clean-shaven. "I'll use my own." When he could figure out a way to afford one.

Citoyenne Bernard shrugged. "Suit yourself." She didn't need to say that his shaving kit, his money, and almost every other thing he owned in this world besides his coat was still in Nantes. "I was only thinking of your image."

Maxence pressed his lips together, suddenly sympathetic to Citoyenne Colbert's fatigue, and a measure of his goodwill retreated under her teasing. Perhaps this emotional shaking from one direction to the other was why he had never felt the desire to marry. Deep in his bones he must have understood that kissing girls was one thing, but living with one day after day with no reprieve, constantly subject to her observation and teasing, was enough to drive a man to irreversible madness.

White sheets billowed like sails along the Loire, and Armelle buried her nose in their clean freshness before she pulled them from the line. Mère always shook her head when Armelle acted this way, but she couldn't help it. Recollections of long days of washing and mending alongside her mother and sisters swirled, with strong soap, bright sun, and jovial song to make the workload lighter.

She tossed the sheets in Alana's basket and pocketed the pins. How could she miss that tiresome work so much? When would she have another day like that in the company of her family?

"I'll take these inside," Alana said, hefting the basket piled high with white linens. "Then we can finish the line."

Armelle nodded and moved to the other line strung between the workshop and house as her friend headed to the door. She unpinned a little red petticoat and draped it over one arm. At home this was Jacqueline and Cécile's job. They'd have to take on more of the work now that she was gone.

And she wouldn't be able to return to Nantes very soon to take over her responsibilities, perhaps not for many years. Neither would Père or Henri, especially not if anyone discovered what her brother had been up to the last several months. She'd be like Étienne, going years without seeing parents or brothers or sisters, although she'd be sorrier for it than he. Her stomach twisted, forcing her to swallow hard to keep down her breakfast. Standing in the chill of the yard with none of her friends beside her, the weight of the distance between her and her family made her drop to her knees.

A pair of girls Jacqueline's age passed on the road, their voices echoing in the yard. Armelle sat still to not draw their attention. When they'd gone, she glanced toward the workshop, which Étienne and Jean-Baptiste had entered that morning. Would anyone report them if they saw a strange man entering the carpentry? Alana wanted to trust the discretion of their friends and neighbors, but Jean-Baptiste urged caution. As such, Étienne was confined to the house or the workshop during daylight hours. Étienne was to help Jean-Baptiste with some tasks, though she wondered how productive he was with Noël's steady chatter. Or perhaps that was Jean-Baptiste's design—using Étienne as a distraction for the talkative four-year-old.

The house door opened again. Armelle jumped back to her feet and brushed the dirt from her petticoat. Her face warmed like it had a few days ago when Alana had walked in on her conversation with Étienne. She should have taken more than one article of clothing off the line in the time it took for her friend to empty the basket.

Armelle pulled a pair of Noël's trousers from the line and tossed it with the petticoat into the basket Alana held.

"Thank you for helping," her friend said. Armelle had always adored Jean-Baptiste's wife. And now that Armelle had crossed the threshold of adulthood, the ten years that separated them did not seem quite as large as they once had.

"Of course. It is the least I can do with all you have done for us." And all they had risked. Jean-Baptiste hadn't brought the matter up again once the Colberts had decided to shelter her and Étienne, but she couldn't forget the strain in his voice when they'd discussed it the night of their arrival.

Alana tilted her head, watching as Armelle snatched a shift and shirt from the line. "May I ask a perhaps impertinent question?"

"Impertinent?" Armelle laughed. She'd never witnessed anything rude from this woman, word or deed. Alana wasn't capable of unkindness.

"You might see it that way." A grin flitted across Alana's face. "When you arrived, you said that Citoyen Étienne was your friend. That you hadn't taken a liking to him."

Que diable.

"I simply wonder if that is as true as you made it seem."

"Of course it is," Armelle said quickly, gathering the last of the clothing. She shoved the pins in her pocket. "I could never give my heart to someone who left dozens of pining girls behind him in Marseille." Never mind that he had certainly exaggerated his estimation. "Can you imagine someone like me sharing a life with someone as gloomy as he?"

"I suppose not."

Armelle finished loading the basket, fighting to keep an unaffected demeanor. If she protested too much, Alana would continue to disbelieve any assertion of neutrality.

"You simply seemed flustered the other day when I walked in while you were taking his measurements."

"He . . . he had just told me something rather shocking about his friend." Before that conversation, Armelle had found it difficult to believe Étienne could love anyone. Standing in the barren woods and old snow with her life in his hands had given her one glimpse of his character. Walking with a rumpled, hurting, exhausted version of him over damp roads had given her an entirely different view. Hearing his usually gruff voice laced with such immense grief and feeling his body tremble against her fingers had cast new logs into the fire by which she attempted to decipher him. He was a conundrum, to be sure.

"I see." Alana studied the laundry in her basket. "Will you follow him to Saint-Malo?"

Armelle let her shoulders fall. "Not because I have any interest in him."

Her friend turned slowly, an unreadable expression gracing her features. Armelle fell into step beside her. She shoved her hands into her pockets and stirred the pins about. Étienne would groan if he heard Alana's questions. The thought made her lips twitch. She could almost hear his protest about being erroneously matched with a girl he saw as nothing more than a little flibbertigibbet.

"You can hardly blame us for wondering," Alana said as they walked. "Two young people traveling alone under strange circumstances. Especially when the couple is handsome and lively."

Armelle held up her hands. "Please, do not ever refer to the two of us as a couple again." Her pulse had picked up speed since the start of this conversation, and she did not like how the pace restricted her breath. She would freely admit that Étienne was attractive, even if he looked more like a Renaissance prince with his unshaven face than an enlightened man of the eighteenth century as he purported to be. In truth, the short beard gave him a surprisingly appealing ruggedness. Or was it the brooding glower and challenge in his eyes? "That could not be further from reality. We are friends. Nothing more. We've known each other for hardly more than two weeks."

"But you are going to Saint-Malo?"

Was she? Grandmère and Grandpère didn't even know she was supposed to come to them. Their tiny house would provide her with quiet, safety, and a sense of the familiar. It wouldn't be home with her parents, but it would be close to it, with its mundane routines and childhood memories. Saint-Malo was risky and uncertain. She knew little of the city except what her brother had mentioned in his few letters. And if things went poorly on the journey north, she wouldn't have an easy way to return to southern Brittany. But Henri was in Saint-Malo, and perhaps Père as well. Could their entire family find a place to be together in that crush of privateers and smugglers? There was a better chance of it there than in Nantes.

"Yes. I think I shall."

Alana halted at the door and threw her a probing look. "How can you say you have no feelings for him, when you are practically following him to the ends of the earth?"

Armelle crossed her arms. "I have my reasons. And they are not what you think." She opened the door and pushed it wide for her friend to enter. The soft murmur of Louise's halting reading drifted over to them from the sofa. Armelle lowered her voice. "I do have feelings toward Étienne. Occasional annoyance, frequent amusement, immense gratitude, and even pity. I do not, however, have any silly notions about love, nor am I practicing writing my name as Armelle Étienne."

"Love is not a silly notion." Alana hefted the basket to the middle of the sitting room floor and waved for Louise to come help fold.

With a sigh, Armelle joined them around the basket and pulled hers and Étienne's clothes out from the mix. She still hadn't convinced him to borrow Jean-Baptiste's shaving kit, but she'd talked him into borrowing clothes twice now so she could wash the tattered ones he'd worn from Nantes. They really needed to get him more changes of clothing. These would only continue to wear until there was nothing left.

"I of course did not mean that all love is silly. I simply meant that the thought of loving Étienne was. We are far too dissimilar and want such different things." She wouldn't bother folding Étienne's clothes. He'd just change them again as soon as he could. She gathered them up and took them to his mattress in the corner of the room. "I wish nothing more than to have my family whole and well once again. He could not care less about seeing his family."

"Yes, I can see that," Alana said, nodding in a way that seemed like she truly believed Armelle. She rolled a pair of stockings into themselves and tossed them on the sofa.

Armelle laid Étienne's breeches across his bed, then draped his shirt atop them. The linen shirt was terribly wrinkled despite her efforts to hang it neatly on the line. Perhaps she should iron it for him, though she knew he'd resigned himself to his unfashionable appearance almost to the point of indifference.

"And yet, you are still going to Saint-Malo."

There was no convincing her. Armelle shook her head. "I am simply taking advantage of his company to get where I'd like to go." She still needed to inform him of this new decision. Would he protest the company? "I promise, Alana. There is nothing between us, and there will never be anything between us." The cravat would need ironing as well. She returned the shirt over her arm with the neckcloth and deposited the rest of his clothing on the bed. There wasn't good reason to try to satisfy his vanity—cleaning his clothing and ironing his shirt and tailoring his waistcoat. Maxence Étienne could use a few lessons in humility. But watching the eagerness in his eyes when she worked on his waistcoat had given her an odd satisfaction she didn't care to crush.

He would help her get to Saint-Malo, providing the appearance of protection to dissuade wrongdoers on the long road through the middle of the region, and she would help him look his best while getting there. Surely this sort of reciprocity would prove beneficial to both parties.

Reciprocity. She winced. It would just put her more in his debt. He hardly needed her help now that he was healing, but she'd try to do her part, all while making sure their friendship stayed, as she insisted, platonic.

Armelle shook her head and hurried off to locate the iron. Of course it would stay platonic. What a . . . Well, what a silly notion that it could be otherwise.

7 March 1794
Savenay, Brittany
Chère *Nicole,*

I instructed you to send a note for me to Lorient, but now I beg you to send word to Saint-Malo. Direct it to my brother Henri at number 6 rue Saint-Michel. *I must also ask that you not disclose these directions to my family. They think my brother is at the barracks. So far I have been responsible for posting letters to him, and they haven't suspected anything yet. I suppose we shall have to tell them now that I am gone, but I cannot divulge the secret without first seeking his permission.*

You will think me daft, mon amie, as I have fixed something in my mind and cannot let it go. My family may never be together in Nantes again, but perhaps we can be in Saint-Malo. It's only a dream. I know it. But how can I not reach for this dream if there is even a hope of it coming true? It means I shall keep company with our surly friend a little while longer. The poor man. I think he has had quite enough of me.

How I wish I could hear from you before we reach the coast. I will simply have to trust in God's mercy for your protection.

A. B.

Maxence closed the door against the evening cool and tried not to limp as he crossed the sitting room toward his mattress. Another week and he would be practically healed. At least he hoped so. Colbert and Citoyenne Bernard would be off for Lorient in a week, and he would need to be well enough to walk all the way to Saint-Malo. He was earning Colbert's trust a little more each day as they worked together in the shop, but he didn't want to test that by asking to stay with the man's wife and children while Colbert was away.

The fire in the hearth crackled as it slowly died. Maxence moved to poke it down, since the Colberts had already gone to bed for the night. That evening had been a spectacle, with the parents' rushing to get their children into bed and a chorus of shrieks and giggles and wailing. It had been followed by several rounds of requests for water and extra blankets and last kisses, leaving the poor Colberts with only just enough fortitude to retire themselves.

He smiled. As exhausted as he felt on their behalf, he found himself craving their chaos. To have a place to belong, to be needed, was certainly worth the fatigue. Perhaps his sudden removal from the army, the one place he had belonged, made him vulnerable to such notions. He'd never thought much of having a family before.

As he rounded the couch, a figure seated on the floor made him pause. "*Citoyenne?*" She looked up from her sewing, the firelight painting her face with its amber glow.

Citoyenne Bernard grinned. "I've almost finished." She held up the waistcoat, which had shrunk considerably since he last wore it. Perhaps it wouldn't drown him.

"It's late. Surely you could finish tomorrow."

She lifted a shoulder. "It won't take me long."

He'd wait to bank the fire, then. Her fingers moved methodically, pushing and pulling the needle in a rhythm not unlike sailors hauling on the sheets on *le Rossignol*. In light of her usual unpredictability, the steady movement mesmerized him. Soothed him. How many nights had he wandered to the kitchen to find his mother in a similar attitude mending Père's clothing? She'd pause her work and ask him to sit, then sometimes make him chocolate or coffee. Some nights she'd ask questions. Others they'd sit in companionable silence. He'd felt a sense of belonging then. And when he started his studies at Montpellier, those moments happened less frequently. When Gilles returned from the sea and their father's employ, they'd stopped altogether.

"You can sleep," she said. Maxence blinked back the memories. "I'll see to the fire." She sniffed and wriggled her nose, then went back to her work.

Maxence nodded once. His weary limbs wouldn't let him argue. He moved the blanket and sank onto the mattress with a sigh. The taste of Maman's chocolate coated his tongue as if he'd just taken a drink. He swallowed to clear the phantom sensation. He pulled off his boots before burrowing under the covers.

A lye scent from freshly washed clothing and bedding hung in the air, so different from the washday smells at home. Marseille's olive oil–based soap gave off a much earthier aroma. Sometimes Gilles would bring home lavender- or herb-scented varieties from the *savonnerie*. A lump welled in Maxence's throat, sudden and unexpected. He'd only felt homesick for southern France a few times since the *fédérés'* march to Paris. Why did it rear its head now?

"You're walking much better," Citoyenne Bernard said.

Maxence shifted to his side to face her, thankful for a distraction. He cleared his throat. "I thought I was supposed to sleep."

"If you wish to."

He waited. She wouldn't stay silent. Tonight he didn't want her to. Thoughts of the Colberts had left him vulnerable to memories of his own home and all that had once been. He couldn't fight the melancholy without her.

"You still must take care and rest," she said after a few moments. "We'll make better time to Saint-Malo the more your knee has healed."

He narrowed his eyes. "We?" But she was going to her grandparents'.

"I have decided to come with you." Her head bobbed with a finality that meant whatever he had to say on the matter, she had made up her mind.

"I do not plan on traveling in comfort. Wouldn't you rather ride in the cart with Colbert to Lorient?"

Her shoulders sagged, and she threw him a withering look. "What do you think I am, *une noble*?"

The image of her scrubbing the church floors in the wake of that yelping clergyman sprang to his mind. Definitely not a noblewoman. "But do you often walk all day for many days at a time?"

"I can do it better than you can at the moment." She sniffed indignantly.

Touché. "But why would you want to go to Saint-Malo?"

"I also have family in Saint-Malo."

Maxence pursed his lips. She'd said it too quickly. Either she was lying, or there was something about this family she did not want divulged.

It didn't make sense that she'd want to continue traveling with him unless she had a good reason. Generous as she was—impetuous as she was—she wouldn't decide to join him just to keep him company.

He rubbed the scruff on his chin. She'd fill the hours with stories and questions until his head spun, but it would be better than lonely, silent travel. He frowned. It had been a long time since he desired another person's company. Strange that she would be the one to fill that desire. "*Si vous voulez.*"

"You should sleep. You seem tired."

"It's difficult when someone continues talking to me." Maxence rolled over, putting his back to her. How was he to sleep with her in the room? Even if she didn't say anything else, the anticipation of her talking would keep his mind working. He closed his eyes and breathed deeply. Simulating the actions of sleep had sometimes tricked his thoughts and body into relaxing. He imagined the heat of a Mediterranean sun on his face, a sharp breeze in his lungs, a piercingly blue sea before him. Gilles's contagious grin at his side.

That would not do. His eyes flew open, and he turned again to watch Citoyenne Bernard's work. "You have not kept up your tradition."

Her brows rose. "Which tradition?"

Maxence propped himself up on one elbow. "The one you had with your brother. One question before sleep. You made it seem like a serious duty."

Her face softened. "It is, of course. I've been asking Noël and Louise each night."

"Have they told you anything interesting?" Anything to keep his mind from his family.

"Louise's greatest desire is for her *maman* to make her a new doll because Marie is too small a doll for a girl of seven." She frowned at a tangle in her thread. "Noël finds a way to turn any question into a question about his new bed."

Maxence chuckled. They'd never hear the end of that. "The question

of the night is our greatest desire?" He couldn't say how he would answer that one.

"Oh, no." She gave him a sidelong glance. "It was what they would
do with their family if they had a day completely free of work."

He stiffened. "And Noël said he would finish his new bed." This
conversation had hit dangerous waters. Time to tack this ship and head
for calmer seas.

"*Bien sûr.*" She smiled but quickly sobered again. "Étienne, might I
ask—"

"I don't have an answer to that question."

"I think you have an answer to this one. Whether you wish to respond to it is another matter." She pulled the thread straight and examined its length before returning to her stitches.

He already knew what she would ask. He flipped to his stomach,
burying his arms under the misshapen pillow and resting his chin atop it.

"Why does talking about your family bring you so much distress?"
She spoke softly, as if for the first time in their acquaintance she was
hesitant to offend him.

"Do you ask such difficult questions to your brother each night?" he
asked. "That must be exhausting for him."

"Julien is only seven. But he sometimes asks me things that are very
hard to answer."

Maxence lifted his head. "I did not know there was an option to ask
you the questions."

She put a hand in her pocket and drew something out, which she
clutched in her fist. "We roll this die Julien . . ." Her voice caught. Her
lips pressed together, and the slightest quiver touched her chin. "Julien
made it with my father." She opened her hand. A little cube sat on her
palm. "Even numbers, I ask the question. Odd numbers, he asks the
question." She sniffed and fished a handkerchief from her pocket to wipe
her nose.

"Are you falling ill?"

She shook her head quickly. "I always get sniffles and sneezes in the spring."

It wasn't quite spring yet, but he didn't mention that. "I think I prefer asking the questions."

Citoyenne Bernard held up the die. "Shall we let chance decide?" She tucked the handkerchief into her pocket, then tossed the little die to the floor. Tap, tap, tap. It skipped across the floor then teetered to a stop. She leaned forward to see, firelight giving her hair a metallic sheen. "Five."

"*Parfait.*" She wouldn't push his answer. He settled his chin back on the pillow. "Now I want the truth. Why do you wish to come with me to Saint-Malo?"

She opened her mouth to speak, but the words didn't come. Her chest rose and fell.

"Is it a rule that you cannot lie in this game?" He cocked his head like she often did. It earned him a glare. The corners of his mouth twitched. After all the times she'd rendered him speechless, he enjoyed the few moments he got to return the favor.

Citoyenne Bernard tugged on the thread before cutting it off with little shears close to the fabric. She spread out the waistcoat across her lap, inspecting her work. "Finished."

"We shall both keep our secrets, then." Maxence let his head fall to the pillow.

She used the couch to help her stand. "My older brother is in Saint-Malo."

"You didn't mention that before. What took him there?" Perhaps he'd misinterpreted her earlier response as being secretive. She'd have a roof over her head and food to eat in Saint-Malo.

"The *levée en masse.*"

Maxence frowned. If her brother was part of the Army of the West, she wouldn't be able to stay with him. "But . . ."

"I have another family member I anticipate being in Saint-Malo. I hope in the next few months."

"Someone not in the army?"

She shifted her weight side to side, hugging the waistcoat like a blanket. "My father."

Hoping to find her father's ship in port. Maxence winced. He pushed himself up to sitting. Biting back the instinct to scoff, he ran a hand down the side of his face. How did he tell her the impossibility of showing up to a random port city and expecting to find someone's whereabouts? He didn't want to crush the yearning in her hazel eyes. "Do you know what ship he is on? Even if you did, there's no knowing for certain when the ship would make land in Saint-Malo, or if it would at all."

She chewed her lip, then met his eyes. "My father is on a ship called *le Rossignol*."

Maxence froze, breath catching. His father's wasn't the only vessel of that name. "Does she hail from . . ."

Citoyenne Bernard nodded. "Provence."

He held his head. His fingers tangled in his curls. "No wonder you were so interested in my father's brig." And she hadn't thought to tell him. Why should she? She owed him nothing. Still, it stung that she'd known the connection and kept it to herself.

"I know you don't wish to see your father. I won't ask you to meet him. I only need to make the journey to Saint-Malo. And if you have any other information, I would be so grateful."

He wanted to give a resounding refusal. Why should he help her if she didn't trust him enough to tell him things? He looked up. Her pleading eyes melted the iron walls he'd tried to raise inside. How could he say no? "I can help you." His voice held more gruffness, more weariness, than he'd intended.

"Thank you, *mon ami*." She practically ran the finished waistcoat to him. He almost expected her to kiss his cheek in her excitement. If she'd been that sort of girl. "I promise not to tease you quite so much as on our first journey."

He found himself, in this moment of fatigue, wishing she *were* that sort of girl, but he quickly swatted that thought away. "You'll pardon my disbelief."

Her lips pulled into a frown that remained only for a moment. "With that confidence, I may forget to try." She dumped the waistcoat on his head. "Here. You'll be more comfortable."

"*Merci.*"

She gave a small smile of approval, bid him good night, and hurried up the ladder. Shortly after, he heard the muted shuffling of her preparing for bed. Then the house quieted. He sat motionless on the old mattress, eyes locked on the fire. What did it matter that her father was on *le Rossignol*?

The threadbare wool of his waistcoat prickled against his fingertips. Père had helped someone who wasn't himself. Somehow it was difficult to make sense of that. And that person had risked his life for a family he didn't agree with. His daughter had endangered herself for someone *she* didn't agree with and dragged him with her to hide at the house of friends, also imperiling their future. Maxence let the waistcoat drop beside his mattress.

None of it made sense. He slid back into bed, wondering if sleep would find him at all that night.

CHAPTER 13

Maxence stood on a log suspended horizontally over a pit, gripping one end of a vertical saw nearly as tall as he was. In the pit below, Colbert held the other end of the tool. The sawyer he usually hired to cut planks hadn't come through Savenay recently, and Colbert's supply had dwindled. Repairs from the battle in December had taken more resources than planned.

Though hardly an experienced sawyer, Maxence had agreed to help him with the task of turning the pile of logs in the carpenter's yard into usable planks. His responsibility was easy enough—he pulled the saw upward and positioned it for Colbert to make a downward cut. He pulled, then Colbert pulled, up and down until they'd traveled the length of the log and sawed the plank free. The work had the same steadiness as most labor at sea, with enough focus and effort to drive out troublesome thoughts. He'd enjoyed that about life on *le Rossignol*. One of the few positive things.

The last few days Maxence had faltered between accepting Citoyenne Bernard's company on his journey and trying to change his plans to avoid Saint-Malo. But whichever way he looked at it, he couldn't think of a better place for him to start trying to piece his life back together.

His uncle would help him. And Citoyenne Bernard. They'd both get what they wished. But with her there actively looking for *le Rossignol*, he had a terrible feeling a meeting with Père was inevitable.

"Hold," Colbert said as he made a final cut. He set his handle on the ground, and Maxence braced the saw from above. He swiped his sleeve across his brow. The weather wasn't terribly chill for mid-March. Mid-Ventôse, rather. A few hours of work had left them both covered in sweat and wood dust. "Thirsty?"

Maxence nodded. He sat and stretched his knee as Colbert hopped out of the pit to fetch the water bucket. The work was more intense for Maxence's torso and arms than his legs, which was the only way Colbert's wife had agreed to allow him to help. He could brace himself with his uninjured leg to take some of the weight off his knee.

"We've made good work given this is your first time acting the part of a sawyer," Colbert said as he lifted a ladle of water toward Maxence.

Maxence took it and guzzled the cool water. It washed the grit of dust from his mouth. He handed the ladle back to his host, who took his own drink. When Colbert returned the ladle to the bucket, he fixed Maxence with one of his unnerving stares.

"You leave for Saint-Malo in two days."

They'd already established that. Maxence didn't move a muscle.

"You've given me no grounds to distrust you."

That was a relief, as Maxence had no doubt Colbert could cause him serious harm if he had a mind to. Yet his host's glare did not relent, and neither did Maxence's urge to squirm.

"I've attempted to convince Armelle to come with me to Lorient, but she will not listen." Colbert shook his head, finally breaking eye contact. "I shouldn't expect any less from her, I suppose. She's always been stubborn."

Maxence started to agree, but another look from Colbert silenced him.

"I don't like this arrangement. If any harm comes to Armelle, especially if it is at your hand . . ." His brow rose. Maxence gulped. "I will hunt you down and see that you pay. And I know several men and boys who will be even more eager to see you strung up."

The hate in young Julien's eyes in the church courtyard when he was trying to protect Maxence's sister filled his mind. He could only imagine what the rest of the Bernards would do. He raised his hands. "I would never—"

"My wife mentioned Armelle talking about dozens of broken hearts in Marseille." Colbert took another drink. "A man that sure of himself can't be trusted to know boundaries."

Dozens of . . . Maxence clapped a hand to his face. *Diantre!* What had she been telling them? "*Citoyen*, that is far from true. I simply—"

"I'll take your word and say nothing else on the matter."

"I will not harm her in any way," Maxence said quickly. Would the trouble this woman brought him ever cease? "What's more, I will do all in my power to protect her until she has secured a place to stay."

Colbert nodded once and offered him another drink. Though his mouth had gone drier than dust, Maxence shook his head. His host had accomplished his goal. Maxence scrambled back into his position at the top of the saw. All pride he'd built from doing a good job on his first try had vanished.

The scrape of the saw started up again, as accusatory as Colbert's glower. Maxence resolved to run to Saint-Malo, never mind his knee. The sooner he delivered Citoyenne Bernard to wherever she wished to go, the sooner they could part ways. No more accusations, no more knowing glances, no more distrust from those who loved her. He would be on his own again, which was just the way he preferred.

Alana linked arms with Armelle as they walked into town. "I cannot believe it is already time for you to leave. It seems you arrived just yesterday."

Armelle buried a cough in her elbow. A night of constant sniffling had left her throat raw and scratchy. She was sure it would pass in an hour or two. "I think Jean-Baptiste would have preferred we stay for a shorter period."

Alana's mouth contorted. "He has been worried."

"As he should be." Armelle squeezed her arm. "You shouldn't worry about us. We are in your debt for so many kindnesses."

"Do you think Citoyen Étienne will be well enough to travel?"

Dear Alana. So worried about everyone. "You should have seen him in the prison. He could hardly walk. Now he's helping Jean-Baptiste. I think Étienne will survive. We may have to travel a little slower, but we will make it to Saint-Malo."

Her friend sighed. "I am not pleased that you are all leaving tomorrow. What am I to do with those little ruffians by myself?" She gestured ahead to Louise and Noël running along the road ahead of them. The lavender ribbons of Lousie's bonnet had come untied and now trailed behind her. Noël had lost his cap and didn't seem to notice. "They are always wild the day after visitors leave."

Armelle laughed, which her throat did not appreciate. She tried to swallow back a cough. "I will miss those two."

Her friend let go of her arm and crouched to retrieve Noël's cap. Armelle took the chance to muffle her cough and clear her throat.

When Alana straightened, she said, "I think you are very sweet to do this for Citoyen Étienne. He doesn't have much, does he?"

"He may not be very happy I'm spending money like this." Armelle lifted a shoulder. "But when has anything I've done made him happy?"

Her friend poked her arm. "I think he was made very happy when you helped him escape prison . . . and by your alterations to his waistcoat. Have you seen him strutting about the carpentry yard?"

She had seen that. Like a little boy in his first pair of breeches. Her lips tugged upward. "Who knew a waistcoat could change a man?"

"I think he's softened quite a lot in the last two weeks," Alana said. "He seemed so angry at everything when he arrived."

"I think he was." With an understandable, if not good, reason.

Armelle tilted her head back, taking in the clear sky. Spring was on the way, with its promise of relief from the cold. The day was nearly too warm for a cloak. They'd have a very pleasant walk north if this weather held.

"I hope he finds what he's looking for in Saint-Malo," Alana said.

They walked on in silence as the houses lining the road grew closer together and the little shop they sought came into view. Armelle adjusted her bonnet low over her eyes, even though she wasn't very worried about someone recognizing her. After two weeks, the army wouldn't be actively looking for a girl who affronted the *représentant* and fled. Still, she didn't want to make an impression on anyone.

They pulled the shop's rickety door open, and they had hardly crossed the threshold before Noël and Louise asked for sweets. Hushing did little to calm their pleas. Julien would have done the same thing, despite having such a frugal mother. Armelle requested the kit she needed from the shopkeeper and could not help quietly asking for a few lemon *bonbons*.

The grey-haired man motioned to the paper-wrapped bundle he'd set on the counter. "Will he need soap as well?"

Oh. Soap. That would be important. How stupid she'd look if she forgot soap. "Yes, *s'il vous plaît*."

"Would you prefer lye?" the man asked. "Or we have some *savon de Marseille* left, if that interests you."

Savon de Marseille? It would cost far too much. She glanced at Alana, who was ushering her children toward the door under a chorus of complaints. It only had to last him until they reached Saint-Malo. Then he could take care of himself from there. "Do you have a very small piece of the *savon de Marseille*?"

"Cinnamon or without scent?"

She stared at the counter. It was Étienne. The man who couldn't let go of his fine army coat, no matter the risk. He didn't need to be coddled with scented soap. And yet . . . With a sigh, she nodded. She could practically hear Mère's scolding. "I will take the cinnamon."

Armelle laid down the precious coins and took up the kit, the soap, and the little packet of boiled sugar treats. There was a reason Mère always sent her to the market with a specific list and the exact amount of money for the things they needed. Julien would be spoiled rotten otherwise.

"*Trugarez*," she said in Breton as she left, tucking her purchases into her pocket. If this didn't earn her a smile, she didn't know what would. If nothing else, she would get plenty of smiles from Alana's "little ruffians." Knowing Étienne, she might have to be content with that.

Maxence had done all he could to give Colbert the impression of his polite disinterest toward Citoyenne Bernard since the man had expressed his suspicion. He liked their host, liked his blunt honesty and logical patriotism toward the République, but Maxence was eager to start toward Saint-Malo tomorrow to escape the awkward wariness that had settled on him when in Colbert's company.

Shadows had started creeping across the workshop as Maxence helped Colbert pound the last few nails into a door, constructed simply of several planks. The iron latch was nothing to gawk at either. When they'd finished with the nails, they lifted the door and leaned it against a wall.

"Will you help me deliver this?" Colbert asked, returning some of his tools to their proper places.

Maxence wiped his hands on the half apron Colbert had loaned him. "I thought we wanted as few people to see me as possible." He'd hurried to the house any time they thought someone was approaching the carpentry and the reverse if they thought they had a visitor to the house. On the eve of his departure, he didn't see any less of a need for secrecy.

"I need to get this door fitted and hung before I leave tomorrow." Colbert grasped one side of the door. "I do not think it's necessary to worry about secrecy where we're going, so long as you keep quiet."

That wouldn't be difficult. Maxence took the other side of the door, and they tilted it onto its side, shifting the weight until it was evenly balanced between them. They must not have far to go if they were walking it to the customer. He followed Colbert out into the cool evening. The road that passed the house had only a few distant travelers but was otherwise empty.

They turned down a smaller road leading to a more densely populated area. It was then Maxence started to notice the damage—a smattering of bullet holes in the side of a house, a mangled fence in front of an empty paddock, a nearly unrecognizable wagon left in shards near the street.

Colbert halted near a small half-timbered house. Its smashed-in door looked ready to buckle. A blue blanket peeked through the many slits in the door. The occupants must have hung the blanket for protection against the winter cold. Maxence glanced over his shoulder. None of the dwellings on this little road had escaped damage from the recent battle. He'd seen destruction in Paris, but it was usually targeted and aimed at upper-class edifices. Savenay's destruction had no rhyme nor reason.

"The area around the church is worse," Colbert said, lowering his side of the door so they could stand it up.

Maxence had seen what a broadside could do to the hull of an English merchantman. He could only imagine the destruction to a village in point-blank range. "And some residents stayed?"

"Those who did were rounded up and taken to Nantes." The first night after their arrival, their host had spoken with little emotion about the Chouan situation. Maxence had taken it as a lack of feeling, for which he did not fault the man. War had deadened Maxence inside as well. It made one want to care for his own and not be bothered with the affairs of others.

Colbert hailed the occupants of the house, and a moment later a girl of fourteen or fifteen parted the makeshift curtain and pushed open the battered door. "Citoyen Colbert?"

"I've come with your door," he said.

She stared at him blankly. "But we cannot pay this month."

Maxence didn't doubt it. The windows of the humble house had no glass or even oiled paper, just rags. Chunks of plaster littered the ground beneath cracks in the walls.

Colbert left Maxence to hold the new door and began pulling at the hinges of the old door, which were rusty and in poor shape. His tools clinked against the old hinges, the only answer he had for the girl. She retreated into the dark house. Murmured conversation in Breton drifted out the holes and gaps.

"Will these people ever be able to repay you?" Maxence asked quietly. With fewer and fewer wealthy landlords in France, the upkeep of tenant dwellings fell on the shoulders of the common people.

"We all have to do our part to rebuild this land." Colbert went down on one knee to pull the lower hinge apart. "We have to help each other, or we'll never survive."

Maxence tapped his fingers against the wood he held. It wasn't a fancy door, but it was sturdy. Colbert used hours to build it that could have been spent making things that would earn him money. For so long Maxence had only had himself to care for. His future to think about. His duty to perform. Then he'd joined the Jacobins and changed his focus to building the République. If he were honest, his real focus had been finding a place where he could excel. Before he'd escaped Nantes, he'd been trying to find his way into the *chef-de-brigade*'s good graces.

"Are these your wife's relatives?" The girl's skin was too pale to be a blood relative of Colbert's.

The man shook his head. "I've spoken with them a few times."

How could someone be so concerned with the cares of a family he had few connections to? The old door creaked as the last hinge pulled free. Colbert turned it away from the house and let it crash to the ground. Then he motioned for Maxence to bring the new door.

"These hinges should fit the original pintles," Colbert said. "They should go on easily."

Maxence helped him lift the door into place. They fit the new hinge pieces into the old ones with only a little trouble. When they'd finished, a shriveled old woman came to the front of the house, her tears hindering her speech. She spoke to Colbert in Breton. The carpenter said little in response, mostly nodding and repeating the same Breton word.

On the road toward home, Colbert broke the silence with a chuckle. "You seem incredulous, *citoyen.*"

Maxence realized he had been glaring at the ground and quickly unfurrowed his brows. "How do you have the resources to just give doors to people?"

Colbert flipped the hammer in his hand once, then again. The handle slapped against his palm with each rotation. "A new *république* cannot stand if her people do not band together."

"The République is supposed to take care of her people." But *had* she taken care of these people? Of course it wasn't the République's fault the Chouans decided to make a stand in Savenay. The rebels brought war to these people, not the country. Many of those rebels had paid with their lives in the Loire's waters. Each time he thought of it, Maxence's stomach twisted. The République saw him as nothing better than a traitor, exactly the same as those people who hadn't had his luck.

"But, *citoyen,*" his companion said, "we are the République. We are one family united in the cause of liberty." They reached the door of the carpentry, and Colbert paused. "We all take care of each other as though we are family. At least that is how it should work."

Maxence laughed mirthlessly, shoving his hands into the pockets of his breeches. "I suppose I do not have a family that takes care of each other, so I cannot understand it." His mother mending Père's clothing in the kitchen shot once again to the forefront of his mind. He could almost imagine the pain in her eyes if she had heard him say such a thing. Or perhaps he was just imagining the unexpected sorrow she'd displayed that hot summer evening in Marseille as he set off for death and glory.

"I'm sorry to hear it." Colbert's voice held sympathy but did not drip with pity. Maxence appreciated that.

"Dinner is ready," said a voice behind them. Maxence glanced back at the house to see Citoyenne Bernard, her head tilted as she did when she was deep in thought.

That night after dinner, she and the Colberts retired early, leaving Maxence alone to his lumpy mattress for the last time. He sat slowly.

Who knew the next time he'd have a mattress to sleep on? He should enjoy it, even if it was old and contorted. Something crinkled against his side. He pulled back the blanket to find a package secured with string. The hint of cinnamon touched the air.

Who would give him a gift? He tugged on the string. Not Colbert. They'd agreed Maxence's work in the carpentry was payment for shelter and food. His wife, perhaps? Surely Citoyenne Bernard wouldn't have spent her meager funds on something . . .

The paper opened. In it sat a wood-handled razor, a simple soap brush, and a small rectangle of soap. In the light of the nearly dead fire the letters M-A-R-S-E-I-L-L-E marched across the top of the soap, stamped into its surface. *Savon de Marseille.* Pencil markings filled one corner of the paper wrapping. Maxence squinted to read them.

You look like a bear. Shave your face.

An unbidden smirk sprang to his mouth, and he closed his eyes, rubbing his forehead. He quickly wiped the grin from his lips and let his hand fall back to the mattress. She had used her money to buy him a razor. It wasn't finely crafted, not like the bone-handled instrument he'd left in Nantes. Froment had most likely claimed it with anything else he had of value. The brush's bristles were uneven. The soap was only a scrap. But she'd thought of him. She'd sacrificed for him.

Suddenly he found it hard to breathe as some strange emotion welled up from his chest. The shaving kit in his lap blurred as the fire waned. When was the last time someone had given him a gift, and not because they were compelled or felt it was their responsibility? Colbert's words from earlier rang in his head. *We all take care of each other as though we are family. At least that is how it should work.*

Citoyenne Bernard might have been a prater, but somehow compassion came so easily to her. Even for people such as he who hardly deserved it. How would he repay her for the services she'd rendered? He stared at the razor and its accessories. Just like the family with the broken door, he wondered if he ever could.

CHAPTER 14

Armelle drew in the crisp morning air as she stood just outside the Colberts' front door. Pink wisps of dawn drifted above the trees and fields that encircled Savenay. Mist that would soon dissolve into a pleasant spring day clung to furrowed earth.

It was as if southern Brittany were trying to bid her to stay, to not venture toward the rocky northern shores. The scene was almost as convincing as Louise and Noël's pleas to stay until their papa returned. But the Loire country, with its castles and vineyards, could not be her home anymore. The thought should have hurt, but strangely she'd awoken early that morning with a fire in her belly and spring in her step. And an irritation in her throat that exceeded yesterday's.

Footsteps drew near, and in a moment Étienne rounded the corner of the house. He'd shaved his cheeks clean, and the sharp angles of his jaw were now much more pronounced. He wore his well-fit national guard breeches as usual, with the waistcoat she'd altered and his shirtsleeves rolled up to his elbows. Though still in a state of undress, he'd suddenly transformed from rough vagabond to the severe soldier she'd met on the church steps.

She stood paralyzed and watching, unsure of what to make of the strange sensation in her chest. Was it the return of the clawing fear from that fateful morning?

He stopped beside her, gaze down. In his hands he held a small towel with the shaving kit cradled inside.

"You must think me an ingrate for not thanking you for these at breakfast."

Armelle tore her eyes away, back to the safety of the misty fields. "Gratitude is difficult for you. I didn't expect anything."

"You didn't have to do this for me. In fact, there are many things you've done that you didn't have to do. And I'm . . . I'm very grateful."

She raised her brows. "*Very* grateful? *Sacrebleu*, what has happened to you?" Her voice trailed off into a cough.

"Are you unwell?"

She shook her head emphatically as she recovered. "Of course not. I'm always well."

"Perhaps the Colberts wouldn't mind if you stayed for—"

"I'm going with you to Saint-Malo," Armelle said, her hands on her hips. "You cannot be rid of me over a little morning cough." Was that a flash of concern in his eyes?

"Then let's bid our hosts farewell and be off."

True to her expectations, Louise and Noël whined their complaints until Armelle produced the little packet of lemon *bonbons*. Alana gave her a thankful smile, eyes shining with tears as she drew Armelle in for a hug.

"We shall miss you terribly," her friend said, drawing back. "Do be safe. And don't push Citoyen Étienne too hard."

"Or let him push himself too hard." Armelle laughed. That was more likely. But she quickly sobered. Goodbyes. How she hated them. "I don't know when I shall see you next."

Alana nodded sadly. "When the war is over."

Whenever that would be.

"Jean-Baptiste wished to have a word with you before you left." Alana dabbed at her eyes. "He's hitching Pierre's horse to the cart."

Armelle nodded. She gave Louise another squeeze and kissed Noël on the cheek, though he was too busy asking Étienne if he would return to see the new bed.

Outside in the carpenter's yard, Jean-Baptiste was buckling the last harness straps on the neighbor's horse. Armelle walked up beside him and patted the old brown horse's nose.

Jean-Baptiste fixed her with a stern gaze. "You can still change your mind, Armelle. I can deliver you safely to your grandparents."

She shook her head. "I've made my choice." Jean-Baptiste's lips twitched, and it didn't take much of a scholar to tell that he thought her choice a doltish one. Perhaps it was. "You needn't worry about me."

"You hardly know this man," he said, gesturing toward the house. "He's a soldier and an admitted *charmeur*. Just because he saved you does not mean he will not take advantage of you."

Armelle pressed her lips together, battling the urge to bristle at his accusation. "I will be on my guard." Étienne could be trusted.

"Take this." Jean-Baptiste reached into his coat and pulled out a handle that resembled the razor. He flipped it open to reveal a sharply pointed blade, only a little shorter than her hand, that glinted in the sunlight just peeking over the rooftops. "I made this handle shortly after I started my apprenticeship with your father. Keep it in your pocket." He snapped it closed and handed the knife to her.

She ran her thumb over the handle.

"Hold it in front of you, like you're shaking someone's hand, not pointing down. It takes more effort and time between stabs," Jean-Baptiste said. "Hit fast and hard wherever you can."

Armelle went cold. "How . . . many times?"

"As many as it takes."

She slid it into her pocket with stiff fingers. "*Merci*." She couldn't imagine stabbing Étienne, or anyone, but if it made Jean-Baptiste more comfortable letting her go, she would take it.

"Stay alert on the road. You never know who you'll meet between here and Saint-Malo. Soldiers, Chouans, travelers who wouldn't think twice of—"

Armelle took his arm. "You have been more than generous with us, despite your own misgivings. *Merci, mon ami.*"

"Your parents will never forgive me if something happens."

"We'll look out for each other. I promise."

Jean-Baptiste looked away. Without a word he turned, and Armelle followed him back toward the front of the house as Étienne exited with Noël hanging onto his arm. She hated leaving the Colberts to worry.

Étienne extracted himself from the four-year-old, the ghost of a grin on his lips, which he quickly banished when he caught Armelle watching. They bid farewell to the little family and set off down the road. To avoid potential meetings with the soldiers housed in town, they skirted around it before meeting the north road.

Somehow it felt so natural, walking side by side. Like they'd returned to their normal routine, even though they had spent more days recovering at the Colberts' than they had walking to Savenay. Whenever they passed the occasional traveler, they made sure to give the person or group a wide berth and keep their heads down as they had on the first part of their journey. This time Étienne took her bedroll and market bag—into which he'd promptly stuffed his bundled coat.

"I can carry at least one of them," she said after they'd turned onto the road heading north.

"You carried them both for two days. I can take my turn." His gait was slow for a man of his height, but he walked with very little limp. That wouldn't last the whole day if they didn't rest frequently. She'd have to pay close attention to when he started to favor his injured leg.

"We can share the load." She reached for the bedroll, but he sidestepped her effort. Very well. If he wanted to tire himself out faster, so be it. She was already fighting labored breathing, and they'd hardly made it out of town.

"You look very different without your beard," she said after they'd covered more ground. Beards weren't the fashion among any circles in the new République, poor or rich, but a part of her missed the coarse recklessness it added to his appearance.

He looked down at her, a glint in his dark eyes. "Ah. Now you will not be so embarrassed to be seen with me."

She reached out her arms. "Walking on this practically empty road? Yes. I am much relieved. Heaven forbid I get shunned by my elite friends for keeping company with an unshaven mariner."

"I am *not* a mariner." He didn't say it as intensely as before.

"What are you, then?"

He turned his focus back to the road ahead. "I studied medicine for a time at Montpellier." Something about his voice made it seem like an unhappy memory. Though from what she knew of him, she wondered if he had any happy memories at all.

"But . . . ?" she prodded.

Étienne's mouth twisted. "Does this fulfill your question for to-night?"

Armelle bit her lips to keep back a grin. "I will allow it." He wasn't protesting.

With a great sigh, his shoulders fell. "I was not a scholar. In fact I was a terrible medical student. I went into it with great ideals, but I let myself get distracted when the studies became difficult."

"Distracted by young women." A laugh escaped her defenses at his glower. "You cannot deny it, *monsieur* 'The-kisses-that-followed-suggested-they-were.'" She deepened her voice to mimic his and puffed out her chest like the swaggering seamen she'd seen near the docks.

It was much easier to see him flush now that the beard was gone. "I should think you wouldn't bring up that incident, as you had the greater embarrassment."

"I did?" she cried.

"You were the one caught ogling a man without his shirt."

Armelle snapped her mouth shut as a heat flooded her skin. "That was . . . I mean, I wasn't . . ."

"You were staring. Admit it."

She would never admit to that. Never mind that his instances of ogling most likely far exceeded hers. She shoved her hands into her pockets and focused intently on the road. There was no response, though she grasped for some witty return to throw back at him.

"Étienne three, Bernard fourteen," he said.

"Fourteen of what?" She cast him a sidelong look.

"I don't often win these conversations." He lifted a shoulder.

"You are keeping track of how often you win?"

He ducked his head with a chuckle—light, carefree, and entirely too short. "It clearly doesn't happen often."

Did he just laugh? A real, true laugh from this surly former soldier who didn't think anyone cared? Who only laughed in sarcasm or derision? "No." She grinned. "Not often at all."

Maxence stood and stretched, then rubbed his bleary eyes. Shadows still enveloped the barn they'd slept in, but hazy light was peeking through the windows and cracks around the doors. The cows and plow horses below the loft had begun to move about. Wind whistled lightly past the stone building's walls. He'd promised the reluctant farmer, who lived in a small house attached to the barn, that they'd be gone before the sun rose. They should make it to Nozay by the end of the day, even with their slow walking.

Citoyenne Bernard lay on the opposite side of the hayloft, her back to him. He didn't know how well she'd slept with all her coughing. Her cough had finally settled, but that couldn't have been more than an hour or two ago. Yesterday on the road she'd called for rest frequently, and while she cited his injured knee as the reason, she'd been the one who seemed more and more drained as the day rolled on. They hadn't even made it to the town of Blain as they'd intended before she suggested they stop and inquire about staying the night in this barn.

"Shall we start?" he asked. She didn't stir.

Maxence crossed the loft, his boots thumping against the wood floor. Bits of hay drifted about, stirred up by his movement. He went down on one knee beside her. She'd pulled the wool blanket up so that only a bit of her white cap showed above it. The mass of hay and heat from the animals below had kept them reasonably warm, but she lay huddled as though freezing.

"Citoyenne Bernard? It's time to wake up."

She finally groaned and rolled over. "Is it morning?" Her voice was huskier than usual, no doubt from the long night. She touched her throat and swallowed.

"Yes. I told them we'd leave early." She was sick. There was no getting around it. She needed rest and good food, not a journey across the province. But they were far from friendly territory, nor did they have the funds to pay for a room at an inn.

She sat up and was instantly set upon by a fit of coughing, which she buried in her sleeve. Maxence's stomach sank. Perhaps in Nozay they could find someone who would take pity on them and let them stay for a day or two while she recovered. Thank the stars the last few days had been warm.

Maxence slipped the waterskin from their market bag. Well, *her* market bag. They were both using it for the moment, but that did not give him joint ownership. He uncapped the waterskin and handed it to her. After drinking a few sips, she gave it back and pushed herself to her feet, brushing hay from her jacket and petticoat. She cleared her throat. "Shall we eat on the road?"

He picked up her blanket to fold and roll up with his. She shouldn't have left Savenay. One more day and the rest of them would have realized this wasn't her usual spring sneezing. The worst thing she could do when sick was exert herself by walking a dozen miles on a road that wasn't well maintained.

She reached into the slits in her petticoat that allowed access to her pockets, then seemed to rummage around in a strange manner. "Do you mind?" she asked when she caught him staring. She quickly turned her back on him.

"What are you doing?" He secured the bedroll and slung it across his chest.

"Adjusting my stays." Her hoarse voice made the indignant tone almost comical.

"Oh." He turned his back to her. "I didn't realize you could do that without . . . you know." Not that he had ever been in a position to watch a woman do this. Perhaps most didn't, and this was simply another Citoyenne Bernard peculiarity.

"Pocket slits are a remarkable thing." She retrieved her bonnet and moved toward the ladder.

Maxence put the waterskin back in the market bag and withdrew the bread Citoyenne Colbert had packed for them. Its greyish hue testified that it was a true *pain d'égalité*. Knowing that didn't make him eager to eat it. "Never mind that a few weeks ago when I was changing—"

"Don't say it." She descended with swift movements.

The corners of his mouth lifted. He must be learning the way her mind worked without realizing it, for he'd flustered her once again.

She paused just before her head disappeared below the hayloft floor. "And you cannot count it as another win if it is on the same subject."

"Why not? There are not rules to this." He descended after her. "Besides, the game is in my own head. You have no authority there."

She pushed open the barn door and faltered back a step at a large gust of wind. The influx of light made the white patches on the cows' hides practically glow. "You cannot tease me about a thing multiple times. It's hardly fair." She pushed the door wider and stepped out into the yard, then held the door for him to exit.

"And yet you tease me for my accent and my demeanor and my dislike of my seafaring past more than once a day." Despite her lack of sleep, she seemed to have more energy this morning than she'd had the night before. Maxence split the bread between them as they found the road and started off. She didn't have a response, so they munched the dense, lumpy bread and walked in silence.

After a few minutes, Citoyenne Bernard cut the distance between them and reached for his hair.

"What are you doing?" He didn't flinch as her fingers teased his curls.

She held up a piece of straw. "This was in your hair."

"Oh. *Merci.*"

A moment later she moved close again, her fingers back in his hair.

"Another?" He couldn't say he minded it—the proximity or the sensation of her playing with his curls.

She tossed away a bit of straw. "I don't think looking like you slept in a barn is quite the style among the fashionable set." She nodded once and put a safe distance between them again.

Maxence ignored the urge to brush at his hair to get out any remaining straw. He'd much rather she do it.

Shadows faded around them as they walked. Wispy strands of clouds hurried past high above. He shoved the rest of his bread into his mouth. His father had taught him to be wary of those thin, innocent-looking puffs, especially when they moved fast.

His observations put him behind her a few steps. A little bit of straw clung to the ruffle on the back of her cap, just under her bonnet. With a grin, Maxence increased his pace and plucked the straw from her cap, his knuckle grazing the back of her neck.

She whirled, clamping a hand over where he'd touched her. He stopped short to keep from bowling her over. Her surprised glare demanded an explanation for his actions.

Maxence held up the piece of straw with an innocent shrug. She stood so close, it almost grazed her nose. "Returning the favor," he said. His skin tingled where it had met hers.

"Oh. *Merci.*" She hurried ahead before he could tease her about repeating his response. Maxence let the straw flutter away, mirroring the odd commotion inside him that had lingered since she had started fussing with his hair.

The wind picked up sometime after they'd finished their breakfast, adding to the already cooler morning. Citoyenne Bernard proved far less talkative than usual, though her coughing made her equally noisy. She retrieved her handkerchief from her pocket upon finishing her bread and never returned the little square. The constant dabbing quickly turned her nose pink.

By noon two things were clear—Citoyenne Bernard's zeal to start the day had been the last of her energy, and nature had sent a storm fast at their heels. She sat against the trunk of a tree, eyes closed and arms resting limp at her sides despite having stopped not five minutes before.

Maxence pulled her cloak from the market bag. He thought about bringing out his army coat as well. It was thick and much warmer than the cloak. But they passed other travelers often enough that they couldn't risk it. "Put your cloak on. If we don't find shelter soon, you will need it."

Citoyenne Bernard cracked her eyes open. "I'm wearing two jackets. You take the cloak."

"I'm not ill." He pushed it toward her, and she hesitantly took it.

"But you'll be cold."

"This is nothing compared to furling in a gale." He'd barely survived that. As one of the better topmen until Gilles came along, he had been sent aloft by his father to bring in the sails during a storm that had caught them by surprise. He'd never truly understood what it felt like to be chilled to the bone, as drenched as a drowned rat, until that moment. Numb fingers trying to roll and tie unruly canvas, feet slick against the ratlines, eyes stinging with rain and saltwater. A little storm on land was nothing to that.

She stuck out her hand. He grasped it and pulled her to her feet.

"How much longer do you think we have until we reach Nozay?" She fumbled with the strings of her cloak while trying to close it around her neck.

They'd passed Blain not long ago and couldn't have made it even halfway yet. "We should be there by the end of the day." Maxence rubbed the back of his neck. The end of the day could be midnight at this rate. He rubbed his knee, which was reminding him it had only just recovered from injury and didn't appreciate so much exercise.

Citoyenne Bernard nodded, then her illness took over again. He attempted to deflate his alarm at the scratch in her coughs. When she bid him to start walking, she was already out of breath. Maxence didn't comment with his concern. He didn't want her to expend any more strength on arguing with him.

"Oh no," she muttered an hour later. Thick, low clouds had replaced the wispy cirrus clouds, and a nip of ice had infiltrated the winds.

"What do you see?" It didn't take long for him to notice. A tiny, white flake circled and then dropped to the ground. Oh no. It couldn't be that. His gut tightened, and it was all he could do not to swear. March—or Ventôse, rather—storms never carried as much intensity or stayed as long as winter gales. They'd have to hope this storm would merely sprinkle a few flakes for a moment and then carry on its way.

"I thought we were done with snow," Citoyenne Bernard said, her voice flatter than he'd ever heard it.

"Once in a while it does like to surprise us, doesn't it?"

"I would think you haven't experienced many spring storms in Marseille."

More spots of white swirled around them. It was too early to tell if they'd stick and make the roads harder to travel. "No, we do not have to suffer this insanity."

She made a noise he couldn't tell was a cough or a laugh, and Maxence started scanning the road for turnoffs and paths that might indicate a village or farm nearby. He couldn't say how long this snow would last, but he had to get her out of it soon. The tightness in his core would not let him forget that illness and prolonged exposure to the elements could make a terrible combination for the young lady beside him.

CHAPTER 15

Maxence hated snow. It made him miss the warmth of Marseille with its mild winters, and very few things were able to accomplish that. But as he and Citoyenne Bernard trudged through the ankle-deep whiteness that covered the road, with more fat snowflakes continuing to fall, he resolved to never so much as visit a place as potentially frigid as Brittany again.

The air had grown icy cold, and his companion had taken to covering the bottom half of her face with the edge of her cloak. Snow had hidden any paths to potential help. Maxence could see little through the trees. He'd lost most of the feeling in his feet despite his boots. He couldn't imagine how frozen she must be with wet stockings and shoes.

"I am half expecting to hear bells calling us to midnight mass for Christmas," she said, voice muffled by the wool of her cloak.

"France doesn't celebrate Christmas." It wasn't entirely true. Even after the start of the revolution, he'd spied little terra cotta crèches in the windows of wealthy homes around Marseille toward the end of the traditional calendar year. As boys, he, Victor, and Gilles had loved going to the church with their mother to see the magnificent displays.

When she didn't respond for a long time, Maxence looked back.

Surely she'd refute that, as he was fairly certain the Bernard family did still celebrate Christmas despite not being true counterrevolutionaries. She was barely moving her feet. Her head was bowed, and at some point the hood of her cloak had fallen. Snow gathered on the top of her dark bonnet. She'd drawn her hands into her middle, and her whole body trembled.

"Citoyenne Bernard." He retraced his steps. "We need to keep moving." The sooner they reached shelter, the sooner they could get warm and dry.

She lifted her head, eyes half closed. Her cheeks and nose were rosy from the cold. "I'm sorry. I'm just so tired."

"Let me help you." Maxence took her mitted hand and pulled her forward. Beneath his hand, the skin of her fingers burned. He halted. His hands were freezing, but she shouldn't feel that warm just from a few more layers. He took her face in his hands, looking into her sleepy hazel eyes. Hot. Far too hot.

She flinched, her breath rushing out in a little cloud. "Your hands are cold." She grabbed his hands, and he let her pull them away.

"Are you hot or cold?"

"Freezing."

She had a fever, no doubt about it. Maxence searched the road ahead of them but found no sign of even another traveler. What if they'd missed farmhouses or even roads into town because everything was covered with snow? He took her hand again. "We need to move quickly." Ignoring the protest of his knee, he plunged forward down the road that had practically disappeared. Only brush and trees marked the path.

Citoyenne Bernard stumbled along behind him. "I can't . . . It's too fast." She tried to pull her hand from his, but he tightened his grip.

"You need shelter. We have to try."

In a matter of minutes her ragged breathing made him slow their pace. The steady sinking in his chest would not ease. Ahead and behind lay only snowy, picturesque countryside veiled with a steady curtain of cottony flakes. Finding a roof to cover them seemed impossible; finding a roaring fire to warm them was nothing short of a distant dream. He considered himself a resourceful man after several years at sea and almost two in the military, but none of his experience had prepared him for this. Perhaps he could lash some branches together to form some sort of shelter, but he had neither rope to lash nor ax to cut branches. Citoyenne Bernard didn't have anything to start a fire in her market bag. All of his skills were useless without the proper tools.

Her breathing only worsened the farther they traveled, intermingled with more severe bouts of coughing. She stopped protesting, but it was all he could do to keep her from tripping and falling to the ground. Her actions turned so stiff that he finally stopped, pulled out his coat, and shoved her arms into it. Even inside out, it wasn't hard to tell it was a military coat. The red collar stuck out sharply against the blank snow. He pulled the edges to overlap in front of her and paused. Red against the snow. Her wide, fearful eyes catching his.

His breath hitched as images of their first interaction jumbled his mind. He couldn't have imagined a few weeks later he'd be tromping through a late snow fighting for this woman's welfare. He'd preserved her life once, even if for selfish reasons, and he'd do it again, this time he hoped with more selflessness.

The sleeves of his coat only showed the very tips of her fingers as she held the coat closed in front of her. "You . . . take the . . . cloak." He could barely hear her, even in the silence around them.

"I don't need it." But she shook her head and shuffled away from him when he tried to wrap her in it.

With a sigh, he put it around himself and awkwardly tied it with fingers stark white and stiff. Perhaps he was colder than he thought. Then he took her burning hand in his freezing one and pushed on. He lowered his head to keep snowflakes from catching on his eyelashes and sending water into his eyes, checking their direction every few minutes to make sure they stayed on the road.

"What . . . is that?" Citoyenne Bernard had released his coat to point.

At first he couldn't determine what she meant. Had she gone delirious? That could only mean serious complications. But his eyes finally settled on a stone off to the side of the path, its top clearly rounded by tools. A milestone. *Remercie le ciel.*

He dragged her toward it then dropped her hand to clear away the snow caught on its surface. *Vay 2 leagues.* The indentation of at least a path, if not a small road, stretched off to the side.

Maxence stood and released a breath that twirled before him then dissolved. How far were they from Nozay? At the pace they were traveling, it had to be more than two leagues, but he couldn't be certain. Staggering into a town as large as Nozay wearing a soldier's coat would bring suspicion. Could they care about that now? But if their destination was farther than expected, things would only get worse for his companion. "What do you think we should do, *citoyenne*? Take this chance, or try to push on to Nozay?"

She opened her mouth to speak but drawing in the cold air set her coughing. That was answer enough for him. He put an arm around her shoulders. "Come. Let us see if we can find help in Vay." At least this way was more certain, even if it was off their path.

The white afternoon light faded to blue as they struggled along the new road, whose dents and divots caught their shoes through the snow. The snowflakes finally stopped, though clouds still blanketed the skies and added to the growing dusk. A little dark spot appeared on the horizon as they rounded a gentle bend.

"*Regarde!* A house." His body ached from cold and effort, but he felt as though he could run toward the little building.

Citoyenne Bernard sagged against his side. "*Dieu merci.*" Her voice came out as a croak he might have teased her for had he not been so worried.

"We can make it." An ember of hope kindled inside him.

What Maxence thought to be a chimney on a grey stone structure gradually took on the shape of a steeple. Not fancy by any means, but far more elaborate than the rest of the building, which aesthetically resembled the barn they'd slept in the night before. He hoped there was a hamlet of some sort behind it, or his excitement would be in vain. With all that had happened to expel religion in France, this church could be ransacked and empty. Abandoned. He immediately banished the idea and its rising disappointment. It *had* to be occupied.

They stopped at the base of a gentle hill leading up to the tiny church. Trees at its flank blocked any view of the surroundings. The snow prevented them seeing any sign of whether the churchyard was well kept or wild.

Maxence took her hands and squeezed them. "Even if it's empty, we'll at least have shelter from the wind and snow."

Citoyenne Bernard shook her head. "It's not empty."

He looked over his shoulder. A figure had appeared at the door of the church. Faint light filtered through the opening behind the person.

They were saved.

Maxence pulled his languid companion up the slope and through the gateless opening in the stone wall. The ground leveled out as they neared the church. The occupant of the building was clad in a long, black coat. No doubt a constitutional clergyman. Citoyenne Bernard would hate that, but they couldn't be too discriminating about who helped them. Maxence certainly couldn't be bothered if it meant a fire and a roof. That would be if the clergyman let them in.

"*Bonsoir, citoyen!*" Maxence hailed him. "We're seeking—" His boot caught something solid under the snow. He keeled forward, landing face first despite flailing his free arm to catch himself. His elbow slammed into the ground, the snow bit his face, and a moment later Citoyenne Bernard tumbled on top of him with an "oh!"

Maxence lay still for a moment, too drained of energy to fully comprehend what had happened. He turned his head and blinked ice out of his eyes. She didn't move, either. Her bonnet brim dug into his shoulder, and her breathing rattled against his back.

"Merciful heavens, those footstones like to trip everyone," came a raspy voice. "The little imps. Let me help you." The clergyman arrived at their side and assisted Citoyenne Bernard to her feet. "I would have put the graveyard a greater distance from the church—it isn't as though we have a shortage of land—but no one asked me when they made the plans."

Maxence raised his head, coming face to face with a carved headstone. The skulls on its surface seemed to laugh at his predicament. He'd narrowly missed knocking his brow against them.

Someone hooked an arm through his and hauled him to his feet. "We do have a new cemetery north of the village that causes much less mischief," the man said. Maxence reached down to massage his knee. That jolt hadn't done it any favors. He collected the market bag and straightened to face their rescuer.

Maxence stood nearly a head taller than the clergyman, whose grey strands of hair barely covered the sides of his head. He couldn't be sure if the man intentionally shaved his hair into a monk-like style or if it were the result of losing most of it. The clergyman looked to be perhaps sixty and lean as a bowsprit.

"What a handsome couple we have here," the clergyman said, looking between them.

Citoyenne Bernard's cheeks reddened further, to the clergyman's apparent delight. He rubbed his hands together. "Newly married? I guess three, perhaps four, months."

Maxence drew in a breath to soundly refute the accusation, but an arm slipped through his. Citoyenne Bernard nuzzled her cheek against his shoulder. His heart skipped in a bizarre way that left him unable to respond for a moment. Blast. What was she doing? Now *he* was blushing.

"You are very astute, *monsieur*," Maxence managed. *Monsieur*! He mentally kicked himself. The shake in his voice made him sound like a fourteen-year-old boy. Before the clergyman could make another knowing comment, he blurted, "She is sick. We need a place to stay." Clergymen, whether constitutional or nonjuring, were meant to help people.

The clergyman's eyebrows shot up. He reached for Citoyenne

Bernard's arm. "Come, child! Come around to the house. I'll return to lock up the church."

A lump formed in Maxence's throat at the sight of the small home at the back of the churchyard with a thin trail of smoke coming from its chimney. Hours of fear lifted from his shoulders. He had finally found what she needed, and now they could focus on getting her well.

"What a terrible day to be on the road," the clergyman said as he unlocked the plain but well-made door to his house. Oak, Armelle thought it was, but the pounding in her head made it difficult to think.

"Where are you traveling from?" The older man took her arm again and ushered her into the house. A cramped hallway led past a small sitting room on one side and a study on the other. Farther back was a dining room and kitchen.

"Nantes," Étienne said after a moment's hesitation. Did they want him to know? It would be easier to keep things straight the closer they stayed to the truth. Ideas passed unhindered through her head. Her mouth was dry, her throat on fire. She wanted nothing more than to sleep.

Their host led them to the farthest door in the passageway. "You should change out of your wet clothes. You'll have to excuse my humble abode, as I have only one small bed for guests." He turned with a twinkle in his eye. "Somehow I think that won't be a problem."

Armelle swallowed, sending a fresh shot of pain down her tender throat. That would be a very big problem.

"Of course not." Étienne said it firmly, clearly recovered from his previous surprise.

The clergyman opened the door and motioned them in. "There are blankets in the trunk. Bring out your wet clothes when you are done, and I shall hang them in the kitchen. I've been roasting a small chicken, but I think there will be enough for three."

Armelle sniffed, trying to smell the cooking food, but her nose didn't work. She followed the priest's direction and entered the little bedroom. It had one narrow bed against the opposite wall below a curtained window, a trunk in the corner, and not much else.

"My name is Quéré."

"Rossignol is ours," Armelle volunteered before her companion could say anything. It would be easy enough for them both to remember.

"Please do not hesitate to ask for anything."

"We are in your debt," Étienne said, shaking the man's hand and following Armelle into the room. He shut the door behind them, leaving the room in partial darkness.

Armelle sank onto the bed. Her fingers began to prickle as they warmed. "This is hardly a—"

"We need to get you warm and dry." Étienne deposited the market bag and bedroll on the floor.

She wrapped her arms around herself, the too-long sleeves of Étienne's inside-out coat flapping. "I'll warm soon enough."

He dug into the market bag and retrieved her extra pair of stockings. "Stockings and shoes first. Then we'll assess the rest of your clothes."

She started with her bonnet, removing the pin and setting the hat beside her on the bed. Then she shrugged out of his coat; the exposed linen lining had absorbed a good amount of damp. Taking off her stockings would be difficult to do modestly. Sitting on the edge of the bed, she lifted the back hems of her petticoats, which were wet from the snow, until she could reach the garter tied above her knee. The prickling in her fingers turned into stabs from a hundred tiny needles as she tried to pull the garter free. Instead of loosening, it tightened into a knot.

Fichtre.

She tried to bring her other hand over to help, but she couldn't grasp the individual strands of the knot with either set of fingers. She groaned and shook out her hands. That didn't cure the needling.

"Do you need help?" Étienne knelt before her.

"The knot won't come out." How terrible her voice sounded, all rough and whining.

He reached for the garter tentatively, eyes flicking to hers as though asking permission.

She sighed and nodded.

"It is lucky for you that I am an expert at tying knots," he said. "And as such, I am also rather good at untying them." The garter tightened against her leg.

"From your time at sea?" Her mind was starting to fuzz again, but she couldn't tell if it was from illness, fatigue, or the tickle of his touch as he worked on the garter.

"A mariner has to know his knots." The garter slid free, but before she could take over, he slipped the stocking down. Was that the hint of a smile on his face? The wet part, about halfway up her calf, stuck to her skin. With cool fingers he peeled back the wet wool. Armelle's heart leaped into her throat at his touch. He finally got it off and shook the stocking out.

Cold air hitting her foot sent a shiver up her spine. She quickly brushed her petticoats back into place.

He gestured. "The other one?"

Reluctantly she hiked up the other side of her skirts. Her pulse raced erratically. She must be more ill than she thought. This time Étienne didn't bother with the knot, but pulled her stocking through the garter and off, then wiggled the garter down after it. Armelle gasped. What a dolt she was. "I could have done that myself." Never mind the knots. It wasn't as though she'd never taken them off that way before.

Étienne lifted his shoulders as he straightened her other stocking. "I don't mind helping."

Of course he didn't. He, Maxence Étienne, who had rubbed lips with half the young women of Marseille, and heaven only knew how many in Paris. She jerked her hems back down. "You could have suggested, but instead you decided you wanted to . . ." She couldn't bring herself to say it. Do it himself. For the thrill of it.

He stiffened, eyes wide. "I wasn't . . . Come now. You know I'd never . . ."

Did she? He hadn't explained his escapades. "*Dozens of broken hearts, Étienne,*" she hissed. Is this what Jean-Baptiste had seen in her companion, what he'd tried to warn her of? Her head throbbed, from the anger or from the cold, she couldn't determine. She pulled her legs up onto the bed to hide her tingling toes under her skirts.

"Citoyenne Bernard, I was helping you and that is all. I did not think of it in any other way." He stood and snatched up her bonnet and his coat.

"How am I to believe that?" The knife Jean-Baptiste had given her weighed heavy in her pocket. They'd slept in the same barn twice, and he'd never made any advances, but now they were sharing a bedroom. With one bed, which after sleeping in a barn, felt like a soft, warm patch of heaven. Would he take advantage of the close quarters?

"Why did you choose to come if you thought so little of me?" he growled, backing toward the door. "Put on your stockings and get under those blankets. You need rest." The look of betrayal on his face cut her to the core. He exited and pulled the door firmly shut behind him.

She pulled on the new stockings, not bothering with the garters on the floor, and burrowed into the blankets. She closed her eyes, her entire body yearning for the oblivion of sleep. But the cogs in her head churned relentlessly, revolving through the near smile when he'd helped her, the look of hurt when he'd left, and his grim determination in the clearing that day when he'd decided to lay down his life for her to run free.

CHAPTER 16

"I suppose the best thing about snow is that it does not quite drench a person when walking in it," Quéré said while hanging the few items of clothing Maxence had given him on the line strung before the kitchen hearth.

Maxence settled into one of two simple chairs in the room. Citoyenne Bernard thought him a cad, and as much as he wished to believe her wrong, the longer he thought, the more he agreed with her. Bakers' daughters, tavern maids, the girl at the last Jacobin meeting he attended in Marseille. How many wagers had he and Émile made? It had been all for sport. He'd been annoyed when Gilles had cut off his advance on the girl at the meeting and then furious when he found out that instead of trying to win Émile's wagered money for himself, his brother had done the gallant thing and warned her to stay clear of them. But that irritation had quickly vanished in Gilles's greater offense of deciding not to join the march to Paris. Utter disloyalty.

The priest continued talking about snow, but Maxence didn't hear him. He settled his chin in his palm. The Parisian girls they'd met in cafés had been even more eager to play around, kissing and fawning over the *fédérés* in hopes of earning a coin or at least a drink. Whether truly attracted to them or not, Maxence hadn't cared. He hadn't been very selective. That had all ended at Émile's death.

But what did it matter that he'd stopped spending his free time in cafés? Or practically stopped looking at young women at all now that his friend was gone? Why wouldn't Citoyenne Bernard expect the worst of him, if that's what he'd once been? And perhaps still was.

"*Citoyen?*"

Maxence blinked. Quéré stood by the hearth with an expectant look. "Pardon, what did you say?"

"I asked if there was a coat you wished to hang with this cloak. The one your wife was wearing when you arrived."

He shook his head quickly. "Oh, no. It would be too heavy for the line. It will dry well enough in the room."

"As you'd like," the priest said. He paused, inclining his head. "You know, *citoyen*, you needn't fear my asking questions. However you came by that military coat, your secret is safe with me."

Maxence stared, unsure how to respond. If the priest had guessed the truth, they'd need to run. Soldiers wouldn't be stationed in so small a hamlet as this, but they couldn't be far. The army had a strong presence in Brittany.

"However, I am not entitled to knowing the details of your life. If you have no wish to share, I will not press you." Quéré lifted the cloak to glance at the chicken, which was trussed and hanging just to the side of the flames. The scent of meat and herbs hit Maxence's nose with such force his stomach rumbled. "Your clothes may smell like chicken, but I think there are worse things." The man chuckled as he dipped a spoon into the pan below the meat and drizzled the drippings back over the bird. "It should be nearly done." He set down the spoon and straightened, letting the cloak fall back into place.

"If you'd like, we can take down the clothes until you've finished cooking," Maxence said, letting his shoulders relax. The man had seemed to dismiss the topic of the coat without much thought. As though he weren't concerned.

Quéré waved a hand. "I don't mind them at all. I generally hang my laundry to dry in here during the cold months and am quite used to working around the wash lines." He clasped his hands together. "You look quite chill, *mon ami*. I have a coat left by my predecessor which practically drowns me. Allow me to fetch it for you."

Before Maxence could protest, his host had left the room. How much charity would he be forced to accept before he could finally provide for himself? Quéré returned a few minutes later with a black coat. Its construction was simple, but Maxence could tell it was cut from well-woven cloth.

"My predecessor had fine taste in clothing but not so fine a taste in company. He was not here very long."

"The Catholic priest you replaced?" Maxence took the coat. "After you swore the oath?" He didn't believe the coat was quite large enough to *drown* Quéré. Had the man said that to make him more comfortable using it? He pulled it on. It was a little wide in the shoulders, but not enough to feel sloppy.

"There is an odd story to that," the older man said, taking the other chair, which sat closer to the fire. "You see, I was the Catholic priest I replaced after taking the oath."

Maxence's eyes narrowed. "They allowed you to stay in the same parish?"

"I have been blessed with very few problems compared to my brothers." A false lightness tainted his voice. "But that is a tale for another time. I've forgotten to close up the church, and I needn't incur the wrath of Saint Josse any more than I already have."

A fit of coughing sounded from the bedroom down the corridor. Maxence tensed. He needed to tend to her. If she'd let him.

"Do you think your wife would like some broth? I had a little extra from my dinner last night which I can bring from the cellar."

"Yes, if you please."

The priest nodded. "I will return shortly." He left, humming a tune that sounded both ancient and familiar.

Maxence located a bucket of water and a bowl, which he filled and carried to the bedroom. He held back for a moment. There had not been many opportunities to act as physician during his time at Montpellier. His schooling mostly consisted of lectures rather than real experience like that of a surgeon's apprentice. Physicians tended to play more of a counselor role, befitting the higher classes, while lower surgeons did the dirty work. Regardless of his level of experience, Maxence determined to enter this interaction in a polished and detached manner. She had every right to react the way she had earlier, but he would prove to her and himself he could act with dignity.

He tapped on the door. "Citoyenne Bernard?"

"Come in." Her voice had an added nasally tone.

He entered. She'd kicked off the blankets, which lay rumpled at her stockinged feet. Her face was pink, even in the dim light. Her fever clearly hadn't broken. "We need to get your fever down."

She dabbed at her nose with her handkerchief and nodded.

He rested the back of his fingers against her cheek. Still hot, and she wasn't sweating as she should when this warm. She tried to breathe through her nose, which just made her cough again.

Maxence set the bowl beside the bed and sought out her clean hand-kerchief in the market bag. He dipped it into the bowl, wrung it out, and placed it across her forehead. She closed her eyes wearily, or was she avoiding his gaze?

"Should I run outside and bury myself in snow?" she asked. "Surely that would bring it down faster." She opened one eye and glanced at him.

"Shocking your body will only leave you more vulnerable. Besides, we tried that earlier." When he'd led them off the hidden path and across the graveyard.

Her haggard breathing was still cause for alarm. He wouldn't ask to get a better listen for fear of outraging her again, but he'd have to pay close attention. If that hitched breathing was the first warning of an

168

onset of pneumonia . . . He chewed his lip. He wouldn't worry her about it now, but the thought twisted inside him tighter than a ship's cable.

"I'm thirsty," she said.

"Quéré went to close the church, but I will see if I can find something to warm up." He turned to go.

"Étienne, you cannot call me Citoyenne Bernard. I told him our name was Rossignol."

He held onto the side of the door, ready to pull it closed. "I shall try to remember to call you Citoyenne Rossignol." That would be awkward to explain if he slipped.

"Is that what your brothers call their wives? Citoyenne Étienne?"

The feminine form of "citizen" sounded so odd when paired with his surname. It rhymed, like a character from a comedic play or song. He hadn't thought of that before. But then, he hadn't been near his sister-in-law or mother since the movement had done away with previous titles.

"I have only one married brother. He calls his wife Rosalie."

She reposed straight and unmoving, her arms resting on her stomach. For a moment he thought she'd drifted to sleep. "Perhaps you should call me Armelle, then, for the sake of our disguise."

Armelle. It was easier than "Citoyenne Rossignol," and he agreed it felt less stiff, as one would expect from a young and freshly married couple. And he'd been wanting to call her that, as the Colberts did. "Armelle" suited her far better than the austerity of "Citoyenne Bernard." But the intimacy of using her given name left him in an odd state he couldn't quite describe.

"I can still call you Étienne," she said, "as it won't be suspicious."

"Whatever you wish." In the end he didn't care as much what she called him as he did what she thought of him.

Étienne didn't say anything when he came in to change the rag on Armelle's forehead and bring her a full cup of watered-down broth. The first time she'd watched him, noting the wall that seemed to have gone up behind his eyes. The second time she feigned sleep so she wouldn't have to see it. Her accusation from earlier had unsettled him, and while she couldn't guilt herself for it, she did wonder where his thoughts had taken him. Was he angry at her? Embarrassed? He seemed as distant as he'd been upon arriving in Savenay.

The murmur of the men's voices through the stone wall behind her head kept her from sleep. She wanted to know what they said, but they talked so softly she couldn't make it out. At least Étienne had someone to talk to, if he wouldn't talk to her.

The next time Étienne returned, he brought a chair and a lantern with him. He set the chair near the head of the bed and the lantern on top before going back to the kitchen. The lantern sent funny shadows about the room fit to worry any child. She didn't move until he came back with a steaming bowl in his hands.

Food. If only she could smell it. Armelle sat up quickly, making her head pound. The wet handkerchief tumbled down her face and into her lap.

"You don't have to do everything with so much energy," Étienne grumbled, retrieving the handkerchief and plopping it back in the water. He handed her the bowl of food, but before she could bury her face in it, he caught her wrist. "Quéré let me borrow his pocket watch to check your pulse." He knelt by the bed and positioned two fingers just below the base of her palm. "Relax your arm, *s'il te plaît*." He turned the face of a simple watch toward the light.

"Can you not do it without a watch?" she asked.

"I cannot keep count with you talking. *Chut*," he hushed her.

Armelle eyed the food. More broth with a few chunks of chicken and vegetables floating about. Her mouth watered. "Did you have a nice watch before . . ."

He closed his eyes, giving her wrist a squeeze. "Yes, I had a very nice one, and it was the first thing Froment took when they arrested me. You, *mon amie*, are as bad as my nieces."

She glanced in the direction of the kitchen. "Is that something you would call your wife?" she whispered. His long-suffering sigh made her lips twitch.

"Can you close your mouth for two minutes, *ma femme*?"

My wife. That would do. She pulled in her lips and clamped her teeth over them to keep the next thought at bay. His hand was still cool, but not as terribly cold as it had been on the road. She focused on it, on the feel of his strong hand encircling hers. He held onto her firmly but with care. Perhaps Nicole would not be terribly wrong in finding him attractive. Étienne was more gentle than he let on. And less irritable in certain settings.

"That wasn't so difficult," he said, snapping the watch closed. "Your pulse is higher than I would like, but it is not as bad as I feared." He smoothed the back of his hand across her brow once more. "Quéré brought in a bottle of *cidre* as well. I'll bring some when you've finished."

"*Merci*, Oncle Étienne." Is that what his rambunctious nieces called him?

He arched his eyebrow. "Is that any way to address your husband?"

She grinned and took up the spoon. As fun as it was to tease him, she needed this soup in her belly. But she couldn't help a parting shot. "*Merci, mon chou.*" My cabbage. She bit her cheek to keep from snickering.

Étienne groaned and dashed from the room. Armelle retrieved her handkerchief and wiped her nose, which had started to run from the mounting pressure of trying not to laugh. She held the bowl up to her face, attempting to breathe in the swirling steam through plugged nostrils. The broth didn't have as much flavor as she'd hoped. Blast this cold. But the soup settled comfortably inside her, and when she had finished, she was finally able to doze into contented oblivion, the memory of Étienne's gentle voice humming in her ears.

The priest had pulled down the hanging clothes by the time Maxence returned from collecting Citoyenne Bernard's empty bowl and spoon.

"Will you join me in the salon for a dish of *cidre*?" Quéré asked. He stirred a little pot over the reducing fire.

"*Bien sûr.*" Maxence rinsed the dirty dishes in a basin in the corner and set them to dry on the table. Then he followed the older man into the front room. Quéré walked with more energy than a man half his age. Besides his hair, he seemed to have aged well, though his high, raspy voice contrasted his sprightly movements.

Quéré sat in an old wood chair with a cushion only on the seat and not on the back, leaving the more comfortable-looking, though equally old, armchair for Maxence.

"Oh, no. I couldn't."

Quéré nodded. "You are my guest. I insist." After Maxence had reluctantly settled into the chair, Quéré handed over a bowl of *cidre*. "Apple harvests were not as good as hoped last year, but it is not a bad batch considering."

Maxence took a drink and allowed his muscles to loosen for the first time that day. Had it been only a day? It might have been a week for all the worry.

"How is she?" the priest asked.

"Resting." Her humor had not stayed away for long. That woman would be the death of him, one way or the other. The way she whipped his emotions back and forth . . . Now he understood the warnings some well-meaning older sailors had given him about marriage. He was only pretending to be married, and he was worn out from a few hours.

"How long will you stay in Ilizmaen?"

Maxence swirled his drink. "Until she is fully recovered, if we are able." It was a great request, especially if the priest had suspicions about Maxence's ties to the army. If he wouldn't let them stay that long, they would take as much time as they could and be grateful.

"My house is at your disposal. Stay as long as you wish." The priest gave a kind smile.

Maxence leaned his head back into the chair, the weariness of the day overcoming him. "Thank you. I don't want her traveling until there is no fear of relapse."

"Of course, of course." Quéré took a long drink, then smacked his lips. A simple man who took pleasure in simple things. Maxence couldn't help but like him. "You know, I was just reading this evening in the Gospel of Saint Luc. A marvelous book, perhaps my favorite of the holy word, if I am allowed a favorite part as a clergyman." He chuckled. "I was reading in the second chapter. Are you familiar with it?"

Maxence drew circles with his thumbs across the sides of the bowl. "I cannot say I am a man of religion." He waited for a bolt of lightning to strike him through the roof. Taking advantage of a clergyman's hospitality without actually being a believer was certainly some sort of sin.

But Quéré brushed it off. "No matter. It begins with Caesar's decree of the world tax and follows Saint Joseph, the Nazarene carpenter, and his wife, the Virgin Mary, as they arrive in Bethlehem."

Maxence narrowed his eyes. He *did* know the Christmas story, even if he did not know much else.

"And I was contemplating the dire straits of this poor young couple, far from home and without friends. How scared they must have been, seeing as she was so great with child. And weary from travel. They couldn't even find a roof to cover them." He shook his head. "Sometimes the things that God asks of us are great indeed."

What was the man getting at? Maxence lifted his bowl to his mouth.

"And in the midst of this pondering, I had the thought that I should go to the door of our little chapel. Curious, I followed the inclination, as who knows but it was a nudge from higher beings, and who should I find but a poor young couple, weary from travel, the wife in such a dire state, imploring for whatever shelter I could provide them." The man gave a questioning smile.

Maxence choked on his *cidre*. He turned away, sputtering. He'd reluctantly agreed to playing the part of husband, but he had not signed his name to playing the part of father. "She is . . . She is not with child." His lungs couldn't expel the drink. Now he sounded as bad as Citoyenne Bernard.

Quéré threw back his head and laughed. "No need to fear. I have heard that children are not as difficult as they sound." He tapped his chin. "Or perhaps it was the other way, that they are more difficult than they sound."

Maxence cleared his throat, his face aflame. "Citoyenne B—" He swallowed. Idiot. "Rossignol is not having a baby in the next nine months, that is for certain." And he did not want to continue down that path of thinking.

"Oh, you needn't be formal on my account. Just call her whatever you do at home."

He licked his lips. "Armelle."

"Ah, a good Breton name. After Saint Armel." Quéré set his empty bowl on the mantle. "But you. You are not from Brittany."

Obviously not. "Provence," was all he volunteered.

"What happy circumstances that brought the two of you together."

Maxence wouldn't exactly call them "happy." He shifted in his chair.

"She is quite the catch. What a handsome pair you make." The older man winked.

Maxence didn't know how to respond. They were not actually a pair, but two travelers planning to go their separate ways at the end of the journey. The thought did little to cheer him.

"I am engaged myself, as it were."

"I suppose you are at liberty to do that now," Maxence said. "Not being under Catholic rules."

"At liberty." Quéré's expression grew serious. "Or forced to comply."

Maxence sat up straighter. "I take it you are opposed to marriage?"

The older man put up his hands. "Not for others, surely. But I try to adhere to vows I have already made, even if I am cast out from among my true brothers."

"You do not sound like a constitutional clergyman."

Quéré leaned forward, planting his forearms on his knees. "I suppose I am not. But when one loves his parish as though they were his own children, how can he leave them to the wolves?"

Outside the narrow windows, the misty outline of snow was the only thing visible. Clouds still shrouded the sky, damping the hope of stars. "You took the oath so your parishioners wouldn't have to suffer under a real constitutional clergyman."

The priest closed his eyes, as though hearing those words pierced his soul. "What is my own salvation if I abandon my flock? I convinced them to allow me to stay. Ilizmaen is an inconsequential hamlet, and our Chapel of Saint-Josse is of little worth in the eyes of the world. I didn't do it for honor or even my own protection. Only to ensure my dear ones would not stray from light and truth."

Maxence stared at the floor with its uneven boards. How could a man be so selfless as to give up all that was important to him for the sake of his neighbors? He had seen men openly sacrifice quite a lot for the cause of the revolution. He and Émile had thought they were doing the same, but what had they left behind? An education that suited neither of them, lives of unending triviality, and families who didn't . . . Maxence plucked at a loose thread on the arm of the chair. Nearly two years of repeating to himself that his family didn't love or support him, and tonight he couldn't think it.

"The woman to whom I am engaged," Quéré went on, "is the widow of a miller who left her in a very comfortable position. She owns the mill, and her grown sons run it. She approached me when word spread of clergymen being forced to marry and offered her hand, should the need arise." He rubbed his hands together. "Sixty-one years of celibacy, and now women are throwing themselves at me!"

It was an odd image, women chasing an old priest. Maxence laughed with his host for a moment, but the laughter died quickly, leaving a quiet sobriety to fill the space between them.

"In plain honesty," the man said, "we both hope the engagement is enough to satisfy the République until the ashes of revolution settle."

"Will they settle?" They hadn't for Maxence.

"They must if France is to survive."

Maxence agreed, but in his time in the *fédérés* and then the army, he had seen no indication of a turn in that direction. It would take one of Quéré's miracles, or several, to bring about peace.

He heard Armelle coughing from the bedroom and pushed himself to his feet. "I hope she doesn't wake you tonight." He'd had trouble sleeping the previous night, but his current fatigue suggested he'd sleep through most of it.

Their host gestured for Maxence's *cidre* bowl. "At my age, *mon fils*, it is I who should worry about waking you. I've woken myself up snoring more than a few times."

Maxence bid him goodnight and found his way to the bedroom. She'd snuffed the lantern, leaving the room in utter darkness. He closed the door behind him and listened. No movement suggested she was asleep. Good. He felt around for the roll of blankets and spread the thicker one across the floor. The priest had mentioned something about extra blankets in the trunk. He crawled in that direction. His hand bumped the old wood. It took him several seconds to figure out the clasp, and the lid creaked loudly as he opened it.

Stacks of ratty quilts and thick wool met his fingers. One more to lay on the floor, another to roll for a pillow of sorts. It wouldn't be a luxurious bed, but he'd survive. He closed the lid and crawled back to his blankets.

"Where are you sleeping?" came a whisper.

"Right here." He put the fluffiest quilt he found on top of the wool blanket and arranged the pillow as best he could. Then he removed his boots, jacket, and cravat.

"On the floor?" she asked. He pulled the top blanket over himself before laying his head down. It wasn't a grimy prison floor, so he'd be grateful.

"If you weren't ill, I'd take the bed and make you sleep here." The silence that followed told him he'd said it too dryly for her to take it as the joke he'd intended. "It really isn't so bad."

"I thought doctors bled their patients." She'd already slept some, so of course she was ready to talk. "You've just been shoving food and drink at me."

"That isn't how I learned to care for colds," he said, shifting his position to try to find something more comfortable. He'd get used to this after a few days.

"Did you learn it from your medical school?"

"No, from my mother." She had spent her adult life in a steady cycle of nursing three boys back to health.

"She must be proud of you."

He rolled to his other side away from her. "Hardly." She'd been too caught up in the lives of his brothers.

Sleepiness crept in, blurring the edges of his consciousness. He reached for it, willing it to block the memories that threatened.

Tap. Something hit the floor near his head. Tap, tap, tap, tap-tap. He opened his eyes. With one hand he felt along the floor until his fingers closed around the wooden die. He ran his forefinger against the top surface. "Three." She had to answer. But that meant he had to think of something to ask.

"May I answer your question from earlier?"

"Yes." He drew his arm back in and closed his eyes, not remembering what question he'd asked.

He nearly fell asleep during the pause before she answered. "I chose to come with you because I trust you. I'm sorry for how I reacted to your . . . help . . . earlier. My mind was fuzzy. I don't think little of you. In fact I think the world of you."

He rotated to face her, even though he couldn't see anything. The strange words pushed sleep from his grasp. Why would she say that? She knew what he was. "Do you still?"

"Yes." Soft but fervent.

An odd pang struck his heart. "Perhaps that isn't wise."

"I respectfully disagree."

"That isn't how you usually disagree." He lifted his head from the makeshift pillow. "You had good reason to react the way you did."

"Just because I suspected you took advantage of the situation does not mean you did or would. I've thought about this quite a lot since we've met. You're a good man, Étienne. Someone whose family should be proud of him."

His eyes stung, from the exhaustion certainly. The memories flooded in of a glorious Mediterranean sunset peeking through a crush of people, some in crimson liberty caps. His mother waiting near the line of trees planted to commemorate the revolution. Émile's face, so full of excitement. Gilles and Émile's sister Caroline whispering together. When it had come time for goodbye, Maxence had tried to break away quickly, but Maman had held tightly to him.

I'm so proud of you, mon fils. *Never forget how far you've come.*

The memory still rattled him, as though she'd taken him by the shoulders and shaken him senseless. She couldn't be telling the truth. He'd watched her dote on his brothers, watched Gilles take his place in her affections. Witnessing this desperate goodbye—it hadn't fit the narrative he had constructed in his head.

Then he'd turned to see Gilles's face full of regret and longing to make things right, as he had done with Émile moments before. But Maxence wouldn't let him. Gilles had gone back on his word. Everyone adored Gilles—Maman, Père, Monsieur Daubin—even Caroline had seemed to be giving him notice. Maxence wouldn't be one more adoring devotee. So he'd nodded and turned his back on his life in Marseille. Forever? Time would tell.

He didn't respond to Armelle's *bonne nuit.* One thought tumbled through his head and would not let him surrender to sleep. After all that had happened in the last dozen years of his life, how could his family be proud of him like she said? Especially when he couldn't be proud of himself.

CHAPTER 17

Armelle woke up drenched in sweat, but she could breathe easier than she had yesterday, which really meant she could breathe just fine out of one nostril, but not both. In times such as this, she found it more beneficial to be grateful for the one than greedy for two. Her throat didn't sting as intensely as the night before, and when testing her voice with a cheerful *demat*, she sounded a little less like a frog.

She leaned over the side of the bed. The floor was empty. No trace that Étienne had spent the night there. She hadn't heard him get up. She pulled back the curtains from the window, and light flooded the dim room. Outside a little stream of water poured from the roof. Snow still covered the land, but the clouds had moved on. A woman and child walked in the opposite direction of the church with a basket between them. They both nodded to a man tugging at the lead of a disgruntled donkey pulling a cart. The country had its charms.

A knock sounded on the door, and Étienne poked his head in. "Did you sleep well?"

"Well enough." Armelle stretched her arms above her head.

Étienne crossed to the bed and felt her forehead, then moved his hand to her cheek. He'd done it half a dozen times the day before, but this morning she had the curious desire for him to not remove his hand as quickly as he did. She must have been craving a caring touch. "I think your fever broke."

"Then I don't have to stay bedridden?"

Étienne dropped to his knees and leaned his elbows against the bed. "You were very sick yesterday, *chérie*. If you exert yourself too much today, you'll regress to a similar state."

Chérie? He was taking his role in their disguise seriously. Never mind that the clergyman seemed sympathetic enough that they probably did not need the protection of deceit. Yet how would the poor man react if he learned they'd shared a room unmarried? As a clergyman, he might not be so sympathetic. "May I at least have a few minutes outside, *docteur*? It's a lovely day." She lifted the curtain again to let in the sunshine.

"Husband, uncle, doctor. What am I supposed to be to you?" He sighed. "Five minutes. But you must eat your breakfast first."

Armelle sneaked out of bed as he went to get the food and took her brush from the market bag. She removed her cap and slid out the pins and ribbon. Her hair must look a sight, but she didn't have a mirror to view the horror. She could remain blissfully ignorant of the disaster. It took less effort to brush through her hair than she'd feared. She tossed the brush down and had just sectioned her hair when boots sounded in the corridor.

Étienne entered with two steaming bowls and stopped to watch her hurriedly braid her hair. Having his eyes on her made her fingers clumsy. She twisted the braid into a low knot and jammed the pins back in, scraping her neck in the process. She winced, feeling the scrape to see if it bled.

"What is this?" she asked, sitting back on the bed.

He hadn't moved from the doorway, eyes still on her. Then he blinked as though coming out of a trance and held out one of the bowls. "*Potage citrouille*. Quéré was pleased to point out that he had saved a little nutmeg for a special occasion such as this."

Armelle took the bowl and eagerly dug into the soft bread soaked in stewed pumpkin and sugar. "What is the special occasion?"

Étienne snorted. "Our recent marriage."

She plopped the thick, creamy bite into her mouth. The velvety notes of pumpkin and heat of spices exploded across her tongue, cutting through her illness-induced inability to taste. The food dissolved too quickly, forcing her to scoop up a larger morsel for the next spoonful. "That was very kind of him."

"And fraudulent of us," he muttered. At her look, he added, "He's gone to visit some parishioners."

Thank the heavens. "It cannot be helped now. He would think we were sinning."

"Are we not sinning, lying to a priest?"

Armelle huffed. "Yes, but it is not as grave a sin as *that*." Her neck warmed under her fichu.

His lips curled as he suddenly showed particular interest in his own bowl of *potage*. She pointed her spoon at him. "That does not count as a win."

"Why would it not?" He finished off the last of his breakfast. "It is very difficult to take anything you say seriously when your voice is so gruff."

She made a face at him.

"Citoyen Quéré is rather interested in our marriage for someone who has sworn not to take that path." Étienne stood and held out his hand for her bowl. Armelle frantically scraped the last bit of *potage* from the bowl before he could take it from her.

"I think it's sweet."

"Perhaps it would be if the marriage were real." For a man who had professed to not have much of a conscience, he seemed to be struggling to maintain this lie. Were all men as confusing as Étienne? Her brothers and father never had been. He must be a rare breed.

"Go have your five minutes of freedom." He glanced down at her red-stockinged toes curled against the wood floor. "Don't forget your garters."

Her nostrils flared. She snatched them from the floor where they'd stayed through the night and threw them in his direction. The ribbons floated harmlessly to the ground as the door shut behind him.

Armelle pursed her lips. He'd count that as a win, *le rufian*. And he'd run away like a coward before she could refute its validity. She scowled and retrieved her garters. As she tied the ribbons above her knee, she concentrated to be sure the bows were well tied so as not to risk knotting and needing the help of so nefarious a friend again.

Sure enough, Armelle's fever returned within a few hours and with it her lethargy. Maxence had to bite his tongue to not tease her about it. The rest of the day she kept to her bed without his prodding, and any time he went in to check on her, she was genuinely asleep.

The priest did not talk so long over *cidre* that night since he had a service and sermon early the next morning. Maxence didn't regret retiring early, even if it was just to a bed on the hard floor. The ache in his knee had increased after the difficulty of walking through snow the day before.

Armelle wasn't breathing well, so he rolled his coat to prop up her pillow. When that wasn't quite enough, he fetched a couple more blankets to nestle under her head. The faint moonlight peeping through the curtains traced her copper brown braid along the side of her neck and the smooth skin of her hands resting on her middle. He grudgingly admitted that she had a playful attraction that was growing on him. There was an ease about her that reminded him a bit of . . . Well, of Gilles.

He pulled his gaze away, not wanting to face the awkwardness if she awoke to finding him watching her, but his mind lingered on his companion as he loosened his neckcloth. As much as he hated to acknowledge the sentiment, he'd liked caring for her these last two days.

He felt needed in a way even the army hadn't been able to satisfy, and she certainly showed more heartfelt gratitude than any captain he'd followed.

A loud knock rattled the front door. After a moment, Maxence opened the bedroom door to see Quéré exit his room with a small lit candle.

"Would you like me to see who it is?" Maxence asked.

"Oh, of course not. You get to bed." He made his way down the corridor in a thin banyan over his shirt. "It is most likely Citoyen Goff with news of his sister's baby."

Maxence closed the door again and removed the waistcoat their host had loaned him. In addition to the coat and waistcoat, Quéré had given him a set of clothing so his other could be washed. Though still used, this shirt was not so worn as the one Armelle had brought him to wear from her friend's rag pile. The softer linen against his skin might have been silk in comparison.

"We regret bothering you so late at night, *citoyen*." The visitor's voice boomed down the hallway.

Maxence pulled the blanket over him and rested his head. No question tonight since Armelle was sound asleep.

"I am a loyal servant of the République," came Quéré's reply. "Of course I will help in any way I can."

That didn't have anything to do with a baby. Maxence raised his head.

"We are looking for a soldier who deserted his unit at Vay," the intruder said. Cold shot through Maxence's body. They weren't searching for him, but what if they'd heard his description? In their search for one deserter, they could discover another. "We have reason to believe he passed this way. You will not protest our searching the house and church to ensure he hasn't taken refuge here."

"Of course not, only I must request that you do so quietly. I have two friends asleep in the back room. The wife is very ill. Do not startle her."

Boots echoed down the hall. *Ciel.* What if they knew him somehow?

He didn't know how far word had spread of his escape. Those soldiers could burst in here and drag him off, shoot him, and be done with it. The knocking and shuffling of rooms being searched seemed deafening to Maxence's ears. His heart thundered in his chest. Would he have a chance to say farewell to Armelle? Should he wake her and do it now? His limbs wouldn't move. Nearly a month of hiding wasted.

He fought to steady his breath. No, Quéré wouldn't allow that. He would stand by the story that they were a recently married couple. Married men, even young ones, were not forced to go to war. A recent deserter could not have married so quickly. They'd open the door and find a new husband and wife . . .

With one of them asleep on the floor. *Imbécile.* That wouldn't look suspicious at all. Maxence sprang to his hands and knees, ripped the blankets out from under him, and shoved them under the bed. Then he lifted the covers and dove in beside Armelle. Low voices rumbled in the kitchen.

"What?" The whites of Armelle's eyes shone in the dim moonlight as they flew open. She drew in a sharp breath.

He clamped his hand over her mouth before she could scream. Her body went rigid. Her hands clawed at his.

"Soldiers!" he hissed.

Her fingers stilled around his hand, clinging rather than tearing. He slowly pulled his hand away from her mouth.

"Pretend to be asleep," he whispered. "I'll talk."

She pressed his hand between hers, then let go. Her eyes closed, but her whole frame stayed tense against him.

A terse knock on the door preceded a request to open it. Before Maxence could respond, the door swung open and lantern light inundated the room. Maxence grunted as though he'd just awoken and exaggerated stiff movements getting out of the bed.

Something clutched his sleeve. "*Chéri,* what is it?" Armelle gave a convincing show of fear and disorientation.

He brushed her cheek with his thumb. "I will see what they want.

Lie back down." It was only a game, this relationship of theirs. And yet somehow the protectiveness of a new husband toward his sick wife had sprung to life inside him. Even if they uncovered the truth about him, he'd do all he could to keep them from harming her.

He ran a hand through his hair with an air of trying to tame it, hoping it hid the fact his curls didn't look like he'd been asleep. His hand shook. These men had no way to prove he was a deserter. He *wasn't* a deserter. He'd essentially been kicked out. But the possibility of arrest hung menacingly before him.

"What is this?" He mimicked Armelle's scratchy voice. His mouth had gone dry enough that it wasn't too difficult. "Is something wrong, *citoyens?*" He walked slowly toward the door. If he somehow blocked them from entering, could he and Armelle get out through the window? He couldn't hold off two men in boots with guns and who knew what else. Not in his current state. Perhaps just long enough for Armelle to run.

For the briefest second, Froment materialized in the doorway. Maxence stopped in his tracks, blinking. No, it wasn't Froment, just someone with a similarly square face. "We're looking for a deserter and are conducting a search of the house." The man carrying the lantern pushed past Maxence and scanned the room.

"Your names, *citoyen*," said the soldier who resembled Froment.

"Étienne and Armelle Rossignol." They should have come up with different names. It couldn't be helped now. He kept his eyes on the searcher, daring him to get closer to Armelle.

"You are from Ilizmaen?"

"No, from Nantes. We are traveling to Saint-Malo for work." The man in the room completed his circle, and Maxence slackened his fists. Clearly there was no one else in the room. These soldiers could leave now.

"What work?"

The soldier with the lantern picked up the market bag, dumping the clothes sitting on top to the floor, and shook it. Maxence's stomach lurched. "We . . . I am to be a clerk. My uncle's shipping company." His coat. Where was his coat?

"I see. You've been married how long?"

The soldier shoved his hand into one side of the bag and jostled things around. Any moment he'd pull out the incriminating coat. Why hadn't he listened to Armelle and left it behind? "Three . . . Or is it four?" What had she told the priest? The memory had fled. "Months, that is. About four months."

"The date?" He'd caught on that something was not right. Maxence swallowed.

"The twenty-third." It was the date of his parents' anniversary. He counted back the months of the Republican calendar. "Of Brumaire." He ventured a glance at the second soldier scouring the other side of the market bag. He hadn't found the coat yet?

"How old are you?" The first soldier looked at him intently, as though trying to see if Maxence had evaded the *levée en masse*.

"Twenty-six." Or he would be in a month. The République only drafted men between the ages of eighteen and twenty-five.

Armelle's hacking cough interrupted the soldier's next question. His companion dropped the market bag and turned. "What is wrong with her?" He didn't see the coat. How had the man not seen it?

Maxence glanced at the bed, which the second soldier was illuminating with his lantern. Armelle curled up against her elevated pillow, fighting against her coughing fit. A blanket's corner peeked out from under the pillow.

The coat was under Armelle's head. Of course. The pinching in his stomach calmed for a breath. But they could still find it if they searched the bed. He had to prevent that. An idea pricked at Maxence's mind. "She has a putrid fever she cannot seem to shake." He let all the worry from the past two days seep into his voice. That would alarm them. Her fever wasn't putrid, but they wouldn't know that. Maxence hurried to her side and sat on the bed. He took her trembling hand and rubbed her back.

"Putrid fever? Has she seen a doctor?" The soldier with the lantern retreated from the bed.

"We haven't the money."

"Nothing of interest here," the second soldier muttered, inching toward the door.

The one who resembled Froment nodded. "We're sorry to have disturbed you." He nodded briskly, then both men marched down the corridor.

"I doubt that very much," Maxence mumbled.

The soldiers spoke to Quéré at the other end of the house. Something about searching the church. The voices receded as the door shut. Maxence slid off the bed and to his knees. They'd escaped. He buried his face in the blanket, breathing in the musty wool in slow, steady gusts.

Armelle touched his shoulder. "Luck is still on our side."

He lifted his head. While he couldn't make out her features with the moonlight behind her, he could feel her comforting gaze wash over him, banishing the panic from his heart, soothing the tensity from his limbs. A lulling heat seemed to flow through her fingers into him.

"You said just what you needed to," she whispered.

Maxence covered her hand with his, holding it against his shoulder, and rested his head back on the bed. He focused on the sensation of her touch with all his mind and willed the other possible outcomes of their encounter with the soldiers to leave his consciousness. All that mattered was they were here, they were together, and they were safe.

Étienne kept his head nestled in the blanket so long, Armelle wondered if he'd fallen asleep. His hand loosened its grip on hers, but she didn't take it back. The muscles of his shoulder eased.

Just when she was about to waken him for fear he'd do harm to his knee, the front door opened. Étienne leaped to his feet. Only the sound of Père Quéré's mules tapping down the passageway cut through the stillness.

"They're gone," she whispered. *Dieu merci.*

Candlelight crept into the room as the priest came to their doorway. "Is everyone all right?"

Étienne nodded. "Thank you."

Père Quéré waved a hand. "I was worried. But you know, there is one thing I have found always works." He pointed skyward. "Prayer, *mes amis.* I was praying from the salon." The older man winked. He bid them goodnight and closed the door.

Étienne crouched to pull his blankets from under the bed and rearranged them. He lay down without another word.

Armelle frowned. They'd just cheated trouble, and he wasn't going to say anything more? She sat up. "*Bonne nuit, mon chéri.*"

He turned toward her. "We don't always have to use endearments."

But she liked how he cringed when hearing some of the names she thought up. "Very well, you may say good night without anything attached to it."

"*Bonne nuit.*"

Satisfied, Armelle lay back. Père Quéré was right. It was a miracle the soldier hadn't found Étienne's coat. She said a silent prayer of gratitude. Then she popped her head up again.

"What if they return? Do you think they will?" she asked.

"It would depend on how much they want to find the deserter." Étienne's voice was muffled.

"I wonder where he's gone." Armelle lowered her head. The poor man, running for his life. She and Étienne knew the feeling only too well. She stared at the ceiling. After not wanting to do much of anything all day, why was sleep suddenly evading her?

She repositioned to her side. It must be nerves from the encounter with the soldiers. Nerves from being awoken and thinking herself in danger from a man she trusted. Nerves from being so close to him, smelling the spicy hint of his shaving soap and feeling the tickle of his breath on her ear. Nerves from appreciating his warmth, his strength. Nerves from sensing his deep desire to do the right thing, to not make a mistake, and to protect her at all costs.

She lifted her head and peered over the edge of the mattress. Étienne didn't move except for the faint outline of his chest rising and falling. Nicole would suggest perhaps there was something more than friendship on his part, that he would so selflessly risk himself for her.

Which was completely nonsensical if a person in her right mind thought about it for more than sixty seconds. Étienne was really more like a brother to her than any other form of relation. Henri would have protected her with the same disregard for himself. So would Gabriel. Julien *had* risked himself trying to protect her, the little rascal. And she would do the same for each of them, as she had done with Étienne.

Besides, a woman didn't love to tease her suitors with jokes to make them grumble then giggle about it to their faces. A man didn't growl and snort and keep track of how many times he won a conversation with his beloved. Brothers and sisters did that. This connection she felt with Étienne, born from saving each other and then traveling together, looked nothing like the romances she and her friend had devoured as girls.

"When do you think we shall reach Saint-Malo?" she asked. They would part as grateful friends. She would of course be sad to see him go, but there would be no more of this speculation of his motives or late-night confusion.

"Ask me in the morning." He didn't sound as asleep as she'd expected.

She sank back into her pillow. She needed to sleep. Sleep would help clear the mists from her brain. In a day or two she would be well again and not have to rely on him as though she were a child. No wonder Étienne had been so irritable when Alana forced him not to do anything while recovering.

Her stomach gurgled. She sighed. Now how was she supposed to sleep? She'd be dreaming of *potage citrouille* until morning light.

She lifted her head. "What time do you think it is?"

His hand reached over and cupped her face. She startled at the un-expected touch and the curious flutter it sent through her body. Étienne lay propped on one elbow to reach her. He gently pushed her head back down. "Rest." He didn't immediately remove his hand. His thumb traced softly across her cheek.

She let her eyelids fall and fought the urge to hold his hand there, then stifled the disappointment when his hand was gone and buried the tiny sparks in her chest that begged to burst into flame. She needed a brother and a friend. Anything more, she wouldn't know what to do with.

CHAPTER 18

Maxence awoke to the scent of batter and sausage frying on a griddle. He glanced at the bed. Sure enough, Armelle was gone. The last couple of mornings she'd managed to tiptoe out of the room before he awoke. He pushed himself off the hard floor, his joints protesting the continued mistreatment.

They'd been in Ilizmaen nearly a week by the republican calendar. More than a week by the rest of the world's reckoning. Armelle's recovery had been slow, but she seemed to be mostly healed now. What he'd worried to be early symptoms of pneumonia when they arrived had gone. She should be well enough to travel.

He dressed and made his way to the kitchen, pausing in the doorway. Armelle stood with her back to him as she mixed something in a bowl with one hand, humming that song about the prisoner of Nantes. She'd pulled the table up beside the hearth. A wide, three-legged frying pan sat above the fire. On the table was a large plate of rolled black flour *crêpes* and a dish of cooked onion and sausage. The sizzling and popping that filled the room suggested more filling was on its way.

Maxence narrowed his eyes. Armelle wore her striped jacket today, the one better fitted to show off her figure. Her blue petticoat swished against red stockings, but where were her shoes?

"You seem to be missing something on your feet."

She looked over her shoulder at him and beamed. "I took some *galettes* to the Goff family earlier. The grass in the churchyard was rather wet, so I put my shoes by the door to dry." She pulled her shoulders up to her ears as she turned back to her work. "Their new baby has the most deliciously round cheeks."

"Are we talking about a sausage or a human?" He plucked up one of the *galettes* and bit into it. The rich sausage burned his tongue, and he sucked in to cool it. The buckwheat *crêpe*—or *galette*, as she'd called them—kept the heat in a little too well. "Where did all this come from?"

"A farmer brought the meat for Père Quéré to give to the poor. Before the revolution he liked to make *galettes* each week for Ilizmaen. He thought it would be a good memory for all, so we made them this morning. He's delivering some."

Maxence nodded. Her hands flew from the skillet where she spread the batter into circles to the table where she wrapped the thin, grey *galettes* around the sausage and onion mix. She always did tasks so quickly.

"You can come do this." She motioned to the unassembled *galettes*.

Maxence shrugged. "If you'd like." There wasn't room on Armelle's side of the table, so he pulled the dishes to the other side and took up his task. His rolls came out awkward compared to her neat ones.

"You don't need to scowl so," she said. "They taste the same whether they look nice or like they've been stuffed in someone's pocket."

The buttery morning light through the kitchen window did her all sorts of favors, and Maxence couldn't help watching her as much as he watched his abysmally rolled galettes. She moved like a sparrow hopping from branch to branch in practiced dexterity and merry spontaneity. He could never quite guess where she'd land when she moved or how long she'd be there. Little wisps of hair that peeked out from under her cap rippled with each movement.

For a moment, Maxence let himself imagine a lifetime of mornings just like this—the comfortable and happy chatter, the tantalizing smell of good food, the clack of utensils on sizzling pans. And Armelle's bright face in the middle of it all. His heart hammered in his chest in much the same way it had when he'd first climbed aloft on *le Rossignol*. The overwhelming harmony of both freedom and danger pulsed through his soul, daring him to let go and see if he could fly.

But a man had to measure the risks.

Armelle dipped a ladle into her bowl and lifted it high, the ash-colored batter trailing in a long stream. She gave another stir and then checked the consistency again before turning to the hearth. A little grease, a spoonful of batter, a few twists of the wooden spreader. She pulled another skillet off the fire and dumped more sausage and onion onto the filling plate.

"This is enough food for a king's feast," Maxence remarked.

Armelle set the skillet beside the hearth. "Alas, we don't have one of those anymore thanks to a band of *révolutionnaires* storming the Tuileries Palace." With a gasp, she straightened, face pale. "Étienne, I'm so sorry. I didn't think before I said that."

He shook his head, letting himself fall into a stupor of scooping and rolling until the threatening thoughts of Émile subsided. The memories hadn't come forward as often in the last month. Perhaps leaving the army had taken away the worst reminders of that day. He reached for the spoon to add more onion and sausage, but she caught his hand in hers. Their eyes met.

"I'm truly sorry," she said. She seemed to see right through his walls to the pain and faults and shortcomings he tried desperately to hide. He hoped she couldn't also see his desires. If she did, she'd let go and walk away. If only he could so easily do the same, because the desire burning brightest right now was to pull her across the table and kiss her as he'd never kissed anyone before.

He squeezed her hand and resumed his task. Holding her hand felt too natural. They'd held hands so often since coming to Ilizmaen. He feared he'd miss the feeling when they left. "The more we pretend to be married, the more we will get used to it."

She laughed, going back to the flat pan to flip the *galette* with a long, narrow spatula. "There may be some habits to break. I'm sure once we're on the road again we will become so sick of each other's company that things will return to normal in no time."

Why did he not like the sound of that? "Who are the rest of these for?"

She sighed. "There are so many just barely getting by. If they are getting by at all." She carried over a finished *galette* and set it on the plate. "One of the local landowners was recently arrested and taken to Paris under suspicion of being an ally to the Chouans. Some of these people rely on their landlords for financial help with the harvest, and last year's harvest was very bad."

"It sounds like the perfect opportunity to change their lives." He leaned into the table.

Armelle paused in the middle of spreading another *galette*. "If they can hardly feed their families, I'm not certain it is the best time to throw lofty ideals at them."

"This *is* the time to do so." That old, familiar Jacobin fervor ignited in his gut. He latched onto it. This feeling was much safer than whatever distracted musing had caught hold of him a minute ago. "They have good reason to start a new life. They're free from their oppressors."

She cleaned off the spreader and straightened. "Not all Bretons appreciate the life being forced on them by Paris." Her voice had an edge to it.

"No, they prefer a life of servitude." The intensity of his earlier emotions transferred seamlessly into his rising frustration. She almost seemed to side with the Chouans when she talked like this, even if she claimed not to support them. "How can a life of living under someone's thumb bring anyone fulfillment?"

She snatched up a towel and threw it over the plate of filled *galettes*. "We cannot all go to prestigious medical schools to sit in cafés with our glasses of Burgundy and ogle what does not belong to us while plotting how to enlighten the poor, miserable peasants of lands we've never visited."

Maxence gritted his teeth. She knew how to rile him. He did not know how to sidestep the bait. "There is more to the values of the République than that."

"Ah, you are right." She flipped the cooking galette, the turner scraping dully against the iron surface of the pan. "I forgot the part about killing those who disagree with you."

"What happened with you and me in Nantes was a misunderstanding." He grasped the edges of the table. She wouldn't look at him now. Her actions had suddenly grown methodical. "I'm not about to go join the Chouans. My commitment to liberty runs deeper than that."

Armelle snorted. "A misunderstanding doesn't send someone to the bottom of the river." Before he could respond, she surged ahead. "If everyone's commitment to liberty runs so deep, why do they not let Bretons decide how they want their new government to look?"

He'd sparred with myriads of people—students at Montpellier, Jacobins in club meetings, Émile's sister Caroline, his father, even Gilles. But Armelle threw cool daggers that got under his skin in ways none of his previous adversaries had managed. He could feel the torrent spinning within her, its frenzied pace increasing by the second. "It is very clear by the war being waged in the West that Bretons have hardly a dozen intelligent minds among them."

"*Breizhadez on.*" Her hazel eyes turned icy and hard.

"I don't know what that means."

"I am Breton."

Maxence slowly let out a breath. Yes, she was, with her chestnut hair and independent spirit. He hadn't relished the thought of coming to Brittany a few months ago. Brittany was seen by the rest of France as a backward region even before the revolution.

"We started your revolution," she snapped. "We started your Jacobin club. All of that was born right here in our land. And what have you done with it?"

He threw up his hands. "We've turned it into something that has changed a nation—maybe the world—forever."

"You've turned it into a beast that threatens our livelihoods, our culture, and for some of us our lives."

The fire within him died, doused with the reality that they'd never see this the same way.

He'd never wanted to give up a fight. It wasn't his way. But the sudden fatigue that hit him rivaled the state he had been in when they first arrived in Ilizmaen.

Armelle focused her attention out the window. "Père Quéré is back. You should take these to him to deliver." She went back to her cooking as though he weren't in the room.

Maxence scooped up the plate of *galettes* and fled. He'd walked into that kitchen a complete and utter fool, his head filled with the fluttering fancies of the youth he'd long since left behind. Love, like the sea, was such a romantic notion, but it never took long for the waves of reality to cut down even the most starry-eyed of souls. He'd been a fool to let himself forget.

Armelle tossed her utensils on the table and sat in the middle of the kitchen. A black-coated form stalked past the window without a glance.

He was right. This revolution did have the power to change the world, or at least all of Europe. She crossed her legs under her petticoats and planted her elbows on her knees, resting her chin on her fists. The things she'd said rang in her mind. Even if she believed them, what a terrible way to present them to a friend. She'd known what to say to make it hurt.

She moaned and rubbed her eyes. They'd been together too long. That was it. She'd learned how his mind worked, and now it had backfired. Instead of feeling elated that she had silenced him, a pit had formed in her stomach.

"A sharp tongue cuts deeper than a knife," Mère always said. Armelle had learned that lesson many times over.

The fire crackled. Tiny fingers of smoke wafted up from the pan, bringing with it the acrid scent of burnt *galette*. What had come of that conversation? Nothing. She stretched out her legs before her. She'd become so used to him, she didn't care if he saw her in a sloppy state, and she didn't care if she told him exactly what was on her mind.

With a sigh she pushed herself back to her feet to deal with the burnt food. As she scraped it onto the table and wiped out the cindery residue, she amended her thought. Nothing had come of that conversation except the realization that she still had many things to learn about being a friend.

Maxence was hardly in the mood for Quéré's optimism. The older man's friendly greeting to anyone they passed in the street made for a long walk through the hamlet.

"Are you much familiar with farming, Citoyen Rossignol?" Quéré asked. His spry step outpaced Maxence's trudging.

"I come from a long line of seafarers."

"Ah. Quite the opposite then. Oh, *demat, citoyenne!*" He raised his walking stick to a middle-aged woman. "How do you do this fine morning? And your daughter, she is well?"

Maxence didn't mind the interruptions in conversation. It was the interruptions in walking that did nothing for his mood. Not that he wished to return to the house, but the constant starting and stopping was grating. Ahead, large hedgerows lined the fields, practically closing in the road like a tunnel. How different from Provence, with its wide-open lavender fields.

"Yes, and do take care of yourself. *Kenavo!*" The priest turned back to him. "As I was saying, the agriculture of Brittany is very interesting when you compare it to that of other provinces. Rather than having all the peasantry working as a large group on the same land, Brittany has always preferred its independence, its individuality. You'll see here." He pointed to where a hedge jutted from the road across the field. "The Bosser family works this land to the south, and Citoyen Menez owns the plot to the north. Each farmer decides what he wishes to do with the land."

"That is very interesting." Maxence was beginning to feel boxed in, like he needed to extract himself from these hedges in order to breathe.

"Some landowners here have land to lease. Some have only land for themselves. But we did not have such a concentration of wealth as did many regions before the revolution."

"I see." He hadn't the faintest idea why the priest was telling him this.

"I couldn't help overhearing the end of your conversation with Citoyenne Rossignol."

Maxence's face grew warm. That wasn't something he'd wanted anyone to hear. "There are a few things on which we do not agree." Many, if he were being truthful.

"If you told me there weren't, I would not have believed you." Quéré stopped to survey the hedges. He went up on his toes. Maxence doubted that gave him any better of a view. "I don't think we passed it yet." He continued walking. "I have heard that the first year of marriage is the most difficult. Though of course I have no experience in the matter. Perhaps soon I will be able to come to you for advice on how to survive it." The priest chuckled.

It was even more difficult when you were just pretending to be married. "I thought you didn't want to get married."

Quéré slowed, nodding thoughtfully. "If I make light of the situation, it doesn't leave me room to sorrow or worry. It doesn't work for everyone, of course, but levity is how I have dealt with many of the trials God has seen fit to allow in my life. A hearty laugh can carry one far."

Laughter brought up thoughts about a certain young woman cur-
rently making *galettes* at the house. And then it brought thoughts of
Gilles's infectious laugh, and Père's deep one during long, cold nights at
sea. Perhaps Maxence simply did not get on well with people who liked
to laugh.

"When do you think you shall continue your journey?" Quéré
asked. "Not that I wish you gone. I have enjoyed our evening conversations. And your wife, she is incredibly charming."

"*Merci.*" He'd enjoyed their evenings as well, but the fumes of the
argument still wafted inside him, preventing an enthusiastic agreement.
"We will leave tomorrow," Maxence said. Armelle was clearly recovered.
"We need to make it to Saint-Malo as soon as possible. We've delayed
long enough." He wouldn't find any relief until the end of their journey,
though exactly what the relief was from, he couldn't say.

"Ah. Well, I shall enjoy our last few hours. Here we are!" He turned
them through an opening in the hedges toward a run-down little house
surrounded by a patch of dead plants which might have been a garden
the year before. The field around them was bare, as though waiting to
be plowed.

Maxence stayed outside while Quéré took the *galettes* in to the family. It felt as though the field were enclosed in a leafy fortress. It was
difficult to see the landscape beyond the hedges except for the very top
of the church's spire to the south.

The priest returned with an empty plate and a large grin. "I think
that should fill a few empty stomachs." They made their way back to the
road, and Maxence slumped at the thought of having to return to the
house.

"You know, Rossignol, there is some truth to what you say."

"What do you mean?"

"Tradition is a powerful thing that can be used for both good and
bad." Quéré tapped his walking stick against his leg. "On the one hand,
it creates a very strong connection between groups of people. The Celtic
traditions of this land have a fierce hold on the Bretons. That spirit and

fire are in our very blood." He motioned toward a path that led toward the back of the church grounds. "But if we hold so tightly to our past that we do not let in new ways of thinking, our ways will grow stagnant and eventually fade into the dusts of time."

"Yes, that is exactly right." The ways of the old regime had grown rancid, slowly destroying its people. Armelle understood that, but what she couldn't understand was that in order to build a new France, they all had to give up their old ways.

Maxence followed Quéré down the other path. The man must wish to visit someone else before returning.

"In these parts, the Chouans are mostly revered," the priest went on. "The people tend to overlook their violence, though some do so for fear the rebels will prevent them from selling their harvest."

"The Chouans will stop at nothing to prevent the army's success," Maxence said. He'd heard of Chouans stopping grain convoys and even murdering farmers for selling food to the army.

"I can hardly blame their anger, however much I disagree with their tactics."

Maxence gave him a sidelong glance. What did he mean by that? The Chouans were vagrant troublemakers, incapable of logic.

"Have you ever been separated from your community?" Quéré shook his head. "Of course you have. You're from Provence. You should know then, the strangeness of being forced into a society so different from your own."

Brittany was certainly that.

"The people of this region feel as though their community has been taken from them. Their religion, their priests, their family, their liveli-hood—so much of that has been stripped away, as Citoyenne Rossignol said this morning. This isn't simply a matter of getting too comfortable with their lot in life. Traditions help form their very identity. It is diffi-cult to want to align with those from Paris who do not understand what it means to be Breton."

"We should all be French." Maxence had a community once, all tied up in seafaring, where the conversations centered on brigs and frigates, halyards and sails. Men would leave for months on end to brave the ocean while women kept homes running tighter than any ship. The hard life created a sense of companionship. Everyone had a place and a duty to perform. He'd upset that when he fled to Montpellier, and then again to Paris.

"Perhaps there is a way to be both."

Maxence pulled a leaf from a bush as they rounded a bend in the hedges. Is that what he'd been looking for in the cafés—that community he'd lost when he turned his back on his past? Had he joined the Jacobins and *fédérés* really to find that sense of belonging? He ripped the leaf, letting bits flutter to the ground. He'd felt like an outcast, unstable and unsure. A little inkling of understanding for the Bretons' sense of loss flared inside him.

A rough-hewn stone taller than Maxence came into view at the back of the churchyard. Long with angling sides, it looked both a strange feat of nature and a relic of human imagination.

"Magnificent, isn't it?" Quéré walked up and patted it, as a farmer would a beloved horse. "This *menhir* has stood here for centuries. It was thought to have been placed here by the druids, or perhaps Merlin himself if the stories are true." Quéré winked. What a strange clergyman he was. "We may never know anything about the people who made this. But I have found something rather interesting."

He led Maxence around to the side of the stone facing the church. Maxence avoided looking at the house, though only a small corner of it was visible through the trees. On this side of the stone a large Christian cross had been carved, which looked completely out of place on the monument.

Quéré pointed with his walking stick at the base of the stone. Maxence went down on his knees to better see. A series of swirls and lines etched into the rock filled one corner.

"I'm not sure what this individual intended by these carvings," the priest said. "It looks as though he or she were interrupted in their work.

But even though it is small, this person we will never know left his mark."

Maxence straightened, brushing off his breeches. "It's incredible it has lasted so long." Armelle would find this interesting. He'd have to show her before they left.

Quéré leaned against his walking stick. "I don't think we know what sort of effect, good or bad, this revolution will have on history. I think it will be better determined five or ten years from now. Perhaps more. But we have the power to make our mark on it, however small. We must make sure it's an honest effort."

Maxence's eyes finally strayed toward the house. He'd made an honest effort with so many things. Even though Quéré was talking about their argument over the revolution, he couldn't help thinking of all the relationships he'd failed to maintain and all the pursuits at which he'd failed to succeed. He couldn't even preserve good standing with one of the friendliest young women in Brittany for one month. "What if we can't make the mark we wish to? What if we aren't good enough, no matter how hard we try?"

"Then I suggest trying another way. There is *always* another way."

How could he believe that? Maxence fiddled with the buttons on his borrowed coat. Surely someday he would run out of chances. If he hadn't already.

CHAPTER 19

Maxence followed Armelle and Quéré out of the little house the next morning. The snows that had driven them to Ilizmaen were a distant memory, melted into the ground by the warming spring days. He twisted the market bag to make a handle and slung it over his shoulder. The anxiety to leave had dwindled just a little now that they had reached the time of their departure.

Armelle turned back toward Père Quéré and took his hand. "You have been too kind to us. I wish we could repay you." Her eyes glistened in the sunrise.

"You can repay me by helping someone else when you are in the position to do so." He patted her hand. "Have a safe journey, *ma fille.* No more illness."

She nodded. "*Adieu, père.*"

"Oh, I do hope we meet sooner than that." He turned to Maxence, but instead of shaking the hand he proffered, Quéré pulled him aside. Armelle wandered off toward the church, the bedroll on her back and a kerchief bundled with his extra clothes in one hand. She'd insisted on at least sharing some of the load.

The endearments had completely stopped since their argument, as had the spontaneous taking of his arm or hand. She hadn't said good-night, nor had she asked to play the silly question game. Near silence pervaded most of their interactions. Maxence hated to admit that the distance hurt.

"I am glad to have met you, Citoyen Rossignol," Quéré said. "We have talked much the last week, and I am grateful for our conversations. As such, there is only one more thing I have left to say to you." He leaned in. "Marry that girl."

Maxence flinched. "But . . . we married four months ago." Or was it three? Blast, how long ago was the twenty-third of Brumaire?

Quéré set his lips and raised one eyebrow almost to the heavens. What had given them away? How long had he known? Maxence rubbed the back of his neck, suddenly as hot as the *galette* pan. He had the urge to shrivel into the ground.

"New husbands do not sleep on cold, hard floors when there is only one bed in the room."

Maxence had never been religious, so the shame of standing before a priest with his lie exposed was a completely new sensation. But he was more concerned about Armelle's reputation with the priest. "I can assure you," he said, waving his hands before him, "that nothing has ever happened between us. It is strictly business. We both needed to get to Saint-Malo, and Armelle thought that—"

Quéré clapped him on the shoulder. "I am not condemning you. I hope you have a safe journey with no more disruptions. But I meant what I said." He wagged a finger in Maxence's face. "Sometimes young men don't know the good things in plain sight before them."

"Oh. Yes. That is . . . That is a good reminder. *Merci.*" Had Quéré forgotten their terrible argument? It had been made very clear to Maxence that the strange magic this place had held over the two of them had blinded him to the truth—the truth that he and Armelle Bernard were not well suited. That union would never happen.

The priest shook his hand. "May the path be smooth and swift, *mon fils.* And may you find the peace you seek."

Maxence hurried down the hill after Armelle, who waved and called farewell until they'd cleared the church gate. Ilizmaen lay like a dream behind them, foreign and so removed from his true life. How, then, did it also feel like a vision he didn't want to wake from?

The hedges and trees that had been destroyed in southern Brittany were still very much alive between Nozay and Rennes. New leaves reached through the branches and twigs, adding color to the dull landscape. Armelle walked along practically by herself, as Étienne lagged behind. He wasn't limping, just walking much slower than his long legs should carry him.

She had hardly spoken to him since their argument. Sometimes her anger at his unfeeling words made her want to ignore him the rest of the journey. Her humiliation at letting her tongue get carried away also kept her from starting conversation. She hated the gulf that lay unaddressed between them. They couldn't travel like this.

"How is your knee?" she asked over her shoulder, starting with an easy question to reel him in.

"Never better." He didn't lift his eyes from the road.

That was a lie, but if he wasn't limping, it couldn't be causing him much discomfort. They weren't walking quickly, but if she slowed, he slowed. He didn't wish to walk with her. "Is something wrong?" she asked.

It was as though he hadn't heard her. Several minutes passed. A laborer walked by in the other direction, and she greeted him, but she received only a grunt in return. And Étienne said nothing.

"This is going to be a quiet journey," she thought aloud. No response. She'd surely go mad with three more days of this. A mischievous grin spread across her face. Or *he* would.

"What a fine day we are having, Monsieur Rossignol. Do you think we shall have many more like it? I do hope so. Traveling in a downpour, whether it be rain or snow or even hail, is certainly one of the worst misfortunes a person can live through. Do you not agree, *monsieur*? Just think of the inconvenience we would have should it happen to rain to-day. And look ahead at those hills before us. Can you imagine walking up and down them in mud? I'm quite sure the rain pools in the roads in this part of the country, with how deep the roads are dug out. Why, I do think we should be slogging through a river should we meet even a small amount of—"

"Armelle."

She spun to face him. "Well, if you will not talk to me, you cannot fault me for finding a way to fill the silence."

"I will throw you in the ocean myself when we get to Saint-Malo if you prattle the whole way there."

Armelle walked backward, keeping in front of him in hopes she would catch his gaze at some point. "I can't swim. You're not that cruel."

"Try me."

"You know that I will." That earned her an unexpected smile that melted a little of the ice that had formed inside her since their argument the day before. He didn't look as severe when he smiled. "Have you been to Saint-Malo many times?" She would break him down, bit by bit. When he was comfortable talking to her again, they might be able to make amends over yesterday's disagreement.

"A few."

"Did you stay on the ship?" She stumbled on a rut in the road and nearly fell backward. Étienne reached for her but pulled away when she quickly righted herself. She turned to walk forward beside him. This time he didn't hang back.

"No, we got to see a bit of the city. Mostly we stayed by the beach."

"Is it a fine beach?"

He lifted a shoulder. "I suppose."

"That doesn't paint a good picture." Henri hadn't given much de-scription the few times he'd written either.

"You would have to ask Gilles. He's the one who waxes poetic."

"Gilles. He is your brother?" Armelle tried to keep her voice mildly interested. He rarely volunteered information about his family and had never brought up names.

"My younger brother. We enjoyed exploring the old fort ruins on one of the islands. That was on our last voyage together."

How to keep him talking? The hunger to know more about his family made her quicken her step. "Exploring ruins! I cannot think of anything more enjoyable to do with a brother. Is he very close to you in age?"

"Just less than two years younger." His eyes took on a faraway look. "We were inseparable."

"That is how Henri and I were before the *levée en masse*." Now he couldn't tell her anything, and his letters were riddled with lies only she saw through.

"My brother was likely drafted as well." Étienne shifted the market bag to his other shoulder. "It's a shame, as he's saved money for so long to attend medical school at Montpellier."

"Following in your footsteps." She grinned, but it wasn't returned. Clouds hastened across his eyes.

"If only he had."

There it was, that pain. She hadn't seen it very often since he told her about Émile's death. Seeing it jostled her, just as it had then. Without thinking, she looped her arm around his. "Where was he sent?"

"I don't know." He pulled his arm from her grasp as though to adjust the market bag and drifted toward the middle of the road, away from her.

"How do you not know?" Surely the rest of his family would have informed him.

Étienne stopped and turned to her. "My brother and I did not part on good terms. He went back on his decision to join the *fédérés* with me and Émile. He should have been there with me when . . ."

When Émile was shot.

Étienne stared, as though he wanted to take back what he'd said.

Armelle's eyes smarted. He blamed his brother for leaving him alone when he needed him most. Had he shared this with anyone before? What a burden to carry, along with all his others.

She touched his arm. There was little to say. Nothing she said could take away that pain.

He pivoted and continued walking. "We aren't married anymore. I thought we were breaking those habits."

Touching his arm was hardly a romantic gesture; she did that to family and friends alike. Armelle watched him, trying to decide how to verbalize the feelings in her heart. Then she ran to catch up with him. She could take away a different pain. The one she'd inflicted. "I've wanted to apologize. For yesterday."

"No need." Now he was walking fast. She practically took two steps to each one of his.

"There *is* need. I purposely said things that I knew would make you angry, and I'm sorry."

The path had started up an incline, and his breathing came faster. "Everyone does that at some time." His eyes narrowed as though he were bracing against some internal gale.

"That doesn't mean we shouldn't apologize." She took his arm again, pulling to slow him to a more manageable pace. She took a moment to catch her breath. "I'm asking your forgiveness because you are someone important to me."

He flinched at her last words. "You only stated truth as you saw it. That's hardly something to apologize for."

"But the way I stated it was inexcusable."

He licked his lips. "I'm sorry as well." It came out almost as a whisper, as though the words were foreign and he wasn't certain of getting them correct.

"Can we be friends again?" She hugged his arm. "Instead of indifferent traveling companions?"

"We have been a great many things to each other over the course of this journey, haven't we?" His voice gained in confidence, though he'd started to breathe hard up this hill.

"Rescuer, companion, doctor, spouse." She ticked them off on her free fingers.

"You forgot tailor." He squeezed her arm against his side like he had done a few times when in company with Pére Quéré. She liked it when he did that. It made her feel as though he enjoyed having her beside him. "And also confidante. I haven't had many of those."

Confidante. She did like the sound of that. They walked on in comfortable silence, neither pulling away from their connection. The ravine that had formed between them was filled once again with cozy companionship, and Armelle was starting to wish they'd never arrive in Saint-Malo. She didn't try to consider what that wish could imply.

Maxence sat with his back against the wall of the abandoned house they'd happened upon a short way outside of the town of Nozay. They'd managed to make a fire in the hearth, as the evening had already grown chilly. Now that dark had fallen, they couldn't see outside the small windows. The inability to see anything or anyone who might approach sent prickles across his skin. Once Armelle returned, he'd bolt the door as best he could and try to rest. He still got chills when he thought of the soldiers' search in Ilizmaen and how close they'd come to being discovered.

He hadn't expected to enjoy the walk today, though he should have known Armelle couldn't let things lie unfixed. Somehow she'd tricked him into sharing many things about his family. More than he'd ever shared with anyone except Émile. He didn't regret it either.

Maxence gnawed the inside of his cheek, then reached for the market bag. Finding the breast pocket of his national guard coat wasn't difficult since it was turned inside out. He drew out the little white rosette that had resided in that pocket since the attack on the Tuileries. It had been nothing short of a miracle that Froment hadn't found it when searching him after his arrest.

They would have shot him on the spot if Froment had seen it.

Maxence sat back against the wall. He traced the looped ribbon with his thumb, pausing at the brown stain on one side. The rosette was a symbol of the monarchy, an old way of life that valued only a few lucky individuals. This one was stained with the blood of a patriot who had given everything to pull that monarchy down. In that context, the little ornament was a paradox.

But it had greater meaning than just politics. Maxence enclosed the rosette in his hand and brought his fist to his lips. Marie-Caroline had given this to Émile just before the *fédérés'* departure from Marseille. She was a staunch *royaliste*, heavily influenced by their mother's noble relations. Émile was the only one in the family who saw reason and justice in the revolution. But they'd still managed to put aside those differences when it came time to leave. Maxence and Gilles were not so opposite in beliefs as the Daubins—they were both Jacobins after all—but they hadn't been able to cross that smaller divide. Maxence's pride hadn't let him try.

He ran his hand through his hair, then released the rosette to examine it again. He'd pulled it from Émile's coat after the carnage, thinking to send it to his friend's family with Émile's few belongings. But in the aftermath of battle and recovery from his own wound, he forgot. The symbol was a dangerous thing for a *révolutionnaire* to carry on his person. Maxence didn't know why he'd never thrown it in the fire. Something about the hope of reconciliation that the rosette stood for had stayed his hand.

Voices sounded outside, and Maxence crammed the rosette back into his coat pocket in the market bag. He hurried to the door, pulse racing. Not every traveler they passed on the road would be a threat, but any of them could be.

It opened before he reached it, and Armelle came through with an older man in a threadbare cloak. "We have room in here for one more, do we not?" she asked.

"I am very sorry to intrude," the man said. He carried a pair of saddlebags over one shoulder and a large pack on his back. A lantern shone weakly in one hand. "My donkey insisted on traveling slower than I wished, and we did not make it to Bain-de-Bretagne as planned." Something seemed odd about this man. Maxence couldn't decide if it was his probing gaze or the disheveled appearance. Not that he and Armelle looked any better.

"I'm sorry to hear it." Maxence wiped his hands on his breeches to keep them from knotting into fists. Dirt from travel spotted the man's face, but it did not soften his sharp eyes, which seemed to be taking far too much pleasure in watching Armelle.

"If you don't mind, I would appreciate sharing your fire for the night."

"But of course!" Armelle motioned him in.

What was she doing? They didn't know him. Chouan or *révolution-naire*, he could prove a threat. "My wife cannot leave anyone out in the cold." The words rushed from his mouth.

Armelle's eyebrows shot up. If she was going to toss out invitations to anyone without a thought, she couldn't fault him for trying to protect her. They could pretend for one more night.

The newcomer's expression became instantly guarded. "You have a lovely wife, *citoyen*."

"I agree." *And would appreciate you not trying anything that would force me to beat you within an inch of your life.* "Come in."

The man set his things near the fire on the opposite side from where Maxence had spread out his blanket. "You are most generous." The stranger's voice seemed more uncertain than a moment ago. Good. "If you will excuse me, I wish to tether my donkey a little closer to the house." His gaze flicked from his pack to Maxence before he slinked out the door.

Armelle hurried to Maxence. "I was under the impression you were tired of playing that game." She spoke softly, leaning in as though to keep the sound from carrying through the glassless windows.

"It won't look so strange with you sleeping next to me if he thinks we're married." Armelle's blanket was already set up on the other side of the room from Maxence's.

"He is not going to hurt me," she said.

"He's less likely to if you're my wife."

She sighed and retrieved her blanket. "He's a kind man alone on the road. There's no need to distrust him." She walked around Maxence to put her blanket near his, leaving a foot-wide gap between them.

"'Alone on the road' gives me every reason to distrust him." He settled back down in his original seat, and she took a place not far away.

She tilted her head, giving him a patient smile. "Jean-Baptiste didn't think I should trust you."

Maxence threw his arms wide. "And he was right. Look where it's led you."

She huffed and shook her head. After a moment, she looked over her shoulder toward the door. Still no return of the stranger. "You didn't have to say that, you know."

"I completely agree that Jean-Baptiste was correct." Traveling with him put her in far greater danger than traveling with Colbert would have.

"No, that isn't what I meant." She shifted, eyes falling to her hands. She pulled out the little wood die and rolled it through her fingers. "When you agreed that you had a lovely wife." Her cheeks pinked, or perhaps it was just the fire's light.

How else was he supposed to answer? But if he'd had a choice, would the answer be any different? The flames' glow turned her hair almost red beneath her neat cap. Her soft lips pursed, twisting at whatever thought had crossed her mind. Around them, the abandoned house— with its dirt floors and rough stones—lay dark and drab. Armelle was the only light, the only color amidst it all. "I meant it."

Rather than coaxing out a smile, her visage grew more serious.

"Étienne, you know that though we're *married*, I don't want . . ." She rubbed the back of her neck.

"There are lines you don't wish to cross." He knew. She'd made that quite clear, not just at Ilizmaen, but in Savenay. He'd laughed at her then, with her grand ideas of saving her very first kiss for her husband. It was so different from the life he'd led.

"Well, yes. Of course. But also . . . sometimes it seems as though we forget this isn't real." The die flicked from her fingers. She grabbed for it, but it rolled out of her reach on the packed dirt and landed beside him.

Maxence picked it up. "Four."

"I don't want us to forget what is real and what isn't."

He stretched out his legs and attempted an unaffected look. Inside he felt as though he'd taken a battering ram to the chest. She hadn't stated anything he disagreed with. They both knew this was part of an act. The intensity of the blow left him fighting to breathe. "We won't. We're both too stubborn to allow that."

"There we are," the stranger said as he entered. "My beast is settled." He sat, nonchalantly inspecting his bags before arranging them behind him.

"Where are you headed?" Maxence asked.

"To Rennes. I have just been in Nantes and procured some goods at a fine price." Something about the set of his mouth gave him a calculating aura.

"We are off to Rennes as well," Armelle said. "Perhaps we can travel together the rest of the way."

Maxence scowled. If she didn't want to keep up this ruse any longer, why was she volunteering to extend it? Curse her friendliness. If they had more than a day left to travel, he would have flatly refused. At least they wouldn't need to extend their lie too long.

"I always appreciate company." The man reached into his pack and retrieved something wrapped in a handkerchief. "Can I interest you, *citoyenne*, in a little something?" He pulled back the cloth to reveal a small ceramic jar. "A pot of rouge? I will trade."

A peddler. Maxence folded his arms. Peddlers especially couldn't be trusted.

Armelle laughed as the man opened the lid to reveal the deep-red pigment. "I've never been one for cosmetics. My mother didn't allow us such luxuries."

"Surely she told you that once you've caught a man, you must work to keep him." The peddler arched his brow suggestively. "A little rouge has helped many a woman keep her husband's eye from wandering."

Maxence's gut twisted. Husband or not, he didn't like what the peddler was insinuating. It hit too close to the cad he'd chosen to be at Montpellier.

"Oh, I don't worry about that," Armelle said, voice tight.

"I do have a few other things." He sifted through his pack, pulling out pouches, a knife, a pair of combs, and various trinkets. A fold of pale-green cloth that shimmered in the dimness poked out, but he hurriedly pushed it back down. A gown, perhaps? It looked too expensive for a simple peddler to sell. "Face paint? Or perfume? It's from the finest *parfumeries* in Provence. I also have needles and thread."

"I think we have all that we need, and we have nothing to trade or buy with, for that matter." Armelle stifled a yawn.

"A cream for the hands? For wrinkles? An ointment to cure wounds?"

"*Merci, non.*"

"Are you tired, *chérie*?" Maxence asked. Couldn't the man see they weren't interested? Armelle nodded through another yawn. "You should sleep. We have far to go tomorrow."

"Yes, good night, *citoyenne*." The peddler scowled while returning his wares to his pack.

Maxence caught her hand as she walked past to get to her blanket. She met his eyes. "*Bonne nuit*," he said. Her face dimmed with an emotion he couldn't make out. She squeezed his hand and pulled away. Then she lay down on the hard ground and pulled her blanket over her, cradling her head with one bent arm. If only they'd found a barn when it had started to get dark. Hay made a far better bed.

"Why do you travel to Rennes, *citoyen*?" The peddler shook his pack, trying to make more room.

"We're passing through."

"On your way to where?" He tried to shove in one of the pouches, but it stuck out the top.

"The northern shores. I've found work." Maxence stayed planted where he was beside the fire. He wouldn't try to rest until the peddler slept. It would make for a long day tomorrow, but he wouldn't risk the stranger doing something nefarious while he was asleep.

"Yes, of course." The peddler reached into his pack, moved things around, and finally got the pouch to fit. "There are many places to find work in Saint-Malo." The sidelong gaze told Maxence he was searching for information. For what purpose, Maxence couldn't tell. He didn't confirm or deny the implication.

"Does Nantes not have an abundance of peddlers?" he asked. That was enough questions about Armelle and him.

"Oh, yes. I never sell my wares in Nantes." The man picked up the last item that needed to go into his pack—the knife. "But Nantes has had more executions than Rennes." He turned the leather-cased blade over in his hands.

A chill shot through the house's single room. "What does that have to do with peddling?"

"Where do you think I buy these things for so cheap a price?" He held up the sheathed knife. "From soldiers and looters. I was in luck this week. They had several rather wealthy patrons, if you will."

These were the personal effects of prisoners. The thought soured his stomach, though it never had before. It wasn't uncommon for soldiers to collect what they felt were their dues after an arrest or before an execution. His comrades had boasted of things they'd taken or found before. Froment had taken everything he could from Maxence the moment he was detained. How else would they supplement their meager soldiers' pay? But after being the victim of this sort of plunder, Maxence couldn't support the practice.

"Terrible business, but we all do what we must to survive." The peddler slid the knife into the pack. "Perhaps someday my work will not be so morbid." The scoundrel chuckled. "But isn't that what we say of everything? Someday the fighting will stop, someday we will be able to afford bread, someday we will see the ocean—on and on until we're dead."

Armelle's breathing had deepened, but Maxence couldn't tell if she was asleep. Her stiff shoulders made him think not, but that could just have been a result of sleeping on hard dirt.

"How did you convince a girl like that to marry the likes of you?"

Maxence's back went rigid against the wall. "Bewildering, isn't it?" He hadn't convinced her of anything like that, and he couldn't imagine he ever could. She knew what he was. Who he'd once been. *Dozens of broken hearts.* Just the thought made him wince. He'd had either humility or sense kicked into his head, probably by the girl with the impish eyes resting nearby.

A strange flutter overtook his heart, so powerful it took his breath. The urge to curl up beside her hit just as strong as the urge to run from the house. He'd found himself attracted to plenty of women since leaving his father's ship as a youth. He'd flirted and carried on, practically played the part of a suitor with many of them, but nothing had hit him as violently as this baffling draw to Armelle Bernard.

He could almost hear Émile's teasing. *Maxence Étienne, has someone finally caught your eye for more than two seconds? I can hardly believe it. She must be some woman to make you want to give up our little games.* His throat tightened. She was a wonderful woman. He wondered what Émile would think of her.

"I hope to be back on the road early tomorrow," the peddler said, rolling out his bed. "Thank you again for allowing me to share your shelter."

Maxence nodded curtly. He watched the still room until the peddler seemed to have fallen asleep before creeping under his own blanket. He pulled the market bag and bundled clothes over to sit just above his and Armelle's heads. They hadn't bothered with trying to protect their things while they slept since they'd been in places with little danger of it being stolen. But the peddler's understandable protectiveness of his goods had set Maxence on edge.

Armelle turned toward him after he lay down.

"I thought you were asleep," he whispered.

She tried to find a comfortable rest for her head against her elbow.

He pushed the clothes bundle toward her. "Here."

She laid her head on top of it. "You will make someone a fine husband someday," she said so softly he could barely hear it.

He made a face. "More likely a terrible one."

"I didn't get my question."

Maxence rolled onto his side, resting his head on his arm like she had. "You didn't actually roll it."

"It still counts."

"Then ask so we can both sleep." Tomorrow was going to be a long day.

She brought the blanket up to her chin. The room was a little cool despite the fire. They'd be warmer if . . . Well, no. That wouldn't work at all. They were better off with space between them.

"What happened between you and Gilles? When he refused to go to Paris."

Maxence scrunched his eyes closed as Gilles's troubled face when they said goodbye filled his mind.

"I'm sorry," she said. "You don't have to tell me."

When he slowly opened his eyes, her head had come up off the makeshift pillow. The fire reflected in her large eyes.

"It's too long a story to tell tonight. In short, I was an imbecile."

"We all are sometimes." After a few minutes, her eyelids drooped and her eyelashes fell dark against her cheeks, and it wasn't long until Maxence fell asleep to the rhythm of her breath and the comfort of having her near him.

CHAPTER 20

Night still prevailed when Armelle awoke. The fire had died down to tiny orange tendrils and pulsing embers. She lay unmoving, searching the shadows. All she could hear was Étienne's breathing beside her. How curious. Nothing seemed amiss to have woken her.

Something scratched against the floor above her head. Rodents? She swallowed slowly. Or perhaps the peddler had left the house to check on his animal. If it was a rodent, she needed to scare it off before it ate their food. She slowly turned her head. While she didn't hate the little invasive creatures as much as Jacqueline, she had no love for—

A steel blade glinted faintly above Étienne's exposed neck. Angled at his throat.

Armelle pushed herself up and lunged for the peddler's hand. She snatched his wrist and shoved the knife away. Pounding filled her ears. The demon! The *murderer*! The peddler jerked back, muttering an oath and partly dragging her with him. He broke her grasp, and she fell across her sleeping companion with a belated shriek. Étienne startled, throwing her off of him. She landed in the dirt on his other side, gasping. Her head spun.

"You knave." Étienne leaped at the peddler, who was scrambling to his feet. He caught the peddler's ankle and pulled, leveling him. A barrage of curses filled the room. Étienne pounced at the man's fist.

Armelle sat up, feeling her pockets. Jean-Baptiste's knife. He stole it. She'd kept it in the market bag instead of her pocket as her friend had instructed.

Her stomach lurched. The men grappled for the weapon, Étienne's fist locked around the peddler's wrist, and the peddler threw all his weight into trying to get a hit. What could she do? She pushed herself to her feet. They didn't have any other weapons, and she'd be worthless even if they did.

Étienne yanked the man's arm back and scrambled to pin him. "Armelle," he shouted, "get the knife."

She sprang forward and dropped to her knees. The peddler tightened his grip on the handle, twisting as if to take a stab at her, but she was out of range. Étienne pressed the peddler's wrist, the veins on his hand and neck popping out with the effort. Their attacker's hand paled as Armelle grasped the end of the blade and pried his fingers off. He screamed and swore at her, calling her filthy names she never wished to hear again.

When the blade was free, she dashed away. If she'd followed Jean-Baptiste's advice, they wouldn't have been in danger. She flipped it shut with shaking hands and crammed it into her pocket before turning. Étienne was on his feet, arm out. She couldn't tell if it was in protection or to warn her back.

"You're a soldier." The peddler wheezed, rising. "From the Army of the West. I saw the coat."

"Not anymore."

Their attacker bent his knees, looking ready to leap at Étienne at any sign of weakness. Étienne stood his ground.

"I don't think the Chouans housed down this road will care if you are a deserter or not." The man inched toward his belongings. "They'll string you up and be done with you."

Ice shot down Armelle's spine. Chouans.

The peddler put his arm behind him, feeling for his pack and saddle-bags, but he wasn't in reach yet. She hoped he'd go and leave them be. He wouldn't carry many weapons, would he?

"How do they feel about thieves?" Étienne asked.

Armelle's heart jumped to her throat. "His knife!"

The peddler froze. Étienne dove toward the pack, a half second faster than the attacker. The peddler locked his arm around Étienne's neck, but her friend managed to snatch one strap of the bag and fling it toward her. She flinched out of the way. It hit the wall opposite the hearth, shattered pottery tinkling.

"Devil!" the peddler howled.

She scuttled over to the pack and thrust it behind her as far from him as she could get it. Étienne pulled at the man's arms. He got one arm loose, but the peddler pounded him in the back, just below his ribs. Étienne cried out, knees buckling. Swinging his elbow, he managed to knock the peddler away. The man raced for his lantern and saddlebags and swept them over his shoulder as Étienne stumbled to his feet. He put himself between Armelle and the peddler once again.

"Leave."

"Give me my pack, and I'll leave you in peace."

"You have a knife in there," Armelle said. "And who knows what other weapons."

"I will not—"

"We trusted you," she said. "We won't be fooled again." *She* had trusted him. Étienne had been right not to.

"Leave now, or you won't have another option." Étienne breathed heavily. He was the taller man, but catching him by surprise had nearly given their attacker the upper hand.

"You'll have every Chouan in the region tracking you before sunrise. You really want to risk your dirty little wench falling into their hands?"

"Get out now."

The peddler made one last lunge for his pack, but Armelle cut him off, her blade in hand as Jean-Baptiste had showed her. "Go."

The man glanced at the blade, then at her face. She stared back with all the hatred she could muster, stamping down the trepidation that threatened to overwhelm her defenses. He backed away, looking from Étienne to Armelle.

He halted in the doorway. "*Vivre le roi,*" he hissed, then dashed out into the blackness.

Etienne moved to the door, watching until the muted sound of the donkey's hooves carried into the night. Armelle glanced out one of the small windows. A little spot of light appeared toward the road. He'd lit his lantern. It quickly disappeared.

She released a breath, limbs suddenly weak.

Étienne ran his hands down his face, then let them fall to his sides. They didn't say anything. Armelle's mind churned over what had happened in the last few minutes. The pieces wouldn't fit. That peddler, who had been kind and flattering, turned on them in a matter of hours. He would have slit Étienne's throat if she hadn't awoken.

She gagged, a hand flying to her mouth. In a moment she was before Maxence, throwing her arms around his waist. Could he feel her quaking? "He almost . . ." Her voice caught. That man had meant to kill him.

His arms encircled her and pulled her tightly against him. "But he didn't. Thanks to you." She laid her head on his chest. Her eyes stung, and she begged them not to release tears all over the front of his shirt. His heart thundered in her ear. Safe. Reassuring. They hadn't taken him tonight.

With a sigh, but with his pulse still racing, he rested his head atop hers and squeezed her tighter. For a moment the danger disappeared, and with it the worries of tomorrow, replaced with warmth and understanding and care. It felt so familiar. Almost like . . . like she was home.

Blast. He'd dozed. Maxence couldn't find a part of his body that didn't ache as he forced his eyes open. Sitting up the whole night to

watch for the peddler's return hadn't led to restful sleep. A stiff back and legs were the price of safety. His shoulder was the worst of all, and the arm attached to it was completely numb. But he couldn't mind those ailments as much as the rest.

Armelle sat curled against his side, her head nestled into his shoulder. Her face tilted up toward him, catching the fresh rays of early morning tiptoeing through the window. She slept with a faint smile. Her arms wrapped around her middle with fingers barely peeking out from under the sleeves of his coat.

They'd grown so familiar with each other at Quéré's that the closeness seemed second nature. He hadn't questioned it last night when she'd found her way to his side in the dark and snuggled against him for comfort after the attack. Now in the clearness of dawn, he was all too aware of the fire in his chest. He not only enjoyed her nearness but also dreaded waking her as it meant they would separate. He'd held women in his arms before. Why did this time feel so different?

Maxence, you fool. This was hardly the right moment to fall in . . . in love. If that's what this was.

"We should get moving," he murmured in her ear.

Her brows rose, but she didn't open her eyes. "Hm?"

"We need to figure out how to get past the Chouans."

She sat up, rubbing her eyes with sleeve-covered hands. "What are we to do?" Her peaceful features had tightened.

Maxence stretched his arm and shook out his hand behind her to keep the numbness from her notice. "My first thought was to take another route, but I don't know the land. We could get lost taking the wrong road."

"And fall into the hands of Chouans in other places."

He nodded. They didn't know which paths were held by counter-revolutionaries. "If we traveled separately, you might make it through unharmed. You have nothing for them to hold against you." But it meant she'd face potential dangers of traveling by herself.

She quickly shook her head. "I'm not leaving you to be captured by the Chouans."

"If it's inevitable, there's no sense in us both getting—"

"You've made that argument before," she said flatly, cocking her head.

He shrugged. "I thought perhaps I could convince you this time." In truth, he'd expected this exact reaction.

"If I didn't leave you behind when we were practically strangers, what makes you think I would leave you behind now that we're friends?"

The question crashed into him like a white-capped wave hitting a sandbar. He was used to being left behind. It had happened much of his life, with his father and Victor constantly leaving for the sea, and Gilles going without him after Maxence had decided to end his career as a seaman. Then Gilles had left him to fight for the cause of freedom alone. Leaving was the Étiennes' way of life.

She wanted to stay with him.

"We must assume our friend has given them our description," Maxence said, trying not to grin since the words weren't funny in any way. His heart felt so weightless, he couldn't help it. "They'll be looking for a young couple."

Armelle put her chin in her hand. "So we must disguise ourselves somehow."

"I have a national guard coat."

That earned him a glare. "That is not helpful, Étienne."

"Maxence. You might as well call me that, as I've been calling you by your given name." He nudged her with his shoulder.

"I suppose you have." She nudged him back, eyes lowered. A pretty pink ran across her cheeks. Then she tapped her fingers along her chin. "We have some extra clothes, but nothing that would change our appearance greatly. They won't be looking specifically for a girl in a blue petticoat, so changing to my green one will not fool them."

"Perhaps if we switch clothes that will confuse them."

"We might be able to tie my petticoat to fit you, but somehow I do not think my jackets will fit over your shoulders." She squinted at him. "You are rather jovial this morning given the circumstances."

"Me? Jovial?" He didn't remember the last time he'd felt so carefree. He shouldn't feel this way. They faced very real danger. Maxence ducked his chin.

"By your standards, quite." She sighed. "Even if we could exchange clothing, we would still be a couple under suspicion. A lot of suspicion."

Maxence scanned the one-room house. Nothing had been left by the previous inhabitants. Or it had all been looted. His eyes fell on the pack lying against the wall where he'd thrown it during their midnight scuffle. "Shall we see if he left us anything useful?"

He brought it over to where she sat and pulled it open. The knife lay toward the top. He plucked it out and tossed it to the ground. It could prove useful should they meet with a very small group of Chouans. But threatening more than one or two with only a knife would be asking for worse trouble.

A few of the cosmetics jars had broken and sullied the handkerchiefs wrapped around them. Maxence set them beside the knife and wiped black powder from his hands. Kohl, most likely. The next time he dug in, something smooth and soft enveloped his hand. He drew out a long stretch of sage green silk, the end of which formed a bodice and sleeves.

"This has potential." He held it up. It was a round gown with a gathered bodice and high waist after the new style. He'd seen many similar gowns during his time in Paris.

Armelle pulled the skirt straight and smoothed it over her lap. "This is lovely." The silk had plenty of wrinkles and a stain on one side from the kohl.

"It should fit you, I think." In truth he had no idea. He had an eye for women's styles but little sense of fit.

"I couldn't wear this. I'd look like a hen trying to impersonate a peacock."

Maxence leaned forward. "Oh, come. They'll be looking for a poor couple in travel clothes. If you are a nobleman's daughter running from soldiers after your parents were captured by the République, the Chouans won't harm you."

Armelle paled. "I couldn't play that part."

He lowered the dress. "You can harass clergymen and smuggle rogue soldiers out of prisons, but you cannot pretend to be a nobleman's daughter?"

"Why would I be running in such a fine gown?" Her voice came out small, uncertain.

"This is a day dress. Look how the neckline is higher."

She eyed it as though it were a cannon ready to fire. "I couldn't."

Maxence rummaged through the pack. Silver candlesticks, an old-looking bit of needlework rolled haphazardly, a wooden plate, a porcelain dish now in several pieces, forks. Nothing else of use. "Do you have a better idea?"

Armelle fingered the dress. "It doesn't solve our problem that they are looking for a man and a woman traveling together."

She was right. Blast that peddler. He ran a hand over his stubbled jaw. The sun was getting higher. If they wanted to reach Rennes by sundown and have the possibility of procuring a real bed at an inn with the little money they had left, they needed to get moving. The longer they stayed, the greater the chance the Chouans would seek them out. They couldn't defend themselves here.

"You change. We'll decide what to do with me after I shave." He handed her the gown and moved to their market bag. It took longer than it should have to find his shaving kit after the peddler's ransacking. He froze. Where was the coin purse? He tore everything out of the market bag.

"What is it?" Armelle sat with the dress in her arms.

"Did you put the coin purse in your pocket?"

"No."

Maxence checked his breeches pockets, both the ones he wore and the ones in the bundle. It wasn't in his coat pockets either. "*Quel démon.*" He sat back on his haunches. "He stole the money." That good-for-nothing villain. "I suppose we'll be looking for a stable in the city tonight." Quéré would have found that funny given his recent Bible reading. Or perhaps he'd see it as some sign.

"We've survived worse."

It was true. With a groan, Maxence got to his feet and retrieved his shaving kit, towel, and a waterskin. He quit the house, calling over his shoulder, "It's a dress, not a snake." And it could be their only way of convincing the backward-thinking, militant *royalistes* not to kill them on the spot.

CHAPTER 21

Maxence wiped the last of the water from his face, then shoved the towel and his other shaving supplies as best he could into his pocket. He plucked up his shirt from the little tree and shook it out. Wanting to give her privacy, he'd gone around to the back of the house where there were no windows. A breeze tripped by him, cool against his skin, bringing with it the scent of raw earth. Dew twinkled from the tips of weeds throughout the neglected field.

"Maxence?"

He pulled his shirt over his head and hurriedly tucked it in. Running a hand through his disheveled hair, he strode around the house toward where she stood in the doorway. She backed inside as he approached, hem whispering against the dirt.

It took a moment for his eyes to adjust to the dimness of the house. She stopped in the center of the room, hands wringing before her. The gown's long, fitted sleeves accentuated the curve of her arms. The soft hue of the silk drew more green from her eyes than usual. A timidity that he'd rarely seen graced her features. "You see? I'm nothing more than a carpenter's daughter in an elegant gown. They will see through the act in a moment."

"I think you look fine." Stunning, more like it. But he couldn't bring himself to say it. He crossed the room and laid his hands on her shoulders. "But you must relax." Her shoulders lowered a couple inches.

"The sleeves are far too long, and so is the skirt. I'll be treading on it the whole way."

"The style is supposed to be long." That's how the women dressed in Paris these days.

"The back needs padding," she went on, her pitch rising. "The skirts hang so limp." Well, he wasn't going to investigate that one. "And my shoes look ridiculous. They're not quality and terribly scuffed. Never mind that they are too practical to be fashionable."

Maxence squeezed her shoulders until she met his gaze. "I don't think anyone will see your shoes."

"How do you—"

"You said yourself that the skirt was long." He let go of her. "But I know of a few things we can do to add to the effect." He knelt by the peddler's pack.

"You cannot turn this Nantais into an *aristo*." She sat facing him, brows knit.

He picked through the cosmetic pots set out on the ground, unstopping the ones that hadn't broken. No pomatum or hair powder. It looked like only powders and paints for the face. "Take your hair down."

"Down?" She removed her cap and pulled pins out of the knot she'd just created that morning until she was left with a braid.

"Unwind it." Maxence mimed the motion of unbraiding.

She untied the ribbon before slowly pulling the strands apart until her soft, wavy hair fell around her shoulders.

"It's usually puffy and curly on top, but we don't have anything to help with that," he said. Armelle fluffed the hair near her scalp, then raised an eyebrow. "Now tie it together at the back with the ribbon."

"And just leave it long like this?" She pulled her hair over one shoulder. "Mère would think this terribly impractical." She set the cap back on her head and secured it with a pin.

"Now a little rouge, and no one will be able to tell if you're a baron's or carpenter's daughter." He held out the little jar the peddler had shown them the night before.

Armelle shrank back. "I don't know what to do with that."

Maxence laughed. "Surely you've at least tried wearing it."

Her head swung side to side. "Mère wouldn't allow us to spend money on such things."

"But your friends must have had some." Nobility weren't the only members of society who used cosmetics. "That girl from the prison?"

"Her family could never afford it." She wouldn't take the jar.

"Just dab some on your cheeks and lips. It isn't hard." He'd watched his mother do it plenty of times.

"Is this essential? I'll look ridiculous. I don't know how." She covered her cheeks with her hands. "I don't even have a mirror."

It wasn't essential, but it might help the Chouans see her as someone other than a humble traveler. "I could help you."

She fussed with the neckline of her gown, then brought her hands together and tapped them against her neck. "Very well," she huffed. "If it will add to the disguise."

"Come around here to get the light from the window." He crawled closer to the window and waited for her to follow. She finally scooted into the brightness, the orange rays lighting her face. She kept her eyes on the hearth as he opened the little pot and swiped his thumb across the creamy carmine pigment. He slid the rouge over her smooth cheek, keeping it toward the front of the face as he usually saw women do.

"Have you worn this before?" she asked.

His mouth twitched. "It isn't my style."

"Too *aristo* for a Jacobin."

He dipped his fingers in again and rubbed the color on her other cheek. Her face reddened under the rouge, and she looked anywhere except his eyes. The air around them grew harder to breathe, as though someone had suddenly sealed all the open windows. "I might have thought that."

He kept moving his thumbs in little circles over her cheeks, lighter and lighter as the color blended into her skin. She'd pressed her arms together, fists at her chest as if she were cold. Or scared. "Are you all right?" he asked. "Do you need a blanket?"

Her throat seemed to tighten as she swallowed. "No."

He set down the pot and cupped her face in his hands to survey his work. She didn't flinch. It was a passable job.

"How does it look?" she asked.

"You wouldn't believe a man had done it." Wisps of hair played across her brow. She slowly turned her eyes to him. Sunlight glittered in their green and brown depths, edged by misty grey, like a spring morning he never wanted to end. He drew his thumbs across her cheekbones, whose lifted shape made her look as though she always had a grin hidden just below the surface, waiting to break free.

"And now just the lips." His voice was husky, his mind fuddled, but whether from lack of sleep or the enchantment of dawn, he couldn't tell.

She licked her lips, catching her bottom lip between her teeth for a moment before releasing it full and soft. He took her chin in one hand and dipped his fingers in the little pot. A tiny dimple marked her chin, so faint he hadn't noticed it until now. He brushed the pigment across her upper lip, tracing the gentle curve. Her short breaths tickled his fingers.

A rising force within him, powerful and thrilling, insisted he close the gap between them. It compelled him to kiss her, to lose himself in the savor of Armelle Bernard. He'd never had such an intense desire to kiss someone. He'd always felt so in control of what he wanted. Now he held back with waning strength.

Why did he hold back? The man he'd been in Marseille wouldn't have given a second thought. If he wanted to kiss someone, he kissed them shamelessly and never regretted it. He eased the rouge over her bottom lip. Of its own accord, his finger went back to stroke the length of her lip once more.

The previous Maxence Étienne didn't hesitate. He'd kissed girls dozens of times—the reward for his assertiveness had been a flash of pleasure and a few *livres* from Émile. His friend almost always lost when wagering against him.

But it wasn't a game this time. There was more at stake than a little money and his pride. He'd thought his heart was securely beyond the reach of the tides of love, treading recklessly with no thought of the future. How unprepared he'd been to trip and fall, to lose himself along a Breton shore. Maxence slid his hand to the side of her face, searching her features for any sign of disgust.

Her gaze flicked to his mouth, and a question lit her eyes. The look dragged him in. The edge of his lip grazed hers, the barest connection, and he paused. She could pull away. She could run from this and all the terrifying things it would mean. Instead she sat still as the *menhir*. He slipped his hand down to her neck. Beneath his palm, her pulse raced in time with his.

He shouldn't do this. Their comfortable pretending would change to uncomfortable reality in an instant, bringing with it all the questions he hadn't wanted to consider yet.

Then he kissed her, and a thrill coursed up his spine like nothing he'd ever experienced.

Her lips stayed still, receiving the kiss but not giving anything back. Was she uncertain?

Dizzying energy pulsated through his body. How could she not experience this same acute sensation? He tenderly coaxed. Did she not feel anything for him?

Her hand rested on his at her neck. He halted his pleading kiss. She would run, and he'd be left to pick up the pieces of shattered hope. It would serve him right. He didn't deserve her love.

He tried to pull his hand away, but she held it there. Her lips parted against his as she drew in a breath. Then they pressed to his. He urged her closer, covering her lips, alive with the encouragement. Practically mad. Something was there in her careful heart. A place for him to belong.

She squeezed his hand, gave him one last timid kiss, and withdrew.

The reverie dissipated, its sparks scattering across the expanse of his captured mind. She got to her feet and wandered toward the window. She hugged herself as she looked outside, no sign of either elation or turmoil.

Maxence's hand fell to his lap, and he knelt where she left him, breathless. What had he done? And why hadn't he done it sooner? She'd hate him. Or love him. Both held complications he did not know how to navigate.

"I'm sorry," he said. "I just . . ." Just what? Lost his head.

"We need to get past the Chouans."

Blast the Chouans. He cleared his throat, pushing down the disappointment. Did she need a moment to make sense of what had just occurred? The thrill pulsing through him had morphed to agitation at her sudden stoic air. Barriers around her emotions had risen, walls he hadn't seen before. Perhaps he needed a moment to make sense of it too.

Very well. They'd pretend it hadn't happened. For now. And he'd try to be grateful at least one of them had kept their head. "We have half a plan."

"I think I have the other half." She turned from the window, that impish twinkle once again in her eye. This did not bode well for him. "If I must play the part of a noblewoman, then you must play the part of my servant." She put her hands on her hips.

He got to his feet. "That doesn't solve our problem of a young woman and young man traveling alone."

She nodded at the jars of cosmetics. "You will not be a *young* servant."

Maxence snorted. If they could get him to look old with what they had, that still didn't solve their problem. "An old man traveling with a young woman is worse. And it's still a man-woman pair they're looking for."

She folded her arms in front of her, nose in the air. "We won't be the man and woman they are looking for, because you will be my *gouvernante*."

His jaw went slack. Surely she was not asking him to play the part of her governess. But the look on her face read that she certainly was, and that there was no room for arguing. If he wanted her to take the safety of posing as an *aristo*, he had to accept her terms.

Maxence snapped his mouth shut. *Ciel.* This woman.

Armelle could not hold back her laughter. Whether it was giddiness from the . . . incident . . . or simply lack of sleep, it bubbled up inside her without relenting.

Maxence stood before her, one of her petticoats held about his waist, attempting to tie it on. "Is this how it goes?"

"And you call yourself a mariner." She pulled one of the bows out and retied it while he held the skirt up.

"*I* do not call myself a mariner. You do."

She set the tie on the other side to rights, then adjusted the skirt so the slits in either side weren't so gaping. It didn't quite fit him, but she hoped the bedgown would help cover it. "There. That should stay."

"Is it quite appropriate for a woman of my age to show this much boot?" He stuck his leg out from under the petticoat, revealing his black boot.

"I cannot help that you are much taller than I am." Armelle frowned. "You will need to hunch, it would seem."

"Very comfortable," he grumbled.

Armelle held up the bedgown her mother had given her before leaving. It was blue and striped and an utterly sensible garment with no shape to it. The long, baggy sleeves mostly fit over Maxence's shirt. "You'll have to roll up your sleeves." She unbuttoned his cuffs and rolled them part way up his arm, purposely avoiding touching his skin. The front edges of the bedgown crossed in front, and she made him hold it together while she tied her apron over it.

She stood back to survey her disgruntled friend's disguise. He looked ready to take back his kiss.

His kiss. The thought killed the giggle she had almost released at his indignant expression. His kiss had to wait for the spinning in her head to settle. How could she think about what had happened when their lives were in danger? He'd been a fool. Hours before, a man had nearly slit his throat, and he was back to his university games. A sour taste permeated her mouth. She had to make sense of it later.

"Your collar sticks out of the top. Can you tuck it in?"

"You won't do it? You've been doing everything else." He didn't sound like he particularly wanted her to do it, so she stayed where she was. He released the button at his throat and flipped the collar under. "Do you want it like this?"

She stepped forward and tried to make the edges of the bedgown overlap more, but his shoulders were too broad to allow much adjustment. His well-defined neck was still exposed to his collarbone. And it certainly did not look like that of an old woman. "My kerchief." She pulled it out of the market bag to tie around his neck.

Heady cinnamon from his soap wafted between them as she adjusted the kerchief to cover him. For an instant the thought he might kiss her again paralyzed her. She kept her gaze lowered. That's what had put her in trouble earlier—looking into his intensely dark eyes. He seemed distracted enough now by the humiliation she was putting him through.

"I have too much hair on my arms to be an old woman." He extended his hands. The sleeves didn't reach his wrists.

"We'll have to pray they let us through quickly. You can hide them under the cloak." She retrieved the white face paint and tried not to snicker.

"I didn't make you put paint on," he said, drawing back.

She cocked her head. "This isn't for your face. It's for your hair." She made him kneel as she swiped paint from the broken jar and raked it through his curls. When she was done, his hair was puffy and greying. "You look far more fashionable than I do." He tried to rise, but she hadn't finished. She retrieved the kohl and smeared the black powder under his eyes.

"I should have dark enough circles already," he mumbled.

She dragged the powder across the lines of his scowl, unsure if she was making him look old or simply dirty. "And now just a touch of rouge."

He threw up his hands. "I draw the line at rouge."

"Oh, come. You already have some on your lips from kissing . . ." Her. She turned away quickly.

"That is the only way I will accept the application of rouge, if you want me to wear more."

"You're right. I think you have enough." She glanced over her shoulder. He looked absolutely clownish. She hid a giggle with her hand. This had been a wiser plan than she'd realized. She didn't want to think about what they'd done that morning, not until she was far enough away from him to think clearly. In the meantime this disguise would keep her laughing and entirely too distracted to entertain the strange desire—one she was trying with all her fortitude to restrain—to kiss him again.

After a few hours of walking, Armelle let her fears ease. They'd expected to meet the band the peddler spoke of by now, but no militant rebels had appeared. Maxence had stopped them a few times, thinking the Chouans were upon them. So far they'd slinked past many of the Breton peasantry, but no one who cared about their bedraggled appearance or seemed to be looking for them. She'd never appreciated being ignored before.

Armelle stopped short as Maxence caught her hand once more. Thick stands of trees lined the road, but she couldn't see anything amiss. The hood of her cloak he wore cast his face in shadow.

"Did you see something?" He'd jumped at anything that moved all morning.

"*Chut*, Mademoiselle Savatier." His hand tensed around hers. They'd decided names and a story as they walked, and she hoped they wouldn't forget what they'd come up with should the Chouans appear. Perhaps the peddler's words had been hollow. Or the band of Chouans hadn't come to the road today.

"It might have been nothing." He urged her forward again, limping along beside her in a hunched position to hide his boots. All the crouching seemed to have aggravated his knee.

"Are you all right?"

He didn't reply. That wasn't a good sign.

Something moved up ahead, this time in the trees, and Armelle's stomach leaped into her throat. A lean figure sauntered into the road, a musket slung casually over his shoulder. Young and plainly dressed. Unmistakably a Chouan.

She shrank back against Maxence. It wasn't difficult to pretend fear. Maxence's life was forfeit if the disguises didn't work. She could face a similar fate if this proved one of the more violent bands who called themselves Chouans.

"Who are you?" the young man asked.

"Please don't hurt us," Armelle whined. If only she were as adept at bursting into tears as Cécile.

"Tell me who you are, and I will let you pass."

She could hardly believe that. She looked to Maxence as though for reassurance. He nodded under the cloak. She could barely see his face, he'd pulled the hood so far forward. "My name is Claire Savatier, and this is my servant, Florence. My father . . ." She covered her mouth with her hands. Heaven help her, she was a terrible actress. "They took my parents. Arrested them for helping the *chouannerie*." Armelle's eyes blurred as she forced forward images of her father being dragged off. They'd cowered before the République's soldiers. Now they cowered before the Chouans. Would they ever be safe?

The young man hesitated. "Where are you from?"

"My father's estate is near Châteaubriant." *Please let him not be from Châteaubriant.* "What is left of it."

Rustling in the brush announced the arrival of another young man. For a moment her heart leaped, as he had the same short build as Henri. But of course Henri was in Saint-Malo. With how spread out the various Chouan cells were, it was unlikely they'd even heard of her brother. A third form, and a fourth, joined them, and a fifth came from behind.

"Where are you traveling?" The first young man looked concerned, but the one she'd mistaken for Henri looked unconvinced.

"I have family in Rennes. I must find them." She blinked rapidly, but even though her eyes were wet, she could not get a tear to fall. "I have nothing left."

"Filthy *patriotes*," the man behind them snarled.

"I am sorry for your loss, *mademoiselle*." How strange to hear that address. In Nantes, a city fully under control of the République, calling the wrong person *mademoiselle* or *monsieur* could get the perpetrator landed in the coffee warehouse prison. He looked at her long and hard, and it felt as though he could see through every disguise. Then he nodded sharply. "We will escort you to your relatives in Rennes."

"Oh." Her tongue refused to work. No, they didn't want that. They wanted to part ways and get rid of their disguises.

"Stay here with the others," he said to the one who looked like her brother. "I'll take Prado. We'll be back before it's time to leave."

"When will Tanet return?"

The first young man, who appeared to lead the group, shrugged. "Perhaps we will meet him on the road."

"You are too kind," Armelle said. Her voice squeaked terribly. "I do not wish to trouble you. If the road continues on to Rennes, I believe we shall make it on our own."

The leader's face darkened. "We've been warned of a rogue soldier on these roads. Violent and thieving. We can't allow you to travel unguarded."

Rogue soldier. They must mean Maxence. She dug her fingernails into the too-long sleeves. Praise heaven she'd convinced him to leave the peddler's pack at the house with any of the goods they weren't using. "We are very grateful."

The leader bowed. "May I take your bag, *mademoiselle*?"

Armelle's hand tightened around the twisted handle of the bag. If she let him carry it, they couldn't run if needed. She glanced back at Maxence, but she couldn't see much of him with how far he'd retreated under the cloak.

"Let her carry her own bag," one of the others said. It earned him a glare from his leader.

"She has had a trying few days, can you not see that?" He offered her his arm. "Keep your bag if you are more comfortable. We will see you safely settled."

She carefully took his arm. To refuse would be rude, and a woman of her pretended station would be used to such gestures. Though perhaps not from plainly dressed ruffians? She hardly knew. No one had showed her such deference before. Bowing and offering his arm. Only her father had ever treated her in such a way.

"I shall send to Châteaubriant to see if anything can be done for your parents," he said as he led her forward. She listened for the sound of Maxence and the other Chouans following. The footsteps seemed no more than a few paces away, but the distance felt vast in the midst of men who would wish Maxence harm. "The Chouans have very little concentrated force, but we have our ways of protecting what is ours."

The market bag thumped awkwardly against her back, threatening to slip off her silk-coated shoulder as she tried to lift her excessively long skirts and hold to his arm while she walked. The hem must be in shreds by now. It certainly had not been made to travel in.

"You must tell us all you remember. Names, descriptions, what they said." The leader didn't look much older than Armelle. He had light hair and a kind look to his face, though serious. "It will help us find your parents and determine how to help them."

"Yes, of course." These young men didn't act like killers.

"I am Evennou. I'm glad we found you before someone else did." He kept his arm sturdy, guiding her at a polite distance to not be forward rather than pulling her close. "We sometimes get patrols from the army and the Territorial Guards. The latter is especially ruthless. Though, you would know that, as I'm sure they were at your father's arrest."

"I am incredibly grateful." At least she would be if they made it to Rennes undetected.

"May I help you, *madame*?" someone asked behind them.

"*Non, citoyen.*" Maxence's attempt at an old feminine voice was so terrible, she almost laughed.

Evennou stilled. Armelle went rigid. *Citoyen*! Her breath halted in her throat. Evennou whipped her around. His companion, Prado, grabbed Maxence's arm and jerked back. In his unstable stance, Maxence stumbled and fell, the cloak's hood flying back. The boots he wore poked out from under the petticoat.

"We don't speak that way here, *monsieur*." Prado spat out the last word.

The Chouans they'd left a few paces up the road ran forward. One pulled a pistol from his waistband, and another fixed a bayonet. Armelle's scream caught in her throat as visions of another bayonet— one meant for her demise—glinted across her memory, Martel's jeering face looming behind it. Prado's expression rivaled Martel's as he hauled Maxence to his feet. She tried to jerk away from Evennou, her only thought to get between Maxence and the Chouans.

"Run!" Maxence shouted.

But Evennou had her by both arms and dragged her back toward the others. The market bag fell to the ground. She dug in her heels and thrashed, but she couldn't break his grip.

Maxence landed a facer, sending Prado reeling. In moments the other three Chouans surrounded him, bayonet to his throat. He struggled but stilled when they pressed with the bayonet.

"Say another word, *patriote*, and you're finished."

"No, stop!" Armelle cried. She wrenched against Evennou's hold.

"He's the soldier that old man was talking about." Prado rubbed his jaw, staring daggers at Maxence. "We should dispose of him and be done."

Dispose of him. Bile rose in Armelle's throat. That's what Maxence had been instructed to do with her. Secluded wood, bullet to the head, problem solved. Her knees threatened to buckle. "Please. My brother is a Chouan."

Evennou ignored her. "What would we do with his wife if we shot him?" he asked Prado, voice even.

"The same thing the *révolutionnaires* have done with wives of *royalistes*. They usually get the same fate."

"Or they're left to their own devices," Evennou said.

Prado folded his arms, clearly not appreciating his leader's implication. "Let her go on to family in Rennes."

"My brother is Henri Bernard," Armelle said, raising her voice. Its shrill desperation rang through the trees. How could they know him? The Chouans' small cells scattered about the region operated according to their leaders' whims and rarely interacted. "He has been a member of the *chouannerie* in Saint-Malo since last spring."

"You will forgive us, *madame*, if we do not believe you," Evennou said. He didn't know Henri. Her hope shattered against the ground. "Bind them."

One Chouan ran to the edge of the brush and brought back some lengths of rope. The Chouans wrestled Maxence to the ground when he wouldn't hold still for them to bind his wrists.

"Evennou, please," Armelle said as the leader tied her hands behind her. Her words came out in gasps. "This isn't what it seems."

"Nothing is anymore."

The Chouans opened the market bag and clothes bundle, and it wasn't long before they found the national guard coat, which Maxence had carefully stuffed into the coat from Père Quéré.

Armelle's pulse rang in her ears as Prado waved the condemning

wool like a flag. "Now can we shoot them? I feel that's evidence enough."
They hauled Maxence back to his feet. Dust from the road coated the
clothes he'd borrowed.

"Let her go," Maxence said. "She has nothing to do with the army."

"She's your wife," a Chouan said. "She has plenty to do with the
army."

"The peddler was misinformed. We are not married." He didn't look
at her. His tone came out flat, defeated, and the pang that shook her
heart took her breath away.

"More lies."

"If I was married, why would I be in the army?" Maxence said. "The
levée en masse only extended to unmarried men."

"There are plenty of married zealots," Prado said.

Armelle rounded on Evennou, swallowing back the sudden ache.
"He was taking me to Saint-Malo to find my brother. My brother evaded
the *levée*." Henri was too far to be of use. How could she hope they'd
know him?

The leader searched her face. He gave no hint as to what he found.
"We are not barbarians. Blindfold them and take them back to the
house. Bring their things."

A chance. She stared at Maxence, who focused on the ground. One
of Evennou's men tied a handkerchief around her eyes, cutting off her
view of Maxence's despondency. Prickles ran up her neck. He thought
they were only delaying the inevitable.

"What will we do with them there?"

"We wait for Tanet. He was in Saint-Malo until December. If he
can confirm their connection, we'll send her on her way." Only her?

"Maxence?" she cried, like a little child afraid of the dark. She
wanted to trust the goodness she sensed in Evennou, but his palpable hatred for all Maxence stood for threatened that trust. She wouldn't leave
without him. Not after all they'd been through. If they let her go, she'd
have to find a way to bring him with her. Evennou pulled her forward,

and she fought to breathe. What was she thinking? There were too many Chouans. They couldn't escape.

"And if he can't confirm her story?"

Evennou halted her. "Step up."

Armelle reached out with her foot and found the incline where the ground banked at the edge of the road. She tripped on her skirts as they climbed, and Evennou steadied her.

"If he can't speak for her, then we can all expect an unpleasant evening. But I think our new friends will get the worst of it."

CHAPTER 22

"Your companion is not very trusting," Evennou said, settling onto the floor a few paces from Armelle. She sat with her back against the stone wall of a very small cottage, even smaller than the one they'd stayed in the evening before.

They'd allowed Maxence to go wash his face and hair with three of the Chouans to guard him. As they left, he'd threatened to wring Evennou's neck if he laid a finger on her, earning Maxence a cuff from one of his guards.

"He's been through many difficult things." She fiddled with the ropes that tied her hands, not expecting to loosen them. Evennou had taken pity after her attempts to pick her way through underbrush in long skirts. He'd retied her hands in front of her so she could at least lift her hem to keep from tripping.

"If he is not your husband, what relation is he to you?"

That was getting more difficult to determine. A friend, certainly. One she'd met in the worst of circumstances. But had it become more than that? He seemed to want it to. Or perhaps he was just missing his old ways. The thought sent her heart on a downward spiral. "He rescued me."

Evennou scratched his chin. "What did he rescue you from?"

"Execution."

The Chouan waited. Armelle sighed and related Maxence's decision to not follow his orders, his arrest, and their escape. Evennou didn't interrupt, only nodded from time to time.

"He has family in Saint-Malo, and I wish to find my brother," she finished. "We aren't causing trouble for anyone. The peddler attacked us last night."

"He isn't the most honorable man." Evennou stretched his legs out across the dirt floor. "I admit, you had us fooled for a few minutes."

"Can you blame us for trying to survive?" The afternoon was still bright through the narrow windows. A thought sent icy dread through her heart. What if they took him out there to shoot him? She couldn't say how long they'd been gone. From where she sat, she could see only blue sky through the windows, no view of the stream. She straightened, but it did little to help her see.

"He'll be back." Evennou got to his feet and went to the hearth. "We are not such villains as the Jacobins."

Armelle couldn't wrap her arms around herself. It wasn't a very cold day, but the stone house suddenly felt frigid. She wanted to believe him as much as Evennou seemed to want to believe her, but this conflict had brought too many surprises. "Some Chouans have done terrible things."

He knelt and gathered kindling. "Not as many as Jacobins have." They agreed on that point. He went quiet as he started the fire. "Your friend, is he a *sans-culotte* or Jacobin?"

She hoped not a *sans-culotte*. The radical group of lower-class *révolutionnaires* had wreaked havoc throughout France in the name of freedom. Smaller and more disorganized than the Jacobins, their leaders could whip them into a frenzy with little effort. Many had met their end at the hands of the *sans-culotte* mobs, some without reason. "He has never said." But he had been a *fédéré* at the Tuileries. That would not win him affection among this royalist bunch.

"He seems to still believe in the cause of the République, despite the fact it has turned its back on him," Evennou said.

"His superiors wronged him, not the country he believes in." At least not in Maxence's eyes.

Evennou added sticks to the fire. "I suppose I can understand that."

In other circumstances, she might have befriended this man. What was supposed to be an interrogation felt more like a conversation between new acquaintances. He seemed rational, careful, and honest, not prone to brash outbursts. Like her mother. Mère would much rather she bring home a young man like Evennou than one like Maxence, with his fierce passion and uncertainty. She squirmed at the bizarre feeling that accompanied that idea. A part of her wanted to bring home a man like Maxence.

"Where does your allegiance lie?"

She leaned forward. "My allegiance lies with my family and the people I love. As long as they are safe, I couldn't care who has power."

Evennou nodded as he poked the fire with a stick, pushing the flames back farther in the little hearth. "A relatable sentiment."

The door opened, and Maxence entered, his hair and shirt wet. His eyes instantly went to her. Did the worry in them mirror her own?

"You see?" Evennou said. "You are both safe."

Maxence sat clumsily beside her, hands tied once again behind his back. One of the Chouans brought in her clothes he'd been wearing and set them atop the market bag. Maxence dipped his head toward her. "You are sure he didn't—"

"Yes." She drew her attention away from how the wet shirt clung to the lines of his chest.

Prado grunted. "Should we separate them?" Armelle's gaze darted to the leader. Voicing displeasure could make separation more likely.

Evennou stepped away from the fire and brushed off his trousers. "They won't try to escape unless they want to be shot. Leave them be." How different Evennou and Prado were. Prado was a large young man with a dark scowl that read he'd just as soon beat a person than look at them. The leader was of a much slighter build with a hard-to-decipher expression.

Maxence's shoulder met hers. The touch steadied her, and the coiled tension inside her eased.

"Get food on the fire," Evennou said. "Tanet will be back soon, and then we're off."

"What will we do with them?" Prado nodded at their prisoners. One Chouan brought over a pot, and another pulled open the lid of a nearby chest.

"We can bring them with us, or I will stay to guard them."

"Bring them?" Prado cried. "We can't bring them."

An owl hooted in the distance. The Chouans paused in their work, listening to the signal of one of their own approaching.

"Roulin, watch the prisoners." All the Chouans except the one she'd mistaken for her brother quickly exited the house. Roulin followed them and stood in the doorway.

"Their friend must have returned," Armelle whispered. Her chest constricted. Their fate would be decided on whether or not this man knew of her brother. Never mind Saint-Malo could be swarming with Chouans.

A lock of wet hair tickled her temple. His breath warmed her cheek. Suddenly sitting near him brought a strange electricity to her skin, one she couldn't tell if she adored or regretted. The close proximity had never affected her like this before.

"When were you planning to tell me your brother was a Chouan?"

She bristled at the accusation in his question. "Does it matter what he is?"

"It does matter. He's a traitor."

Henri, a traitor. She drew in a sharp breath, battling the hot flames that had erupted inside her. "And you are not?" She leaned away from him so they no longer touched. "You are very bold to say that aloud, given the situation you are in. Some of these men would not mind dol-ing out revenge for their many grievances suffered at the hands of your comrades." And if they asked her just now to join them in thrashing Maxence, there was a high likelihood she would.

How dare he suggest Henri was anything less than an honorable man fighting for what he believed to be right. And how dare he expect her to tell him everything about her life. As much as they had pretended, he was not her husband or anything close to family. That kiss had proved the ruse had gone too far.

"They can't hear me."

"While we are on the topic of things we are entitled to know, why did you feel you had any right to kiss me this morning?" she hissed. "I thought you were joking about the girls at home."

"Kissing you . . . That was not one of my games."

The fire kept rising. "Games?" She scoffed. "That's what kissing is to you?" Her eyes burned. He'd teased her that first night in Savenay, belittling her desire to kiss only the man she'd marry.

"It might have been once." His eyes widened at the slip.

"How many girls have you kissed?" she demanded before he could amend his admission.

He'd confessed to breaking dozens of hearts, but surely that was boasting. "I . . ." He groaned. "I don't know, Armelle. I can't remember."

Her brows shot up of their own accord. "You can't remember?" Jean-Baptiste had warned her, hadn't he? She had refused to listen.

"But I promise you, Armelle, that was not what I meant by kissing you. This was different."

"How was it any different from what you inflicted on all those girls back home?" What was taking the Chouans so long? If she didn't think they'd shoot her for trying to escape, she'd make for the door.

"You are not like them."

She ground her teeth. "Am I not? Perhaps you should have tried to know them better, and you would have found that I'm not so dissimilar; you were just an oaf." She scooted away, keeping her gaze straight ahead.

"Armelle." His pleading made her eyes smart. She didn't know why.

"I didn't want it. You *knew* I didn't want it." She'd told him in

Savenay, in the darkness under the light of one persistent star. He should have remembered. She shouldn't be reminding him after the deed.

But that small piece of her, the one she wouldn't acknowledge, murmured her words might be lies. She leaned her head back against the bumpy stone wall and closed her eyes, trying to breathe away the torrent within that threatened to come out as tears.

Maxence stared. The words wouldn't come. Refutations, pleas, reasonings—they all died on his tongue. She'd returned that kiss. Hesitantly, it was true. But she had. He tore his gaze from the light that trailed down her long hair and the way the silk of her dress smoothed over her shoulder.

Perhaps this was why he'd been satisfied with the games. Committing nothing in a kiss hurt far less than pledging all and having it thrown back in his face.

She didn't want it. "I'm sorry," he said, almost whispering. "I misunderstood." What an idiot he was. He'd wanted so badly for her to love him, it had muddled his reasoning.

Voices grew louder, coming toward the house, and Roulin stepped back in.

"You imbeciles!" came a voice from outside. "Bernard is going to skin us alive." A red-haired man burst through the entrance and blinked before locating Armelle against the wall. "Mademoiselle Bernard, you have my sincerest apologies. Let us get you out of those." So he did know Armelle's brother. Whatever they decided to do with Maxence, she would be safe. The relief didn't flow into him like it should have.

Tanet helped her to her feet and tugged at the knots on her bindings. "You know Henri?" she asked breathlessly. The rope fell, and she massaged her wrists.

"It has been a few months since we last met a supply shipment from the islands, but I left him quite well in Saint-Malo." Tanet laughed.

"You look like him. He spoke of you so often, it's almost as if we've already met."

She took the man's arm, face glowing. Maxence's stomach twisted. "You must tell me about Saint-Malo. I have been longing to see it for so long."

"What about him?" Prado asked, motioning with his head toward Maxence.

They could leave him in the corner, and he would be content. It was where he always got left. The corner of everyone's mind.

"Can Mademoiselle Bernard speak for him?" Tanet said. He led her to the one chair in the house.

"He's on the run from the République," Evennou said, arms crossed as he regarded Maxence. So she'd told the leader everything. Something about that grated against Maxence's nerves. "That should make us allies."

And yet it didn't. He believed removing the king had been the best course of action for France, and they wanted their royalty, with its erratic spending and disregard for its subjects, put back in place.

"I think we all know that isn't how alliances have worked in recent years," Prado said.

Evennou considered Maxence, then Armelle. "Keep a watch at all times. But we can let him loose."

"Oh, yes. He is no threat to you." She did not look at Maxence when she said it but waved a hand in his direction. It was as though she'd embraced the role of nobleman's daughter and was assuring her subjects of the harmlessness of her pampered pup. She folded her hands in her lap and leaned forward. Tanet and the others had the whole of her focus. "Are there many Chouans in Saint-Malo?"

"More than here, certainly."

Prado grudgingly untied Maxence. "If you try anything, I won't hesitate to shoot," he muttered under his breath.

"Understood." He had nothing to do with his newfound freedom but make himself presentable. Not that he had anyone to impress.

Maxence went to their pile of belongings, most of it Armelle's, and pulled out his waistcoat, neckcloth, and the coat Quéré had given him. The sense that someone was watching him was unnerving, but he pretended not to notice as he knotted the cloth at his neck. When he lifted his head, Armelle turned away quickly.

The gown did become her. The rich sage silk brought out the green in her eyes, the looseness of her hair and its gentle wave gave a sense of elegant ease, and the gown's cut accentuated her figure in ways that drew all the men's eyes. For once, despite the style being the height of fashion in Paris, Maxence found he hated it. This wasn't the Armelle he knew. Instead of impish and carefree, she suddenly seemed grand and coy.

"Our soldier friend looks ready to go to a wedding," one of the Chouans said.

"No one is going to a wedding." Maxence went back to where he'd been sitting and leaned against the wall. These men would watch him carefully until they sent him on his way, but he wanted nothing more than to be alone.

"Everyone is going to a wedding," Evennou said from his place near the hearth. He tended the fire as one of the others added to a pot sitting above it. "We will take you on to Rennes in the morning."

"Hirel's sister was married this afternoon," Tanet said to Armelle. "He is the seventh member of our band. We're attending the celebrations tonight."

Maxence cringed. A wedding celebration was the last place he wanted to go.

After a simple vegetable soup, Armelle asked to be allowed to change. Maxence stood with the other men outside the house, the Chouans giving him suspicious glances and Maxence silently vowing harm should any get too close to the windows. She practically sprang from the house in petticoat and jacket, her hair twisted out of the way in her usual style. She sighed and smiled. "Shall we, *messieurs?*" She'd taken off the anger from before like she had the silk dress, replacing it with her usual merry self.

As she walked along beside him, it was as though she'd forgotten everything that had happened between them, from the kiss to the argument. But things couldn't go back to the way they were before, no matter how badly he wished it.

Maxence found himself sitting at the edge of a little square in a nearby hamlet as the sky darkened, a bowl of *cidre* in his hands. The low drone of *biniou* bagpipes and vibrato of the trumpet-like *talabard* rang through the gathering, most of whom were dressed in brightly embroidered and trimmed costumes. Armelle had stayed near him when they first arrived, telling him about the foreign music and dance despite his lack of enthusiastic response. When their captors had invited her to join them, she'd eagerly bounded into the chaos without a backward glance.

Now she talked and laughed and twirled before him, and Maxence wished he had something stronger than *cidre*. With no more delays, they would make it to Saint-Malo in a few days. And then . . . what? If she meant to stay with her brother, she would get involved with the Chouans. He could never be part of that. He'd work for his uncle and wait for an opportunity to leave. Perhaps if he went back to Marseille, he could put her out of his head, but he did not know if he could stomach living with his mother again. Things could never be the same, even if Gilles had left.

The song ended, and Armelle cheered with the rest of them. She said something excitedly to Evennou, who'd danced at her side. Tanet joined them from the other side of the circle, and Maxence wondered if he could make it back to the Chouans' dwelling on his own. They hadn't made it easy to remember the path—he suspected on purpose.

Armelle broke herself away from the gathering and scampered toward him. Maxence corrected his slouch, attempting an unconcerned visage. She sank to the ground next to him, out of breath and beaming.

"I haven't enjoyed myself this much in years," she said. "This never happens in Nantes anymore."

Thanks to people who believed as he did. He passed her his bowl of *cidre*, and she drank thirstily. She handed it back, licking her lips. "Why do you not dance? I'm certain you are an excellent dancer."

"I'm unfamiliar with these." He and Émile had participated in celebrations of the revolution in Paris, but he hadn't had the heart to dance since Émile's death.

"They are easy to learn." She folded her legs under her skirts and rested her elbows atop her knees. "So much has happened today."

They'd gone from fearing for their lives to celebrating with their captors. He'd shown her his heart, and she'd run from it. Yes, this day had lasted far too long.

"Maxence." She held up the wood die.

"Do you not think we've answered enough questions today?" He finished the *cidre* and set down the bowl. The square before them undulated with orange torchlight and blue shadow, like an early dawn on a sleepy sea. Laughter and conversation filled the space the *biniou* and *talabard* had vacated. They were in the midst of civil war. France was tearing itself apart while also attempting to stave off invasion, yet here in the niches of Brittany was true contentment. A contentment he couldn't be part of.

"I still have a question I'd very much like answered."

Why was she doing this to him? "Ah, yes. You wanted to know what happened with Gilles. Well, there isn't much to tell. He refused to come with us, I told him I couldn't care if he lived or died, and neither of us tried to reconcile before we left. Though I fear I was the most to blame, looking back." He always seemed to be the most to blame.

"But you did care, didn't you? You care for Gilles very much."

Maxence picked up a stick at his feet and snapped it in half. "Yes. His refusal felt like a betrayal."

"It is very difficult to act kindly when you feel you have been wronged." Her brows pulled together.

"And yet you do it at every turn." Maxence spread his hands. "These Chouans captured you and took you to their quarters, threatening to end you. Here we are a few hours later, and you're dancing and laughing and carrying on with these same men. Colbert offended you with his words, and you quickly reconciled. I dragged you out of town to . . ." His stomach soured. He couldn't think about what would have happened if he'd been bold enough to follow orders.

"Most people could use a little more forgiveness." She nudged him. "I do not think the clergyman back in Nantes would agree with your assessment of me."

The corners of his mouth curled, but he quickly reined them in. "Meanwhile I hold onto perceived wrongs for years."

"Perhaps you do not know everything that was going on in your family's lives."

"Perhaps not." But Gilles had always confided in him. Maman had too for a time. The last letter she'd sent had been full of emptiness, despite her many words. Even at such a distance, he could tell they all held things back from him.

"I think your family misses you."

Maxence dropped the pieces of stick to the ground and kicked them away. "I don't know if I believe that."

"How could they not?" She reached for his arm, then retracted her hand. An instant of anticipation withered, but limiting their touch was wise. "I hope in Saint-Malo you are able to reconsider your life and your family." She rested her chin on her fist. "I know I'd give anything to see mine again."

The revelers gathered for another dance. Armelle made no move to stand.

"That was not the question I was going to ask if I won the toss," she said, holding up the die again.

He took the little cube, turned it, and set it in her palm with two dots pointing up. "What is your question?" He didn't want to ask the question burning in his mind. He didn't know how he would form it into words, and what's more, he already knew the answer. She didn't want him the way he wanted her.

"Can you ever forgive me for not feeling as you do?"

He let out a mirthless laugh. "There is nothing to forgive. I wouldn't want to force you to feel something you don't."

"I don't know how I could have survived this separation from my family without your friendship, Maxence."

He nodded. She'd been the bright spot that pushed away all the despair at losing his place in the army and the future he thought he'd wanted.

"We are nearly to Saint-Malo. Let us put it behind us and be friends." She stood and brushed off her skirts. Then she reached a hand toward him. "Come, let's dance this *passepied* with the rest of them."

He hesitated before taking her hand. She yanked him up and dragged him to the circle. The music began as she explained, and it wasn't long before he picked up the simple steps. The swinging arms and stomping and jumping washed away some of the weight he carried in his heart. Armelle's grin should have taken the rest of it, except that her vivacity had caused so much of the hurt. He didn't know what could purge that burden. Time had already proven it couldn't heal his wounds.

CHAPTER 23

Half-timbered houses, with their intricate patterns of beams and plaster, greeted Armelle and Maxence as they made their way through Rennes. Though the day was cloudy and threatened a spring rain, the many-storied buildings seemed to smile as they crowded together, watching people passing below. They had weathered many a storm in the last few hundred years and could attest the sun always shone again.

Armelle swung the bundle of clothing on her arm. She and Maxence had mended things quite well the night before. The kiss could be forgotten, as though it never had happened. She didn't have time to fantasize about such things as men and marriage. She was going to Saint-Malo to bring her family back together, or at least to figure out a plan to do so. A man stepping into the picture, even a man as wonderful as Maxence Étienne, would upset things forever. Yes, she had to reunite her family before she let herself entertain such thoughts.

Maxence left her in the street as he entered a shop to ask for directions to the inn his uncle frequented when in Rennes for business. A little way down the road, a unit of soldiers marched before a carriage. A piper and drummer accompanied them, the piper playing a stirring tune she quickly recognized. It had spread throughout France the last couple of years and was known as "La Marseillaise."

"Did I tell you I was there when this was introduced?" Maxence appeared beside her.

"'La Marseillaise'? No, you didn't."

He nodded. "It was at a banquet when they first called for *fédérés*. Gilles and Émile were there as well."

"They named it after you, then." The impulse to sidle up next to him hit her stronger than it should have. He would take that as flirtation. She couldn't do something so heartless. "You are one of the Marseillais."

He shrugged. "I suppose."

"It's a beautiful song." She leaned forward to see the carriage better. "I can see why it would make someone wish to join the fight."

Maxence's hand clamped around her arm. "We need to get out of the road." His ashen face as he stared at the coach gave her gooseflesh. She'd seen that look too many times.

He dove into the crush of people lining the road, and she followed him. His long legs put him many steps ahead. "Maxence, wait!" She lunged for his hand and finally caught it. He pulled her into an alley as the carriage and soldiers passed.

"That's Voulland." He pressed his back to the wall.

"Who?" He looked like a military leader from the glimpse she got. Fine coat and gold buttons like the ones on Maxence's uniform.

"He's the reason we're in this mess." He sighed when the coach disappeared from view.

"I thought *I* was the reason we were in this mess."

"He's the one who gave me my orders."

Armelle stuck her head out of the alley to stare at the coach continuing to the center of the city. "From Nantes?" She remembered him and the rage in his eyes as he had helped the *répresentat* she'd battered with her water pail.

"I forgot he was to head north. It's a wonder we didn't pass him on the road." Maxence swiped a hand down his face. "Let's find the inn. I do not want to be in the streets if Froment is here."

They located the Chapeau Rouge, and Maxence suggested they eat before the masses descended on the inn for evening merriment. They had a small amount of money from selling the dress Armelle had worn to a modiste, who had greedily taken the silk without asking questions earlier in the day. Maxence had said in prime condition the dress would have cost twice as much. The thought of wearing something so expensive made Armelle a little ill.

"We might be able to afford a room for tonight," she said as they ate. The inn was quiet, with only a few patrons. Mugs chinked, and conversation murmured. After the crowds in the street, the corner they shared felt like a haven.

"That would be terribly expensive, given our funds." Maxence tore off a piece of the dense bread. "I thought we decided a stable would suit us. It would certainly be better than a barn."

"You haven't slept in a real bed since Nantes," she said. "And haven't had a mattress since Savenay. We can afford one night."

He furrowed his brow. "We cannot afford two rooms. Where do you plan to sleep?"

She lifted a shoulder. "The floor."

The door opened behind her. She turned to see a large man stride through it. He had greying hair and a stern set to his mouth.

"I do not mind sleeping on the floor," Maxence said, pulling back her attention.

Did he always have to do the noble thing? Even when she was trying to give him something. "I can take my turn once in a while." The bean soup before her had little taste and too much broth, but it was as hearty a food as they'd had since leaving Père Quéré's.

Maxence inclined his head. "Or we could find a stable where we'd both at least have hay to sleep on."

"Maxence Étienne," a deep voice said, practically in her ear. The hair on her neck stood on end. Who knew him in Rennes? They both bounded to their feet. Maxence grabbed for their bags. "*Que diable!* What are you doing here?"

The man who had just walked in stood at their table, arms outstretched. "Oncle Oscar?" Maxence cried.

The stranger seized Maxence's hand and pulled him in, thumping his back. Armelle's mouth fell open.

"I knew you were an Étienne the moment I walked in. What are you doing in Rennes, *neveu*? You are the last thing I expected to find here. We all thought you were in Paris."

Maxence scanned the room. "Many things have happened since then. We are on our way to Saint-Malo, but we are trying not to draw attention."

His uncle nodded gravely. "We can speak in my room when you've finished. And who is this?" He arched his eyebrow, interest twinkling in his eye.

"This is my friend, Armelle Bernard."

His uncle bowed grandly, and Armelle bobbed a curtsy. "Your friend, or your *friend*?" He had the same olive skin and curly hair as Maxence. They were of similar height as well, though Maxence did not have his uncle's girth.

"Friend," Maxence mumbled, and Armelle winced at his discomfort. It would grow less awkward the further they got from the incident.

Oncle Oscar stayed standing while they quickly finished and gathered their things. As he led them up the stairs, Armelle felt her spirits soar with each step. They'd found help. They'd found family. And soon they'd find safety in Saint-Malo.

"Do you have rooms for the night?" Oscar asked, ushering them into his room. It was clearly the nicest the inn had to offer, large and with a view of the street and a church not far away.

Maxence sat on the bed, letting Armelle take the chair by the writing desk. "We hadn't decided where to sleep yet."

Oscar stepped back out into the hall and called for the chambermaid to prepare two more rooms. Armelle looked ready to burst, her eyes round and a grin lighting her face.

"Can you believe it?" she whispered. "We found your family."

"We were going to find him in a few days regardless," Maxence said. But an early meeting was a stroke of luck. They hadn't had many of those on this journey, between his injury, her illness, and the run-ins with the peddler and Chouans. Fate owed them a good hand after all that.

Oscar returned and closed the door. "It is all settled. You will have the next two rooms down this hall."

"You are very kind, *monsieur*," she said.

"*Citoyen*," Maxence corrected. They weren't in the countryside anymore.

Oscar chuckled and sat on the bed next to him. "*Citoyen, monsieur*, it is all the same to me." He removed his cloak. "Now, before you tell me how you came to be here, I must ask . . ." The man sighed. "How is Gilles?"

Maxence's eyes narrowed. How was he to know? "He's well, I suppose." Not that his mother had said much about his brother since he left.

"I haven't been able to see him for a couple of months, but Jeanne sends food every so often. I think she visits as well, but who can blame her?" His grave expression lightened with the hint of a smile.

Maxence blinked. "Gilles is . . . in Saint-Malo?" He glanced at Armelle, whose brows shot up. How could that be? His mother had never mentioned it. What would convince him to remove to Saint-Malo?

Oscar reared back. "For more than a year now. How did you not know?" He blanched. "Then you . . . You don't know about . . ."

"About what?" Maxence's mind spun. He'd been preparing himself for a potential meeting with Père, not a certain meeting with Gilles. Bile rose in his throat.

Oscar dropped his head to his hand. "I should not be the one to tell you. There's too much. Go visit Gilles."

Gilles was supposed to be in Montpellier studying medicine. Or conscripted into the army. At the very least back working for their father.

Oscar wiped at his mouth and shook his head. "How long has it been since you last wrote to your family?"

"A few months." At least six since he'd responded.

"Maxence!" Armelle cried. "It's been so long?"

He could only nod. He should have written from Nantes, but there wouldn't have been time to get an answer before he left. Gilles had moved to Saint-Malo a year ago. There had been plenty of time, plenty of letters, that could have informed him.

"Are you from Rennes, *mademoiselle*?"

"No. We are on the run from Nantes."

Maxence raked a hand through his hair. He couldn't make sense of it. Armelle told their story, but he didn't register the words or his uncle's reaction. Somehow his younger brother had evaded the *levée en masse*. Their mother would have mentioned something in her last letter if he'd married. Wouldn't she, as his mother, afford him at least that small courtesy? It seemed too large a thing to forget to include. As did his brother's moving across the country. His family's lives had changed dramatically, and they hadn't considered him worthy of the information.

"You may stay with us as long as needed, *c'est naturel*," his uncle said. "Saint-Malo has a reputation for welcoming the outcasts of society." He winked.

The noise from below had increased since they'd ascended to Oscar's room. Dark had crept in through the window. Oscar lit a candle on the desk, and the maid came in to start a fire.

"I think I should retire," Maxence said, rising.

"You've had a long journey," Oscar said. He stood and grasped Maxence's shoulder. "Get some rest. Tomorrow's journey I hope will be much easier. I'll bring you back to Saint-Malo with me, of course. We'll leave as early as we can, as I have business to attend to."

Maxence nodded and scooped up the market bag. Armelle thanked Oscar enthusiastically. Maxence agreed that the service to them warranted such thanks, but he did not have the fortitude to give it. In the corridor he exchanged the market bag for the bundle Armelle carried.

"Are you well?" she asked.

"Yes, of course." It was as though someone had tied rope around his chest. His lungs wouldn't expand as they should.

"How will you sleep in a room all to yourself?" Her grin didn't shed any light into his soul like it usually did.

"I will manage." He bade her goodnight, reminded her to bolt the door, and took the room farthest from his uncle. If something threatened her, he or Oscar would hear it.

There wasn't a fireplace in his room, and he didn't bother figuring out how to light the candle provided. He fell back onto the bed after removing his coat and boots. It wasn't very soft, but compared to what he'd slept on for the last two years, it should have felt like heaven.

Gilles's face wouldn't leave his mind, the shattered expression he'd worn when Maxence slammed the bedroom door. How could he hope for forgiveness? If anyone in his family had wanted to bestow it, they would have shared their lives with him.

He didn't have Armelle's incessant chatter to distract him tonight. His ear strained for the sound of the die hitting the floor. As the night closed in, so did the emptiness. Emptiness he hadn't felt since before seeing Armelle's face through the prison bars that fateful morning when providence reminded him there was at least one soul on the earth who cared whether Maxence Étienne lived or died.

CHAPTER 24

Maxence had never entered Saint-Malo by road. It always took a long time to dock *le Rossignol* after seeing land, but this journey into Saint-Malo seemed to last an age.

He sat beside Armelle with Oncle Oscar across the coach. Her face stayed glued to the windows throughout the day as she told them how rarely she'd ridden in coaches, all about her brothers and sisters, and how much better their current situation was from walking.

At every milestone, his stomach knotted a little tighter. Oncle Oscar insisted he take them to Gilles the moment they arrived, but he wouldn't hint as to why. He either badly wished for the brothers to reconcile or something had happened to one of their parents. It was the only thing Maxence could think of that made sense.

The carriage came to a stop on a bustling street. Not far down the road, soldiers in blue and *fédérés* in red caps stood about in front of a building. A barracks, most likely. The sight didn't help Maxence's mood. They'd have to find Gilles's house quickly.

"I'll send the coach back as soon as I can spare it," Oscar said.

"Oh, no," Maxence said. "We can find our way to the house." He hopped out, the clothing bundle in one hand, to help Armelle down. "You can go with him if you'd prefer."

She shook her head quickly. He hadn't expected her to agree.

"If you're certain," Oscar said. "Perhaps I will call later tonight. Give Gilles my best."

The coach rolled away, and Maxence turned toward the side street his uncle had indicated, away from the barracks. The third door on the right.

A group of soldiers shoved their way down the street. Armelle grabbed his arm and pulled him away from the men. He ducked his head. After the near encounter with Voulland yesterday, his nerves were frayed.

A middle-aged woman bumped into them, pushed out of the way by the crowd in the soldiers' wake, and Maxence caught her by the shoulders before she tripped into the building. She carried a little bundle in her arms.

"Ruffians," she hissed, adjusting the blankets around the bundle.

"Are you all right?"

"*Merci, citoyen*." She spoke with the melodic accent of his home that sent waves of homesickness through him. The woman looked up. Her grateful smile slowly died.

He knew that face. Light brown hair, high cheekbones, dark eyes. Memories of dinners and parties sprang forward. Long nights of deep conversation with his closest friend. Her eyes widened, and she clutched the bundle closer. With a gasp, she tore away from him.

"Wait, stop!"

She lost herself in the crowd. Armelle stepped in front of him. "What is it? Did you see a ghost?"

Maxence shook the memories from his head and rubbed his brow. "No, I . . . I think we should come back another day. I don't know if I'm in my right mind." Émile's mother couldn't be here. The Daubins had no connection to Saint-Malo. And she was dressed so plainly. Émile had inherited his mother's taste for high fashion. Everything Maxence had ever seen Madame Daubin wear was dripping in expensive lace. How had his mind imagined Madame Daubin here?

"Maxence." She took his arms and turned him to face her fully. "You look like you did that morning outside of Nantes."

"How did I look?" He searched once more for that woman. He needed to see her again to satisfy his memory. It was not Madame Daubin.

"Terrified. Nervous. All the same things I was feeling."

He swallowed. "I am not nervous."

"Then why are you clenching your fists with your arms rigid as sticks?" He forced his limbs to relax, but his pulse still raced at a terrible speed.

Armelle shook him gently. "This is your chance, Maxence, to make things right. To restore your place in your family."

"What if he doesn't want to make things right?" He counted the doors. That one. That unassuming wood door was supposed to be Gilles's.

"Let it start with you. If you offer reconciliation, the door is open for when he is ready." She tilted her head until Maxence brought his gaze back to her. "What is the worst that could happen?"

"He could say, 'I don't want to see your ugly face, Max. Get out of here.'"

Armelle pursed her lips, but he could see a laugh at the corners of her mouth. "Or he could ask where you've been and why you haven't written, and he could tell you they've been searching everywhere."

Doubtful. "He has every right to hate me. I have to ask him for forgiveness." He pulled out of her grasp to brush his hair from his face.

"You can do it." She smiled. "I'll be with you." She steadied herself against his arms, rose up on her toes, and pressed a faint kiss to his cheek. A shiver crossed Maxence's skin. It was a sisterly gesture. She'd made it clear that all her gestures were sisterly. But he barely kept at bay the desire to embrace her, to bury his face in her hair and drink in the scent of her.

A couple dozen steps, and they were at the door. Maxence could hardly hear Armelle's encouragement through the pounding in his ears. He mounted the steps, rapped on the door, and waited.

Voices came, but he couldn't tell from where. A moment later the door opened, and there stood Gilles. His disheveled hair had a wild look to it, and he glared with red-rimmed eyes.

"*Mon frère*," Maxence said. What had happened to him? Gilles always had a carefree look about him, but not like this. An almost feral shadow loomed over his features.

"Leave," Gilles growled.

"Gilles, what is wrong?" Maxence stepped toward him. The worry of rejection vanished, replaced by numbing fear. "Tell me."

"I said to leave." Gilles retreated, closing the door.

Two years ago, Maxence had been on the other side of that door, slamming it in his brother's face. The reverberations still echoed inside him. He lashed out, palm slapping the wood and stopping the door before it could shut. A closed door would do nothing to mend what lay between them. "I'm not leaving until you tell me what's happened." If it had something to do with their parents or Victor's family, he deserved to know. The door opened again, and Maxence's shoulders sagged. Praise the skies. "Gilles—"

He didn't see the fist until it slammed into his mouth. Maxence reeled backward and stumbled down the steps, nearly knocking Armelle to the ground. She steadied him, face pale. The door shut with a resounding and all-too-familiar crack.

Maxence swiped a hand across his mouth. A little smear of red marred the back of his hand. He swore and turned on his heel. Gilles was an imbecile. They all were. They wouldn't give him the smallest chance.

"Maxence, you cannot just give up."

"You said I only had to open the door." Steam rose in his chest, hot and stinging. What a ridiculous idea to try to patch things up with his spineless brother.

Armelle seized his sleeve. He rounded on her, wits muddled. She was no different from the rest of them. She'd leave without a second thought the moment they found her brother. No chances to win her over. She'd walk out of his life forever.

And he did not want to stay to watch.

Armelle stared, the things she wanted to say disappearing from her memory. The fire in Maxence's eyes paralyzed her. He tugged his arm out of her grasp.

"You cannot take that as his final answer," she said.

Maxence stormed down the street. "I don't know why I shouldn't."

She adjusted the market bag on her shoulder and ran after him. "Did you not see him?"

"Yes, he was clearly drunk."

Gilles's response had overwhelmed him, and she couldn't blame him for it. "Something was wrong." He wasn't listening. "Will you stop? Please?"

Maxence paused, jaw taut. Veins stood out on his temples.

"He was in pain, Maxence. Could you not see it?" Her voice came out desperate. "The things your uncle said last night . . . I think something horrible happened. You cannot quit trying. I haven't given up on gathering my family, even though so many things have torn us apart. You cannot let one instance ruin everything."

"This is the reality, Armelle," he said, throwing up his arms. "You can't wish happiness and peace on everyone and expect it to be so. Perhaps your family is perfect, but the rest of ours are not."

Armelle recoiled. "How dare you say that." She knew her family wasn't perfect. She also knew they were all she had. "You cannot give up."

"Sometimes you do have to give things up," he said, volume rising. "Things you wanted more than anything. The sooner you realize that life is only kind to an elite few, the easier it will be." His eyes glistened, and Armelle's teared as well. "You cannot control people, and because of that it is foolish to dream."

"I never said that life wasn't difficult. It is still worth it to dream."

"Dreaming is for fools."

Blue coats with gold buttons filled her vision. Soldiers, their sights set on Maxence. They advanced behind a smirking leader. She reached out to stop Maxence, but he turned and walked into them before she could scream.

"Ross. I thought I recognized you."

Maxence jerked to a stop, then lunged back toward his brother's house. A wave of soldiers caught him and threw him to the ground as he shouted for her to run. Her mind slowed. Her shoes seemed made of lead. His eyes locked on hers, but she couldn't hear the words he screamed.

Caught. With no plan.

She'd already seen this. Some of the soldiers' faces matched those from her memories.

They'd been looking for him. She and Maxence had walked into a trap.

He caught her gaze, and while she couldn't read his lips, the intensity in his eyes was enough. Leave. Hide. Don't get caught.

Her legs finally moved of their own accord, and she took off down the street instead of launching herself into the circle of men tying and gagging Maxence. The people she passed hardly glanced at her. She wanted to shriek at them to help, to stop what was happening in front of them. Her mouth wouldn't open.

She darted between carts and down alleys until she was hopelessly lost. When her feet couldn't run anymore, she collapsed against the side of a building and slid to the cobbled ground. The market bag fell from her shoulder. She threw her arms over her head. Her body quivered uncontrollably.

"Max," she choked out. The grey buildings rising above her shut out the sky. Another closed door.

He was gone. And she'd abandoned him.

CHAPTER 25

Dark had fallen by the time Armelle found *rue Saint-Michel* and knocked on the sixth door. Ocean mists wound through the streets like the shrouds of the *kannerezed noz* she and her friends would tell stories about in hushed tones. A woman with a face so stern she might have been one of the ghostly washerwomen answered the door without a greeting.

For a moment, her mind did not function. The sobbing that had wracked her body not long before made it difficult to think. "I am looking for . . . for Henri Bernard. Is he here?" The skin of her face felt dry and stiff, her throat scratched and raw. She could only imagine how red her face was. After wandering the streets trying to make sense of an unknown city for hours, she must look like a miserable wretch.

Armelle clenched her teeth to keep back the tears and brought a hand to her mouth in case another sob escaped. She *was* a miserable wretch. Maxence. Her knees knocked together. She hadn't realized how much she'd leaned on him through their journey. Now that foundation had been swept out from under her, leaving her grasping for anything to keep her standing. Only the thought of Henri forced her onward.

"Who are you?"

The woman hadn't denied he was there. Armelle lowered her hand. Did that mean she'd found the right place? A tiny flame flickered to life in a heart that had been listless for hours. "Armelle Bernard."

"Wait." The woman half shut the door, leaving Armelle in the street. She pressed her hands together, bringing them to her lips in silent prayer. Her brother. He was here.

Citizens of Saint-Malo passed behind her, some not watching where they walked and bumping into her. She stayed as close to the door as she dared. They were on the opposite side of Brittany from Nantes, and still the masses looked the same—weary, downcast, praying for relief.

The sound of thundering footsteps down a set of stairs met her ears. In moments the door was flung open, and Armelle met uncombed brown hair, wide eyes, and a splitting grin.

"Armelle!" He pulled her through the doorway and shut it. "I received a letter from Nicole, but I didn't—"

The surge she'd tried to lock inside her spilled forth. What should have been pure elation at this reunion with her brother now hung heavy with terror for the person who had somehow, unbeknownst to her, crept into her circle of loved ones. She threw her arms around Henri, buried her face in his shoulder, and wept.

22 March 1794
Nantes, Brittany

Chère *Armelle,*

I've sent this to Saint-Malo as you instructed with the hope that it finds you there and that you haven't changed your plans yet again. I am well and have not come to any harm over the incident. I only hope you have not. I do not understand your decision not to go to your grandparents. While I do not fault you your dream, this is hardly the time to reach for it. Now we must keep our heads down and push forward to survive this.

Your mother is worried sick. She received a letter from your friends the Colberts about your plans to travel with that man and sought me out for confirmation. I could not lie. I beg your forgiveness. To say she is furious would be a gross understatement. I beg you to write to her.

It seems to all of us that, rather than your family, you have sacrificed for one person of no relation who should be of little interest to you. My dear friend, is this really worth it? I fear there are things you have given up that cannot be replaced.

I pray for your safety. Please be careful.

Nicole

Maxence stood in a salon that had been turned into a makeshift office. He'd had little sleep. His feet were shackled, his hands were cuffed, and his limbs threatened to give out after an hour of standing solitary in the cramped closet they'd thrown him in the night before. Froment sat in a chair to the side of the desk, making no attempt to hide his glee. He sipped at a cup of coffee, his fourth since hauling Maxence here. Froment hadn't received Maxence's promotion to lieutenant. Voulland made him an *aide-de-camp*, and it appeared Froment intended to remind Maxence of his superior position for the rest of his short existence.

"I should have shot you in that little clearing, you know," his former comrade said. "No one would have doubted my actions were justified."

There would still have been an investigation, but one could do practically anything under the excuse of defense of *la patrie* these days.

"I'm surprised Voulland hasn't come in yet. He must have received important news this morning." Froment pulled out his pocket watch, and Maxence recognized its face, painted with *tricolore* flags, instantly. Until the accident with Martel, the watch had been his.

Strange how insignificant the theft seemed now. Maxence clenched his jaw to hide a yawn. He didn't have the energy to get angry about the watch, even if he'd wanted to. His head pounded from where they'd struck him. His arms and legs throbbed. Cramped quarters, a hard floor, and little food the night before gave him a different perspective. Or had it been the journey from Nantes?

"I had the most curious encounter while we were in Rennes," Froment said. "A man came to us with information, and of course the *chef-de-brigade* always accepts reports of counterrevolutionary activity."

Surely the halfwit would have to relieve himself soon and grant Maxence a little peace.

"The man said he had been attacked by a deserter and robbed of a large amount of valuable goods." Froment downed his cup and poured another. How was he not running circles around the room with all the coffee's energy? "Of course I asked him how he came to believe this man was a deserter. He said he glimpsed a blue army coat among the man's possessions."

The hairs on Maxence's arms raised.

"Naturally this news interested me, as this criminal either was truly a deserter or had stolen it, both serious crimes against the République." Froment stood and crossed to stand before Maxence. "I inquired if he had any more information, to which he answered the man's name was Rossignol and that he was traveling to Saint-Malo to work for his uncle." A wolfish grin crossed his face. "Come, Ross. Surely you can be more clever with your alibis."

Maxence stared at the wall beyond Froment. The peddler had gone to both the Chouans and the army to get his revenge.

"Voulland did not care much to investigate, but I sent word around our companies to watch for a man of your description traveling with a young woman. We were on our way to question your uncle when we spied you in the street." He stepped forward until his face took up all of

271

Maxence's vision. "I could not be more pleased with the speed it took to locate you. And perhaps in an hour or two I will have the pleasure of—"

Voulland swept into the room, and Froment jerked into a salute. "At ease, Froment." He spared Maxence a glance. "Étienne, I did not think I would see you again." Voulland made an impressive figure in his *habit national*. He sat at the desk and pulled out papers, clearly uninterested in the issue his aide had brought before him.

"I request permission to carry out the justice that was not served in Nantes, *chef*," Froment said.

Voulland grunted. "I do not remember the circumstances." He brought out a writing box and uncapped an ink bottle.

"Étienne disobeyed your orders to execute a girl in Nantes. A soldier named Martel tried to stop him, but Étienne killed the man with his bayonet."

"Ah, yes." The *chef-de-brigade* raised his head to study Maxence. "What do you have to say to the accusations, Étienne?"

Would he listen to the truth? Either way Maxence had grounds to be shot by the end of the day. A trickle of sweat ran down the inside of his collar.

"We had orders in Nantes to capture and shoot him," Froment said. Maxence shifted. He wouldn't get a word in with Froment in the room. It was just as well. He had little left in this world. Immobilizing cold settled into his chest.

"Is your name Étienne?"

Froment reddened. The chill within him didn't allow Maxence to enjoy the reprimand.

"What happened, Étienne?" Voulland asked, emphasizing his name.

Practically the only thing he had left was the truth. "I disagreed with the order and chose not to follow it. Martel tried to use my bayonet against me but tripped and was stabbed in the process. He was still in possession of the bayonet."

Voulland opened a drawer and sifted through its contents. "The girl

I instructed you to execute. What was she to you?" He pulled out a paper and set it to the side.

Maxence's throat tightened. "Nothing, *chef.*" But she'd come to be everything. Her accusatory eyes from the Chouans' hut burned into him. He'd betrayed her trust. And then in his anger and confusion at Gilles, he'd berated her hopes. He didn't deserve her. How had he deluded himself?

"He's been traveling all over Brittany with the little wench," Froment cried.

"She followed me." How could he persuade them not to pursue her?

Voulland raised a hand. "I am not concerned with my men's indiscretions." Maxence winced at his dismissal of Armelle's importance, even though he had tried to convince him of just that. "Froment, will you arrange a messenger for this answer to General Turreau?"

Froment took the proffered letter and put it in his coat pocket, then resumed his position next to Maxence.

"That missive must start its journey immediately, Froment," Voulland said. "See to it."

The muscles in Froment's jaw worked. He was being dismissed. Maxence turned his gaze to the floor. His former comrade's presence would not affect the outcome of this interrogation, but the fewer of his last hours Maxence had to spend with that doltish fop, the better.

Froment saluted, threw Maxence a scathing glare, and stormed from the room. The *chef-de-brigade* watched him go, then shook his head. "That man is impossible."

Maxence couldn't agree more, but he was not in a position to criticize anyone.

"Why did you disagree with my orders?" Voulland pulled out a letter and broke the seal.

"She was trying to defend her brother, not attack the République."

The *chef-de-brigade* nodded slowly as he read his letter. "These Chouans are nasty little mongrels, aren't they? Disorganized and undisciplined, but they've been a thorn in the side of the République for too long." He took the paper he'd set to the side. "The République needs discipline if she is to stand the test of time. She needs superior military power to defend at home and abroad. She needs young men willing to sacrifice their personal convictions for the good of *la patrie*."

Why was the man drawing this out? He didn't act as though he was toying with Maxence, not like Froment had done all morning. "Your captain sent me the report after you went missing," Voulland said. "There are some grave accusations."

Maxence bowed his head. They were grave, and he did not feel remorse for all of them. He only regretted Martel's accident and the part he played in it. On the other accounts, he had done what his conscience dictated. A month of running, and he would still suffer the consequences of saving Armelle. If fate put the choice before him again, he would not hesitate doing all he could to protect her.

At least she knew where he'd gone, and she would try to tell his family. Even if they did not care to leave space for him in their lives, they would know what happened. Perhaps they would mourn.

Armelle's pallid features as she watched them drag him to the street would haunt him until his last breath. She would mourn him, if only as a friend. He squeezed his eyes shut against visions of the things that would never be.

"There is testimony from some of the soldiers involved in your first arrest that supports your story of an accident. A few of your former comrades believed you, based on what they found."

Maxence lifted his head, unsure if he had heard correctly.

"Insubordination is serious, but not so serious as murder of a comrade." Voulland steepled his fingers before him. "You were one of the Marseillais *fédérés*, were you not?"

"Yes."

"You were at the Tuileries Palace when they brought down the king."

"Yes." Those images had not plagued him so much in the weeks since he'd left the army.

The *chef-de-brigade* sighed and sat back. "In reviewing the evidence against you and your captain's thoughts on the matter, I wish to pass my judgment. It is fortunate that you have caught me in good humor this morning. I just received news of the birth of a grandson." His lips curled faintly. "How can I be old enough to have a grandson?"

The clock behind the man's desk ticked. Footsteps echoed somewhere in the house. Voices came from outside. Maxence held his breath.

"I conscript you once more into service. The army is hurting for men, and one cannot question the loyalties of one of the Marseillais." His eyes narrowed. "Or am I mistaken?"

Maxence started. He was offering it back. The life Maxence had built for himself, free from the risk of disappointing family and free from living under the shadow of his brothers. A place to belong. A place he was needed.

But what of Armelle? Accepting this meant turning his back on all they had and leaving her here, perhaps never to see her again. A panic seized his heart. He couldn't abandon her.

You Étiennes can't resist a pretty face. Martel's words thundered back. How could he spurn this more-than-generous forgiveness for a girl who didn't return his love? He wouldn't be turning his back on much if there was nothing between them to begin with. Her brother lived in the city. She wasn't Maxence's concern anymore.

"I am loyal to the cause of liberty," he said, forcing the words through a mouth that for once didn't want to speak them.

"Very good." Voulland stood. "I will assign you to a different company, in case there are any lingering issues with your previous one, and issue you the supplies you don't have."

"Thank you, *chef.*" Maxence's head rang as though he'd been hit again. Not many were handed a second chance like this.

"You know, I've regretted selecting your comrade as my aide," the *chef-de-brigade* said. "My eye was on you. I will give you the opportunity to earn my trust. When I feel you have proven your commitment, we will discuss other opportunities." *Aide-de-camp* to a *chef-de-brigade.* It was more prestigious a position than a company lieutenant. His brain struggled to put the pieces together.

"Are we to stay in Saint-Malo?" he asked.

"We were to go on to Saint-Brieuc, but it seems we have been called back to Nantes."

Nantes. It would be far from Armelle, from Gilles, from any connection he thought he had. A true new beginning at the place where the nightmare had begun.

"General Turreau needs help in his purge of the Vendée." Voulland walked to the door and stuck his head out. "Cellier, find someone to get these shackles off of Étienne."

"Thank you, *chef*." The purge of the Vendée. Rooting out counter-revolutionaries for the good of *la patrie*. Maxence's mouth went dry, the elation at his restoration instantly plummeting. He would show his loyalty before then. Become an aide who didn't have to participate. But as he was led away to take his place among the République's finest, it was Armelle's terrified face in a snowy clearing that filled his waking eye.

CHAPTER 26

Armelle leaned into the wall outside of the candle shop, her cloak's hood pulled as far forward as it could go while still allowing her to see the house across the street. It was one of the places repurposed for the use of the army. Henri had pointed out several similar buildings throughout the city over the last few days.

The jailer at the nearby prison had given her the same news again that morning. No one by the name of Maxence Étienne had been brought since her last visit. Armelle chewed her lip. The army must be keeping him in one of its own buildings. She didn't allow herself to think her search might be fruitless, that Max's fate was irreversibly sealed. Most enemies of the République waited at least a few days between conviction and execution.

Most.

Henri had called her a fool every morning she went out to search, but she refused to stagger under the grief that had nearly incapacitated her when Maxence was arrested. Not until she knew for certain.

A few soldiers exited the building, which Henri's sources said housed some of the soldiers accompanying Voulland. They didn't lead any prisoner, though. Armelle shoved her hands into her pockets, instantly finding Julien's wood die and then the two letters from Père and Nicole.

Her friend's words wound through her mind. A little piece of her hissed that she'd made a serious error. Following him had been reckless. Getting caught up in Henri's *chouannerie* could be equally so. She should have gone to Grandmère and Grandpère to quietly wait out the danger.

No. She would not believe that. Even if her doubts grew stronger by the hour.

She pressed her back into the wall of the shop and closed her eyes, willing the cold stone to ground her. Saint-Malo was not under the thumb of a *représentat-en-mission* as villainous as Carrier, with regular mass executions. Maxence wouldn't have faced execution so quickly.

More soldiers exited the building. Did she dare ask them? What if one of them knew Maxence's story and somehow connected her to it? She rolled the die through her fingers. It wasn't as though she had anything to go back to. The carpenter Henri stayed with, the one pretending her brother was his seventeen-year-old apprentice, had nothing for her to do.

The soldiers crossed the street in her direction. Armelle ducked her head and slid away from the door of the shop in case that was their destination. There were three of them, all dressed for duty and armed, but they did not seem to be in a hurry. Armelle didn't know which was worse—République soldiers on a mission or République soldiers with nothing to do. She prayed they didn't see her.

Two of the soldiers conversed as they went; the third hung back a little behind the others. She gave them a quick peek from under her hood. It wouldn't hurt to learn their faces. The first two passed without looking at her, and the third soldier's eyes were glued to the ground, his dark curls poking out from under his hat.

Armelle's stomach leaped. "Maxence!"

His head snapped up. He jerked to a stop, throwing a wary glance at the soldiers ahead of him. The buttons of that blasted coat he'd dragged from Nantes to Saint-Malo glinted in the sunlight. The blinding white-ness of the straps across his chest made it hard to look at him. Worse was the barrel of the musket poking out behind his shoulder.

"What is this?" She tried to keep her voice low. A soldier? She'd imagined him in chains, beaten, waiting for a sentence. Not this.

"I had the luck of catching the *chef-de-brigade* in a generous mood." Maxence shifted. A bruise marred his cheek. "What are you doing here, Armelle?"

"Looking for you. What else would I be doing?" She scanned the street, trying to breathe.

Somehow seeing him like this hurt. It wasn't that he didn't look fine in his apparel. Even she could admire the way the coat perfectly fit his form. The entire ensemble gave him a dashing air that made her heart flip. But this wasn't the Maxence they'd hauled away. This was the one who had hauled her away.

"I thought you'd be reuniting with your brother." He stood stiff. Official.

"Yes, I already have." She rubbed her forehead. "I've been going to the prison every day. I've been waiting outside of the army headquarters and barracks hoping for any hint as to your whereabouts." And each day a little piece of her hope had died as she believed that the longer it took, the smaller the chance of finding him alive and well.

He turned as though to gauge how far ahead his companions had advanced. "Well, you may stop looking now. Everything is right, as you can see. I must report with my comrades."

Armelle threw out her arms. Her mind would not make sense of it. "What are you doing? How could you go back to this?" The longer they'd traveled, the more at ease he'd become. Less proud, less obstinate, more understanding, more gentle. "Come back with me."

He closed his eyes, kneading his brow as though he had a headache. "This is what I desired from the beginning, Armelle. To give my all in the defense of *la patrie*. I have that back now. You are here in Saint-Malo with your family. We both found what we wished to in this city. It was always the plan to go our separate ways."

Was it? "I did not think we had discussed plans beyond arriving." She shrank back, wishing the wall would swallow her. She'd known the potential of difficult news, but she hadn't prepared herself for this.

"Be reasonable, Armelle. I am happy. I'm needed and wanted here." He didn't meet her eye.

"You are needed and wanted elsewhere," she cried.

"By whom?" he shot back.

"Your family. Your friends." *Me.*

"I've received enough rejection in the last few days to find that difficult to believe." The bitterness that tainted his tone pierced her soul. Her arms itched to wrap around him, the way they had that night after the peddler had attacked and she'd come so close to losing him. She longed to feel his heart pounding against her cheek through his worn shirt, the weight of his head resting on hers. How could she put that into words, here in the streets of Saint-Malo, his haunted eyes accusing her of things she couldn't understand.

Mère would say to let him go. Nicole would say to let him go. Henri had said several times in the last few days to let him go. She folded her arms. Why couldn't she? "Where is your powdered hair, Ross?" Her teasing sounded flat, forced.

"I've had trouble procuring hair powder." It hadn't rankled him. He stared back with undisturbed solemnity.

"I cannot believe that you would return to this."

"You thought because I roamed Brittany with you for more than a month that I would stop wanting to make something of myself."

"I thought you would see how unhappy you were." He'd seemed free of the memories and the guilt.

"I am happy, Armelle," he said again. "I don't have to watch my back for fear of capture. I don't have to worry that you . . . are safe." He turned toward where his comrades had stopped at the next street to wait for him. He motioned for them to wait. "It is better this way. I'll leave with the army in a couple of weeks. Our connection cannot endanger you anymore."

"Leave?" Armelle clutched the bow of her cloak. He couldn't leave.

"We are being called back to the Vendée."

Her eyes widened. Henri had spoken of the chaos in the region south of Nantes. The République wished to eradicate its enemies, and many in Brittany feared a similar fate. "To murder families." A heat burst to life inside her, and not the heat of sharing Maxence's kiss on a bright spring morning.

"We won't be doing that," he said fiercely. "We are trying to unify this country. If we cannot come together, we will fall. Great Britain, Austria, and Prussia are all salivating to get their hands on France."

He couldn't really have convinced himself of that. It was just what he told himself to reconcile his true convictions with his current desires. But she'd never make him believe otherwise. The fact that he would let his wounded pride delude him proved he was not the man she believed him to be deep down. Molten disgust roiled within at the betrayal. "That is strange to hear, coming from someone who pushes away the very idea of family unity."

"My family didn't want me, so I found somewhere to belong here." He groaned, removing his hat and running a hand through his hair. Silence spread between them. Dull. Heavy. One of his companions shouted, but she couldn't make out the words. She glared into his dark eyes and might have seen remorse in their depths if his words hadn't cudgeled her sensibilities. "Armelle, can we not part as friends?"

She gave a single nod. "I'm glad that you are happy. That you've found what you are looking for."

"And I am glad you have as well." His tone had softened, but she wouldn't let it break down her defenses. Let him think her perfectly satisfied. If he meant to pretend, so would she.

The soldiers called out to him again, jeering this time. Maxence took her arm. It felt like an age had passed since this same soldier dressed in enticing blue had taken her arm in the street. Her pulse had galloped then, and it thundered now, but not in the same way. His strong hand was gentle. His thumb smoothed over her sleeve. "You should get out of the street. Take care of yourself, *chérie*."

Chérie?

He tugged her closer, and suddenly his lips pressed to her forehead. The tender touch sent a wave of unsteadiness through every limb. Before she opened her eyes, he'd pivoted and strode away, his boots clipping the cobblestones. She wrapped her arms around her middle, pleading with him to look back. Just one look, one assurance that he meant his kiss, was all she asked.

But he didn't turn. When he rejoined his comrades, they quickly turned the corner. She dug her fingernails into her palms as a chasm opened in her chest, a terrifying, gaping hole with no one to fill it.

Two weeks had passed infernally slow. Every time Maxence stepped out of the makeshift barracks, he expected to see Armelle standing against the wall of the *cirier*'s. Sometimes he ventured into the candle shop for a moment to give himself the opportunity to search the street through the window. But she never returned.

Now they waited to follow Voulland's entourage out of Saint-Malo. The stifling morning made his coat too warm. The wait for the *chef-de-brigade*'s party had taken longer than expected, as those things usually did, and by the time the carriage pulled through, sweat soaked his shirt.

Froment rode beside the carriage through the rows of soldiers at attention, his nose in the air and buttons polished. He casually spat at Maxence's feet as they passed. Maxence gritted his teeth. Someday soon Froment would be forced to respect him. Then Maxence would rub his face in the dirt. Whether literally or metaphorically, he didn't care— only that Froment paid for his pompousness.

But his anger fled quickly, replaced by overwhelming dullness. Like an old horse too cranky to follow commands promptly, the army ambled into formation and started its march. He didn't look back as the city, with its ancient ramparts and forest of ships' masts flooding the harbor, faded behind him. Wherever he looked, he'd see specters of his past. Gilles running along the beaches, Père and Victor strolling down the docks, an excited Armelle practically hanging out the window of the coach as it drove through the streets.

His throat constricted, and he cinched his eyes shut at the ache. *You must take me to the shore, Maxence, so I may see these forts you spoke of. Do you think your father will arrive in Saint-Malo soon? I wish to see the docks as well. I think I will like this city.* The longing to hear her voice nearly strangled him.

The road out of town did not make it any easier. He would retrace his and Armelle's steps with his comrades, first to Rennes and then to Nozay, passing the places they camped and laughed and talked. She'd stay in his mind, haunting him at every turn with memories of question games, teasing, and the glow of being so close to her.

The pit in his stomach grew as the hours passed, more intense than it had been leaving Marseille. Saint-Malo should have been easier to leave. Gilles hadn't loathed him when he departed Marseille, or at least he had not shown it. Armelle hadn't existed to him. He'd marched for glory, not to wipe out an entire region in General Turreau's latest military scheme—lines of soldiers sweeping every last inch of land in search of rebels. "Infernal columns," the soldiers were called. And rightly so.

Maxence tripped, nearly bringing down the man behind him. He righted himself and mumbled his apologies, but the sensation of falling did not subside. It spiraled within, stifling and inescapable. He'd only harbored this feeling once before—when he and Émile had run through the Tuileries gates toward his friend's final breath.

CHAPTER 27

The steady hum of merchants and farmers buzzed in Armelle's ears. She loved market days, which is why Mère always sent her, though today she kept her head down as she followed Henri through the maze of vendors. The pungency of fish permeated the street. She had no qualms with fish, but now the scent turned her stomach.

"Armelle!" Henri called from several paces ahead.

A man bumped into her, knocking her toward the side of the street without so much as a pardon. Armelle scrambled toward her brother, skirting around another man carrying wet cages fresh from a fishing boat.

"I wonder how you made it all the way here from Nantes if you can hardly walk in a straight line."

"Maxence kept us going."

Her brother turned and hurried on. Customers already filled the streets, even though the sun had not yet cleared the tops of buildings to the east. Maxence would be marching south this morning, away from the glittering coasts of Saint-Malo.

"Do you think they have left yet?" she asked.

"Jean? If he has, I'll wring his neck."

"No, I mean Maxence. With the army."

Henri wheeled around. "Do you have nothing else to talk about?"

"What do you mean?" Citizens muttered as they moved around the siblings halted in the middle of the road.

"I mean that you've spoken of little else since arriving except this man who left you to fight for the République." Henri's eyebrows lowered, and his eyes clouded. "Tell me of Mère, or Julien, or any of the rest of them. Talk to me about the Colberts. I will even take speculations about Père. But I would not regret it if I did not hear about Maxence Étienne the rest of the day. Better would be not hearing of him ever again." He took her arm and pulled her forward.

Armelle's nostrils flared. "He is the only reason I made it here safely."

"And left you brokenhearted. What a courteous fellow." Henri slowed, investigating each person they passed.

"Brokenhearted! Don't be ridiculous." She pulled out of his grasp. They were just friends.

Her brother leaned in. "Have you heard yourself the last two weeks? People do not obsess over mere acquaintances like this."

"That has been my life for more than a month, Henri. Traveling with Max."

Henri darted out of the street between two fishmongers toward a young man who looked a few years younger than Armelle. She scuttled through buyers to keep up. The young man wore a blue waistcoat and floppy hat that shadowed most of his face.

"Jean. *Demat.*" Henri and the young man shook hands. Her brother pulled a letter folded into a narrow rectangle from his coat pocket. It was small, hardly bigger than her palm. Armelle pressed in and barely made out the words Henri spoke: "Guernsey. Monday night. We'll need it by Tuesday."

What did Guernsey have to do with anything?

Jean nodded, gave Armelle a wary glance, and tucked the letter away.

Henri nodded. "Safe travels, *mon ami.*" Then he turned and headed back the way they'd come, leaving her to run after him, ducking around baskets of wet, slimy fish.

"Henri, what's in—"

Her brother held a finger to his lips, eyes ablaze. "We cannot speak here."

Understanding dawned. Tanet had talked about supplies coming from the islands. He must have meant the Channel Islands.

"Traveling with *Max* is not your life anymore, Armelle," Henri said, as though they hadn't been interrupted. She'd never considered him short before, but as she walked beside him, he seemed small. And young. Of course, Maxence was a few years older and quite a bit taller.

How strange to get so used to someone that walking with her own brother felt foreign.

"Admit it. You're infatuated. And the sooner you forget him, the better."

She squeezed her eyes tight and dropped her head as the words pounded through her heart. He was gone to Nantes, and who knew what else beyond? But no matter what she did, he appeared in her mind, his stern look and guarded grin engraved in every thought. She did love him, and not just as a companion or a friend. Not even as a brother. This empty corner in her soul, little more than a dirt floor and vacant hearth, ached for the man willing to give all for what he knew to be right. Beneath his obstinacy, beneath his self-doubt, lay a heart yearning for love and to be loved in turn. She wanted to be the one to fill that yearning and welcome him into her heart, small and unassuming though it was.

Armelle pressed a hand to her stomach. Not even the Chouans with their unpredictable tactics could stop the line of soldiers marching for Rennes and bring him back to her. What good did this admission do if he was already so far away?

They made their way through Saint-Malo back to the home of the carpenter, with his stern wife and false apprentices. By the time they arrived, Armelle felt sick. She'd had plenty of chances to return his love, but she hadn't been ready. Too late she'd realized she no longer wanted her home and family back exactly the way they were before. Her silly dream of a restored family couldn't be complete without him.

Maxence's company camped just outside Saint-Domineuc that evening on the grounds of an abandoned manor house near the road. His captain had assigned him and a few others to sentry duty. He used to groan about the task before, since he and Martel usually received the same assignment and it meant listening to the man drone on. Before that in the *fédérés*, Émile had done it with him.

But tonight sentry duty meant having something to do besides lie awake in his blankets thinking about Gilles and Armelle and Émile—three people dearer to him than all the world, and three people he'd lost, which was entirely his fault.

He roamed the perimeter of the camp mechanically, searching the trees and brush for any movement. Only an idiotic band of Chouans would dare come close to a group of soldiers this large, but the wagons loaded with supplies would sorely tempt them.

The colors of the day turned to the purples and blues of twilight. Maxence stifled a yawn. He would have thought only having to worry about himself would be less tiring, but not having Armelle to boost his mood, and his fortitude, had taken its toll. He hadn't realized how much he depended on it.

A shout a little ways off brought him to attention. Brush rustled, and muted voices yelled. Maxence rushed toward the sound, scanning the foliage for signs of people. He finally spied the disturbance. Two sentries grappled with a third person. The intruder swung with his elbow, catching one of the sentries in the face. The soldier dropped to the ground with a howl.

Maxence threw himself in, pinning the young man to the ground with the help of the other sentry. Together they dragged him toward the nearest fire where half a dozen newly recruited *fédérés* sat. They wore civilian clothes, a red liberty cap their only uniform. Maxence instructed the *fédérés* to fetch the injured sentry and help them secure their prisoner.

"Filthy Chouan," the unharmed sentry, who wore a national guard uniform like Maxence, said with a sneer.

"Check his clothes, Trouard." Maxence said. This young man they'd caught, whatever his affiliation, had no love for République soldiers. He glared as Trouard checked the pockets of his blue waistcoat.

The *fédérés* arrived with the injured sentry, broken nose by the looks of it. Blood ran down his face and onto his uniform. Maxence motioned for them to take him to the surgeons.

"We found these as well," a *fédéré* said, handing a satchel and wide-brimmed hat to Maxence. While Maxence wasn't the leader by any means, at almost twenty-six he was older than most of these drafted young men. His uniform marked him as a professional soldier, rather than a volunteer, and the new recruits already came to him with their uncertainties. It should have felt nice to have a place of unspoken authority in the company, even without a rank.

Maxence checked the band of the hat but found nothing. The satchel also yielded a fruitless search. Food, a little water, a change of shirt. No money or supplies. He'd meant to take a short journey.

"Get the captain," Maxence said to the *fédéré* who had brought him the satchel. The young man they'd caught stared straight ahead, face impassive as Trouard searched his breeches pockets while other men held him. "Where are you headed?"

"Saint-Domineuc." He didn't sound concerned, but an edge tainted his tone. Hatred.

"Why are you traveling there so late at night?" Though the stars hadn't yet appeared, they very soon would. One didn't keep to the shadows of trees and bushes if they didn't have something to hide.

"My mother is sick."

Trouard straightened and shrugged. "I found nothing."

"Did you check his shoes?" Maxence asked. A sick mother was a compelling, if overused, cover. "Where do you travel from?"

The young man didn't answer. As Trouard reached for his shoes, he kicked. Trouard leaned out of the way just in time to avoid getting his face smashed. The *fédérés* holding the prisoner wrestled him to the ground, and Maxence helped them pull off his shoes. A small rectangle of paper lay in one of them.

"He's a Chouan," Trouard said as Maxence snatched up the paper.

There was no doubt about that. Their prisoner writhed, as though he could break free from four soldiers, each larger than he. The captain arrived at that moment, and Maxence stood to present the message to him.

"Fine job, *soldats*." The captain opened the paper, then frowned. "It's coded. I'll take it to the *chef* and see what his men can make of it. Secure him."

Trouard went for rope. The young man lay on the ground, chest heaving. Maxence felt a twinge in his core. Getting overpowered and roughly thrown down was humiliating at best, but worse was the fear of what the next hours held. When they'd bound and gagged the prisoner, they hauled him toward the manor house where Voulland had made camp. Maxence's spirits sank, as though they led him to judgment rather than this Chouan. In a few days this could be Evennou or Prado or Tanet if they didn't keep away from the road. And any connection to them could lead the République straight to Armelle and her brother.

Once again Armelle stood on a doorstep, hoping, as night set in. This time she prayed for the right words to say. Her eyes kept straying to the spot down the street where the soldiers had captured Maxence. What would he think if he knew of this visit? She pulled her gaze away from the unassuming cobblestones. He'd left. It didn't matter what he thought.

The door opened to a woman who looked about fifty. Her light brown hair was flecked with white around the temples. Her clothes seemed impeccably clean, though they were plain but for a fine stretch of lace edging her fichu. No Breton embroidery and very muted grey. The woman's eyes brimmed with wariness, but they softened as she took in Armelle.

"May I help you?" Men's voices in easy conversation drifted out from behind the woman.

"Is Gilles Étienne here?" She said his name in Maxence's accent, sending a little pang through her heart.

The woman hesitated. Could this be their mother? Armelle's breath faltered. If so, Maxence had missed more than just speaking with his brother. The idea made her ill. Perhaps this was just the woman renting Gilles a room. "Did Dr. Savatier send you?"

"No. I wish to speak with him about his brother."

Even in the dimness, Armelle could see the woman pale. "What is your name?" Footsteps inside advanced toward them.

"Armelle Bernard."

A hand touched the woman's shoulder. "Allow me, Angelique," said an almost familiar voice. It was not as deep as Maxence's but carried that same richness Armelle had grown to adore. The woman backed out of the doorway, and Gilles stepped forward. He was shorter than Max and a little broader through the shoulders. Though she knew Gilles to be the younger of the two, he looked older somehow. Dark circles shadowed his eyes, which held a hard, almost dangerous expression. She wouldn't have recognized him from Maxence's descriptions of his amiable, studious younger brother. "Did Maxence send you?"

Armelle shook her head. "He's gone to the Vendée. He doesn't know I'm here."

Gilles seemed to relax. He rubbed at the back of his neck. "Come in, then."

An airiness filled Armelle's chest as she followed him inside to the orange glow of firelight. The woman and a balding man sat on the couch, watching her. The faint scent of a savory dinner long since eaten drifted through the room. It would have made a cozy and welcoming scene, if not for an invisible gloom that seemed to permeate each corner of the house.

Armelle picked at the stitching on her mitts. She couldn't get this wrong. "May I sit? I have quite a lot to say."

CHAPTER 28

Maxence didn't know if he would have preferred sleeping in the manor house that night. As he stood outside the room Voulland had claimed, the dark corridors and empty chambers seemed to whisper their stories. People had lived and died here, and they'd left it an empty shell with little but its walls as reminders of the past.

The door opened, and Froment beckoned him in. Maxence entered, then saluted. The *chef-de-brigade*'s campaign desk sat in a room far smaller than his office in Saint-Malo. A candle sat atop it, the morning light not quite strong enough. He seemed in no hurry to make it to Rennes.

"You and the other sentries made a worthy discovery last night. It was an easily cracked code, an older one we'd previously deciphered."

"I'm glad to hear it."

The *chef-de-brigade* picked up a paper. "'Dinard. Monday evening. Transport needed Tuesday morning.' Signed H. Bernard."

H. Bernard? The back of Maxence's neck prickled. Henri Bernard. Armelle's brother.

"We assume this is about the weapons and supplies *émigrés* in

England have been sending through the Channel Islands to aid the Chouans."

Bernard was a common surname. And *H* could stand for many given names, could it not? It had to refer to someone else. Maxence couldn't move if he wanted to; his muscles had hardened to stone.

"I sent the original letter and a copy of our interpretation to Dinard by way of Saint-Malo last night," the general said.

Then companies in Saint-Malo would already know, and they'd send to Dinard shortly. If he somehow found a way to post a letter in Saint-Domineuc, it would be too late. He wouldn't know where to send it anyway. Imbecile. He should have asked where she was staying that day she found him in the street. He'd been too caught up in worry.

"I tell you this because I have a task for you to complete," Voulland said. He seemed to consider his words. "You and one of your comrades will return the Chouan to Saint-Malo for questioning. He must have ties to the *chouannerie* in that city, and it will save us the trouble of relaying information."

Back to the city. A part of him dug in his heels. He'd left it behind. He'd *wanted* to leave all the pain and frustration that resided there. The army accepted him, even if only as a pawn. Leaving Saint-Malo meant no more watching for Armelle, anticipating her appearance at every turn and wondering why she couldn't need him the way he needed her.

Voulland tossed the paper on the desk and stood. "We will camp at Rennes for two nights, and I expect you to meet us there in that time."

Maxence nodded. "Yes, *chef.*" The way he needed her. He needed that ray of sunlight through the smoke and fire his life had become since the onset of revolution. They'd hit plenty of discouragements on the road to Saint-Malo, but he'd smiled. He'd even laughed, if not always outwardly.

"Make sure you are well armed. My sources do not think this road is heavily guarded by Chouans, but you cannot be too careful."

"Of course." He could try to find her. Give her the warning. Plead with her to leave the danger surrounding her Chouan brother and come back with him . . . to what? To be a camp follower on their way to the Vendée? He sighed. She'd never agree to that.

"Is something wrong, Étienne?"

"No, *chef.* I'll leave immediately." He'd take Trouard, a nice, if oblivious, fellow who he could easily escape from for a few hours that night.

A few hours? As though he could search an entire port city in so short a time. His stomach sank. He'd have to try.

"*Aurevoir, soldat.* Safe travels." Voulland dismissed him with a wave, and Maxence hurried from the room. The sooner they left, the more time he had to find her.

Armelle had already burrowed into bed by the time Henri entered the little room they shared in the Nadon family's house. The Nadons owned a much larger carpentry business than Père's, with many employees and apprentices. The sounds of other apprentices readying for bed drifted through the walls. Nearly all of them had evaded the draft and involved themselves with the *chouannerie* in some way.

"Are you awake?" Henri asked, closing the door.

She didn't want to be, but lying there wondering how Maxence fared was not conducive to sleep. "Yes."

"I just came from the docks."

She lifted her head and looked over her shoulder. "The docks?" He wouldn't have had to walk far, but why would he go there this late at night?

"We had another message. The shipment is coming tomorrow night, not Monday. It means we'll have to hide the supplies a little longer since the letter Jean carried to Saint-Domineuc said we needed the wagon Tuesday."

"You're going to drive a wagon of supplies through the city without getting caught?"

"No, ninny, we're going to smuggle it out piece by piece and then load it on the wagon."

Armelle rolled back to face the wall, hands balling into fists. He'd called her that all their childhood, but he hadn't said it for many years. How was she to know his plans?

"The muskets will be more difficult, but with the extra time we can make a scheme. We'll have to hide them at the carpentry."

She pulled out Julien's die and turned it until two dots pointed up. What would she ask Julien if he sat beside her right now? Everything. What he'd seen on his walk home that day, what Oncle Yanick made him do in the shop, and what he'd done to terrorize Jacqueline and Cécile. And Max . . . She covered her cheek with her hand, remembering the feel of his touch that night after the soldiers had come to Ilizmaen. She might ask him if his knee bothered him after so much marching or if his barracks were more comfortable to sleep in than their barns. More than anything she wanted to know . . .

"Oh, come. Don't be angry with me," Henri said, sitting on the other small bed in the room, which creaked under his weight.

"I'm not." She hadn't imagined her reunion with Henri would go like this. It was supposed to be a joyous occasion, in which they would plan how to get all of their family to Saint-Malo while they waited for word of *le Rossignol*. But Henri only had plans for securing weapons, and Maxence's arrest had drained all the joy from their arrival.

"You can come with me tomorrow, if you'd like."

She closed her hand around the die. "To get the supplies?"

"It shouldn't be a terribly dangerous operation this time. Few people know of it. And you could enjoy an evening ride across the estuary instead of sitting here alone like most nights."

Except last night, but Henri didn't know about that. She closed her eyes and gripped the die tightly as she recalled the conversation, first at Gilles's house and then when he'd walked her back to the Nadons'. There was so much Max didn't know about his family. So much pain, so much misunderstanding. If only she hadn't caused a scene on the street and attracted the attention of the soldiers.

"Will you come?"

To collect guns that could fire at Max, while he fired against people like Henri. This was madness. "I suppose."

Henri laughed. "My sister's first act for the *chouannerie*. I don't think it will be the last." He kept talking, going on about the plans for tomorrow night.

Armelle brought the die to her lips and kissed it. She offered her usual prayer for Julien, for Mère and Père, and for each of her family members by name. Then for Max, who'd carved his name into that list without her realization. A hot tear escaped her eye and ran down her cheek until it seeped into her pillow. She'd come to Saint-Malo to restore what she once had, but now it lay in tattered and fraying pieces on the floor, never to go back to the way it was.

CHAPTER 29

They'd been forced to camp just outside of Saint-Malo for the night, an inconvenience that nearly drove Maxence to insanity. Now that dawn had broken, his hope lifted. The morning air, steeped with the freshness of the nearby shore, convinced him to spend another minute under covers reviewing his plan. They'd turn in the prisoner, he'd slip out, and he'd . . . find Gilles.

Maxence adjusted the blankets over him, the forest floor crackling as he moved. In the late hours of the night while Trouard and the prisoner slept, he'd decided Gilles offered him his best chance. His brother would know the city, and he hoped his brother would be easier to track down than Oscar. Of course he would have to find a way to apologize before Gilles threw any more punches. He rubbed his eyes. Gilles had never been prone to violence before. Most times they scuffled as children, Maxence had provoked it.

Footsteps behind him heralded Trouard's return from relieving himself. Time to collect the prisoner and move. He'd soon see if his plan was as ridiculous as it sounded in his head.

A gun muzzle swooped in to hover above his face. Maxence went rigid. Somewhere in the distance, men shouted. The pop of gunfire made him flinch. Where was Trouard? The prisoner?

"Get up, *soldat*." The gun raised only enough for Maxence to sit. A sloppily dressed man stood at the other end of the barrel. Some might have taken him as a simpleton from his unkempt appearance, but the way he gripped the musket with a firm but comfortable hold hinted at his expertise. Maxence tried to swallow against the sudden dryness of his throat. One wrong move, and he'd be done for.

Another man untied the prisoner and helped him to his feet. So much for Voulland's assurance of the safety of this road. Maxence and Trouard had taken turns watching through the night, but he'd let his guard down as morning hit like a new recruit fresh from the provinces.

"Get up and raise your hands."

Maxence struggled to his feet and lifted his arms. A slight breeze through his shirt made him shiver. The man hadn't cocked the musket, and for a moment Maxence had the urge to run and try his luck. This marksman wouldn't let him get far without a bullet in his back.

"Tie him up." The prisoner and his comrade eagerly brought the ropes and transferred them to Maxence's wrists and ankles. Where was Trouard? Maxence's stomach twisted. The gunfire a moment before did not bode well for his companion. "Bring their packs and guns, but leave the bedrolls. Where are—"

Two Chouans ran toward them through the trees. "There's a group of soldiers." They halted, breathing heavily. "Six or seven, just off the road. Coming this way."

Soldiers? Why would soldiers be on the road at this hour? "Where's the other?"

One motioned behind them with his head. "He ran off. We lost him."

Maxence felt only a little relief. Trouard had escaped death, but Maxence wouldn't be so lucky. Despite the greater force behind them, he doubted his odds of escape.

The leader swore. Older than the others by at least fifteen years, he didn't seem the brash, reactionary type like the other Chouans Maxence had run into. "You three lead them east toward Saint-Père and then north to the city. We'll hide the prisoner here. Do not return to the dugouts until you know you aren't being followed."

The leader strapped cloth across Maxence's mouth and cinched the gag tightly at the back of his head. Then he and his companion led Maxence away from the road with the packs and muskets. The three Chouans distracting the soldiers, including Maxence's former prisoner, set off toward the rising sun.

He cooperated with his captors as they forced him behind a prickly hedge, but each step came harder. Armelle. He had to warn Armelle.

"Keep a musket on him," the leader said, lashing Maxence's ropes to the base of one of the bushes. It put him too close to avoid getting poked by the spines. "I'm going to make sure we weren't followed."

The Chouan left with him did not seem to know his musket as well as the leader, which both worried Maxence and encouraged him. If he could find a way out of these ropes, he might overpower the man. Maxence dropped his hands to his lap and carefully pulled at the knots as best he could without being conspicuous. What knowledge this Chouan lacked in weaponry he made up for in knot tying.

I thought you said you were rather good at untying knots, Étienne. He could almost hear Armelle's quip in his mind. It hastened his work. He had to get to Saint-Malo. He had to find her before the République did.

Maxence watched his captor going through the packs. After an hour, the man seemed content that his prisoner was unable to escape and began his rummaging. It left opportunity to work at the ropes, but Maxence was getting nowhere.

The Chouan pulled out his national guard coat and tossed it to the ground. The insult against the blasted coat would have enraged him not long ago, but that uniform had since caused more trouble than it was worth. If he hadn't brought it, if he'd listened to Armelle's concerns, there wouldn't have been soldiers looking for him in Saint-Malo. He'd still be free.

Free. At one time that was the army for him, freedom from the constrains of disappointing his family. Now he wished he'd escaped the army when he had the chance.

The hoot of an owl came through the hedge, and a minute later the Chouan leader stepped into the field. Maxence's guard dropped the waistcoat Armelle had tailored on top of his coat. "What did you find?"

The leader raised a brow and glanced at Maxence, who stilled his hands. "Someone wanted you dead, *soldat*."

Dead? Yes, all the Chouans did.

"Or they at least did not care if someone killed you."

The guard stood. "What do you mean by that?"

The older man planted the butt of his musket on the ground. "The soldiers trailing us found the one who escaped, and I heard their explanation." He looked pointedly at Maxence. "They knew you'd be ambushed. Your commander sent you to draw us out with the plan to follow us back to our camp."

Voulland had lied. Maxence reeled, when he knew he shouldn't. What was one life, when Voulland commanded so many? That snowy scene sprang once more to his mind, Armelle's crimson cloak stark against the dead trees. Paralyzing fear had filled those hazel eyes. Weeks on the road lifting, encouraging, caring, had shown him how much one life meant. The men who drove this revolution, this war, had lost sight of their target to build up a France that respected the peasant as it had the king.

"What do you have to say to that?" The leader crouched before him.

Maxence grunted and glared. He couldn't say anything with the gag, clearly. As if reading his thoughts, the leader untied the cloth at his mouth.

His jaw ached. His mouth had gone dry. Maxence swallowed, then said, "I need to get to Saint-Malo. A shipment of supplies to the

Chouans has been compromised. The army in Dinard is waiting to intercept them."

"Are you one of us?" his guard asked slowly, glancing around at Maxence's things, which were strewn over the ground.

Maxence shook his head. "But someone I love is in danger."

The leader pushed himself up with the help of his musket. "I cannot just let you go."

"Then send someone to find Henri Bernard and warn him. His request for the supply transport won't arrive, if he gets the supplies that far. The army intercepted it and broke the code." The idea of not seeing Armelle made him ill, but it mattered more that her brother got the message.

"Do you know this Bernard?" the leader asked the other Chouan. His companion's head wagged back and forth. The leader sighed, stroking his chin. "If I let you go, and you run straight back to your comrades, I will look a fool."

"Who would be the greater fool, a Chouan letting a soldier go," Maxence squared his shoulders, "or the soldier returning to the army that tried to sacrifice him without his knowledge?"

"You don't intend to go back."

He dropped his gaze to the blue coat sitting in the sun. This revolution had been half a decade of constant change. Forming and reforming beliefs until no one knew in which direction to point their gun. But Maxence knew where to aim, and it was anywhere that threatened to take the people he loved from him. "I intend to do what I can to protect my family." Not that Armelle was his family. But maybe someday he could convince her of his worth. "And I cannot do that in the Army of the West."

"I can respect the sentiment," the Chouan leader said. "That is, after all, our greatest motive in the *chouannerie*. To protect our family, our religion, and our way of life." The man slung his musket over his shoulder, then pulled a knife from his boot. "Would you like me to make you disappear?"

Maxence drew back. That sort of disappearance was not what he'd had in mind. "How would you do that?"

The man picked up the national guard coat and held his knife to the sapphire wool. "I can make you a dead man." Sunlight reflected from the blade, harsh and biting. The sun already sat too high in the sky.

Maxence stared at that coat, which had once represented his greatest desire. "Do it."

The Chouan leader slashed his knife through the back of the coat. The sound of fibers wrenching apart shattered the silence of the field. He did it again and again, and when the back of the coat was in shreds, he dropped it to the ground. "We'll feast to celebrate your demise tonight. I think we can spare a chicken." He winked at his companion. "Then we'll leave this where your fellows are sure to find it. Send them a warning."

They untied Maxence and helped him stand. He walked over to the ruined coat. From the little breast pocket he pulled out Émile's rosette.

"What is that?"

"An olive branch." Marie-Caroline had given it to Émile to make peace. Maxence didn't know how much ground he had to recover between him and Gilles, but he had to try. Not just for Armelle's sake, but his family's.

"That isn't something a soldier of the République should carry," the leader said.

A symbol of the monarchy. Certainly not. "We established I wasn't one any longer." Maxence retrieved his waistcoat, brushed it off, and pulled it on. Let them think what they wished about what the rosette meant. If it earned him higher esteem in their eyes and helped him get to Saint-Malo faster, all the better. He quickly knotted a neckcloth at his throat.

"You'll want your pack."

Maxence shook his head. "If you would point me to another path to Saint-Malo, you can keep what you like." He'd lost most things he cared about after his arrest in Nantes.

The Chouan leader nodded toward the west. "You can follow the coast or stick to the main road. The coast will be longer, but you're less likely to run into your friends."

Maxence shook hands with them and dashed out the opening in the hedge. Then he ran, not pausing to worry if they'd shoot him in the back. He had to get to Armelle and had to do so without being seen by his comrades. Hesitations weren't a luxury he could afford.

No one answered. Maxence pounded again and scanned the street. His feet throbbed, he had a stitch in his side, and after everything, Gilles wasn't home. *Ciel.* He kneaded his eyes with the heels of his palms. He'd have to track down Oncle Oscar. With how late in the afternoon it was, his uncle might be at home. Or he could wait for Gilles. Both would take time.

He tried the door. Scraping of a latch not quite secure filled the air, and then the door creaked open. "Gilles?" Shadow pervaded the room behind. Maxence pushed the door open to a vacant salon with one small couch and a chair. He closed the door, blinking as his eyes adjusted. A set of stairs lay behind the door, but no light came from above. The house sat silent, empty.

One long, faint beam of light pointed toward a kitchen window with a table beneath it.

Maxence followed the light. A figure lay slumped against the wall. Maxence stopped short. "Gilles?"

"What do you want?" The haggard voice didn't sound like his brother.

His stomach seized, and he rushed into the little kitchen. "What happened?" Gilles didn't look injured. Maxence dropped to a knee. No blood, but that didn't mean much.

Gilles turned his head toward the curtained window. His bloodshot eyes glistened.

Maxence sat back, the heavy aura of the house suddenly resting on him. "Gilles . . . What is it?" Years had passed since he'd seen his brother cry. The last time he could remember was when Maxence had gone to sea with Père and Victor, leaving Gilles home with their mother. That was when they were boys.

"Why would I tell you?"

Maxence swallowed. "Because I'm your brother."

"That hasn't meant much to you before." Gilles didn't look at him, just kept staring toward the window. A bottle sat beside him, but it was corked and full. He seemed lucid.

Maxence braced himself. Whatever Gilles didn't want to tell him, whatever burden he bore, it wasn't going to be easy to hear. "I know. I am sorrier than I can express." How awkward and forced that sounded.

Maxence wanted to kick himself. Gilles needed something, and Maxence couldn't give it. The sorrow etched into his brother's face knifed at his soul. A hundred possibilities flashed through his mind, terrible things happening to their family that made him want to wretch.

Neither of them stirred. The buzz of the street filtered through the closed window, muted and distant. Gilles's hands rested limply on the floor, and his head leaned into the wall, as though all his strength had fled. He'd always had so much energy as a boy, so much zeal for life, and it hadn't let up when they'd entered adulthood. This shell of a human— how could it be Gilles?

"She's gone," he finally mumbled.

Bile rose in Maxence's throat. "Maman?" Two years of hardly saying anything. Months of not responding to her letters. He'd let his own stupidity ruin so many chances.

Gilles slowly shook his head, then said in a choked whisper, "Caroline."

CHAPTER 30

Armelle couldn't escape the blinding glare of the late sun off the sea. Ships lay scattered throughout the bay, some awaiting high tide to push them into harbor, others sailing south up the River Rance, and others still out to sea. Smaller boats similar to the one Henri rowed wove between the larger vessels. They headed in all directions, like tiny sanderlings scuttling through a colony of lazy gulls.

Henri didn't row in any great hurry. They still had quite a ways to go, having started their journey at a quiet beach south of the main harbor. Not far ahead, two more boats with two passengers each bobbed on the waves. Henri kept the bow pointed in their direction, following his Chouan comrades.

"You haven't mentioned your soldier much the last few days," Henri said. "I'm glad you've put him out of your mind."

Nothing could have been further from the truth. She saw him in the face of every man she passed. At night she imagined he slept on the floor beside her bed, grumbling that she should go to sleep. And when she wanted to be perfectly miserable, she remembered his lips caressing hers and all the things that might have been if she'd only examined her heart.

"We should call on his uncle to see if he has had any word of *le*

Rossignol," she said. Perhaps Maxence would write to him. She shouldn't get her hopes up. If he hadn't written to his mother in months, it wasn't as though he had plans to write his uncle.

"Armelle, I know you want us all to be together again. I want it as well. But it would be better if you didn't count on it happening very soon."

She shrugged. "I can be patient."

"It may not ever happen."

Armelle lowered her brows. "That I will not accept."

Henri paused his rowing. "We are all grateful Père escaped, but sea life is not without its perils, especially in times like these. The ship might go down, it might get captured, or an accident might happen."

Her insides twisted tighter with each word he spoke.

"What's more, how could we get the rest of the family here? Selling the carpentry will not be an easy feat these days, and it would put Yanick out of work. Then Mère would have to get four children and herself across the region."

It felt as though their boat had sprung leaks, water rushing in from all sides. "We have to try."

He started rowing again with renewed vigor. The slap of his oars against the sea sent droplets flying through the air. "I have work to do. Important work. Sometimes family obligations need to be put on hold. Surely your soldier taught you that."

No, he'd taught her just the opposite. Armelle looked out across the bay, ignoring the piercing light that made her eyes smart. He'd needed his family, and he'd cut them off in his overzealous pursuit of ideals. Even if he'd achieved his goals and brought about the utopian France the Jacobins dreamed of, what would it be worth if he had no one to share it with?

"Tomorrow we'll start trying to find you work," Henri said.

Armelle bristled. "I can find my own work, *merci*." Her brother had so quickly dismissed any possibility of reunion without sign of regret. If she could not count on Henri to help her . . .

A wave of melancholy washed over her, cold and wet as the sea. She'd held so tightly to this silly dream. Now she saw it for what it was—a child's fantasy. Who could hope for reunion in a land tearing itself apart? She should have gone to Lorient and let Max go his way. Lonely and quiet as her life would have been, she could have safely waited for others to fix this mess. She wouldn't have known the extent of Henri's obsession with the *chouannerie*, and she wouldn't have known what it meant to be loved by Maxence Étienne. She might have been content.

Armelle lowered her head and folded her arms across her stomach. The void that had enveloped her the last few weeks swirled, blocking out the brilliance of the evening. Waves hitting the little boat's hull pounded her deeper into the abyss. Would that she had never set foot in that wretched church, with her bucket of water and stubborn follies.

Maxence's eyes narrowed at Gilles's words. Caroline? He only knew one, but surely that wasn't who his brother meant. "Daubin?"

Gilles nodded, almost imperceptibly. Maxence dropped his eyes to the floor. Two Daubin children dead in two years. Madame Daubin would be inconsolable, if she'd survived the despair.

"I didn't know you had feelings for her." Real feelings. Émile had teased about it, but Maxence didn't think anything of it at the time. He ran a hand through his hair. How had he been so unobservant to not see it?

"She was my wife."

Maxence lifted his head, breath draining from his lungs. Wife? He steadied himself, hands against the floor. "No one told me," he whispered. Marie-Caroline and Gilles? His mother hadn't said a word.

"The Daubins got into trouble with the Jacobins. We were afraid of where your loyalties lay."

They'd feared him and all his revolutionary fanaticism. Maxence clenched his eyes shut as his stomach heaved. He couldn't breathe against the piercing agony that flooded his entire being. His family couldn't trust him, and he knew they had every right not to.

And may your impure blood water the fields with that of every other enemy of France.

He recoiled as his own awful words echoed through his head. His insecurities and perceived offenses had built walls that never should have existed. He'd held to things he wanted to see.

With a shaky hand, Maxence reached out and grasped his brother's taut shoulder. "I'm so sorry." His voice broke. What words could he say?

A tear rolled down Gilles's cheek. He didn't bother to wipe it away. Maxence watched him, throat too constricted to talk. Gilles was a far better man than he. He always had been. How did he deserve this? How had Maxence allowed himself to get so removed from the people who mattered most that he had no knowledge of these burdens? He'd blocked his own vision, so absorbed in his own zeal, his own grief, his own insecurities. Armelle was right; he was just an oaf, riveted on his sorry life until she had thrown herself into it.

Gilles clasped his hand, and for an instant he thought his brother was going to push him away. He deserved it, as much as he'd deserved to be cursed and thrown out in the streets on their first meeting. But Gilles's hand tightened around his.

"Sometimes I think I have found a way to carry it, the weight of living each day without her. I can tend to my responsibilities and muddle through. Other days . . ." Gilles pressed his lips together as another tear fell. "It hits like a squall out of nowhere, and I wonder if this will be the time I go under with no strength to push myself back to the surface."

"What happened?"

"Childbirth."

Maxence gritted his teeth as his eyes filled. Despite his efforts, his own tears dropped. Gilles had been alone. "How long has it been?"

"Four months."

Four months of this darkness, while Maxence was off playing

soldier, yet another thing he hadn't succeeded at. And fighting his own demons over Émile. Maxence knew that pattern of struggling to right oneself after someone so dear was torn away, if in a different realm. Émile. He pulled the rosette from his pocket. "Gilles."

His brother finally looked at him, eyes red and wet. Maxence held up the white rosette, a symbol of the tyranny they had both once pledged to fight, but now an emblem of so much more. "Caroline gave this to Émile when we left with the *fédérés*. He was carrying it at the Tuileries."

Gilles stared at the looped ribbon for a moment. His chin quivered. Reverently he took it from Maxence and smoothed his thumb over its face. His head fell forward, a sob escaping.

It broke Maxence. He pulled his younger brother in and embraced him. Together they wept. For Caroline. For Émile. For all the things this war had taken from them.

Gilles's shaking slowly subsided. He straightened and wiped at his eyes. "You can keep that," Maxence said, drying his face on his sleeve.

His brother pressed it to his lips, then slipped it into his breast pocket. "What are you doing here? I thought you'd gone south with the army."

Armelle. Maxence lurched to his feet. "I need your help. I have to find someone, and quickly. She might be in trouble."

Gilles reached out a hand for Maxence to help him up. "Armelle Bernard?"

"How do you know—"

"She came here two nights ago." Gilles straightened his rumpled jacket. "I'll take you to where she's staying, but I need to wait for some-one. They should be here soon." He checked his pocket watch.

"Armelle was here?"

Gilles sniffed and rubbed at his eyes. "She wanted to explain your story. You should ask her to defend you more often. She's quite adept."

Maxence let out a breathless laugh. That woman. He'd be lost with-out her. The yearning to see her gnawed at him once more. The same yearning Gilles must feel now, which could never be satisfied. What awful injustice for life to take everything from a man as good as Gilles and give Maxence, who'd done nothing to deserve love, the chance at happiness. If he could find her in time. "Who are we waiting for?"

The door opened before Gilles could respond, and in walked the woman who'd run into Maxence in the street carrying her little bundle.

"Angelique," Gilles said.

The woman hurried into the kitchen. "You've left the house so dark." She halted at the door to the kitchen, eyes round. It *was* Madame Daubin. Gone were her fine silks and extravagant coiffures, her jewels and her painted face. "Maxence?" She glanced at Gilles.

"Would you stay with Lina? He needs to find Mademoiselle Bernard."

"*Bien sûr.*" The top of a little head peeked out from beneath the blankets she carried. Gilles crossed the kitchen and kissed the dark, feathery hair. Two tiny arms extended toward him, pushing away the blanket to reveal large eyes and full, rosy cheeks.

A baby. Maxence's vision clouded again. He'd missed so much.

"You stay with Grandmère, my Lina." Gilles squeezed the girl's hand. "I will return soon, and then you can properly meet Oncle Max." He kissed Madame Daubin on the cheek and thanked her, then strode toward the door.

Madame Daubin moved out of the way for Maxence amid affronted squawks from Lina. They both watched him warily as he followed Gilles out the door. He couldn't blame them.

Maxence closed the door behind him and hurried into the street with Gilles. Something about his brother's presence calmed his instinct to run. They'd find her, they'd warn Henri, and then they'd return home to continue this healing and forgiving.

The woman through the doorway showed no emotion as she said, "Mademoiselle Bernard is not here."

"Henri, then?" Maxence asked. Where would she have gone?

"Neither of the Bernards are here."

Ciel. He glanced at Gilles. "Do you know when they'll return?"

"I am not at liberty to say."

The sun sank toward the horizon. Maxence couldn't beat down the rising panic in his chest. The sooner he delivered his information—and the sooner he confirmed her safety—the sooner he'd rest easy. "We need to know."

Gilles put a hand on Maxence's arm and stepped forward. "Madame Nadon, we've learned something that could put not just the Bernards but others in danger. Can you tell us where they've gone?"

The woman's lips twisted. She looked Maxence up and down, in his waistcoat and shirtsleeves, and then Gilles in his jacket and cravat. "You are the man who brought her home."

Gilles nodded.

The woman scowled. "They have gone to Dinard and will not be back for quite some time."

Dinard! Gilles's hand tightened on Maxence's arm.

"I suggest you call again tomorrow, but if I can have your names—"

Maxence pivoted, not waiting for the rest of her speech. "We need to follow them." Blast it to the skies. He took off down the street, heading west toward the harbor. There would be soldiers waiting for them. Soldiers not as hesitant as he had been.

Gilles ran to catch up. "Max, we need to get to Oscar's. He'll have a boat we can use."

Maxence hardly heard him. How long would it take to cross the mouth of the river? They'd have to search the shore in waning light. The shipment wasn't supposed to be delivered until tomorrow. How had it come early?

"Max, listen!"

He pulled up short.

"Oscar has jolly boats," Gilles said.

Jolly boats? They were made for four rowers, but he and Gilles could manage if they could get one into the water without trouble. "It's late. His men won't be at the docks to help us." But where else were they to find a boat? He tugged at his hair.

"He has them at his house." Gilles darted down a side street in the direction of their uncle's.

Maxence followed. "Why does he have boats at the house?"

"Did Père never take you down to the cellars? In their smuggling days?"

No, but it sounded exactly like his father and uncle to have a secret smuggler's hold.

"There's a hidden exit closer to the harbor so we can carry a boat out unnoticed." Their uncle's house appeared at the end of the street. "We'll find her, Max."

A lump formed in Maxence's throat. He didn't deserve this help, and Gilles was in no position for him to ask, yet Gilles gave it freely. Maxence didn't know how he could repay his brother. He could only pray to whatever deity was listening that they'd all get out of this un-scathed so he could try.

Armelle steadied herself on a rock before stepping onto the next one. Water pooled at the base of the stones, beaten ragged by centuries of tides. Deep in the crevices crabs in white and orange shells scuttled through swaying vegetation. Her foot slipped, and she caught herself on the rough wall of rock beside her.

"Careful," Henri warned, a few steps ahead. He led them onto a pile of rocks with less water trapped around.

"Do you see it?" she asked.

He stopped, turning toward the sea. "Not yet. They're to anchor off that little island and show a white flag." He pointed to a mound a ways from shore, poking up out of the ocean.

"You have to row all the way out there?" After rowing for more than an hour to get from Saint-Malo to Dinard across the mouth of the river, Henri and his companions would be exhausted.

"Nadon isn't making me work tomorrow." He grinned.

They continued making their way along the shore, walking casually and pointing out the scenery as though enjoying an evening stroll. Henri's gaze kept drifting to the small, rocky cliffside that separated the beach from the land above it. Bushes and boulders popped up here and there, which Henri inspected with an air of blasé interest.

Peeking through the rock formations and arches, the sunset's ruby haze seeped into the sky. She might have paused to appreciate its deep hues if Henri's cautions weren't rolling about her mind. He was right, just as Nicole had been right. Though letting go of her dream hurt nearly as much as seeing Maxence walk away, it needed to be done. Perhaps Oscar Étienne had a position for her.

What a dolt she was. She teetered on the edge of a rock, flapping her arms to keep balance. She clearly couldn't let go of fantasies, even in the act of trying to move on from them. A position with the Étienne family would give her a small chance of hearing from Maxence again and an even greater chance of hearing from Père. Knowing she played the fool did little to convince her to stop believing.

They climbed up a large slab of granite sloping upward in the direction of the sea. Its flat surface made it easier to climb than the bits of rock they'd been scrambling over. Henri cut the distance between them. "We will go out in the boats when the signal is given. You'll stay here to watch the shore. Stay where we can see you. If you're not there, we'll assume you're hiding because you saw someone. Should that happen, we'll come back for you when we can."

The cool, wet air sent a chill up her limbs. She hadn't allowed Henri to recruit her so she could spend the night on a beach alone.

"Whatever you do, do not hide in the cave. The tide will come in a few hours from now and fill the entrance. You'll be stranded or worse."

Stranded in a cave or at the mercy of soldiers. Wonderful choices. "I thought you meant to hide some of the supplies in the cave."

"We have means to protect supplies in there, but not people." Henri turned toward the sea, leaning forward and pointing. "Look. There's a schooner off to the northwest. I wonder if that's the one." He hopped down from the large rock they'd climbed, making his way back to the cave where his fellow Chouans waited with the boats.

Armelle watched the little patches of white against the slate blue water for a minute more before creeping carefully down the rock. If aiding the *chouannerie* meant nothing more than evening boat rides and walks on the beach, she could embrace it. But this war wasn't that simple. It turned friends into foes.

She scanned the line of the cliff above, half expecting to see Maxence in uniform ready to arrest them. They'd stayed barely a step ahead of the République for so long, it wouldn't have surprised her to find their plans disrupted again. Worse than the fear of such a discovery was her disappointment at seeing the ledge clear, because deep down the other half of her had hoped to see his face.

The point that formed the easternmost coast of Dinard seemed to stay the same distance away each time Maxence looked back to adjust their course. As the minutes passed, dusk marched across the sky, chasing the sun toward night and taking with it the light he needed to find her.

He and Gilles rowed in familiar tandem. They hadn't worked together like this since Maxence left *le Rossignol*, and yet they'd fallen into routine as easily as if they'd never left the sea.

"Hard to port," Maxence said, turning back around. Gilles followed the command, and the boat responded smoothly. He already felt the satisfying burn in his shoulders of work done well. If not for the tightness in his chest, he might have enjoyed himself. After living inland for so long, he'd forgotten the vibrancy of the sea breeze.

"Will you marry her, then?" Gilles asked.

He didn't want to think about that now. "She made it unquestionably clear that my advances were not appreciated." He focused on the strokes of his oars, matching them with Gilles's. The embarrassment of the conversation in the Chouans' house still heated his face when he thought about it.

Gilles grunted. "She gave a very different impression when I met her."

"What did she say?" Maxence's brows knit. She'd given him strange signs, but he did not doubt the sincerity of her rebuke. She'd meant it when she said she hadn't wanted his kiss.

"Nothing directly. It was more in the way she glowed every time someone mentioned your name. It reminded me of the look I'd see on Caroline's face."

Gilles must have imagined it. Maxence shifted his grip on the oars. "It angered me at first," Gilles said. "I didn't think you deserved it."

Maxence snorted. "I don't." But it was suddenly a struggle to keep his strokes short enough to match his brother's.

"You'd abandoned us." Gilles paused. "We didn't realize you felt abandoned as well."

His woes meant nothing when compared to theirs. Maxence looked back to check their course again and caught Gilles's gaze. Pain filled his eyes. And questions and grief that might never leave. Maxence groaned within. Nothing he did or said could take that burden away. And here they sat discussing Armelle, only adding to the ache. It wasn't doing either of them good. He opened his mouth to ask after Oncle Oscar, but Gilles went on.

"Père said once that I didn't understand women," his brother said, expression softening. Was that forgiveness hiding behind Gilles's tired eyes? "I could be terribly wrong about Armelle, but I think the Daubins would agree with me that that young woman would have thrown herself into your arms if you'd walked through the door the other night."

A smile pulled at the corners of Maxence's mouth. It was too much to hope for, but a little flicker sprang to life where once only the darkness of disappointment reigned. "If you would, please ask her if that's true when we find her, using those exact words." He could do with another sight of a thorough blush on that face. Or any sight of that face.

They worked their way around the point toward the north shore, where Gilles mentioned a series of caves where the Chouans could be hidden. They didn't see anyone through the rocks as they rowed the length of it, so they beached the jolly boat to search.

"I'll go above and look for soldiers," Gilles said quietly. "You look for her down here."

Maxence nodded, and Gilles scrambled up the slope. Stone formations, some as large as the *menhir* at Ilizmaen, stretched along the waterline. He stepped carefully through gravel and boulders. She and Henri could be hiding anywhere. The tide had begun its foray inland, sometimes splashing up his footholds onto his boots. Large black birds called to each other, making it difficult to listen for movement or talking.

He didn't see any blue coats above the foreshore. Perhaps they hadn't taken Voulland's order seriously or they were patrolling another beach. He wouldn't relax until he knew for certain.

The azure-lit shore lay peaceful and unassuming. Had the Chouans called it off? He didn't have much land left to search before reaching the point.

Two rowboats a little way into the water caught his eye. And a masted vessel—a schooner by the looks of the rigging—anchored some distance out. Maxence paused to watch. The boats could turn at any moment and go off in a different direction, but they looked to be making for the schooner. Was Armelle on one of them?

He ducked through an arch, formed by the beating of water and wave. He'd finish searching the beach and then hurry back to the jolly boat. If she was on the water, he and Gilles could intercept her there.

And once those boats were out of musket range, it was the safest place for all of them to be.

Straightening, he caught sight of the striped sleeve of that terrible bedgown she'd forced him to wear to trick the Chouans peeking out from behind a rock. Her arm was low to the ground, as though crouching. The soaring inside carried him over the last stretch of rocks. He'd wrap her in his arms, feel her breathe against his chest, and drink in the scent of her. Only then would he believe her safe and well.

He rounded the outcropping that separated him from Armelle. She huddled between boulders in conversation with someone unseen. Henri, he assumed.

The click of steel against steel made Maxence turn, gut wrenching. A flash of a white cuff through the bushes. The glint of gold buttons. A muzzle.

Maxence bolted and shoved Armelle down. The gun cracked. He slammed against the granite, shoulder erupting in hot, piercing agony.

CHAPTER 31

The shot rang in Armelle's ears as she pushed herself upright on shaking legs. She couldn't make sense of it. One moment she'd been following Henri, the next she'd hit the ground hard. The man who'd thrown her down rolled to the gravel and groaned.

"Hide, Armelle!" Henri hissed. "I'll get him."

A crimson stain bloomed across the man's sleeve. She couldn't see his face, but she knew those dark curls.

"Max!" Bile rose in her throat. She was mistaken. She had to be mistaken. It couldn't be him. She scrambled toward him, refusing to believe her eyes. Why was he here?

Shouts and scuffling from above the beach rang across the water. He writhed, gasping. Her limbs trembled as she crouched beside him. His eyes were clenched shut, his breath short and tense.

"Max." Her voice quavered. She pressed her hand to his face, but he didn't acknowledge her touch. Suffocating terror shot through her, smothering her ability to think.

A whirring sounded above them, then the thud of metal on stone. She and Henri glanced up in time to see a musket plunge into the rising waves, thrown from above. Someone shouted again.

"Help me," she cried to Henri. She stepped around Maxence. How would they get him up? They couldn't carry him easily over this rough ground. The gears in her head picked up speed, sending thoughts tumbling wildly. They were so far. How could they save him?

"You're going to get shot," Henri hissed.

Someone barreled down the slope. Armelle and Henri hunched behind the rocks, her brother pulling out a pistol from the waistband of his breeches.

"Max?" a worried voice called.

Armelle reached for her brother. "Put that down! It's Gilles." Praise the heavens.

Gilles came around the boulders and paused. *"Diantre.* Where was he hit?" He dropped to his knees beside Maxence.

"We need to leave," Henri said.

"I disarmed the lookout." Gilles tore off his brother's neckcloth and unbuttoned his shirt. "He ran back for his comrades, so we don't have much time." He pulled back the shirt and waistcoat. A bloody hole marred the flesh just above Maxence's chest. Armelle's stomach lurched, her body going cold. The brown waistcoat had disguised the rip in the shirt.

"It went through." Gilles pulled the shirt back over the wound. "Max, can you stand?" Maxence nodded, eyes scrunched tight. Armelle grasped his uninjured arm as she and Gilles helped him first sit, then slowly stand.

"The boat is here," Henri said, pointing to where it sat with waves lapping the prow. "Put him in there. But we need to warn the others."

"There's no time," she said. "We have to get him back."

"Our boat is on the other end of the beach." Gilles motioned to her, and Armelle reluctantly let him take her place to support Maxence.

"Can he walk that far?" she asked. Maxence's face had paled in the effort to stand.

Henri glanced between the Étienne brothers and Armelle. "I'll take yours. Get him back to Saint-Malo. Nadon is going to have my head."

Eyes on the land above them, he turned and hurried down the shore as fast as the rock would let him.

"That's not going to be easy for one man," Gilles muttered. He glanced at her as they moved forward. "Watch for soldiers."

"Should we bandage his wound?" The sight of it still burned in her mind.

"Only if we all have a death wish. We'll tend to it in the boat."

Armelle drew in a rattling breath. She worked her way along beside them, scanning the ridge. Every rustle of a bush in the wind made her freeze. Gilles helped Maxence into the boat, positioning him so he faced the shore.

"Get in behind him," Gilles instructed. Water splashed up around her as she ran for the prow and hopped in, careful not to hit Maxence. "No, don't sit on the thwart. Sit below, and, both of you, keep your heads down."

She slipped from the seat to the floor. Blood covered Maxence's left sleeve. Gilles thrust the boat into the water, and Maxence moaned at the jostling. His brother jumped in. He sat on the thwart closest to the stern and positioned the oars.

"What about you?" Armelle asked.

Gilles dug in the oars and pulled back. "Someone has to get us out of here."

Armelle peeked over the side of the boat as Gilles maneuvered them through the maze of rocks near the shore. The light had dimmed enough that she couldn't see very far to the west where the other boat should have been. Shadows of rock looked the same as small boats.

"Armelle, I'll need you to help him," Gilles said. "Get that waistcoat off first. We don't want to risk wool fibers getting in the wound."

She reached around Max and undid the waistcoat buttons. He'd been vexed when she'd tried to help him with these buttons in Savenay. It seemed like a lifetime ago. So much had happened since. Now he responded without complaint as she removed the waistcoat starting with the uninjured arm.

"There they are. Get down." Gilles picked up his pace with the oars.

Armelle and Maxence hunched. He sucked in, clutching his wounded arm close to his side. Popping from the shore echoed across the waves, and he flinched with each sound. She wrapped her fingers around his, and he squeezed them faintly. She whispered a silent prayer, not sure what words she said exactly.

A thump against the hull made them all jump. "Gilles!" Armelle cried.

"Stay down. It hit the boat."

He was going to get shot too. And then she'd have to get them all to Saint-Malo in the dark.

A bullet splashed to their right. Another two to the left. Sea spray flung across the boat. "We're almost out of range," Gilles muttered.

"Can you see Henri?"

Gilles turned his head west. "Not yet, but the gunfire is on this side of the beach. They haven't seen him." The popping continued for another minute, the splashes getting farther away. He rowed in silence a little longer. "I think they've stopped." The oars stilled, and Gilles panted. He pulled them in and took off his coat, laying it across the seat beside him.

"This is madness." Armelle dropped her head, nerves taut. Why had she allowed Henri to drag her into this?

"We need to slow the bleeding as best we can," Gilles said, setting the oars. The steady beat commenced again. "We'll have to use his shirt."

She didn't think her pulse could race any faster than it did until Maxence helped her untuck his shirt and lift it over his head. He tensed as she peeled the linen away from his wounds. The twilight outlined his shoulders in faint blue and turned the left side of his shirt black.

"How do I put this on?" she asked.

Gilles looked over his shoulder. "Fold it in quarters then press it to both sides of the wound."

Her stomach turned as in her mind she traced the line the bullet would have traveled to produce these wounds. It had hit bone, no question. She folded the shirt across her lap, attempting to keep it out of the dampness in the bottom of the boat. The boat rocked when she tried to get to the side of him to place the bandage. She yelped, redistributing her weight to even out the vessel. A swim was the last thing they needed tonight. She held the shirt to the wound on the side of his shoulder and wrapped it around to the front.

"Keep it there as firmly as you can."

"I will." She couldn't see well anymore, but she didn't need a lantern to know he had a large amount of blood along his arm. Maxence swayed, and Armelle released one side of the shirt to steady him with a hand on his uninjured side. The chill of the ocean air sent gooseflesh over his skin.

"Give me your coat, Gilles," she said. He paused rowing and tossed it to her. She draped it over Maxence as best she could, avoiding the makeshift bandage. "Here, lean back."

She guided him to recline with his head on her shoulder. She wrapped one arm around him to press the linen to the front wound and pushed on the side wound with her other hand. The thwart plank dug into her back as his weight settled against her.

"Your brother made it to the schooner," Gilles said, breathing heavily.

Armelle rested her head on Maxence's curls. "*Dieu merci.*" She couldn't make sense of the shadows to the east, but Gilles must have seen something. Now she only had to worry about making it safely back to Saint-Malo to take care of Max. "How will you get us to the harbor in the dark?"

"He'd be a poor excuse for a mariner if he couldn't," Maxence mumbled, earning him a chuckle from Gilles.

She hugged him closer, tears springing to her eyes. Just hearing his voice soothed the gaping void that had opened in her heart since he'd left her in the street. "I've missed you, *mon amour*." She pressed her lips to his temple. They'd get him to shore, Gilles would mend the wound, and in a few weeks he'd be good as new.

"Why are we pretending again?" Maxence whispered. His chest rose and fell weakly but not as rapidly as it had at the start of their escape.

She brushed her cheek against his hair. "No more pretending, Max."

"I don't think my head is functioning well enough to interpret what that means."

A tear slid down her face. "Rest." He was back. He was here. They would answer the questions in the morning.

That morning the torrent of grief had hit Gilles with the fierceness of a fifty-gun broadside. Ripping, tearing, leaving him in a battered heap. He didn't know why the young woman's appearance on his doorstep had incited the downward spiral, but the longer he thought on it, the harder it was to push away the indignation. Maxence didn't deserve the happiness life had taken away from Gilles.

Now as he staggered along the cobbled streets of Saint-Malo, Max leaning heavily against him, he couldn't hold onto the anger. His arms trembled from an hour of heavy rowing, but he wouldn't let them release his brother's weight.

He needed Dr. Savatier. This wouldn't be an easy surgery. Shoulder wounds never were. How would he summon the doctor? This was beyond his capacity. The worries spun through his head, mounting with each step.

Armelle hurried along beside them, holding the shirt against Max's shoulder. "Are we going to your house?"

It was closer. They'd already waited so long. "I need Savatier."

"Where does he live? Is it far?"

"Number 7 *rue de l'École*." Too far for Max. Did he let her take his brother home while he ran for the Savatiers' house? She might not be able to support Max if he lost consciousness.

They came to a cross street, and voices made them pull up short. "We need to hide," Gilles hissed. They led Maxence to the corner of a building where the street lamps created a long shadow. Though they'd covered his brother in his coat, it was still apparent they were walking around with an injured and half-dressed man. They didn't want to make an impression that could be used against them.

The three of them huddled together, watching. Two men passed, the lamplight making their uniforms glow orange. Soldiers, and older ones from before the revolution. They still wore the coats of the previous regime, but they wouldn't be out patrolling in uniform if they hadn't sworn allegiance to the République. Gilles adjusted his grip on Maxence.

"My daughter will be ten years old," one of them said. "I can hardly believe it."

The soldiers would be gone soon. Gilles glanced toward Armelle but couldn't see her face in the dark. They only had to hold still a few moments longer.

"Ten? Surely not."

The soldier halted beneath one of the street lamps. One pulled something from his coat, fiddled with it, then reached up toward the lamp. After a moment he turned, bringing a pipe to his mouth. "It makes you feel old, doesn't it?" He took an easy pose and puffed on his pipe.

Gilles groaned inside. They couldn't wait here until the soldiers had finished their chat.

"Number 7 *rue de l'École*?" Armelle whispered.

"Yes." If they tried to move back down the street and take another route, the soldiers would see. *Diantre.*

"Hold the bandage." Gilles took it, and Armelle dashed out of their hiding place. "*Citoyens!*" she cried in an alarmed voice.

Que diable! What was she doing?

The soldiers straightened, one reaching for the musket at his back. "Help me! Please, help."

"What is it?" Neither soldier relaxed. She was going to get herself killed. If they saw the blood on her hands . . .

"I'm trying to meet my *père*, but I cannot find the house. Can you take me to him?" She stopped running a few paces from the men, one hand in her pocket. "He was to meet me at number 7 *rue de l'École*."

"What are you doing out so late?" one asked.

The soldier with the pipe shrugged. "We can take you, *citoyenne*. It's this way." He pointed back the direction they'd come.

"Oh, *merci*. Papa will be so worried." She glanced toward Gilles and Maxence as she and the soldiers passed their hiding place and disappeared behind the corner.

She meant to get Savatier. There was no changing it now. When they were far enough away that their voices became jumbled, Gilles pulled Maxence forward. The rest of the walk lasted an excruciatingly long time, but the sight of his home, the flicker of light coming through the window, hadn't brought him this much joy in months.

He startled Angelique out of her chair when he unlocked the door and burst through it, knees threatening to buckle. She rushed forward, cap askew.

"What happened? Gilles, you took so long." She gasped. "Is he . . ."

"Get water and wine. And my bag." He practically dragged Maxence the rest of the way to the kitchen and laid him groaning on the floor. Not five hours before he'd sat on this same floor cursing his brother and his fate when Maxence had appeared. His mother-in-law followed him with a candle she set on the small table.

"Shall I send for Dr. Savatier?" Angelique asked, pulling over a water bucket. She plucked up the bottle Gilles had been contemplating earlier from the floor and moved it beside the bucket.

"Armelle went for him."

"Your bag is upstairs?"

"It was in the sitting room." Gilles's hands shook as he rolled up his sleeves. Flecks of sand, the kind impossible to remove, scattered over his hands. He sought out a towel and dipped it in the water before scrubbing at the stubborn bits. Anything that got in the wound would cause infection. He couldn't risk it.

Angelique helped him lay out his tools, which gleamed too brightly in the faint light. He usually used Savatier's when helping with surgeries. They eased an old tarp under Maxence's left side.

"Let's find all the candles," he said. Where were Armelle and Savatier? Had something happened?

When they'd gathered and lit all the lights he owned, a loud pounding came at the door. Gilles rushed to lift the latch and usher them in.

Savatier threw off his coat before Gilles could get the door shut. "Have you given him something to dull his senses?"

"I was about to get the laudanum."

Savatier rolled up his sleeves with the dexterity of someone half his age. "Is it salvageable?"

Gilles swallowed. "I don't know."

Armelle's eyes bulged, and her face took on a sickly hue. "What do you mean?"

Savatier hurried into the kitchen. "Maxence, what have you gotten yourself into this time?" he said in a bright tone. They couldn't hear the muttered answer from the sitting room.

Armelle snatched Gilles's sleeve. "What do you mean?" she repeated.

"I mean that the shoulder is a terrible place to get hit by any weapon," Gilles said with a sigh. "There are too many parts to make a mess of. If we are successful tonight, if he doesn't get infection, if it doesn't require amputation now or later, there is still a strong likelihood he will never have complete use of his arm again."

Her eyes dropped to the floor. All Gilles could think to do was pat her arm. "Angelique, will you help?"

"Of course." She'd helped them on a few surgeries before this when Madame Savatier was not able. The thought of having her there gave him strength to proceed. Gilles made for the kitchen, but a cry from upstairs made both him and Angelique pause. Of all times.

"Lina always knows when she's missing something important," his mother-in-law said.

That little person certainly had a knack for crying at inopportune moments.

"I'll tend to her," Armelle said too quickly, voice strained. He didn't blame her for not wanting to witness this. Angelique handed her a small candle before she raced upstairs.

By the time they reentered the kitchen, Savatier had already given Maxence laudanum, as evidenced by the bottle on the table. He carefully probed the wounds. "Clearly it didn't hit the artery, or he wouldn't have made it this far. That is one mercy."

Gilles went to kneel beside the surgeon but balked. Something rose in his chest, a too-familiar panic that he could not hold back. He stood above Maxence, paralyzed. Seeing his brother pale and limp made the memory of Caroline lying in much the same way, unresponsive with tiny Lina curled against her chest, flood his consciousness. He couldn't save her. He might not save Max. The floor tilted beneath his feet.

"Can you do this, Gilles?" Savatier asked kindly.

"I . . ." How could he not? What good was studying to be a surgeon if he couldn't save the people he loved?

A hand took his arm. "You can, Gilles," Angelique said. "I know you have the strength in you. And *she* knows you do too." The mention of Caroline, her trust and faith in him, relaxed the tightness that wound inside him.

Who would have thought that his mother-in-law would become such an anchor in his life? When they'd left Marseille, she'd gone to pieces over the slightest worry. Losing two children had toughened her, changed her into a woman he hardly recognized. She still dealt with the demons as much as he did, but she'd pulled her grief back behind a wall so that he rarely caught a glimpse of it.

Gilles knelt. Savatier squeezed his shoulder. "The bone is shattered, just here. We'll need to extract the shards and the head of the humerus, as I think it's separated. We don't want it causing problems later."

They set to work while Angelique prepared needles and catgut for sutures. Just like rowing the boat, he found a rhythm and threw himself into it. He'd give this his all, and only time would tell if it was enough.

Armelle sat in a chair beside the window of Gilles's bedroom, gently rocking Lina's cradle with her foot. The baby's thick eyelashes splayed across her cheeks. She'd worked both fists out of her blankets to rest beside her face. Armelle envied this picture of perfect repose.

Gilles's warning would not leave her, and it mingled with Henri's from earlier. Who was she to hope for happy endings? She wanted to have faith. For once in her life, it seemed too great a task.

Below, the murmur of voices drifted through the floorboards, but she couldn't determine what they said. How she wished she had more to offer, but she'd only get in their way. If she could stomach being there at all. She let the cradle come to a gradual stop. She needed to get rid of these unrelenting anxieties. They'd eat her alive.

She crept to a shelf of books and pulled the first one off. Reading would distract her. She positioned the chair closer to the desk where the candle burned low. The simple leather cover looked fairly new. She opened it to the middle.

28 July 1793

Mon cher *Gilles,*

The lavender fields will be in bloom by now. I didn't expect to miss them so much. If I could visit any memory for just a moment, that is the one I would choose, when it was simply the two of us and a brilliant sunset. Neither of us had any inkling that night what the future would hold, not the destruction or the bliss.

Sometimes it is difficult to look to the future with any sort of anticipation when it can only be riddled with heartache, but knowing I have you by my side makes it easier to bear. Together we can weather the storms.

I love you, mon chéri. *I'm so proud of all you have accomplished.*
Caroline

Another letter began below it in a masculine hand, dated a few days later. Armelle snapped the book shut, face heating. This was a diary of letters between Gilles and his wife. She quickly returned it to its place. How terrible she was to intrude on that space.

As she returned to the chair and settled into it, a yearning for that same sort of place of trust and understanding and support sprouted in her heart. There was only one person she wanted to create it with. She rested her head on her arm atop the desk. Whatever happened in the morning, they would face it together.

CHAPTER 32

Armelle awoke to the fuss of a hungry baby. She sat up quickly. Light poured in through the window. Soft footsteps came up the stairs. She rose, brushing off her skirts. What a fright she looked with dried blood on her hands and bedgown and salt stains on her petticoats.

Madame Daubin came through the door with a bowl and cloth. "Ah, *bonjour*." Her bright, fresh face gave no hint that she'd been awake much of the night.

"*Bonjour*." Armelle stretched. Her back and neck protested the movement. "Did you sleep at all?"

"Dr. Savatier walked me home after they finished." Madame Daubin set the bowl and cloth on the desk. "I'm getting old, so I do not sleep much anyway. Here, you can freshen up." She looked barely fifty, so she could not be *that* old, but Armelle didn't contradict her. She dipped the cloth in the cool water and wiped it over her face.

"And *ma petite* Lina, how do you do this morning?" Madame Daubin lifted the baby from the crib and kissed her cheek. As Armelle washed, the woman changed Lina's clothing and rewrapped her blanket. "We are off to the wet nurse, unless you need something else."

Armelle lowered the cloth and drew a breath. "How is he?"

"They're both fast asleep downstairs, poor boys." The woman gave a small smile. "The surgery went as well as they could have hoped. They salvaged the arm."

Dieu merci. So many small miracles.

"I brought over some of our breakfast, if you are hungry. It's in the kitchen."

Armelle thanked her, though she didn't know if she could stomach food. The hunger to see Maxence superseded everything. When Madame Daubin and Lina left, she cleaned off her hands as best she could and unpinned her hair. As she raked through it with her fingers, her eyes fell on the neatly made bed on one side of the room. A night of aiding someone he barely knew and then dealing with the aftermath, and Gilles had slept downstairs with little comfort. She winced. She'd been of no value to anyone last night, but today she would amend that.

After twisting her hair back into place and returning her cap atop, Armelle hurried to the stairs. A pang inside stopped her on the top step. Nothing would be the same as it had been the day before. She wrung her hands. Not for Max or for her. Descending these stairs would plunge her into this new reality, and for a moment the looming unknown felt too great to bear.

She forced her foot down one stair and then another. Maxence was below. Whatever came next, she wanted to weather it with him, as Caroline had said to Gilles.

Madame Daubin had lit the fire in the sitting room when she arrived, and it cast the room in a cozy glow. Max sat on the couch, propped up with blankets and pillows. His head rested against the back of the couch. They'd wrapped his shoulder in bandages and put his left arm in a sling. A blanket lay across him, but it didn't cover his uninjured shoulder with its image of a ship.

That day in Nantes, when they'd hid in the prison and he'd teased her for watching him, she'd had no idea how much that arrogant fop who couldn't let go of his national guard coat would come to mean to her. The miles they'd crossed, the laughter and tears, the caring for each other—she could embrace that for the rest of her days.

She crept into the room. Gilles sat in a chair on the opposite side of the couch, head lolled to one side in much the same way as Max's. The similarity between them brought a smile to her face. She crossed the sitting room and tapped Gilles's shoulder.

He sat up with a start.

"I'm sorry," Armelle said. "You should sleep upstairs. You'll be more comfortable. I'll sit with him."

Gilles wiped a hand across his face. "Yes. Yes, very well." He pushed himself stiffly out of the chair. "Where is Lina?"

"Madame Daubin took her."

He nodded, eyes still half closed. After pausing to observe Maxence, he stumbled up the stairs. Poor boys, indeed.

She eased onto the couch and turned toward Maxence. The lines of frustration, so often present, had lifted from his face. She crossed her arms and grasped the sides of her bedgown. Her fingers itched to grab his hand, but she didn't need to wake him. She would have to content herself with watching over him.

"Enjoying yourself?" came his scratchy voice. His eyes were barely opened, and they quickly closed again.

"Max." She scooted closer, a bubbly lightness filling her chest.

"I can't say I mind."

"You should still be asleep." But she wouldn't complain that he wasn't.

Maxence shifted and grimaced. "I have always found it difficult to sleep with you in the room."

"That does not bode well for us." It popped from her mouth before she could reel it back.

He opened one eye and gave her a sidelong glance. "What do you mean by that?"

Armelle blushed and dropped her gaze. Was she making too many assumptions? Perhaps he'd changed his mind in the weeks they'd been apart. When she looked up, he seemed to have gone to sleep again. "I only meant that life felt empty when you went away," she whispered. She traced the outline of one of the sails on his shoulder. His skin was warm against her finger. "There were so many things I wanted to tell you."

He drew in a deep breath as she followed the line of the next sail.

"Some of them just to see you scowl."

His lips curled faintly.

She ran her finger from the top of each mast to the deck. "I missed the strength of your presence, how it grounded me." She brushed the curve of the ship's bow.

He caught her hand in his, pinning it against his shoulder.

A little grin tiptoed across her mouth. "Most of all I was curious if you ever caught up to my number of wins, since you hadn't mentioned it for some time before you left, and I still had significantly more points the last time you told me the score."

He gave a small laugh and opened his eyes. "Life has been rather dull without you, Armelle." Stubble dotted his face, much the same as when they'd started their journey. How had she resisted him then?

"I can think of a simple solution to ensure our separation doesn't happen again." She dug into her pocket and pulled out the die. The face with two dots pointed up, and she turned it to the side with the single dot before placing it in his hand. The question hung between them, dizzying and electrifying at the same time. Armelle had her answer. In her core she'd known the answer since Ilizmaen. She'd been too afraid of getting distracted from her family to accept it.

Maxence closed his hand around the die but said nothing, letting the question linger. He gave a sigh so filled with longing and frustration and worry that she wanted to gather him in her arms. She would have, if it wouldn't have disturbed his wound.

Armelle looped both her arms through his and squeezed. They didn't need to rush this. She should have waited to bring it up until he'd healed, but she struggled to contain the warmth in her heart. "Does it hurt?"

She could already see the lie before he spoke. "Not very much."

That wouldn't last long with what his left shoulder had been put through. He stared at the crackling fire, jaw taut, and for a moment she considered waking Gilles to ask what to give him before the pain increased.

"If you had asked me yesterday morning as I was racing back to warn you the army knew about the shipment," he finally said, "I would have said I'd marry you in an instant. If I could convince you I was more than a flirt and a cad, which I didn't believe possible."

Armelle touched his face, turning it back toward her.

"I don't know exactly what they did last night," he said, "but I wasn't so terrible a student at Montpellier that I couldn't tell how bad it was. To be truly honest, I am surprised I still have my arm. At sea, Savatier would have taken it."

She smoothed back his hair and relished the feel of it between her fingers. So worried about burdening others, he couldn't see how much he meant to them. How much they simply wanted him near.

"I don't know what will happen," he said, voice pinched.

She rested her forehead against his. "We've made it this far, Max."

He swallowed. "I don't wish to face another day without you."

Her heart galloped in her chest. "Then let us get you strong." She wound her fingers through the back of his curls, suddenly anxious to feel the sweet longing of his kiss once more. "And I will allow you to decide when we should transition from Citoyens Rossignol to Monsieur and Madame Étienne."

"If I've learned anything on this journey, it is to let you take the lead."

She laughed, and the weight on her shoulders and her heart dissolved. So much had been taken by this war, which spread from Brittany to Provence, but miracles still happened. How else could this audacious Breton and brooding Marseillais find each other? "I think this is when you are supposed to kiss me."

"Oh, no." Maxence straightened his neck, pulling away.

She arched her brows. Her breath caught. What did he mean? Her spirits, which had been winding toward the bliss of feeling his lips again, plunged.

"The last time I attempted a kiss, I was thoroughly reprimanded. I will not make that mistake again."

She pulled her mouth into a frown. He couldn't be serious. He leaned his head back against the couch and closed his eyes. She settled her head next to his. He was doing this on purpose to tease her. "If you are trying to win, it will not work."

"I am only capable of the utmost solemnity." At one time she might have believed his words, but she'd seen him in moments of tranquility, when his worries weren't overpowering everything else.

She brushed her fingers along his collarbone. "You are going to make a very grumpy old man." But he'd be her grumpy old man. A little snicker escaped her.

"If you are trying to get me to kiss you, that is hardly the way to do it." But his mouth had softened.

"Then this should do the trick." Before she could dissuade herself, she brought her lips just below the square of his jaw. Stubble tickled her lips. His breathing quickened along with hers. She trailed kisses along his jaw as his head turned.

Then his lips found hers, and a little shiver ran up her spine. He kissed her hesitantly, as though worried she'd get angry like last time. She didn't blame him, but she also wouldn't have it. When he first kissed her, he'd practically begged for her to return it. Now she did without reserve. True to his word, he let her lead. The kisses flowed, one following the next, streaming from behind the walls they'd both made. This warmth between them, both new and familiar, seeped through her until it filled her entire being.

And if Gilles or Dr. Savatier were to walk in at that moment, they'd banish her from the house.

She pressed her mouth to his once more, loving the way he caressed her lips with his, and then broke away.

"There." Her heart pounded. She faced forward on the couch. "At Ilizmaen we proved we were proficient in all the rest of being married. It is comforting to know we are competent in kissing as well."

"All the rest?"

"*Chut*," she hushed him. She took his hand and squeezed it between both of hers. "Your doctors will be angry I haven't let you rest."

"I do not think either of them would fault me. I'm certain they kissed their wives thoroughly when they agreed to marriage." But he closed his eyes.

"What a journey this has been," she whispered. "And our next journey will be even grander."

"What makes you think that?" His voice had taken a weary quietness.

"If nothing else, because you won't have to sleep on the floor anymore." Armelle shrugged.

A smile lit his face. "You should leave before I kiss you again."

She snuggled against him, pressing a kiss to the ship on his shoulder. "*Sacrebleu*, whatever shall I do?"

CHAPTER 33

Four months later
2 August 1794 (15 Thermidor, Year II)
Saint-Malo, Brittany, France

Maxence attempted to set Gilles's telescope so he could see into the tangle of ships in the harbor. To his misfortune, holding still had never been Armelle's forte. She steadied the front end of the instrument for him, but her definition of steady resembled the pitching deck of a sloop in a storm.

He pulled his eye away. "I thought I saw a boat leave *le Rossignol,* but then the telescope hit a gale." He'd tried to see if her father was aboard. He thought he spied him, but he couldn't be sure.

Armelle puckered her lips and raised a brow, as she did when she pretended to get irked by his teasing. How funny that after two short months of marriage, he could anticipate her reactions. She took the telescope, closed it, and put it in her pocket. "I try to help, and this is the thanks I get."

Not many people passed them atop the city ramparts where they stood. Before them lay a small stretch of beach that ran into the harbor, and behind them the bustle of *rue Saint-Philippe*. A small arch below them in the Gothic wall allowed dockworkers, businessmen, and all manner of people to enter the old section of the city.

Armelle bounced from foot to foot like Noël Colbert had when telling them about his new bed. Maxence chuckled. "You will fall off the rampart if you don't hold still." He lifted his left arm just enough for her to slide in against his side. Four months of healing had left him with very little movement in that shoulder.

She wrapped her arms around his waist and squeezed. "I've been waiting for this day for so long. I can't believe it's here."

Maxence kissed her brow and hugged her back. He only hoped her father approved of Armelle's choice. They'd received the written blessing of both their parents before the simple marriage, of course, but that did not mean Monsieur Bernard couldn't regret his decision.

An impish gleam touched Armelle's eye, and for a moment it caught him in a mist of memory that made it difficult not to kiss her senseless for all of Saint-Malo to see. After all that he had been, how could he have earned the heart of this woman? Her eager love had pulled him through many dark times as they worked through the shadows of both his past and his future.

They didn't even have a place to call their own—they lived with Oncle Oscar and Tante Jeanne—and still she kept a smile. Someday they wouldn't need the protection of his rich uncle. Though the biggest threat of recognition had left with Voulland and his troops, they both feared the small chance that someone from another *demi-brigade* knew of him. Few in Saint-Malo, even the army, would dare cross Oscar Étienne without good reason, and they'd made a comfortable hiding place in a room in the attic of his uncle's mansion, only venturing out of the house for special occasions such as welcoming their fathers. Maxence pursed his lips, a small part of him wishing he'd stayed hidden for this event. He didn't know which father he was more anxious to meet.

"Look who we found, Lina."

The voice turned Maxence's head. Gilles hurried toward them with

Lina in his arms from the stairs that led up from the street. He had a partly crumpled sheet of newsprint in his hand.

"I thought you were going to meet us at Oncle Oscar's later," Maxence said. Henri was to meet them there as well after finishing some Chouan business Maxence did not want to know about. Having Gilles here would make this meeting much more bearable.

"Dr. Savatier thought I should come." Gilles glanced at Armelle, who failed to hide a grin.

"Come here, *petite* Lina," she crooned.

"I can keep her," Gilles said quickly.

But Lina was already reaching toward her aunt. "Of course not. Lina needs her time with Tante Armelle." She scooped up the dark-haired girl, who gave Maxence a guarded stare. Now at eight months old she had finally forgiven him for looking too much like her papa—at least enough to not scream when she saw him—but she started every inter-action with a warning look should he think about trying to hold her.

"*Bonjour* to you as well, Lina," Maxence said before Armelle swept her off to point out the ships.

Gilles extended the newsprint to him. "Did you hear about this?" His voice had turned grave. "Robespierre is dead."

"Dead?" The words didn't make sense. Robespierre had ruled the Jacobins, and therefore France, for nearly two years. Had an assassin finally found him? Maxence took the paper, but his head spun too much to read the words.

"Guillotined. On the tenth of Thermidor. Louis Saint-Just as well."

Guillotined. Maxence reeled. As a zealous Jacobin, he'd sung the man's praises as much as any *révolutionnaire*, but in the wake of so much death and destruction across France, the applause had dampened. Robespierre and his friend Saint-Just had finally gone too far.

"He practically put himself forward as a god, then called for heads at the National Convention," Gilles said, not bothering to let Maxence read the newspaper. "The Convention decided it had had enough."

Maxence rubbed his forehead. Robespierre guillotined. Just like that.

"Half the members of the Paris Commune were guillotined after him. It's the September Massacres all over again." Gilles's eyes darkened.

A chill ran over Maxence. He'd witnessed the massacres in the streets of Paris. Gilles had lived it in Marseille. The Daubins had barely escaped with their lives. "Who will rise from the ashes?" Maxence asked.

Gilles shook his head. "I think France still has a long road ahead." Someday they'd arrive at the peace they all longed for. One step at a time. He handed the newspaper back to Gilles. Later he'd read through it, when family reunions had settled and he had a better mind to process what it all meant for France and the little family he'd just begun.

"They're coming!" Armelle hurried back to them beaming. She darted behind him, as though hiding. Gilles also backed away so Maxence was closest to the stairs. What were they doing?

Before he could ask, a woman came up the stone steps. Maxence blinked, unable to comprehend the scene before him. "Maman?"

With a sob, his mother ran to him and threw her arms around his neck. "Maxence. *Mon fils.*" She pulled back, taking his face in her hands.

"What are you doing here?" he managed. Tears fell unbidden, blurring the vision before him.

She embraced him again, and he held her tightly, afraid if he let go, this childish fantasy would vanish. "I've missed you," she said. "Oh, how I've missed you."

The pain of the last two years streamed out of him as his shoulders shook. The doubts, the falsehoods he'd told himself, burdens he didn't realize he still carried eased as they cried together.

"*Je t'aime, mon fils.* Don't you ever forget that," she whispered.

He nodded, unable to speak. Not far away, Armelle swayed with Lina, tears in her eyes. This was supposed to be her happy reunion, not his.

His mother kissed his cheek and finally pulled away, turning toward Gilles, and Maxence stepped back. Gilles needed her as much as he did. Maman gathered him in her arms, and they wept together, Gilles clinging to her like a terrified child. Maxence tried to swallow down the lump in his throat. He'd been a terrible replacement for their mother in helping Gilles.

Armelle slipped her arm around his waist again, earning her a grunt of protest from the baby.

Maxence wiped at his eyes. "You planned this."

"She told Gilles she was coming to help him and see you. Gilles and I thought it would be a good surprise." She nuzzled her head against his shoulder. "Was it a good surprise?"

"I don't deserve you," he whispered, throat tightening again. He kissed her softly, and Lina voiced her indignant objection. He pulled away from Armelle to make a face at the baby. "I can kiss my wife, Lina."

Armelle laughed, bouncing their niece. "Silly Lina. You will understand someday when some dashing mariner sweeps you from your feet."

"Oh, no. Mariners are hardly worthy husbands," a voice said behind them. They turned, and there stood Père, grinning wickedly at his own teasing, with a thick-chested man Maxence guessed to be Armelle's father.

"Papa!" Armelle pushed Lina into Maxence's arms, much to the baby's horror, and ran to her father. The man laughed as words flooded from her. Maxence could only imagine half of them were distinguishable.

Père came and put a hand on his shoulder with a husky greeting that belied emotion he didn't want to show. Lina met her *grandmère* and *grandpère* and happily allowed Maman to rescue her from Oncle Max. Waves lapped against the beach below them, cheering the moment, and a little ocean breeze skipped through the gathering.

Everything whispered of newness, of forgiveness, of chances to begin again.

They filtered down the stairs, the fathers heading back to *le Rossignol* to help with unloading and the rest to Oncle Oscar's. Maxence caught

Armelle at the top of the stairs and pulled her close. His lips found hers, and she fervently responded with a deep kiss of her own.

"You are loved, *mon amour*," she said.

"I know." He embraced her tightly, then let her lead him down the stairs. He'd follow her anywhere she took him, whether across the countryside or along a Breton shore, it did not matter. Though the road ahead—for him, for his family, for France—was riddled with hills and valleys, they would face this life of perfect imperfection together.

ACKNOWLEDGMENTS

Special thanks to my friend and fellow author Jennie Goutet for all her help with the French language and history in this book. I would have been hopelessly stuck without her research assistance and inspiration. I'm grateful for all the time she put in helping me find answers and for our wonderful conversations about the history of a country we both love.

On the topic of research, my friends from the *Chatham* reenactment group have proven to be a vital help in my continued research of nautical history in the eighteenth and early-nineteenth centuries. Thank you for generously answering all my random questions.

I am incredibly grateful for the support of my critique group— Megan Walker, Joanna Barker, and Heidi Kimball. Thank you for your honest thoughts on my work, and to Meg for always embracing my bad-boy characters. Also a great thank you to Deborah Hathaway. Your insights and encouragement have helped me through so many struggles with writing this.

Thank you to Madame McFarland for instilling in me a love of France and its history in high school. And to Monsieur LeBras for taking our study abroad group to Saint-Malo and insisting there was so much more to France than just Paris.

To my family members, thank you for all your support of my work. I'm especially grateful for Grandma Carol, one of my biggest fans, who passed away before this was published. She probably sold more books for me than I ever have for myself.

Thanks to the Shadow Mountain team for all the hard work they did to bring this book into the world. Special thanks to Heidi Gordon for believing in my French Revolution historical fiction, to Alison Palmer for being such an awesome editor, and to Heather Ward for the stunning cover design.

I owe so much to my husband and children for helping me to realize this publishing dream. Thanks for your excitement, your understanding, your encouragement, and your love.

And above all, thank you to a Heavenly Father who gave me a passion, a purpose, and a path to pursue it.

HISTORICAL NOTES

CHAPTER 1

Brittany is a Celtic nation in France that retained much of its autonomy after the union of France until the eighteenth century. Brittany held tightly to its Celtic culture until regions were dissolved to create a more united France in 1789. The Chouans, a Breton royalist group, allied with counterrevolutionaries in the Vendée, the historic region south of Brittany, in an attempt to drive out the armies of the new republic, but neither group had the resources for ultimate victory. Many counterrevolutionaries and their families were hunted down and killed in 1793 and 1794 as punishment for rebelling against the new French government. Nantes was the setting of one of these battles between counterrevolutionaries and republican soldiers, which took place about seven months prior to the start of this story.

There were some survivors of the Drownings at Nantes, but very few were able to escape, and many who did were later captured and executed. These victims were largely Catholic priests and nuns, as well as Chouans, Vendéeans, and their families after the Battle of Savenay.

The Coffee House Prison is still standing. It now has an art nouveau gate that suggests it was once a soap factory after the French Revolution. A plaque in remembrance of the drowning victims is on its wall.

CHAPTER 2

When constitutional clergymen first started to replace Catholic priests, Bretons did their best to show their outrage. Many constitutional clergy experienced harassment in Brittany, from burned effigies to desecrated buildings. Bretons even held grand processions for the outgoing, beloved Catholic priests as the constitutional clergy arrived. One way the Bretons showed their displeasure was having women follow the new clergymen around the church while washing the floors of their "filthy" footsteps. While this had largely ended by 1794, I have Armelle recreate this practice in protest.

Représentat Jean-Baptiste Carrier is a real figure from the revolution. He was in charge of ensuring revolutionary values were practiced in Nantes. There is debate as to whether he or his deputies were more responsible for allowing the Drownings at Nantes. Some profess his complete innocence, some suggest he had to have known and did not stop the proceedings, and others claim he orchestrated the drownings. Records show that he was most likely in the countryside recovering from illness on the day this scene happens, so artistic liberty was taken to bring him back to Nantes to meet with my fictional *chef-de-brigade,* Voulland.

Soldiers did take counterrevolutionaries out of town to shoot them, though generally it was larger groups who would first dig their own graves.

CHAPTER 3

Charlotte Corday was a young woman who assassinated Jean-Paul Marat, one of the more outspoken and radical revolutionaries in the early years of the revolution. Corday saw him as a threat to the nation, since he often made calls for drastic violence. She gained an audience with him by claiming to have a list of counterrevolutionaries and stabbed him to death while he was in a medicinal bath. Marat was seen as one of the first martyrs of the revolutionary cause, and Corday was swiftly executed for his death. Over the years Corday has been viewed as a villain and a heroine, depending on popular views of the revolution.

CHAPTER 4

Bedgowns were loose jackets worn by women in the eighteenth century. Despite the name, they were worn throughout the day as a shirt-like garment that was held closed by the woman's apron.

Petticoats in the eighteenth century were not undergarments. (The term changed to refer to underskirts in the nineteenth century.) Rather, they were more like the modern concept of a skirt and could be layered for warmth and modesty. Petticoats were generally tied on at the sides and had slits for women to access their pockets. Pockets of this era weren't sewn into individual garments but were more like purses tied around the woman's waist underneath her petticoats. Most women of all classes would also wear some sort of padding in the back underneath their petticoats for both style and to help keep their skirts from wrapping around their legs.

CHAPTER 6

There are no records of successful escapes from the coffee warehouse prison. My prison escape was inspired by tales of prison escapes by Jack Sheppard and others in the eighteenth century.

CHAPTER 8

"Dans les Prisons de Nantes" is an old song that is based on a real prison escape from the late seventeenth century. It was popular with sailors in the Loire area.

CHAPTERS 10–13

Jean-Baptiste's history is inspired by the history of Thomas Alexandre Dumas, whose mother was born enslaved in Saint-Domingue (modern-day Haiti). Dumas went on to become one of the great generals of the French Revolution. His son was the author Alexandre Dumas.

The Battle of Savenay occurred in December of 1793, about two months before the start of the story. Counterrevolutionaries did set up cannon at the church but were unable to hold off the republican armies. Those who remained in the city during the battle, some of them very old or very young people, were rounded up and put on trial. Those Bretons who weren't immediately executed were sent to Nantes and became victims of the drownings early in 1794. As part of their attempt to round up counterrevolutionaries after this battle, the armies chopped down trees and hedges along the roads to prevent rebels from hiding.

CHAPTERS 14–15

I took a little artistic liberty with these chapters. Max and Armelle could have passed two little settlements—La Bretonnière and Pirudel—before reaching my fictional town of Ilizmaen.

Ilizmaen is based on a little area between Pirudel and Vay that has an ancient standing stone called *Menhir de la Pierre qui Tourne*. Ilizmaen is a name I created from the Breton words for church and stone. Many early Christian settlers refashioned Celtic monuments for their own religious purposes. My fictional church and town were created to have a similar history.

Most Catholic priests did not take the oath of loyalty to the new republic. I haven't found records of a priest doing what Père Quéré did— taking the oath to protect his parish—but there were several priests who took the oath for various other reasons. The local priest was a huge part of a Breton town's culture, and Bretons were loyal to their priests, most of whom lived very humble lives. As part of the dechristianization efforts in 1793 and 1794, revolutionaries attempting to destroy the church in France forced priests and nuns to marry, thus disqualifying them from being Catholic clergy.

CHAPTER 18

Brittany was one of the birthplaces of the French Revolution; many early figures had Breton ties. In fact, the Jacobins were originally referred to as the Breton Club. But when revolutionaries in Paris took over and abolished Brittany's governmental autonomy, feudal way of life, and religion, many Bretons began to fight the changes. In only a few years, Brittany's revolutionary fervor changed to counterrevolutionary zeal and led to bloodshed that lasted into the early nineteenth century.

Because of Brittany's deep connection to Great Britain, Arthurian legend plays a big part in Breton literary tradition. Some Arthurian legends even take place in Brittany. The Breton people would have been as familiar with these stories as anyone from the British Isles.

The French Republican calendar was implemented in 1793 and replaced the Gregorian calendar for twelve years. The government began its count from September 22, 1792 (Year I), which was seen as the start of the new republic after Louis XVI was removed from the throne. While the new calendar retained twelve months, each month was divided into ten-day weeks, with a few extra days thrown onto the end of the year to make three hundred and sixty-five. Months were given names that corresponded with the seasons (such as Ventôse, which means windy), and days were given names inspired by numbers. The republican months did not line up with the start and finish of Gregorian months. A decimal system of time was also proposed, but French society did not adopt the system.

CHAPTERS 21–22

Information on eighteenth-century makeup came from a class taught by the proprietress of LBCC Historical. Its use for Maxence's disguise came from hands-on experiments with reproduction cosmetics rather than actual historical documentation.

Chouans did watch the roads, sometimes harassing and even murdering travelers they deemed to be supporting the republic. They camped in a variety of shelters, everything from houses seized from people who supported the revolution to dugouts in the ground.

The *biniou* is a high-pitched bagpipe with only one drone (pipe laid across the shoulder without finger holes), rather than three like the more commonly known Great Highland bagpipes of Scotland. *Talabard* is an older name for the *bombard*, an oboe-like instrument with a bell like a trumpet. These instruments are almost always played together. The *passepied* has been around since at least the 1700s. Some eighteenth-century dances at court were based on this Breton dance.

CHAPTER 25

While Voulland and his mission around Brittany is fictional, General Turreau was a real figure, as were his war tactics in the Vendée region. There is some debate as to how intensely he hunted down and eliminated counterrevolutionaries, but he wrote to the National Convention, "My purpose is to burn everything, to leave nothing but what is essential to establish the necessary quarters for exterminating the rebels."

CHAPTERS 30–32

While this particular supply delivery is fictional, *émigrés* from England did try to help the Chouans fighting in France, as did Great Britain. Britain's Channel Islands were in danger of invasion from the republic, so it was in Britain's interest to help the counterrevolution.

Oncle Oscar's house is based on the eighteenth-century mansion *la Demeure de Corsaire*, which is still standing in Saint-Malo and is now a museum dedicated to the city's pirate and privateer history. It was owned by privateer François Auguste Magon and included underground cellars and passageways to aid in his work.

The wound Maxence receives and the surgery Gilles and Dr. Savatier perform are taken from accounts from Dominique-Jean Larrey during Napoleon's campaign in Egypt, in which he outlined how he treated a similar gunshot wound. These techniques are not necessarily the best modern medical practice but were done during this period. The recovery is also based on these accounts.

CHAPTER 33

Robespierre was taken out of power and executed in July 1794. What should have ended the Reign of Terror began a new wave of executions of Jacobins that lasted through the end of 1794 when the laws that allowed for swift executions, sometimes without much of a trial, were abolished.